IN THE DARKNESS

Printed in Australia
First Printing: June 2023

Cover design by Kit Cronk

Paperback ISBN 978-1-7637617-0-4
eBook ISBN 978-1-7637617-1-1

A catalogue record for this work is available from the National Library of Australia

THE BLACKBURN CHRONICLES: BOOK ONE

IN THE DARKNESS

NICHOLAS WETEMANS

This book is dedicated to my long time best friend, Sarah-Jayne. This book would not exist without you. When I came up with this new idea, you pushed me to write the idea. When I came up with any ideas or story elements, you are the first person I go to and when I was having my doubts about writing, you pushed me to be my very best and now look where it has gone, published. So I thank you for everything you have done for 'In the Darkness' and I know you will love it as much as I do.

I want to also thank my parents for everything they do for me and their support with my writing.

CHAPTER 1

Four months. For four months Nicholas had been searching. Tracking the item his father had sent him to find. And now, he had finally tracked down the merchant with it in their possession. This merchant was supposedly perched in a small village within the rainforests of Indonesia. Now in that village, the villager he had just gathered information from nodded and pointed into the forest, indicating the direction the merchant had gone only a few hours before. Nicholas bowed in appreciation, his hands clasped together as a sign of thanks, turning and walking into the trees, following the directions he'd been given. The villagers had warned him that some sort of monster was living in the forest surrounding the village and that they had heard screams coming from the forest after the merchant had ventured in there. So, Nicholas was assuming that whatever the monster was, it had killed the merchant and the item would be somewhere in the vicinity. Nicholas drew the sword that was strapped to his back, an onyx black claymore with three rubies embedded in the hilt.

Nicholas knelt and examined the immediate area around him. He instantly noticed the human footprints continuing in the direction he was going, smirked and continued onward. But as he followed the trail the merchant had left, he held the sword in front of him, ready for anything. It wasn't long before he came into a clearing, the canopy overhead thinner and allowing for more light. This allowed him to better see the footprints he'd been tracking and their change from a calm stroll into a chaotic trail of panic.

Something happened to him here, Nicholas thought, kneeling once more to get a better look. He then noticed a set of lion-like footprints among the human footprints.

A lion? What the...?

Suddenly, there was a snapping of twigs from behind him. He whirled to see a dark shape diving toward him. His training kicked in and he quickly tumbled aside, but not before he felt claws raking down his arm.

'Bollocks...' he hissed in pain.

The thing landed behind him and whirled to face Nicholas. It had the body of a lion, a scorpion-like tail and an almost human-like face, a mane bordering the face.

'A Manticore, that makes sense now,' he muttered, nodding.

It growled, revealing rows and rows of needle-like teeth, and leapt at Nicholas.

But he was ready this time and he ducked under it. Raising the sword, he cut through the belly of the beast, spilling blood and guts everywhere. The Manticore crashed to the ground, almost lifeless. Nicholas approached it, raising the black sword over his head, and brought it down, cleaving the Manticore's head clean off. He quickly wiped the blood off the sword and sheathed it before examining its body. Everything about it was intact and in a healthy state. It'd not been contested for its territory. That was good.

Don't these things usually roam in pairs? he thought, trying to remember more of what he'd learned and what his father had told him about these creatures.

This instantly increased his awareness again. Looking up, he spotted a much darker patch among the trees.

A cave den maybe?

He stood, scanning the area once more before advancing towards the cave. Scavenging its barbs and venom would have to wait until he was sure he wouldn't be ambushed again.

Once he made it to the mouth of the cave, he inspected it. It didn't take him long to find bones, decayed meat and skin littering the floor within.

Yup, this is a Manticore nest alright.

He spotted a tattered backpack with a variety of different items hanging off it.

'Bingo.' He breathed in triumph before making a move towards the bag.

However, before he made it halfway to the merchant's bag, he heard the faint sound of bone clinking on bone coming from the depths of the cave.

'Hello, ugly!' Nicholas taunted as the second Manticore emerged from the inky darkness of the depths. He concentrated, summoning his powers over the weather to push a gale-force wind through the cave, past himself, and into the beast. It spun backwards, trying to cling to the ground with its claws.

The Manticore growled out its frustration, trying to get a better purchase and as soon as it did, it pointed its scorpion-like tail at Nicholas and fired the barb at him.

He cursed and dove to the side, dodging the near-invisible barb that had shot toward him, his hold on the wind dropping. This let the Manticore recover, and it charged back at the intruder, its foul maw opening, ready to feed. Scrambling to his feet, Nicholas reached out to his power; his arms frantically spun in circles, as if he were turning a wheel in mid-air. The Manticore rose off the ground, slowing it down as it started losing traction on the ground, making it growl in confusion.

Nicholas moved his arms faster and faster, and a whirlwind began to coalesce around the beast, picking up bones and other detritus along with the monster, lifting it higher and higher. It roared in anger as it rose further into the air, chunks of its leftover meals pelting the creature.

With the beast completely off the ground, Nicholas flung his arms to the left. The whirlwind spat the Manticore out and dissolved, sending the angry beast flying into the root-covered wall of the cave. He grinned as it fell to the ground in a heap.

The victory was short-lived, however, as the thing began to rise yet again.

He cursed again, the grin dropping off his face.

The Manticore pointed its tail at him and growled.

'Not again…' was all he could say before another barb was shot at him.

Nicholas dove aside once more, narrowly dodging the barb, and rolled to his feet.

Holding his hands out in front of him, he concentrated again. This time, a small but violent storm crackled within his hands.

Sensing the charged air, the Manticore paused, unsure.

This gave Nicholas the second he needed. He pushed the lightning to discharge out of his hands and towards the beast. It struck home. The Manticore roared, but the lightning had not affected it, only angered it.

The storm fizzled out, leaving Nicholas more drained.

Only one option left, he thought as he reached over his shoulder and drew the sword again.

The Manticore roared and dove, scorpion tail lashing out at his throat. Twirling around the beast, he ducked under its tail and cut it off at the base.

'No more barbs for you!' he exclaimed in triumph, dancing back and away from the beast.

The creature shrieked its displeasure as it wheeled about for a brief second before charging him again.

He swung the sword with both arms and the blade came in low, taking off one of its front legs at the knee, downing the creature.

Feeling the fatigue weighing down his body, even more, he knew he had to end this soon. He rushed to it from the rear as it got to its remaining feet, and slashed down at its neck, decapitating it. But unlike the first, this Manticore's body continued, turning towards Nicholas and lashing out at him with its remaining front paw, a couple of claws tearing at his side below the ribs.

He clutched his side and held in the scream of pain that so desperately wanted out. Instead, he darted out of the headless creature's range as it continued to lash out randomly.

'Why won't you bloody well die?!' yelled a very frustrated and rapidly tiring Nicholas. 'I'm going to have to use the sword's powers.'

The shadows leapt from their places and surrounded the sword as Nicholas channelled the sword's power to summon them. He then maneuvered the shadows to surround the monster's body. Turning the shadows sharp, he impaled the body with them, showing no mercy as he used the shadows to tear the body apart.

When he was finished, all that was left were pools of blood, chunks of wet flesh, fur and bone fragments.

As he returned the sword to its scabbard, he felt the familiar sting of the shadows leaving his arm sliced up once again. The sword exacting its price for the use of its power.

The threat now neutralised, he tore off what was left of his shirt and tore it into long strips. He quickly wrapped his wounds tightly in the makeshift bandages.

Satisfied that they'd hold till he could tend to them elsewhere, Nicholas turned back to face the bag.

'Finally,' he muttered.

After picking up the bag, he rummaged until he found what he was looking for. He pulled out a torn page and grinned from ear to ear. He tucked it away into one of his trouser pockets, closed up the bag as best he could and began to slowly harvest what he could from the Manticores.

Using some of the stuff from the merchant's bag as containers, he stored the parts in his remaining pockets and slung the bag over his back.

He'd decided to trade the remaining contents of the bag for a night's stay in one of the local's empty huts. He needed to rest before he flew back home.

***

Nicholas flew below the cloud cover, coming out of the slip-stream he had created. He looked down and saw the beginnings of the outer suburbs of the city of London.

'Ah, good to be home,' He sighed, spinning through the air. *But better to be hidden from prying eyes.*

He briefly concentrated and a cloud formed around him, hiding him from view from anyone who happened to look up. He followed the River Thames below until he flew over the city centre. Flying over the London Eye and Big Ben, seeing plenty of tourists milling around both attractions.

He veered his course and took off in the direction of the Lord's Cricket Ground. His father's mansion was not too far from the world-famous stadium.

Approaching the grounds of the said mansion, Nicholas then nose-dived, enjoying the freefall before he righted himself and landed on the front lawn. The cloud had evaporated from around him as he fell. He ran his hand through his short, dark hair and walked towards the front door.

The Quinzel Mansion was a three-storied sandstone marvel on a rather large estate that was completely surrounded by a tall stone wall made of the same sandstone as the mansion. Glorious gardens dotted the land with a run of garden beds leading up the driveway and to the front door.

Off the front door, a large, triple-height entrance hall and sitting room greeted you; a huge commercial kitchen, also found on the ground floor, supplied three separate dining rooms, one on each floor, adjacent to the nearby elevator. The master's eloquent library and study was on the second floor with two accompanying rooms for business. On the third floor: a cinema room and a gaming room. A large swimming pool, spa and sauna steam room were also on the ground floor, but separate from the rest. The mansion had twelve bedrooms and six bathrooms – four bedrooms and two bathrooms on each floor, one of those bathrooms being an ensuite to the master bedroom of that floor. There was also an extensive wine cellar underground and a hidden secret room. A detached five-car garage completed the whole property.

Nicholas opened the front door and walked into the glorious entrance where he instantly ran into Adam, the butler of the mansion.

'Ah. Good afternoon, Master Nicholas,' Adam lowered his duster. 'It has been a while. Was your mission a success?'

'Yes, it was, thank you, Adam. Did I miss much?' Nicholas said.

'No, sir. Master Norman has continued his research, as usual, and I continue to perform my duties here,' Adam replied.

'That's good to hear.'

'Miss Ryan also has been around a few times, just to "say hello",' Adam teased with a small smile.

'I will see her after I have spoken with Father,' Nicholas replied, not giving Adam the satisfaction of seeing him squirm. 'Is he in?'

'Yes, he is expecting you.'

'Thank you, Adam. Where is he?'

'In his study.'

Nicholas spun on his heel and walked up the stairs leading to the second floor. He knocked on the main study door and waited for an answer.

'Come in,' answered a strong voice from inside.

Nicholas opened the door and stepped inside. He found his father sitting at his desk, conducting research.

'What do you want?' asked his father without turning his head.

'I've returned, Father,' Nicholas answered.

'Oh, Nick! I thought you were Adam,' replied Norman, surprised.

He turned in his chair and stood up from behind his desk. He was a tall, muscular man with short, close-cut white hair, a short, neat white beard and a long scar stretching down his face beside his right eye. The man crossed the room and wrapped his arms around his son.

'I'm glad you are home safe!' Norman said, holding Nicholas out and inspecting him for any injuries.

'I am fine,' Nicholas replied, trying not to groan as he reassured his father.

'So did you find it?' Norman asked excitedly.

Nicholas smiled and reached into his jacket pocket, pulled out the page and handed it to his father.

'Finally…' Norman breathed, examining the page, walked back over to his desk and placed it on the wood.

'Aren't you going to look at it now?' Nicholas asked.

'I can look at it later. Now, come and sit,' Norman said as he gestured over to his small lounge within the study.

They both walked over and sat down in the armchairs that were set up at the fireplace, Nicholas having removed the sword from his back and laying it across his lap.

Norman picked up a bottle of scotch that was sitting next to his chair and poured himself a glass.

'Now, what happened?' Norman asked, taking a sip of his drink.

Nicholas told his father of what had happened over the four months, tracking the merchant to Indonesia and what had happened there.

'How many Manticores did you find there?' Norman asked, curious.

'I found two. One was near the village and then I tracked the other to their lair,' Nicholas replied.

Norman nodded and took another sip.

'Well, it is good you killed them. They are very dangerous creatures and shouldn't be near humans. Did they give you any kind of trouble?'

'The first one was easy to subdue and kill, but the second gave me some trouble.'

'Ah, right. Did you have to use that?' Norman asked, pointing to the blade.

Nicholas nodded.

'And is it still attacking when you use the darkness?'

Nicholas rolled up his sleeve and showed the now-fading cuts on his dominant arm. Norman nodded again, swirling the drink around in the glass, his face pensive.

'Why does it do that?' Nicholas asked, lowering his sleeve once again.

'I am still trying to find that out, but I think it has something to do with the prophecy in the book,' Norman replied, briefly looking at his desk.

Nicholas nodded and looked down at the sword on his lap, pondering.

'I have figured out a few more things, however,' Norman said as he leaned forward.

'Really?'

'Yes, I have managed to whittle it down to which country and possibly even the region of where the next one is located,' Norman replied, excitement now in his voice.

'So does that mean you are close to finding the Sword of Light?'

'Yes, I am very close. And now you have got that page, I should be able to pinpoint the location.' He stood, placed his drink on the table and walked back over to his desk.

'So, you have a rough idea where it is then?' Nicholas asked, turning in his chair.

'Yes. It should be somewhere in the southeast of Australia. Which does bring us to where you are going next,' Norman said, pulling out a map from the organised chaos on his desk.

'Excellent,' Nicholas replied.

'You are to go to Australia and search for the Sword of Light,' Norman declared, walking back over and sitting down, handing Nicholas a map of Australia.

'So, I need you to fly to Victoria,' he stated, pointing toward the south-eastern state on the map. 'We have a safe house in one of the western regions of the state there. I'll get Adam to give you the details when you decide to depart.'

'Right, and once you have more information, you will call me?' Nicholas asked, looking down at the map.

'Yes, of course, I will,' Norman replied.

'Alright, I will leave in a few days then,' Nicholas replied.

'Excellent. And once you find the sword, bring it to me,' Norman commanded.

'I will,' said Nicholas, standing up, strapping the sword back into place and turning to leave.

'Rest up and good luck in Australia, my son,' said his father.

Nicholas walked out of the study and went to his room, quickly disarmed himself, changed into a plain shirt and a pair of faded jeans, and then made his way down the stairs once again.

'Goodbye, Adam,' said Nicholas as he walked through the door.

'Off again, sir?' Adam asked.

'Off to see Kate.'

'Ah, good luck, Master Nicholas. Take care.'

'Thank you, Adam,' Nicholas nodded his thanks and walked through the now-opened door. Running toward the open grounds, Nicholas prepared to take off yet again when someone jumped onto his back. He was about to flip whomever it was off him when he realised that person was giggling.

'You're back!' yelled the person on his back.

'Kate!' He laughed, dropping her to the ground and kissing her. 'Yeah, I'm back.'

Kate Ryan was Nicholas's girlfriend. A beautiful, slightly taller than average girl with crimson-coloured hair, streaked black, and deep brown eyes that he could look into all day if he was able. She was quite fit and strong due to her martial arts training and was a first-year university student at the UCL Institute of Archaeology. She also didn't know about his secret life or his powers. Luckily, she'd jumped on him before he took off.

'Good!' Kate smiled.

'But I have to go again,' Nicholas replied.

'Aww, when?' she asked, sadness now crossing her face.

'In a few days, so we can spend some time together,' Nicholas replied with a grin.

'That's great!' Kate replied with a clap of her hands.

They walked down the path to the gates leading out of the property, Nicholas ordering a taxi on his phone as they walked, their plan to head towards the city centre.

CHAPTER 2

'Come on, Dylan! Push it! Just one more set!' the trainer coaxed.

Dylan took in a deep breath and mustered his strength and performed the last set of push-ups.

'Great work, Dylan!' his trainer cheered, offering a hand to help Dylan return to his feet. Dylan took it gratefully.

'Thanks,' Dylan replied, wiping the sweat from his brow and shaking out the tension in his chest, arms and back.

'Right, to finish up, a quick session in the ring and then we'll stretch down.'

Dylan nodded, running his hand through his shoulder-length dark hair. Dylan was seventeen years old, tall and skinny, with a little build on his frame.

He stepped through the ropes and one of the other trainees also stepped through the ropes on the opposite side of the ring.

'Right, you two, lock up then build a match from there. I want to see how you two look when I leave you to do it yourselves.'

They both nodded and stepped up to each other and locked up. Dylan quickly switched into a headlock but his opponent walked him to the rope and used them to push Dylan off. He ran across the ring, bouncing off the ropes and his opponent clotheslined Dylan to the ground. He tried to get back up, but his opponent pushed his knee into Dylan's back but he quickly rolled, grabbing his leg and spinning him to the ground, then Dylan locked him in another headlock. His opponent reached the ropes and Dylan was forced to break the hold. They both stood up again and locked up again but his opponent pushed Dylan to the ground. Dylan hit the mat hard and rolled over in pain. He reached for the ropes but his opponent lifted him to his feet before lifting Dylan over his head. Dylan wrapped his legs around his opponent's neck and fell backwards, taking his opponent with him. His opponent landed with a thud and Dylan quickly covered him.

'One… two… three,' yelled the referee. The referee helped Dylan up and raised his arm.

'That was great work, Dylan,' said the trainer.

'Thanks,' he replied.

Dylan was training to be a professional wrestler and he was hoping that one day he would make it to the big leagues in America.

'I'll see you next week?'

'Nah, sorry. I will be going on holiday, remember?' Dylan answered.

'Alright then, sorry, I did forget. See you when you get back then.'

'See ya,' replied Dylan, waving and walking out of the gym and heading towards the car, where his mother waited for him.

***

Lance looked up from his maths homework and out his bedroom window. His eyes wandered over the street as he waited for his mother and brother to get home and for his other brother to get back from the gym. He sighed and looked back down at the maths homework again. Lance was also seventeen years old, but unlike his twin brother, Dylan, he had short, blonde hair and was shorter, but was built the same.

'This just doesn't make sense,' he groaned. 'Damn maths.'

He stood, reaching for his phone and called up his friend Jake.

'Hey, man, does that maths homework make sense to you?' Lance asked into the phone.

'Hey, bro. Nah, I have no idea. I gave up on it,' Jake replied on the other end.

'Fair call; want to go for a hit?'

'Always.'

'Good. I will meet you at the nets then,' Lance replied, hanging up the phone. He walked across his room and picked up his cricket bag full of his cricket equipment.

Ten minutes later, at the cricket nets, Lance adjusted the cricket ball that he held with two fingers in his right hand. Jake was in the cricket nets, all of his protective gear on, bat in hand, tapping it in anticipation of Lance bowling the ball down to him. Lance was a better bowler than a batter, but Jake was the opposite, being an excellent batter that couldn't bowl.

Having backed up from the pitch for a nice run-up, Lance sprinted at full pace. He raised his left arm in front of his face, rapidly rotated his arms and released the ball from his right hand as it flew over his head.

The ball flew from Lance's hand, heading straight for the stumps with amazing accuracy.

However, Jake easily fended the ball off.

'Jake, I swear, you are going to bat for Australia one day,' puffed Lance, breathing heavily, brushing his blonde hair away.

'I doubt it. I'm not that good,' pondered Jake.

'Whatever you think,' Lance smiled, shaking his head.

Lance didn't want to mess with Jake; even though they were both the same height, Jake spent a fair bit of time in the gym. So, Jake was more muscular compared to Lance. Jake stepped out toward another of Lance's balls, hitting it straight back at Lance. Lance dived to the side as the ball flew past him.

'Watch it!' yelled Lance on the ground.

'Sorry, Lance, I was testing you,' Jake smiled. 'You were meant to catch that one.'

'That ball was bloody flying! There's no bloody way I was gonna catch that!'

'Oh, come on. I didn't hit it that hard! Plus, you're a bowler – you are meant to be ready for those,' Jake jeered.

'It came off the middle of the bat and with my bowling…'

They continued doing the same for another hour, they swapped roles halfway through and Lance had a go at batting, but it wasn't as graceful as what Jake could do and it was the same with Jake's bowling.

'Alright, I'm beat,' Jake wheezed, leaning over, hands on his knees.

'Same, mate,' Lance replied. 'Let's go get something to drink.'

***

As Dylan and his mum drove into Cobden, he gazed absently out the window wondering what his girlfriend, Kelsey Taylor, was doing. He had tried texting her, but she hadn't replied yet.

She must be busy, Dylan pondered as Rosemary pulled the car into their driveway.

'Home again,' said Rosemary. 'You better go and get your homework done, Dylan.'

'Yeah, I know,' Dylan groaned, heading inside.

Once in his room, Dylan placed his phone on the desk, connected it to his speakers and shuffled songs from his favourite band, Linkin Park. He wasn't very good at school since he didn't understand why he had to go, but his mother wanted him to do year twelve so that he could get a good job in the future.

He pulled out his maths work from his bag and sat down at his desk, starting to slowly work through the problems. However, after a few problems, Dylan dropped his pen as he got up and looked out the window, but something caught his eyes in the shadows of his room. He turned and looked into the shadows but he couldn't see anything.

'I swear I saw something move,' he muttered. He shrugged and looked out the window again.

The town he lived in, Cobden, was a small town in southwest Victoria, Australia. The town had a population of about 1800 people. It was situated a couple of hundred kilometres southwest of Melbourne. Dylan loved the place; the people were friendly and he had some good mates there. As he looked up the street, he saw his twin brother, Lance, walking toward home, a cricket bag slung over his shoulder.

***

Theo hefted the set of weights up to his chest, then up above his head, his whole body shaking with the effort. He held it up for a few seconds, then brought it down and let it fall to the ground in front of him with a long clang.

'Nice lift,' Theo's trainer, Lloyd, said.

'Thanks,' Theo replied, nodding. Theo was eighteen years old and tall – taller than both his brothers, Dylan and Lance. He was more built than both of them, due to his time in the gym, and he had short, chestnut brown hair.

'Is that it for today?' Theo asked, looking up at Lloyd.

'Yeah, mate, you're done for the day. I don't think you could do much more anyway.'

'You're right there.'

He walked away from Lloyd and into the changing room. He showered and changed into a plain blue t-shirt and jeans. He left the gym and began to walk home, but his phone vibrated in his pocket. He pulled out and read the text message.

Hey, I have some big news. Where are you? Want to meet me at the usual spot?

The text message was from his best friend. Theo smiled and typed a message back.

Hey, I just left the gym; I will meet you there in five minutes.

Theo changed direction and began to walk towards the centre of Cobden, heading for the local library, which was their usual spot. Five minutes later, Theo walked into the library, nodding to the librarian at the desk. She nodded back and pointed in the direction of where his best friend was. Theo thanked her and walked around the corner to where the seating area was. Sitting there was only one person: a girl. Theo knew this girl – knew her quite well as he'd had a crush on her. This girl, known as the girl next door and his best friend, was Gabrielle Morrison. The same age as Theo, eighteen; she was tall for a girl but not lanky, her curves easing her slender frame. She looked up and her cute smile softened her face, her warm brown eyes looking back at him, long, silky brown hair swept up into a ponytail.

'Took your time,' she said.

'Hello to you too,' Theo replied, taking a seat across from her.

'Hello,' she said, laughing. Theo felt his heart flutter at the sound.

'How was the gym?'

'The usual, nothing new there.'

'All the girls still ogling you?' Gabrielle teased, running her hand up and down, indicating Theo's upper body.

'Probably, but I don't take notice,' Theo replied, shrugging.

'Of course you didn't.' Gabrielle laughed, shaking her head.

'So, what is this big news?' Theo asked, leaning back in his chair, changing the subject.

'Oh right, I almost forgot. I got in,' she replied, grinning.

'Got into what?' Theo asked, a look of confusion coming across his face.

'Have you forgotten already? I can't believe you; remember the program I entered to go to London and shadow a legendary surgeon?' Gabrielle chuckled, shaking her head at Theo.

Theo's face changed in recognition.

'Oh yeah, I remember now,' Theo replied, nodding. 'So you got in?'

'I did!' she replied, clapping her hands together in excitement.

'Congratulations then. That is fantastic news.'

'Thank you, Theo. I am so excited.'

'I understand. It is your dream to become a surgeon, so this would be a fantastic opportunity.'

'It is. I will be leaving in just over a week.'

'Well, that kinda sucks.'

'Why is that?' Gabrielle replied, now confused.

'Well, you're going to London and I am going away in two days. We aren't going to get much time to hang out before you leave,' Theo replied, a touch of sadness in his voice.

'It's okay. We have today and tomorrow. We can hang out here for a while,' she said, smiling at him.

'That sounds like a great plan,' Theo replied and Gabrielle began to explain to him all about the program while he just sat there and listened, wishing he had the courage to ask her out.

CHAPTER 3

Where am I even going to start looking? Nicholas thought as the slip-stream took him over Western Australia.

He loved being able to control the weather – using the wind to fly, create slip-streams and toss enemies around like ragdolls, using the lightning as a weapon and the clouds to make it rain as hard as he wanted or not at all and so much more.

He was adopted by his father when he was a baby after his parents were killed in a car accident and ever since he had everything he wanted. When he turned seven, his power manifested itself and his training began. He was trained in every combat style known to man, trained in the use of different weapons and trained to use his power. Norman also had power; he was able to control things with his mind, also known as telekinesis.

Nicholas flew over the Murray River, knowing he was getting closer to the safe house his father owned somewhere nearby. Somewhere where he could hopefully get some sleep, eat and change into clothes that wouldn't attract attention. Finally spotting the house, he descended, landing outside the front door. Placing his hand on the hand scanner, it flashed green and he heard the door click open before going inside and heading straight to bed, falling face-first onto it and passing out from exhaustion.

***

Adam dropped a tea bag into a cup, poured in the hot water and added a little bit of milk and cream. After placing the cup onto a saucer, he headed for the stairs.

Adam had been working for Norman Quinzel for over twenty years. He was the only person that knew of Nicholas's and Norman's powers and what they were after. He loved his job; it was good pay and Norman was a great man to work for. Adam knocked on the library door.

'Sir? I have your tea,' Adam said.

'Come in, Adam,' Norman replied.

He opened the door and found Norman at his usual desk.

'How is the search going, sir?' Adam asked.

'I am very close,' Norman replied, studying the page Nicholas had brought to him.

'Where do you think it is?' Adam asked, placing the cup of tea in front of Norman.

'I have now isolated its location to be somewhere within The Grampians, toward the west of Victoria,' Norman replied, picking up the cup.

'With the page?' Adam asked, stepping back.

'Yes… The Grampians are mostly high rock formations, forming mountains and waterfalls,' Norman mumbled, more to himself, turning to look at a map of Australia.

'What if there is a hidden cave or something like that, sir?' Adam asked.

'Actually, that's probably exactly where it is!' Norman exclaimed as he reached for the telephone.

***

Nicholas woke up to the phone ringing. He groaned, rolling over to grab the phone.

'Ah, of course,' Nicholas muttered, seeing his father's name on the caller ID.

'Hello?'

'Nicholas! I think I know where the sword is,' Norman exclaimed.

'Great, where is it?' Nicholas replied, instantly awake now.

'Somewhere in the Grampians, toward the west of Victoria.'

'Alright, I'll head there now.'

'Do not fail me, Nicholas.'

'I won't,' Nicholas replied, reassuring his father.

***

Norman smiled triumphantly as he put the phone down.

'Should I get a bottle of whiskey, sir?' Adam asked.

'Yes, Adam, that is a great idea,' Norman replied. Adam left and headed straight for the cellar.

'Now, to find the Sword of Time,' Norman whispered to himself, walking up to the world map on the wall and marking out a spot on the map, the Grampians.

'The Sword of Darkness was in Madagascar... and the Sword of Light is in Australia...' Norman muttered. 'Where could the Sword of Time be?'

He grabbed a ruler and drew a line connecting Madagascar and the Grampians.

'Wait a minute!' Norman exclaimed in excitement.

Using his telekinesis, he called the stack of photos he'd been studying earlier to him. The photos were images that had been taken of pages within the ancient book that he'd purchased a long time ago, the book that the page was missing from. He flicked through them until he found the page he was looking for. On the page, there was a picture of a symbol. It looked like an uneven triangle, none of its sides being the same length. Grabbing a protractor, he copied the triangle onto the map using the line he just drew as a base.

'I found it!' Norman cheered, as Adam walked in with a bottle of whiskey.

'What, sir?' Adam questioned, a puzzled look forming on his face.

'I found the Sword of Time!' Norman cried out, pointing at the map. 'It's in Japan!'

Suddenly there was the sound of shattering glass and loud noises from upstairs in the mansion.

'What was that?' Norman wondered.

'Sounds like one of the windows on this floor is being smashed by something,' stated Adam, cocking his head to the side slightly.

'Indeed, it was!' someone bellowed from behind them.

Norman and Adam turned, finding a tall and athletically-built man with shoulder-length red hair, a bright red shirt and board shorts standing in the doorway of the library.

'Who are you?' Norman asked as books surrounded him.

'Name's Pyro,' Pyro said cockily, his eyes shimmering like fire.

'How did you get in here?' Adam asked bluntly.

'Like this,' Pyro grinned. Blasts of fire exploded out of his feet, lifting him into the air; as he laughed, some of the embers fell into the carpet, making it soldering and smoke.

'You can control fire,' Norman pondered.

'Yep, now, down to business,' Pyro laughed, dropping to the ground.

'What do you want?' Norman asked angrily.

'What I want is the location of the Sword of Light,' Pyro replied, serious now.

'How do you know about the swords?' Norman growled.

'I have my ways,' Pyro laughed, shrugging.

'Well, I'm not going to tell you anything,' Norman said simply.

'Then we have a problem…' Pyro said, his grin coming alive with mischief, taking a step into the room.

Norman quickly used his telekinesis to pick up a table and launch it at Pyro.

Pyro's eyes widened in surprise as he rolled out of the way.

'That was sneaky, but let's see how you like this!' Pyro laughed again.

Thrusting his hands at Norman, twin streams of fire burst out of his hands like flamethrowers.

Norman used his power to create a protective bubble around himself. The fire flowed around the force field, protecting Norman from the heat, but it lit up the bookcases behind Norman.

'No!' Norman yelled, losing his concentration, which in turn collapsed his force field. Taking advantage, Pyro flung a fireball at Norman, the ball of fire exploding near Norman, sending him tumbling to the floor and into the bookcase with a loud *crack*.

'Master!' Adam yelled, reaching out to a motionless Norman. Pyro used the distraction to walk up to Adam, wrapping his hand around his throat.

'Where's the Sword of Light?' Pyro growled.

Adam choked but didn't answer. Pyro shook his head and looked at the map on the wall that showed the triangle and the circled areas of the three locations of the swords, each location labelled with what swords were there.

'So, it is in Australia,' Pyro muttered, dropping Adam.

Adam crawled away from him, choking. Pyro pulled out his phone and took a photo of the map.

'Thank you,' Pyro smiled. The bottom of his feet ignited, lifting him up into the air. He took off, smashing through the library window. Adam regained his composure and scrambled over to where Norman lay in a daze.

'Master! Snap out of it!' Adam yelled, shaking Norman. Norman stirred but wouldn't focus, his eyelids fluttering.

'Oh, come on!' Adam yelled, shaking Norman harder. The fire roared, surrounding Norman and Adam.

'Norman Quinzel!' Adam screamed.

'What?' Norman muttered, his eyes focusing.

'The library is on fire!' Adam yelled. 'We need to get out of here!'

'What?!' Norman roared, instantly jumping up. 'This is a disaster!'

Norman reached out with his powers to the water pipes in the roof above them. The pipes groaned as Norman bent them with his mind. There was the screech of twisting metal as all the pipes burst and water started to rain down onto the library. Norman used his power to direct the water to put out the flames without damaging the priceless books and artifacts in the library.

'You did it, sir!' cheered Adam as the flames dissipated under the onslaught of water.

'Thank you, Adam,' Norman replied.

'For what, sir?' Adam asked in confusion.

'For not using your power against him,' Norman replied, placing a hand on Adam's shoulder.

CHAPTER 4

Theo looked up from his bag and out his bedroom window as the street lights cast an ominous glow onto the nature strip. He thought about the holiday he and his family were leaving for tomorrow. They were heading to Halls Gap – a small town in the Grampians – to stay for three days.

Turning back to his bag, Theo continued packing until he heard singing outside. His gaze went back to outside the window.

He saw Gabrielle walking down the opposite side of the road from his house. She had headphones in, singing along to whatever song she was listening to, not a care in the world. He smirked to himself, grabbed his phone and sent her a text message.

Nice singing.

He looked back up out the window and watched as she stopped, reached into her pocket, pulled out her phone, then turned towards his house and looked up to where Theo was looking out the window. She waved to him and he waved back, then she looked back down at her phone, fingers typing out a text. Theo's phone buzzed with a text message.

Thank you for your love of my singing, I will take it into consideration.

Theo laughed at Gabrielle's reply and typed out a reply.
You're welcome.

He looked back out the window as Gabrielle looked at her phone. He watched her smile, look back up at him and wave to him. She turned and walked up the driveway to her home.

Theo sighed again and went back to packing when Gabrielle disappeared from view.

***

Lance lay in bed, trying to sleep but unable to with Dylan's music still blaring in the next room. He decided he'd had enough, hopped out of bed and headed for Dylan's bedroom. Lance banged on Dylan's door.

No answer.

Opening the door, Lance found Dylan laying on the bed, playing his PlayStation.

'Can you turn it down?!' Lance yelled at his brother.

Dylan looked up at Lance.

'Why should I?' Dylan sneered back, brushing his black hair out of his face.

'Because I'm trying to sleep, you idiot!' Lance yelled.

'What'd you call me?' Dylan snapped, jumping off his bed and puffing up his chest in anger.

'I called you an idiot; now turn down the damn music!' Lance yelled.

'How about no,' Dylan sneered, getting in Lance's face.

'Then I will!' Lance fired back, trying to brush past Dylan.

'Don't you touch it!' Dylan yelled, grabbing and pushing Lance back the way he came. Dylan's anger continued to rise, his fists balling up, ready to punch Lance.

Lance noticed this, but he also noticed the shadows in the corner of the room seemed to writhe and twist with Dylan's anger.

'Dylan, wait!' Lance yelled in alarm before the shadows in the corner leapt from their place and surrounded Dylan's fists. Lance watched in astonishment as Dylan's eyes darkened as the inky black writhed and coiled around Dylan's fists.

'Dylan?' Lance asked tentatively.

Dylan didn't reply. He looked down at his fists and instead of shock, he smirked an evil smirk. Lance started to back away; he opened his mouth to speak but before he could say a word, Dylan flicked his hand at Lance. A mass of darkness flew off Dylan's hand and struck Lance in the chest. Lance was lifted off his feet and flew into the wall behind him; bouncing off it, he landed on the floor in a heap. Dylan laughed as more darkness surrounded his body. Lance sat up and raised a hand to shield himself, the other propped behind him to hold himself up.

Dylan watched in confusion as Lance's hand began to glow. The glow grew brighter and brighter until a beam of pure light fired out of Lance's hand and clipped Dylan's shoulder, knocking him back onto the bed.

Lance looked down at his hand in astonishment.

***

Theo heard a bang from Dylan's room and sighed in annoyance.

Those two must be fighting again, Theo thought. He got up and headed for Dylan's room. Over the loud music, he could hear Dylan laughing sadistically as he poked his head into the room. Theo's legs nearly gave out as he looked on in astonishment.

There Dylan was, standing in the middle of the room, darkness swirling around his body, Lance lying on the floor.

Theo watched as Lance propped himself up with one arm, the other raised in front of him defensively between himself and Dylan. Lance's hand then started to glow before a beam of light shot out of his hand.

'Oh my god…' Theo's words rushed from his mouth as Dylan flew backwards onto his bed.

He stepped back from the door.

'I must be dreaming, surely,' he breathed in shock.

He ducked his head back into the room as Dylan rose off the bed, fuming, the darkness surrounding him growing more intense as his anger grew.

'Nope, not dreaming,' Theo sighed. 'Well, here goes nothing.'

He opened the door fully and stepped in, smack dab between his brothers.

'Dylan! Stop!' Theo yelled, struggling over the music. Dylan didn't even look his way, his focus solely set on Lance.

'Dylan?!' Theo asked.

Dylan just flicked his hand at Theo. Theo closed his eyes, waiting for the darkness to strike, but it didn't come. Theo opened his eyes and the darkness was frozen in front of him. Looking past it, he found Dylan and Lance were also frozen, everything silent.

'What the hell?' Theo asked himself. He looked around the room and he noticed that the clock had completely stopped. His eyes widened in surprise.

'I… can control time!' he murmured to himself, shocked. He moved to the other side of Dylan and closed his eyes.

There was another loud thud as the darkness continued its path and struck the door behind where Theo had been, slamming it shut.

'What?' Dylan said in shock, the darkness in his eyes evaporating slightly.

Theo opened his eyes. Dylan and Lance both were both staring at him.

'Dylan, stop this!' Theo roared.

'No!' Dylan yelled back. 'I feel so powerful!'

Dylan swung his arms out. A wave of darkness flew off Dylan's arms, straight at Theo. Theo blinked, freezing time again so he could walk out of the way of the darkness. Theo then moved to stand in front of Dylan before restarting time.

'How…' Dylan started as Theo kicked out at Dylan's knee.

The darkness instantly evaporated from around Dylan's body as he fell backward onto the floor. Theo placed his foot on Dylan's chest.

'Do you yield?' Theo asked.

'I yield,' Dylan mumbled, nodding.

'You alright, Lance?' Theo asked, turning off the music before helping Dylan up.

'Yeah, I think so,' Lance replied. 'What the hell is going on with us?'

'I have no idea,' Theo murmured, staring at Dylan.

'Do we have superpowers or something?' Dylan asked.

'Maybe,' Theo replied.

Lance looked down at his hands. 'I can shoot beams of light out of my hands.'

'Light!' Theo exclaimed in sudden realisation.

'What?' Dylan asked.

'Lance controls the power of light,' Theo said. 'And you control darkness, Dylan.'

'What about you?' Lance asked.

'I think I can control some aspects of time,' Theo replied.

'So that's how it seemed you had super-speed,' Dylan muttered in slight awe.

'I think we better get ourselves back in order and at least get back to our rooms before Mum gets home from work,' Lance said, picking himself up from the floor and heading for the door.

'Yeah,' Theo said, leaving too, hearing the door shut behind him.

***

Theo woke up the next morning and found he had a text message from Gabrielle.

Meet me at the library at 10:30

Theo checked the time.

10:15.

Theo cursed and jumped out of bed. He quickly dressed and raced out of the house.

Theo got to the library where he found Gabrielle waiting for him.

'Hey… Gabrielle,' puffed Theo.

'Hey, Theo, did you run?' asked Gabrielle.

'Yeah… I… only just… got out of bed.'

Gabrielle giggled. 'Oh, you're a mess sometimes, Theo.'

'Am not!' replied Theo.

'Yes, you are,' Gabrielle laughed.

'Anyway, you wanted to see me?'

'Yes, I did. Let's go for a walk,' Gabrielle smiled.

'Alright then.'

They left the library and headed for the Cobden dam. The dam wasn't all that big; the creek that flowed from underneath a road about a block away collected within this nice green park to make a bit of a lake. It was quite a nice place.

Gabrielle led them down to one of the benches on the green slope near the dam, where they sat down and looked out over the water.

'Are you all ready for your trip?' she asked.

'I think so, not much to get ready for. It's only two hours away,' Theo replied, looking down at the ducks that swam across the water's surface.

'I know, but it doesn't hurt to be prepared,' she said, waggling her finger at him.

'It's fine. What about you? Are you ready for your big trip to London soon?' Theo asked, looking sidelong at her.

'Not really,' She sighed. 'It's just a long way to go is all, from my family and you.'

Theo looked away, blushing at that.

'Theo?' asked Gabrielle.

'Hmmm?' replied a distracted Theo, still looking out over the water.

'I need to ask you something,' said Gabrielle.

'Wait, Gabrielle, I have to ask you something too!' interrupted Theo, turning towards Gabrielle.

'Well, let's say what we have to say together,' Gabrielle smiled.

'Okay then,' said Theo. 'I'll count down?'

'Go ahead.'

'Five… four… three… two… one,' counted Theo.

'Will you go out with me?' they said at the same time.

They stared at each other, and then Gabrielle lent towards Theo and kissed him. Theo nearly pulled back in shock, but he just went with it. Gabrielle broke it off and whispered in Theo's ear.

'Yes, I will go out with you.'

Theo just sat there in shock.

'Now, don't you have a holiday to get to?' Gabrielle asked, chuckling.

'Yeah,' Theo said slowly. Gabrielle laughed some more.

'Go on, I will see you in a couple of days,' said Gabrielle, smiling brightly.

'Okay then, see you in a couple of days,' said Theo, standing up. He headed home, waving goodbye as he left.

CHAPTER 5

Nicholas landed softly on the football oval, his bag softly swinging from his shoulder. It was midnight and he had landed in Halls Gap, one of the popular tourist towns in the Grampians.

'Now, to find someplace for the night,' Nicholas muttered to himself.

He walked into town and went straight into the first hotel he found that was still open and with a vacancy. He stepped inside, the bell attached to the door jiggling to announce his entrance. Suddenly, a middle-aged man with short greying hair and a robust figure came out from the back room.

'Good evening, sir,' he said politely. 'A bit late for someone like yourself to be out and about.'

'It is, yes. My car broke down and I need somewhere to stay for the night until I can get it fixed in the morning,' Nicholas lied in response.

'Oh, that is unfortunate. Do you need me to call someone?' he asked.

'No, I have it sorted. Just a room would be great,' Nicholas replied.

'Of course. I'll just need to see some ID, sir,' he said, sitting down at the desk and turning on his computer monitor.

'No worries,' replied Nicholas, pulling out his wallet, pulling out the ID his father had made him and handing it over to the man, along with a credit card. After five minutes of the man typing and asking Nicholas a few questions, he turned off the computer once again.

'Thank you, sir. I'll just get you a key card for your room,' the man said, walking away, back into the back room.

Nicholas nodded and looked around the lobby and spotted a woman sitting in the corner, obviously asleep, rugged up in layers of clothes.

That's odd. It's summer here, and how could she be rugged up? And why would she be sleeping out here? Nicholas thought.

'Here is your key, sir,' the man said as he stepped back out, holding out a key card to Nicholas.

'Thank you,' replied Nicholas, taking the key. 'Is she alright over there?'

'Oh, yes, sir. She said she is waiting for someone,' he replied with a nod.

Nicholas shrugged and went straight to his room. He held the key card up to the reader. There was a soft beep and Nicholas opened the door. The room had a couch, a TV, a single bed, a small kitchen and a bathroom.

This will do, Nicholas thought, sitting down on the couch and slinging his bag off onto the floor at his feet. *The Sword of Light must be somewhere around here.*

He picked up some of the pamphlets and started to research the Grampians, hoping it would lead him in the right direction.

***

She opened her eyes and watched Nicholas walk away.

'Finally,' she breathed. She stood up and went straight to her room. She stripped off the layers of clothes, letting her blonde hair fall from the beanie. She then dressed in tight black pants, a white shirt and a black leather jacket.

'It's time,' she whispered to herself, grinning.

She left her room and silently crept up to the room Nicholas was staying in. She pressed her hand against the hinges of the door and reached out to her power. The hinge on the door started to freeze and became brittle. She punched the hinge and it shattered to pieces. She did the same with the bottom hinge. Then she quietly moved the door and snuck inside. Nicholas was sitting on the couch, back towards her, reading pamphlets. She snuck towards him, but then she hit something solid. She reached out and touched something invisible.

'Who are you?' Nicholas exclaimed suddenly, standing up and turning around.

She turned to run, but she struck another invisible wall. She felt around her and there were two more invisible walls on each side of her, completely boxing her in.

'How?' she asked in surprise.

'I'm solidifying the air around you,' Nicholas replied.

'You control the air?'

'No, I control the weather. Now, who are you?'

'I am not telling you anything.'

'Clearly, you know who I am and were waiting for me to show up. You were the women in the lobby, weren't you?'

She didn't respond to that.

'How did you know I would come here?' Nicholas asked.

'This is the only place open at this time of night here and I had received intel that you were on your way here,' she replied with a shrug.

'Who told you?' Nicholas demanded.

'Can't tell you that,' she replied with a shake of her head.

'At least tell me your name. You know mine obviously, but it would be nice to know who my attempted attacker is.'

'Fine. I am Glacia,' Glacia said with a small bow.

'Nice to meet you, Glacia. I am Nicholas Quinzel and now I am going to squish you,' Nicholas stated and started to push the two side walls of air inwards at her.

Glacia concentrated as the walls started to crush her, using her power to drop the temperature of the room down to freezing. Nicholas took his concentration off the walls of air and increased the temperature again, using his own power to do so. Glacia used the brief distraction to create a dagger out of ice and she dove at Nicholas. He dodged back and pushed at the wind, a powerful gust forming, striking her in the stomach and she flew backwards into a wall and crumpled to the floor. He then threw his arms out wide and invisible slices of wind flew off his arms and sped across the room, seeking to slice Glacia into three pieces. She quickly slid under, knowing something was moving towards her, then she crouched from the slide and leapt at Nicholas, a dagger of ice at the ready, but another powerful wind struck her, sending her tumbling back. Nicholas then concentrated and clapped his hands together, but instead of a clap sound, there was a loud crack of thunder, making Glacia cover her ears and the whole room rattle.

With this distraction, Nicholas brought up his hand and a burst of lightning struck Glacia, causing her to cry out as her body convulsed and fell to the ground. Nicholas then dove for his bag, reached inside and pulled the Sword of Darkness out with his left hand. Instantly, the shadows leapt from the places and surrounded the sword. Glacia stood, her super-human body recovering quickly, and summoned two balls of ice and threw them at Nicholas. He dodged one, but the other struck him in the leg, bringing him down to one knee. Glacia dove at him, a dagger forming once again and ready to strike. Nicholas rolled to the side and kicked out at her, catching her in the chin and she fell back, howling in pain and Nicholas was on top of her, sword at her throat.

'Tell me who sent you!' Nicholas exclaimed.

'I don't think so,' sneered Glacia.

She touched the point of the sword and ice started to form, quickly running up the sword and then Nicholas's arm. Nicholas stood up in surprise, holding his now-froze arm and sword up in the air and Glacia rolled away from him and ran for the open door. Nicholas quickly increased the temperature and the ice around the sword and his arm melted. Then he used the sword to throw darkness at Glacia and the darkness struck her in the small of the back, knocking her down. Nicholas turned the darkness sharp and struck at her again. She rolled to the side and threw a blast of cold, hitting Nicholas in the leg, instantly freezing the appendage.

'I think you're the one who is going to yield to me now and answer my questions,' Glacia laughed, summoning an ice sword. Glacia walked towards Nicholas as he struggled with the ice around his leg. A fist of darkness struck her in the stomach, throwing her backwards.

'You forget about this?' Nicholas laughed, pointing the sword at her. Then the ice around his leg shattered.

Glacia lunged at him, ice sword ready. Nicholas raised his sword and the two blades clashed. He came in with two quick jabs. Glacia parried the first and sidestepped the second, responding with a slash that Nicholas blocked easily. They went at it again, blades flashing and singing together.

'You're good,' Glacia complimented him.

'Thank you,' Nicholas responded with a curt nod.

He pressed forward his attack, and Glacia retreated, struggling to keep the blade away. Glacia batted his sword down and swiped at his head. He jerked backwards and stumbled. Glacia moved in, trying to take advantage of the distraction, but couldn't get through Nicholas's defence. Nicholas slashed, just missing Glacia. She snarled and stepped in quickly, her blade seeking him. Their blades scraped together and Nicholas flicked his wrist. Glacia's sword flew from her grip and she had to dive to the floor to escape his blade. She summoned another ice sword and came back at Nicholas and he blocked and replied with a swipe that she blocked, the shrill taps of the blade on ice settling into a rhythm as they moved around each other. Glacia leaned in with a deep thrust that was parried, but she responded with a flick that almost took his hands off.

'Surrender?' Glacia asked, smiling.

'You have nearly beaten me,' Nicholas replied, grinning back at her.

'If so, then why are you smiling?' Glacia asked in confusion, her smile dropping.

'I'm not left-handed,' Nicholas replied and threw the sword into his right hand.

Glacia fell back under his renewed onslaught. She lashed out desperately to keep him away, but his sword was moving faster than her own and she couldn't find her balance. Nicholas slashed downwards and she rolled behind him. Glacia slashed at the back of his neck, but he dodged, whirled, and his sword crashed against hers and suddenly her hand was empty. He kicked her down and he stood over her with the tip of the sword at her throat.

'There,' he replied, panting a little. 'You're defeated; now, you will answer my questions. Who sent you?'

'Fine. His name is Pyro,' Glacia sighed, struggling under Nicholas's weight.

'Why does he want me dead?'

'He wants to eliminate you because he considers you a threat.'

'Threat to what?'

'To obtain the Sword of Light.'

'How do you know about the sword?' Nicholas asked in shock.

'Because your father showed him,' Glacia replied.

This caused Nicholas's eyes to widen in shock.

'But my father wouldn't do that…' he began, looking away.

And with Nicholas's moment of distraction, Glacia managed to get her arm free and threw shards of ice at Nicholas. He stumbled back in surprise and Glacia rolled up, ran and dove through the window, sending glass everywhere, and disappeared into the night.

CHAPTER 6

Pyro stood on top of the local tourist attraction known as 'The Pinnacle'. It was a rock formation that jutted out from the cliff, providing a magnificent lookout over the valley that Halls Gap was built in. Stepping up to the edge of the cliff, Pyro looked down at the darkness below. He grinned, his eyes blazing like fire before he jumped. He howled with laughter as he plummeted towards the rocks and just before he hit them, the bottom of his feet ignited and he was propelled back up into the night sky. He hovered in the air briefly, admiring the view. He smiled and lowered himself towards the town. He landed in the car park near the football oval, careful not to leave scorch marks, and got into his red Chevrolet Camaro, driving to the hotel he was staying at so questions wouldn't be raised.

'Now for a good night's rest,' he said as he stepped out of the car, breathing in the crisp night air. Then he heard glass smashing and he watched as a blonde-haired woman, dressed in black, ran away from the hotel and into the trees nearby.

'Was that Glacia?' He cursed as he took off after her, the room now forgotten.

'Glacia?' he called out, but there was no reply.

'Glacia?' he called again. He lit a fireball in his hand, illuminating his surroundings. He walked further into the trees and then he felt the temperature drop.

I'm close, he thought before calling her name once more.

Suddenly a ball of ice flew out of nowhere and struck him in the chest. Pyro fell backwards, fireball extinguishing as someone pinned him down and pressed a cold blade to his throat.

'Wait! Glacia, it's me!' exclaimed Pyro.

'Oh, Pyro, I'm so sorry,' replied Glacia, jumping off him.

'It's alright,' he muttered, standing back up. 'Is Nicholas Quinzel here yet?'

'Yes.'

'So, I take it, he's dead?' Pyro asked in excitement.

Glacia turned away from him, not replying, knowing that she had failed.

'He isn't, is he?' Pyro asked, now serious.

Glacia shook her head.

'Why isn't he dead?' Pyro asked, turning away from her in disappointment.

'Because you didn't tell me that he had powers and the Sword of Darkness!' Glacia blurted out in a rush and anger.

'He has the Sword of Darkness?' Pyro asked in shock, spinning to face Glacia.

'Yes, he nearly killed me with it!' Glacia replied in a huff, crossing her arms across her chest.

Pyro turned and pondered how this development could benefit him.

'What do we do now?' Glacia asked.

'We get the Sword of Darkness,' Pyro stated simply. 'The swords should be able to sense each other. Having the Sword of Darkness will help us find the Sword of Light.'

Glacia nodded, understanding.

'So, we go after Nicholas,' Pyro grinned.

***

Nicholas vaulted out of the broken window, sword in hand, looking around for any sign of Glacia or where she had gone. His training began to kick in and he searched the ground for anything that might show what he was looking for. Quickly, he found footprints that were flecked with shards of ice, leading away from the hotel and into the trees.

'Bingo,' he breathed, but he quickly stopped as he heard something move in the bushes and voices occupying those noises.

Nicholas immediately used the sword to camouflage himself with darkness, blending into the shadows of the hotel. He watched as Glacia and a man with long, orange hair and eyes like fire emerged from amongst the trees. Glacia walked up to the broken window of his room and looked inside.

'Is he in there?' the man asked.

'No, he isn't,' replied Glacia.

'He must be somewhere around here,' said the man, looking around.

Nicholas slowly circled behind Glacia, the darkness concealing his movements, and raised his hand. He felt the breeze against his hand and pushed at it with his powers, causing it to pulse slightly before striking Glacia in the back, taking her off her feet and flying forwards. Nicholas lowered the darkness around him and threw it at the man. He dove out of the way as the darkness flew over the top of him before he rolled up, a fireball in each hand.

'You must be Nicholas Quinzel,' The man smirked.

'I am, and who are you?'

'Pyro,' Pyro replied with a grin.

'What do you want with me?' he questioned, cautiously pointing the sword at Pyro.

'I want that,' Pyro replied, pointing at the sword. Nicholas started to laugh.

'What's so funny?' Pyro asked, angrily, his mood instantly changing.

'You have no hope,' Nicholas laughed. 'You'll never get this!'

'Oh, but I will,' Pyro grinned with malicious intent before thrusting both hands out, two streams of fire bursting forth, heading straight at Nicholas. Nicholas created a dome of wind around him, blocking the streams of fire. Then he pushed out, the dome becoming a wave that struck Pyro and took him off his feet, landing heavily on the ground.

Glacia suddenly dove at Nicholas, but he sidestepped her and she could only watch as Nicholas's hand, crackling with lightning, touched her on the shoulder. She screamed as electricity arced through her body and she fell to the ground, body convulsing from paralysis. Pyro stood up and laughed. Nicholas turned, eyebrows raised.

'What's so funny?' he asked.

'You're good,' Pyro laughed. 'Better than I thought, but I shouldn't be surprised since you are the lapdog of the great Norman Quinzel.'

'How do you know my father?' Nicholas asked with an edge to his voice.

'Well, I don't know him personally,' Pyro replied with a shrug. 'Only met him once, yesterday actually, when I broke into your home and took the information I needed.'

'How dare you?' Nicholas roared, raising his hand and lightning arced out at Pyro.

He dove out of the way, rolled back to his feet and created a wall of flame that he sent straight at Nicholas. Nicholas pushed at the wind, sending a stream at the wall, creating a hole in the wall of flames and then he ran straight at the wall, diving through the hole he created, rolling back to his feet and running straight at Pyro, Sword of Darkness now raised to strike. Pyro summoned a sword of solid fire and brought it up, meeting Nicholas's sword with a burst of flames and particles of shadow. Nicholas stabbed forward, forcing Pyro to dodge to the side. Pyro then threw up his sword, returning Nicholas's strikes and forcing him back. Nicholas fell back and took up a position, crouched, one arm thrown back. Pyro danced back as Nicholas thrust himself, and the sword, forward. With a flick of his wrist, Nicholas caught Pyro with his blade, opening a nick that bled warm down his side. Pyro dove backwards and reached out to the wound with his power and cauterised it instantly, the blood drying up and leaving a scar. Then their swords met again and Pyro was forced to defend as Nicholas swung his sword in a wild flurry, but Pyro somehow managed to disarm Nicholas in the flurry with a brilliant sweep out of nowhere, the Sword of Darkness flying out of his hand.

Nicholas jumped up and snapped out his right leg, the toe of his boot catching Pyro in the side of the head, causing Pyro to stumble back, his sword extinguishing. He was forced to dive out of the way as Nicholas lashed out with a roundhouse kick that would have taken Pyro's head before kicking out at Nicholas's knee, causing Nicholas to roar in pain as he fell. Pyro ran at the downed Nicholas, tackling him to the ground, and then he hooked his leg under Nicholas's throat and grabbed the back of his head, pushing forward with his leg and pulling down with his hands, applying a choke. Nicholas panicked slightly, gagging and starting to lose consciousness. Somehow, he managed to get his legs underneath himself and used them to push up and flip over, driving the heel of his boot into Pyro's face. Nicholas lay back, breathing in air, but he wasn't given much reprieve as Pyro was already on top of him, raining down punches. Nicholas blocked most of the punches, and then he elbowed Pyro in the face, making him fall back, providing Nicholas with the opportunity to push at the air, blasting Pyro further away from him so he could recover. Standing up, he summoned lightning around his fists, ready to continue this fight.

Pyro groaned as Nicholas stepped toward him. But before Nicholas could unleash the lightning, Pyro turned his head towards Nicholas and two beams of fire burst out of Pyro's eyes, striking Nicholas in the chest. In shock, Nicholas fell back, patting out the flames. Nicholas quickly retaliated though, lightning bursting from his hands and crackling through the air toward Pyro, striking him in the chest. Pyro was thrown backwards, through the broken window, into Nicholas's room. Nicholas stood up and brushed himself off. Realising the opportunity, a now-mobile Glacia quietly slunk up behind Nicholas and placed her hand on the small of his back. Nicholas's eyes widened in shock as ice spread over his body, freezing him in an ice prison. Glacia stood back, admiring her work momentarily before walking over to Pyro as he crawled out of the window, falling to the ground, groaning.

'Like my popsicle?' She laughed, almost hysterically.

'I do,' Pyro groaned with a slight laugh, standing up with the aid of Glacia. Stable on his feet, he walked over to where the Sword of Darkness lay.

'Finally,' he whispered to himself, picking it up and laughing. 'Now to the next one, the Sword of Light.'

CHAPTER 7

Lance woke to the sound of breaking glass in the next room.

'What the hell was that?' he mumbled to himself, rubbing his eyes and slowly getting out of his hotel room bed. He and his family had arrived in Halls Gap that afternoon, ready for their three-day holiday there. Lance walked over to the window and watched as a blonde woman, wearing tight black pants and a black jacket, ran into the trees that surrounded the hotel complex.

'What the hell is going on?' Lance hissed. 'Dylan! Theo! Wake up.'

Dylan incoherently mumbled something and Theo instantly sat up.

'What's wrong, Lance?' Theo asked, rubbing his eyes.

'Come have a look at this,' Lance replied, pointing out the window.

Theo got out of bed and joined Lance at the window. They watched as a teenage boy, about their age with black hair, leapt out the window next to theirs, holding a black sword with three rubies embedded in the hilt in his hand, deep cuts covering his wrist. He briefly looked around the area, and then suddenly looked up as if he had heard something, then he waved the sword and shadows surrounded the sword than him.

'That's what Dylan can do,' Theo whispered.

'Yeah,' Lance whispered back. Dylan sat up and rubbed his eyes.

'What's going on? What can I do?' Dylan mumbled sleepily.

'Come have a look for yourself,' Lance replied.

Dylan slowly got out of bed and joined his brothers at the window. They watched as the blonde woman and the red-haired man emerged from amongst the trees, walking up to the broken window and looking in.

'What are they doing?' Dylan asked in a hushed tone.

'I have no idea,' Lance replied.

The brothers watched on as the blonde woman was knocked off her feet, the black-haired guy appearing behind them before throwing darkness at the red-haired man. The brothers moved away from the window in shock.

'Those people… out there… have powers like us!' Lance exclaimed in shock.

'We should go out there,' Dylan suggested, quickly pulling on some clothes.

'What?' Theo asked, shocked.

'It looked like they were after that guy with the sword,' Dylan returned simply. 'He looked like he needs help.'

'Fine,' Theo reluctantly agreed.

Lance and Theo quickly pulled on some clothes, following Dylan, as they snuck out of their room through the lobby and outside. They ducked low and crept to the other side of the building, where the battle was taking place. Lance poked his head around the corner and watched as the blonde woman rose behind the teenage guy and placed her hand on his back and ice spread over his body, completely encasing him in a prison of ice.

'What's happening, Lance?' Theo asked.

'That woman just encased that guy in ice!' Lance replied, panic in his voice.

Lance watched as the red-haired man and blonde woman ran past their hiding spot, a black sword in the man's hand, before getting into a red sports car and driving off.

'They took his sword!' exclaimed Dylan, watching as the car disappeared down the road. The brothers walked around the corner and stood in front of the frozen statue of the teenage guy.

'We should help him,' Dylan suggested again.

'How?' Lance replied as Dylan walked up to the guy.

'What are you doing?' Theo questioned.

'Helping him,' Dylan grinned, darkness surrounding his hand.

'Wait, Dylan!' Lance warned. But the warning fell on deaf ears as Dylan clenched his fist, darkness forming into a fist in front of him before using it to punch the ice. The ice cracked and Dylan punched again, smashing a hole in the ice. Dylan could hear air being sucked in through the hole, backing away as the ice started to expand and crack. Then the ice shattered; the guy stood there, smiling.

'Thank you for that,' he said, brushing his clothes off, shards of ice falling to the grass.

'Who are you?' Dylan asked, slightly confused.

'My name is Nicholas Quinzel,' Nicholas replied.

'I think those people took your sword,' Theo stated, pointing towards the town.

'What?' Nicholas yelled, the smile dropping as he looked around. Nicholas roared in anger and pushed at the wind, knocking trees over.

'Okay, mate, calm down!' Dylan exclaimed, hands up in placation.

Nicholas turned to face Dylan, face contorted in anger.

'It's okay, mate,' Dylan repeated.

'Dylan, I think you should back away from him,' Theo warned nervously.

Nicholas turned and pushed at the air in frustration, knocking Lance and Theo off their feet. Retaliating, Dylan summoned darkness and threw it at Nicholas. Nicholas dodged to the side and ran straight at him. Nicholas kicked out at Dylan and he blocked it with his left forearm and punched Nicholas in the chest with his right. With the darkness surrounding his fist, Nicholas was lifted off his feet and flew backwards. Dylan smiled and more darkness swirled around him. Nicholas got to his feet and raised his arms and started to swing his arms in a circular motion. Dylan watched, in shock and amazement, as a tornado started to form around Nicholas.

Suddenly, a beam of light struck Nicholas in the chest, sending him stumbling back, the tornado disappearing. Dylan looked back as Lance lowered his hand. Nicholas stood up, lightning crackling between his fingers, and then he froze.

'What the hell?' Dylan asked in wonder.

'That would be me,' Theo breathed, holding out his palm toward Nicholas, deep in concentration.

'What are we going to do?' Lance wondered. 'He isn't going to back down.'

'Going to have to think of something, quick,' Theo said. 'I can't hold him for much longer.'

Dylan summoned more darkness and Lance summoned orbs of light in his hands.

'Release him now!' Lance yelled.

Theo did so, lowering his arm and Nicholas, instantly, unfroze. Lightning arced out at Dylan and Lance, but Dylan blocked the lightning with a wall of darkness, but then more lightning continued towards Lance. Lance watched in horror as the lightning raced towards him. He closed his eyes, waiting for the lightning to strike. Then he felt a sensation course through his body. Tentatively, he opened his eyes, finding he was behind Nicholas. Theo and Dylan stood there in shock. Snapping out of it, Lance threw the orbs at Nicholas, striking him in the back and exploding on impact, blasting Nicholas forward into the ground. But Nicholas stood up and brushed himself off.

'You boys are good,' Nicholas grinned. 'But I don't have time for this. I have to find my sword; we will meet again.'

Nicholas rose off the ground and flew away over the trees.

'That was interesting,' Theo said, watching Nicholas fly away.

'Yeah,' Dylan replied. 'Should we go after that man and woman? I have a feeling that that sword is important.'

'Yeah, I think we should,' Lance agreed.

Theo pondered it for a moment before agreeing as well. 'Okay, let's do it.'

'Still got the spare keys for Mum's car?' Dylan asked.

'Yeah, I have a feeling we're going to need them; they turned onto the MacKenzie Falls turn-off,' Lance chimed in.

'Yup, they're inside,' Theo stated. 'I still can't believe you can teleport, Lance!'

'Is that what I did?'

'Yeah. One second you were in front of me, the next, you were behind Nicholas,' Theo replied with a nod and Dylan hummed in agreement.

'Wow, we are one of a kind,' Lance said in amazement.

'I guess so,' Theo laughed.

Dylan and Lance laughed with him as they continued inside. Theo grabbed the keys as the others got whatever else they wanted before heading out.

Minutes later, Dylan, Theo and Lance drove past the football ground.

'It feels like they are headed that way,' Dylan replied. He pointed just off to the left of the road.

'So they, and us, are heading for MacKenzie Falls?' Lance mused, noticing the sign on the side of the road.

'Maybe. It's in the same direction. How do you know they've gone that way, Dylan?' Theo queried.

'I don't know. It's just this weird feeling I have. Like something is calling to me,' Dylan replied, his brow furrowed as he thought about it.

'Okay… now that's kinda weird, even for you,' Lance said, a disturbing look briefly crossing his face before laughing at his joke. When he noticed no one else laughing, he stopped and murmured, 'Okay, tough crowd.'

They continued down the main road for about fifteen minutes in complete silence until Dylan suggested that they take the turn-off for MacKenzie Falls, following the signs to the car park. Once they reached it, they noticed that there was only one other car there: that man's hot-red sports car.

'Told you,' Dylan said with a snort.

'Alright, I guess you were right,' Theo sighed.

They all got out of the car, Theo locking it, before finding and following the trail that led to the falls. The trail got darker and darker as more foliage blocked out the moonlight that was illuminating their way, and then it opened up to a wooden path that had been built.

'Lance?' Theo called.

'Yeah, yeah,' he muttered, instantly conjuring an orb of light in his hand to provide more light.

They continued, the roar of the falls getting louder and louder until they found themselves facing the top of the falls, the river that fed the falls flowing beneath the wooden walkway. They briefly admired the sight before finding the stairs that lead down next to the falls to the second viewing area. Going down them, Dylan brought them to a stop about halfway down.

Dimming his light slightly, Lance asked, 'What's wrong?'

Saying nothing, Dylan just pointed down at something in the clearing in front of the falls.

They soon spotted the man and woman standing in the centre of the clearing, looking up at the falls.

They quickly made their way down the rest of the stairs, the rock walls keeping them from sight. Lance extinguished his orb as they crept. They got to the bottom of the stairs and quickly hid behind a large rock between the brothers and the strangers.

The woman spoke, her voice barely audible over the waterfall. 'The cave must be behind the waterfall.'

They quietly crept closer, listening for the man's reply. But there wasn't one, only the quiet hum of the drawn black sword that only Dylan could hear.

'Pyro?' the woman called as she reached out to the man. He only grunted as darkness started to surround the sword.

Suddenly, the man called Pyro spoke. 'Glacia, freeze the waterfall and the pool, quickly!'

'O-okay,' stammered the woman, Glacia, as she hurried closer to the waterfall.

'We have to do something,' whispered Theo.

'Yeah! Lance, blast that woman with some light!' Dylan whispered back excitedly, trying to be quiet as he concentrated darkness around his fists.

Nodding, Lance shot out from their hiding place, quickly bringing his palm up to face Glacia's back. His hand glowed as a beam shot out, catching Glacia's shoulder. She screamed as she was knocked off her feet and into the water.

At the same time, Dylan jumped out, darkness surrounding him as he ran at Pyro. Pyro's eyes flashed like fire, a fireball appearing in his free hand. Lance then teleported behind Pyro, catching him completely off-guard and lashed out with an awkward kick that managed to catch Pyro square in the back, sending him stumbling towards Dylan.

Dylan, using his power, leapt over the tumbling Pyro, landing next to Lance. Lance re-ignited a light orb, the size of a basketball, in his hand and tossed it high and it hung above them, providing some more light for the others.

Pyro tumbled back to his feet, spinning back to face the brothers, snarling his frustration. He raised the sword and two tentacles of darkness flew off the blade toward them. The one aimed at Lance struck him in the chest and knocked him off his feet. However, the one that whipped toward Dylan just absorbed into his body.

Dylan looked down as the last of the darkness broke away from the sword, slithering into his chest, before he laughed mockingly. Pyro, not finding it amusing in the slightest, quickly thrust his hand out, the fire bursting out in a continuous torrent toward Dylan. Dylan blocked it with a shield conjured from the darkness as he then summoned a claw and charged forward to slash at Pyro but as Dylan slashed down, Pyro raised the sword and it absorbed the claw into itself, just as Dylan had just done. Dylan frowned, taking a step back. Noticing the slight retreat, Pyro smiled and leapt at Dylan, swinging the black sword, only to be blown sideways by what seemed like a mini-gale wind just for him.

Nicholas descended from above, laughing. 'I believe that sword is mine.'

'Well, come and get it then!' Pyro sneered.

Nicholas dove at Pyro but was then slammed to the ground by a wall of darkness created by a laughing Pyro.

'Stop!' Lance yelled, raising his palm toward Pyro.

'You wouldn't,' Pyro taunted.

'Try me,' came the reply before Lance blasted him, sending him and the sword flying. With the sword out of Pyro's grasp, Nicholas was released, allowing him to dive for the sword, only to be frozen mid-air. Theo walked into the clearing with his palm outstretched toward Nicholas.

'Dylan, take the sword!' Lance exclaimed.

'Why?' Dylan asked in confusion.

'Because it might boost your power! Not to mention you would be better at wielding a sword than Theo or I!' Lance replied in desperation.

'Fine,' Dylan sighed as he walked toward the sword. As soon as he picked it up, darkness burst forth from it, knocking everyone away before returning to swirl around him, surrounding him. Dylan watched in horror as the darkness started to coalesce around individual parts of him. It started with his legs; then his arms, his torso and finally his face before solidifying around him. As the darkness settled, it revealed Dylan; the darkness had formed armour around him, tentacles rising out of it, snapping like cobras at anyone who dared approach him.

'Dylan?' Lance called tentatively as he stood.

Dylan turned to him but didn't reply. The tentacles retreated into the armour and Dylan raised his sword as if to inspect it.

'Dylan?' Lance called again, and again, he didn't answer but lowered the sword.

Pyro rose behind Dylan, fireballs in each hand. Quickly raising his hands, Pyro doused Dylan in flame.

'No!' screamed both Lance and Theo, horror-struck.

Suddenly, a beam-like spear of darkness burst from the fire, knocking away Pyro and ultimately stopping the flames. Dylan just stood in the centre of a scorched circle, armour gleaming in the light, as Pyro stood back up and stepped away cautiously, noticing that Dylan appeared untouched by the fire.

'That should have killed you,' Pyro said nervously.

Again, Dylan didn't reply but stepped toward Pyro. He then raised his hand above his head, beckoning the darkness to him. It swirled around the armour, making it impossible to see Dylan. Then the darkness scattered and Dylan was nowhere to be found.

'What the hell?' exclaimed a shocked Pyro, looking around for traces of Dylan.

'Where'd he go?' Theo asked Lance.

'I have no idea,' Lance looked around, finding no trace of him.

Unnoticed, darkness started to build up in the shadow behind Pyro. Dylan silently stepped out of it. The tentacles of darkness from the armour snapped out, wrapping around Pyro's wrists and ankles, forcing a struggling Pyro to be splayed out in front of Dylan, unable to escape.

'Let me go!' he screamed. He stilled as he felt the point of the blade on his back.

'Is he going to kill him?' Theo questioned.

'I think so!' Lance panicked. 'Dylan, stop!'

Desperate, Lance raised his hand at Dylan. Dylan tilted his head to the side as if he were asking 'why?'. Pyro held his breath as the sword was slowly pushed against his back.

'Don't say I didn't warn you,' Lance yelled as he quickly melded his light into another orb and threw it at Dylan. The orb, just missing Pyro, struck Dylan on the side and exploded upon impact. The blast knocked Pyro forward, Dylan back, and the sword out of Dylan's grasp. As soon as the sword left his hand, the armour evaporated from Dylan's body. Lance and Theo instantly ran to Dylan's aid as he fell to the ground, unconscious.

Unopposed, Nicholas walked toward the sword and picked it up.

'Finally,' he breathed. 'But how on Earth did he summon that armour?'

Somehow Pyro managed to stand, fire in both his hands.

'Nicholas, may I please have that?' he asked sarcastically.

'Like hell,' he snorted, pointing the sword at him.

Suddenly, something was thrown from the pool, landing between the two of them. It was Glacia, now unconscious.

Startled, Nicholas yelled, 'What the hell?'

Simultaneously, Pyro rushed to Glacia's side, screaming her name.

Something started to slowly rise from the pool and progress into the clearing. The creature, whatever it was, was an eight-foot-long marsupial-type beast with flippers, a horse-like tail and tusks protruding from its mouth like a walrus.

'No way. A Bunyip!' Nicholas breathed in shock and fear.

It raised its head and let out a blood-curdling howl. Lance and Theo retreated slightly in fear, dragging Dylan with them, as Nicholas raised the sword, readying for a fight.

Lowering its head, its red eyes flashed before it charged at Nicholas.

CHAPTER 8

Using the sword's power, Nicholas attempted to bring large spikes of darkness down onto the Bunyip, trying to skewer the beast. However, it would dodge the darkness every time. Once it was close enough, the Bunyip launched itself at Nicholas, knocking him down with it now on top of him and it slashed at his face with its sharp claws. Nicholas raised his arms to protect his face, but the Bunyip just slashed at his arms instead, reopening old wounds and making the new ones deeper. Snapping out of his shock, Lance quickly fired a beam of light at the Bunyip, knocking it off Nicholas, and then Nicholas blasted the Bunyip further back with a pulse of wind. The Bunyip skidded along the rocks, quickly finding its footing and renewing its charge toward Nicholas once again. Nicholas raised the sword and ran straight at the Bunyip.

'What are you doing?' Lance yelled.

Nicholas gave no reply, only jumping at the Bunyip, using a burst of wind to get him over the monster. The Bunyip tried to turn but lost its footing and tumbled over as Nicholas landed on the other side of it smoothly, then he turned around and raised his hand toward it, lightning jumping between his fingers before he unleashed it upon the

Bunyip, sending it flying backward into the trees with a roar of anger.

'And that is how you do it,' Nicholas said arrogantly as he turned to face Lance. 'Now to claim what is mine.'

'Which would be?' Lance asked in confusion.

'The Sword of Light,' Nicholas replied dully.

Lance's skin instantly crawled at his words. He knew that the sword must be important.

'I can't let you take it,' Lance said nervously.

'Lance, what are you doing?' asked Theo, still trying to wake Dylan.

'I don't know,' Lance replied out of the corner of his mouth.

'And why is that?' Nicholas smirked, raising the Sword of Darkness toward Lance.

'Cause…' Lance started as another roar sounded and the Bunyip came crashing out of the trees, its red eyes flashing with hatred and saliva dripping from its mouth.

Without delay, Nicholas charged at it, sword at the ready. He swung but the Bunyip only caught the sword between his steel- like claws and swiped him to the side; Nicholas landed on the ground with a sickening thud, unmoving, as the Bunyip howled in triumph. Wary, Lance slowly backed away. However, the sound reached the Bunyip's ears, alerting it to its new prey. It howled again and it charged Lance. He was quick to react, somewhat in a panic; two light orbs flew at the Bunyip, exploding upon impact. However, this didn't deter it at all; it just continued its charge. Lance threw himself to the side, the Bunyip barely missing him. Noticing this, it turned itself around, sliding, before renewing its charge. Quickly jumping to his feet, Lance desperately threw more orbs at it, hoping one just might stop it. Just as it was about to hit, it froze. Lance breathed a sigh in relief as he saw Theo getting up, hand raised toward the Bunyip.

'Thanks,' Lance said, looking over at Theo.

'Don't thank me yet. I can't hold it for long,' Theo growled as he struggled to hold the time around the Bunyip.

'What are we gonna do?' asked Lance, staring at the frozen Bunyip.

'I'm thinking we're going to need Dylan for this,' Theo answered.

'Yeah,' agreed Lance, running over to where Dylan lay. Dropping down to his knees, he began shaking Dylan. 'Come on, Dylan, wake the hell up!'

Dylan moaned but didn't wake.

'Come on, wake!' shouted Lance.

'Hurry, Lance,' Theo winced.

'Dylan!' screamed Lance, shaking him even harder as the frustration and fear boiled over.

'It's starting to move again!' Theo cried out.

'Release it,' ordered Lance, standing up to face the Bunyip. 'Get ready to help me fight it.'

'Fine,' Theo lowered his hand, unfreezing the Bunyip.

As it sped back into its charge, Lance raised both his hands and fired beams of light at its chest. This managed to halt it and knock it back slightly. It howled again, furious and confused, before noticing Theo and charging his way. Before it hit, Theo froze it again, quickly stepping out of the way and unfreezing, dodging the Bunyip as it hurtled toward the trees.

'We need Dylan,' Lance exclaimed. Suddenly, an idea struck him. 'Do you think you could speed up time for Dylan, so he wakes up?'

'I could try,' Theo replied, turning and concentrating on Dylan.

Slowly, Dylan's movements got faster and faster, till he sat bolt upright and Theo brought him back to normal speed.

'What's going on?' asked a confused Dylan before yet another blood-curdling howl pierced the air. 'And what the hell was that?'

'That would be the monster we have been fighting while you've been unconscious,' replied a slightly nervous Lance.

'Great,' Dylan drew out. 'So I'm guessing it's my turn then?'

'Yep,' Lance answered as another angry howl erupted as the Bunyip came barrelling back into the clearing.

Noticing the brothers, it altered its course, charging yet again. Dylan smiled and spread his arms wide, darkness surrounding his arms.

'Bring it,' Dylan grinned and he unleashed two tentacles, the first striking it in the chest and the second under the chin, lifting it off its feet and throwing it backward.

Summoning more darkness to surround him, he smiled as the Bunyip charged again. Dylan readied another attack, but a sudden gust of wind pushed the Bunyip off course and straight into a tree, felling it and a few others with a loud crash.

Limping slightly, Nicholas stepped out from under the trees, pointing the sword at Dylan.

'You can thank me now,' Nicholas laughed as he lowered it.

'I was doing just fine,' Dylan muttered, his prey out of sight.

'Sure, you were,' Nicholas continued to taunt.

Suddenly the Bunyip burst from the trees, letting out a furious roar.

'This thing never gives up, does it?' whined Lance, Dylan's smile reappearing.

'They never do,' replied Nicholas knowingly. It started to circle them. 'You know, we should team up to take this thing down.'

'Fine,' Dylan sighed.

'Count me in,' Lance and Theo added.

'Great, ready?' Nicholas asked.

'Yeah,' answered Dylan and Lance as Theo said, 'I guess.'

'Then let's take this thing down!' rallied Nicholas, raising the Sword of Darkness.

Recognising the call, the Bunyip answered with a fierce growl of its own, its head tipped back to face the sky before charging at them once again. Theo froze it at the last second, giving Lance a nod. Nodding back, Lance quickly created a massive orb of light before pressing it to the Bunyip's stomach as Theo unfroze the Bunyip. The orb exploded and blasted the roaring Bunyip back into the trees.

'Nice work,' praised Theo.

'It's coming back!' Nicholas yelled, readying the sword as the Bunyip leapt out of the trees and ran straight for Lance. Dylan threw darkness at it but missed. Lance concentrated, feeling a familiar sensation run through his body before teleporting behind the Bunyip, causing it to stop in confusion. Nicholas immediately dove at it, swinging the sword for the Bunyip's raised head. But the Bunyip moved, dodging the blade and swiping him away again, sending Nicholas tumbling away, the sword falling from his hand.

'Dylan! Grab the sword!' yelled Theo.

'Why?' he yelled back, throwing more darkness to keep the Bunyip at bay.

'Just do it!' Theo roared.

Dylan dove for the sword and the instant he grasped it, darkness erupted from it, surrounding Dylan and the armour reappearing.

'I think we should stand back,' stated Theo, stepping back and taking Lance with him.

Dylan raised his arm, beckoning darkness to him. It eagerly surrounded him like an excited puppy. Realising the imminent threat, the Bunyip renewed its attack on Dylan, howling. He quickly slammed down a wall of darkness on it, pinning it to the ground before lifting it and slamming it back down again.

'Is he toying with it?' asked Theo in a hushed tone.

The question went unanswered as the darkness morphed into a claw, picking up the Bunyip and flinging it at the waterfall near the base. It smashed through in an explosion of rock and water, the cave entrance behind the waterfall now much easier to spot.

'Is that a cave?' exclaimed Lance, running toward it.

'Looks like it,' Theo followed.

'Let's go in then! The Sword of Light that everyone has been fighting for must be in there!' Lance said, excitement in his voice.

'Maybe. Let's do this then,' Theo nodded to his brother and they both took off towards the cave.

CHAPTER 9

Upon hearing a thunderous explosion and the splashing of falling rock and debris, Pyro looked up to see the Bunyip crash through the waterfall and the rock wall behind, revealing the cave within.

'The cave! Come on, Glacia, wake up!' Pyro shouted, trying to shake Glacia awake. 'Come on.'

He looked up again as a long claw of darkness reached into the cave and pulled the Bunyip back out and threw it into the trees. Glacia moaned but didn't wake up. Pyro continued to watch as the Bunyip dove out of the trees once again and lopped towards Dylan. However, Dylan, darkness swirling around his armour, caught the Bunyip in the claw of darkness as it leapt at him, the claw completely encircling the beast. The claw clenched and crushed the Bunyip into a bloody mess. Dylan threw the remains of the Bunyip aside and began advancing toward the cave.

'Stop!' Nicholas yelled, making his way back to his feet. Dylan turned and threw a fist of darkness at him. Diving to the side, Nicholas flung lightning out of his fingers straight toward Dylan. A wall of darkness rose and blocked the lightning before morphing into spears that were sent flying in Nicholas's direction. Nicholas retaliated with a blast of wind aimed at Dylan, which caught and dissipated the spears. The blast also struck Dylan, making him stumble.

Using the split-second given by Dylan's stumble, Nicholas jumped up, letting the wind catch him so he could fly up and circle Dylan to find a weakness. But before he could, tentacles of darkness rose out of the armour and started to snap out at Nicholas. Dodging and weaving through the tentacles, he sent a powerful gust of wind at Dylan, but this time it didn't affect him at all.

Suddenly, one of the tentacles snapped out and caught Nicholas's ankle, he cursed as it curled up his leg before other tentacles caught his other leg and his arms. Nicholas struggled against the tentacles as he was pulled down towards Dylan, the Sword of Darkness poised to strike. Nicholas closed his eyes and waited for the sword to pierce his body and end it all.

Then Nicholas felt the heat and was abruptly dropped to the ground. Standing up, he turned to watch as Pyro walked towards Dylan, flames surrounding Pyro's fists, eyes once again flickering like the fire he controlled.

Dylan turned to Pyro, the tentacles of darkness now snapping out at him. Pyro smirked and threw two fireballs at him, but he blocked the fireballs with a shield of darkness before sending two streams of darkness at Pyro.

He dove to the side and blasted a torrent of fire, the fire enveloping him as Pyro sent more and more flames, increasing the temperature.

'And that finishes him!' Pyro smirked as he cut off the flames.

The smoke dissipated only to reveal that there was nothing in the burning circle.

'Where is…' Pyro started, shadows swirling behind him.

'Pyro, behind you!' Nicholas yelled.

Pyro turned and watched as Dylan stepped out of the shadows, armour gleaming, sword ready to strike. Pyro spun and Dylan jabbed at him, forcing him to dodge away from Dylan.

Raising his arms above his head, Nicholas concentrated as he swirled his arms, turning them in a circular motion simultaneously as if he were turning something above his head. As he did this, the air around him followed the direction of his arms. Moving them faster and faster, a tornado formed around him before he threw his hands out in front of him, directing it towards Dylan. As it lifted Dylan off his feet, Pyro then poured fire into the tornado, but Nicholas started to move it toward the waterfall.

'What are you doing?' yelled Pyro.

'Fire doesn't affect him, but maybe water will,' Nicholas replied.

Nicholas continued to move the tornado towards the water. Dylan struggled against the winds and flames to throw shards of darkness at Nicholas, only for it to be blocked out of nowhere by a sheet of ice.

The tornado finally hit the water, extinguishing the flames and creating a water spout. The water gushed around Dylan, battering him.

'I think it's working!' exclaimed a shocked Pyro.

Pyro then saw movement out of the corner of his eye. He turned and watched as Glacia crawled to the edge of the water and placed her hand in the water. The whole pool froze over, along with the water spout and Dylan.

'Glacia!' Pyro cried out, running toward her.

'She did it,' Nicholas murmured to himself.

'You okay, Glacia?' Pyro asked.

'Not really,' Glacia moaned, rolling over onto her back and breathing heavily.

***

As Dylan took care of the raging Bunyip, Theo and Lance walked into the cave.

'Damn, it's dark in here,' Theo said.

'I'll fix that,' Lance replied, igniting an orb of light in his hand.

'That's better.' Theo nodded.

'So, what do you think we are looking for?' Lance asked.

'I have no idea,' Theo replied with a shrug.

'Well, whatever it is, it must be up ahead,' stated Lance, pointing ahead of himself.

Theo looked up, noticing the glow up ahead.

Walking further, they noticed the passage opened up into a cavern. The cavern was large and symbols that the brothers did not recognise covered the walls, softly glowing.

'Hey, look!' Theo exclaimed, pointing into the cavern. 'That must be the sword.'

Lance looked up and in the centre of the cavern was a podium. Floating, point down, above the podium was a glowing sword of white-gold, three sapphires embedded in its hilt.

'Yeah, it kind of looks like the other sword Dylan is using,' Lance marvelled.

'I think you should take the sword,' Theo said, looking to Lance.

'Why?'

'I believe that this sword represents light, just like the other sword represents darkness.'

'But, what if I become like Dylan when he holds the sword?'

'You won't. I won't allow you to.'

'Alright, I'll do it,' said Lance, a little hesitantly, as he walked up to the podium before taking the sword in his hand.

***

Nicholas walked up to the frozen water spout and looked up at the black figure frozen in the ice.

'Now, how am I going to get the Sword of Darkness back?' he muttered to himself.

A loud *CRACK* sounded around the area.

'What was—' was all Nicholas could say before the frozen water spout exploded in a shower of ice, water and darkness.

'Shit, he's free,' Nicholas cursed, watching as Dylan descended from the night sky, sword ready as darkness swirled around him. But before any blows could be traded, a blinding flash of light came from within the cave.

'What now?' Nicholas moaned in frustration, turning toward the cave. A softly glowing figure in golden armour floated out of the cave, holding a white-gold sword in his hand.

'Who is that?' Pyro exclaimed.

'Whoever it is, they have the Sword of Light,' Nicholas answered.

The golden figure flew up towards Dylan, tendrils of darkness rising from his armour as if it were wary of this new opponent. The golden figure, now in front of Dylan, pointed the Sword of Light at him. Dylan followed suit and pointed his sword at the golden figure, the tendrils now growing more aggressive and trying to snap out at the new threat.

'This is gonna be one heck of a fight,' Pyro said excitedly, a grin on his face. 'Shame there isn't any popcorn.'

Dylan dove at the golden figure, sword poised, ready to strike. The two swords clashed, the golden figure having raised its sword just in time, and with an explosion of light and darkness, the two were knocked back. Being quicker to recover, Dylan sent tentacles at the golden figure, but the tentacles were blocked with a barrier of light before a beam of light was fired at Dylan in retaliation. Dylan quickly surrounded himself in darkness and disappeared. The golden figure looked around wearily.

Dylan reappeared on the ground beneath the golden figure, unnoticed, and threw a huge mass of darkness up at them. The mass struck the golden figure, hurling him higher into the sky. Dylan quickly summoned spears of darkness and threw them at the golden figure, trying to maintain the surprise onslaught, but it blocked the spears with another barrier of light, before firing another beam of light at Dylan. Dylan dove to the side, narrowly avoiding the beam. He rolled, jumped up and threw more darkness at the golden figure but it disappeared in a flash of light, only to reappear in front of Dylan. Dylan hurled a massive conglomerate of darkness as the golden figure fired a ray of light. The light and darkness struck each other, causing a massive explosion, knocking everyone off their feet.

'What the hell just happened?' Nicholas groaned as he stood.

Looking around as the dust settled, he saw Dylan lying near him unconscious, the Sword of Darkness next to him, and Lance unconscious up the other end of the clearing, the Sword of Light next to him. Walking around, he picked up both swords and let the wind lift him.

'Another successful mission,' he smirked, lifting up off the ground and flying off.

Pyro groaned as he watched Nicholas fly away with the two swords.

'Damn it,' Pyro muttered, standing up, then stumbled toward Glacia and picked her up before exiting himself, igniting the bottom of his feet and taking off into the night.

***

Theo clambered out of the cave, breathing heavily.

'What happened?' He heaved. He walked over to Lance.

'Lance, wake up!' he yelled and Lance's eyes fluttered open.

'What?' Lance mumbled, somewhat disorientated.

'It's okay, you're alright,' Theo said, helping Lance up so they could walk over to Dylan.

'Is he alright?' worried Lance.

'Yeah, he is just worn out,' Theo guessed. Lifting him, they slowly carried him back to their hotel.

CHAPTER 10

Norman pulled his coat on as he stepped through the open door and walked to his waiting limousine. Adam quickly shut and locked the front door of the mansion before quickly opening the door to allow Norman to step down into the back seat of the limousine. Norman leant back into his seat and contemplated the past thirty-six hours.

After putting out the rest of the fire with the aid of his telekinesis, Norman had immediately called his pilot to get his private jet ready for his flight to Japan today.

Adam quickly got into the driver's seat and set off to the airfield. Norman looked out the window, watching the London streets pass by.

'How long till we get to the airfield, Adam?' Norman asked.

'About ten minutes, sir,' Adam replied from the front seat.

'Excellent.'

'Are we going to Japan, sir, to get the Sword of Time?'

'Indeed, we are.'

Adam nodded, humming his approval.

Pulling up at the airfield ten minutes later, Adam stepped out of the limousine and opened the door for Norman. Not a second after having stepped out, Norman's phone rang, a familiar number displayed on the screen.

'I'm sorry, Adam, but I have to take this. I'll be there in a minute.'

'Not a problem, sir,' Adam replied, walking away to check that the plane had been adequately prepared.

'Did you get the job done? What? You didn't? Well, that's disappointing. Your next mission? Just keep doing what you've been doing. I'll talk to you later. Goodbye.'

Ending the call, Norman walked over to his plane.

'Is the plane ready?' Norman inquired.

'Yes, sir,' Adam replied. 'I'll just go get the pilot.'

As Adam walked away to fetch the pilot, Norman's phone rang again.

'Ah, Nicholas. Have you got the Sword of Light? Excellent, where was the sword? Alright, don't worry about coming home yet. I'm going to Japan for a couple of days. Good, I'll see you in a couple of days. Goodbye.'

Norman hung up his phone as Adam came back with the pilot.

***

Smiling, Nicholas put the phone back in his pocket. He stood up again. The sight of the sun rising above the hills and mountains greeted him. The tip of The Pinnacle was a truly beautiful place. Particularly at sunrise. Bending down, he picked up the Swords of Light and Darkness that had been lying on the rocks in front of him. He then floated off the ground and lowered himself into the valley towards Halls Gap.

He landed near his hotel and jumped back through the broken window, packed the two swords into his bag then turned back to the broken window.

'How am I going to explain this?' Nicholas mused, looking at the broken window. A grin broke out across his face as an idea formed in his mind. Concentrating, a ball of wind started to form near the window. He compressed the wind ball further and further, the pressure inside the ball building up. Letting go of the ball, the compressed air exploded out, destroying the wall, sending wood, mortar, metal, glass and other debris everywhere, also blasting Nicholas off his feet.

'Well, that turned out stronger than I thought,' Nicholas muttered in a daze before standing up. A knock sounded at the door.

'What's going on in there?' came the manager of the hotel's voice. Nicholas moved the detached door, letting the manager into the room.

'What happened?' the manager asked, shocked at the sight of the damaged room.

'Well, I turned on the heater, turned around and there was an explosion,' replied Nicholas, faking shock.

'Are you okay?' the manager asked.

'Yeah, I'm fine.' Nicholas nodded, reassuring him.

Nicholas and the manager walked outside, through the newer and bigger hole in the wall. The few people awake had started to crowd around with curiosity.

'Have you got insurance on this place?' asked Nicholas, looking over the small crowd of people.

'Yeah,' replied the manager. 'This is going to be fine. I will call them now.'

'Don't worry about it. I will have someone call you for the damages, how about we go and sort that out now?'

The manager nodded and walked back inside.

Nicholas continued to look over the crowd, then he spotted the three brothers from last night. They spotted him and their eyes widened in shock. Nicholas grinned at them and put his finger to his lips, indicating for them not to tell anyone. They nodded but continued to stare. Nicholas smirked and walked back into the hotel room, grabbed his bags and went to check out of the hotel.

***

'Would you like any food, sir?' Adam asked.

'No, thank you, Adam,' Norman replied.

'We shall be arriving in Tokyo in approximately two hours,' stated Adam before he walked to the back of the plane.

Norman leaned back in his chair and reminisced about his life.

He was born on the ninth of July in the year 1950 in Norwich. At the age of ten, in a silent fit of rage, he discovered his power of telekinesis. However, instead of accepting his power, he chose to deny its existence and continue his normal life. Norman excelled at school, graduating at the top of his class and joining the British army, training to become a surgeon. Norman was trained in both combat and surgery. He graduated in the army as a top surgeon in 1971 before being shipped out to the Dhofar Rebellion in Oman. There, he applied his surgery skills but his skills just weren't enough, so he secretly started using his powers to help out with his surgeries. After the Dhofar Rebellion ended in 1976, Norman was honourably discharged from the army, despite the pleas of reconsideration from his superiors, so he could become a professional surgeon.

Norman worked around the world and at the age of 45, he adopted Nicholas. Five years after that, he retired and began his research into legends, myths and superpowers. This ultimately led to his discovery of the book that contained the legend of the three brothers and their swords. After that discovery, he dedicated his riches to finding the swords and training Nicholas. Then, two years ago, Norman discovered the location of the first sword. Norman had left immediately and travelled to the island of Madagascar, where he spent three days searching for the sword to no avail. Until, on that fourth day, when he discovered the ruins that had glowing symbols from the book etched all over them. Walking through the ruins with a new spring in his step, Norman continued his search. The symbols on the crumbling walls guided him to his location; he finally found the room he had been searching for. Not taking any chances, Norman entered slowly, checking the entrance and the rest of the room for traps. Satisfied, he allowed himself to gaze upon the Sword of Darkness, floating point down above a podium in the centre of the room.

Hearing something move behind him, Norman quickly turned around. Standing barely three metres away was a creature with three heads, a lion body and a scaly tail with an arrowhead tip. Its heads – one of a snake, one of a lion and one of a goat – all stared at him menacingly.

'A Chimera,' Norman breathed, marvelling at the sight of the creature up close.

But his time of wonder was cut short when it growled at him, ready to pounce. More than confident that he could handle it, he smirked at the creature before using his telekinesis to lift the Chimera off the ground and throw it through the wall. Thinking that would be more than enough to knock it out for a bit, Norman laughed and turned his attention back to the sword.

But the Chimera jumped back through the hole in the wall, straight toward Norman. Dodging to the side, he shoved the Chimera away using his telekinesis before using it again to pick the Chimera up by the throat of its lion's head. However, the goat's head turned to him and spewed forth a cascade of fire from its mouth. Dropping his hold on the Chimera, Norman erected a force field to hold the fire at bay. It then lunged at him, claws outstretched. Norman dove to the side, rising as the Chimera prepared to attack again. Not prepared to face more attacks from its claws or heads, he reached his hand out and with his power, forced the Chimera against the wall, splaying it out with its back to the wall. It struggled against Norman's mental grip, roaring and hissing its disapproval at being held. Knowing he couldn't hold it for long, Norman grabbed his machete off the side of his backpack and one by one, chopped its heads off, the lion's head being the last to fall.

With the Chimera defeated, Norman turned around and grabbed the Sword of Darkness. Norman smiled, remembering he had returned to London the next day and presented the Sword of Darkness to Nicholas for his next birthday.

Suddenly, there was a *bing* and then the pilot announced that they would be arriving in Tokyo shortly and to start the landing procedure.

'Excellent,' Norman muttered under his breath, eager for the retrieval of the final sword.

CHAPTER 11

Dylan was jolted awake by the muffled sound of a small explosion. Jumping out of bed, he immediately got into an attack position, darkness swirling up and surrounding his fists in an instant, ready to take on anyone or anything. But upon surveying the area, he realised he was not in the clearing where he'd been fighting the Bunyip but in their hotel room.

How did I get back here? he thought, scratching his head in confusion.

The sound of glass, wood and other debris still falling snapped him out of his thoughts as he remembered the noise that woke him.

What's going on now?

Quickly, he got dressed and just as he was about to investigate what was happening, there was a knock at the door. Dylan opened the door and found his mother standing there.

'Ah, Dylan. You're up,' she said, slightly panicked.

'Yeah, I was woken by a loud noise,' he replied.

'That's why I'm here. Go wake your brothers up!' she said hurriedly.

'Why? What's going on?' Dylan asked, beginning to panic himself, fearing that the people from the night before were attacking them all now.

'The hotel is being evacuated. There's been a gas leak and explosion. Now, hurry!' Rosemary said before she took off towards the exit.

Dylan turned around, breathing a small sigh of relief and yelled, 'Hey, wake up!'

Theo moaned and Lance rolled over, mumbling some creative words.

'Come on! The hotel is being evacuated. Move your asses!' Dylan yelled again, now frustrated, wondering how they could have slept through that.

'What?' mumbled a confused Theo as he sat up.

'The hotel is being evacuated. There's been a gas leak,' Dylan said, motioning to the door.

'Right, let's go, Lance,' Theo said sternly, now wide awake, getting out of bed.

Lance groaned and sat up before rubbing his eyes and stretching.

Lance and Theo quickly got dressed and before long, the three brothers were outside with the gathered crowd. Dylan looked out over the crowd and noticed someone that nearly made him fall back in shock, his fear and panic instantly rising again.

'Hey, guys, look over there!' Dylan exclaimed.

Lance and Theo looked over to where Dylan was pointing. The sight of an obliterated wall greeted them and beside the destruction was Nicholas, standing there next to the manager, who was having an animated conversation on the phone.

'It's Nicholas from last night!' Lance replied in absolute shock. 'He must have been staying here too!'

Nicholas then turned away from the manager and spotted the brothers.

'Oh, crap. He's seen us!' Theo gasped.

Nicholas grinned at them, putting a finger to his lips.

'I get the feeling that we're meant to keep quiet about him,' Dylan murmured.

They gave a quick nod toward Nicholas before he grinned, turned and walked back through the hole in the wall.

'Well, I guess we better find our mother,' Theo suggested. 'I wonder where she is.'

The brothers split off from the crowd and searched around for their mother. They found her in the lobby of the hotel, reading through the pamphlets of things to do in the Grampians.

'What did you find, Mum?' Lance asked.

'This!' she replied, holding a pamphlet for Halls Gap Zoo. 'This is where we are going today.'

'Really?' all three brothers replied in unison.

'Yep. I think you will enjoy it,' she replied with a warm smile.

So, the three brothers and their mother hopped into their white Holden Commodore and took the ten-minute drive out of town to the zoo.

'Here we are,' Rosemary stated as she found a car park. They all stepped out of the car, walked inside, paid for their tickets and went into the open park.

'Oh, wow. Look, boys!' Rosemary exclaimed, walking over to the monkey enclosure.

'Cool, Mum,' replied Lance.

They walked around the zoo, their mother rushing ahead of them.

'What are we gonna do?' Theo asked.

'About what?' Lance questioned as they walked past an aviary of a variety of birds, all caged separately by species.

'Our powers,' Theo replied with a scowl.

'What do you mean?' Dylan asked, briefly looking at the lemurs in their enclosure.

'I mean, what are we going to do?' Theo paused, drawing a breath. 'Last night, we discovered a whole new world with other people with powers, deadly creatures and mystical weapons. A world we had no clue about and yet are now a part of.'

'I didn't think of it that way,' Lance said, a touch of wonder to his voice.

'Yeah, neither did I,' Dylan said with a smirk.

'Exactly. So, what are we gonna do?' Theo asked once more.

'Well, maybe we should explore this new world,' Dylan said, an excited gleam in his eye at the new idea.

'What?' A look of shock crossed his brother's faces.

'I mean, come on. We have powers too. It's obviously where we belong!' Dylan replied, his excitement building.

'But Dylan, that world is clearly very dangerous,' Theo cautioned. 'We were nearly killed last night, not only by the creature but also by those two guys.'

'Yeah, but we weren't killed and that creature was killed in the end,' whined Dylan.

'Or so we think,' muttered Lance.

'So what? We still had to carry you back, unconscious, to the hotel!' Theo stressed.

'Really? I did wonder how I got back there,' Dylan mused, trying to remember.

'Yeah, that's what happened,' Lance reaffirmed.

'What knocked me out?' Dylan asked, trying to piece it all together.

'Well, when you touched that black sword, a black armour formed around you and you changed, became a different person,' Theo replied, shuddering at the memory. 'While "you" kept the Bunyip at bay, Lance and I found a golden sword in the cave, behind the falls. Lance grabbed it and the same thing happened. You guys engaged in battle, then there was an explosion and you ended up unconscious.'

'Well, that explains a few things,' Dylan replied, nodding.

Lance walked ahead of his brothers and tried to remember the moment he touched the golden sword. The last thing he remembered was reaching out for the sword, then waking up on the ground with Theo shaking him awake. He scowled and continued walking. Eventually, they found their mother at the exit, waiting for them.

'You boys took your time,' she taunted.

'Sorry, Mum,' they replied.

'It's fine, boys,' She smiled. 'Time to head back though, as surely the hotel is open again.'

They all piled back into the car and drove back to Halls Gap. The hotel was open again; people were already working on fixing the damage from the explosion.

'They were quick onto that,' Rosemary muttered in disbelief as they stepped out of their car. They all grabbed their keys and headed back to their rooms.

Dylan instantly laid down on the couch and turned on the television. Lance and Theo sat at the table and began to play cards.

About half an hour later, Dylan sat up and looked at his brothers.

'What?' Theo asked, feeling Dylan's gaze.

'I was thinking,' Dylan began.

'That must have hurt!' Lance mocked, a smirk on his face.

'Shut up!' Dylan growled. 'I was thinking that we should go find Nicholas.'

'Uh, why?' Lance replied, confused.

'He might be able to train us to use our powers,' Dylan replied, the excitement in his voice back in spades.

'Argh, not this again,' Theo groaned.

'What?' Dylan asked.

'We don't belong in that world, Dylan! We belong in the normal world with normal people,' Theo stated, a little frustrated.

'We don't! We have powers! We aren't normal anymore,' Dylan replied angrily.

'Dylan, those people are trained killers. We aren't! We are just three guys who have no idea what we are doing,' Theo shot back, his anger also rising.

'I don't care. I'm gonna go find Nicholas and if you don't wanna come, that's fine by me!' Dylan shouted, standing up and leaving the room, slamming the door.

'Wow,' Theo exclaimed, turning to Lance.

Lance looked at his brother and stood up.

'Where are you going?' Theo asked.

'I'm going with Dylan,' Lance said calmly.

'You can't be serious! You believe in what he is saying?'

'He has a point, you know.'

'Fine, go, be idiots!' Theo stormed into his room, leaving Lance there for a second before he too left the room.

He found Dylan knocking on the door of the room where the explosion had happened that morning.

He must assume that is his room because that is where he walked back into this morning, Lance thought as he walked up to his brother.

'Anything?' asked Lance.

'Nah,' Dylan replied with a shake of his head.

'Maybe we should go ask at the reception?' Lance asked.

'That's not a bad idea,' Dylan replied with a nod.

Dylan and Lance took note of the room number and headed for the reception. The manager of the hotel was behind the desk.

'Good afternoon, boys!' the manager asked, a smile warming his face. 'What can I do for you?'

'We are looking for someone who we met last night,' Lance said. 'He was in room ten.'

'Ah, the room with the explosion, yeah? A young man, about your age,' the manager said as he sifted through his memory. 'I'm sorry to say, boys, but he checked out this morning after the explosion and paid for the damage.'

'He paid for the repairs?' Dylan questioned in shock.

'He did. Got an associate of his to call us. I just got off the phone with them and they are going to pay for everything, can you believe it?' the manager replied, the shock evident in his voice.

'No, I cannot believe it,' Lance replied.

'Thanks for your help, anyway,' Dylan said, nodding.

'No worries, boys,' The manager nodded and went back to his work.

'What do we do now?' Lance asked his brother, unsure of what their next move was.

'We go into town and see if he is still around,' Dylan said.

'Surely he's long gone by now.'

'Still worth a shot.'

'Alright then, the town it is.'

Dylan and Lance left the hotel and headed into town. They searched for an hour but found no trace of Nicholas.

'Well, that's that I guess,' Lance sighed.

'Yeah, I guess so,' Dylan murmured, disappointed.

'Back to the hotel?' Lance asked. Dylan nodded and they began their walk back.

***

Nicholas floated above Halls Gap, bags slung over his shoulder as he watched two of the brothers walk back to the hotel. Nicholas had been watching them search the town for the last hour.

I wonder what they were looking for? Me, perhaps? he thought.

Nicholas shrugged.

Those three boys are quite interesting.

CHAPTER 12

The next morning, the brothers and their mother packed the car, checked out of the hotel and started their two-hour drive home.

About halfway home, Dylan looked out of the window and spotted something unusual in the sky. He looked closer and it looked like a human flying through the sky with two bags strapped to his shoulders.

What the hell? Dylan thought. He looked again, making sure he wasn't going crazy, but all he could see were clouds.

I must have been dreaming.

An hour later, the car pulled into their driveway and they unpacked their car.

***

Nicholas, having followed the brothers, landed on the outskirts of a small town that he didn't know of. He could see a factory by the name of Fonterra ahead though.

This must be where they live, he thought.

He walked into the town, passing the factory, fire station and surprisingly, the local golf club. Looking further ahead, he saw a service station with a small motel off to the side. It was single story and made of brown brick with a white 'Motel' sign facing the road.

'That's what I am after,' he grinned.

He walked into the service station, booked a room for a few days, choosing the fifth room out of eight. The clerk handed him the key and Nicholas carried his bags back out and walked over to the motel. The entrance to each room was out in the open. A veranda ran along the length of the building and a small table and chairs sat out the front of each room. He opened room five and stepped inside. It was a simple room containing a single bed, a small tv, small kitchen and fridge and a table and chairs. Nicholas dropped his bags on the bed, removed the two swords – now wrapped in a cloth he had brought with him – and slid them under the bed, hiding them from any prying eyes. Satisfied that they were safe, he left the room, locking it behind him and heading back into town for supplies.

***

Theo dumped his bag on his bed and started unpacking. Before long, he glanced up and out the window. He found himself staring across the road at Gabrielle's house.

I wonder if she's home, he thought.

After grabbing his phone, he sent her a message.

Hey.

He put the phone down and continued unpacking but not a minute later, his phone vibrated.

Hey. You home yet?

Yeah, just got back.

Good! Meet me at the park in five minutes?

Sure, see you soon.

He was quick to change into a clean shirt and pair of shorts before dashing out of the house. In his eagerness, he made it to the park in less than five minutes but found no one there. Confused as to why she wasn't there, he looked around a bit more before hearing the wolf whistle behind him. He grinned and spun around. She was dressed in a blue floral dress that went to the knee, with one hand on her hip and the other up by her face, chewing on a nail.

'Hey,' he said shyly.

Moving toward him, she replied, 'Hello, handsome.'

'What's up?' he asked.

'Not a lot,' she said, closing the distance between them and planting a kiss on his lips. Then she whispered in his ear, 'I missed you.'

'I missed you too,' he breathed back, his words almost not leaving his lips.

They walked to a park bench and talked to each other about what they had been doing over the past few days, Theo leaving out the parts about their powers and facing off against the Bunyip.

'So yeah, it was a good holiday,' he laughed.

'That's good,' she smiled. 'But I'm getting hungry. Let's go get something to eat.'

'Alright.'

They stood up and, hand-in-hand, walked the streets of Cobden to the local bakery. But about halfway there, three boys came flying around a corner on their scooters. Theo's eyes widened and knowing that they wouldn't be able to move out of the way in time, he slowed time almost imperceptibly so he could move himself and Gabrielle out of the way. He sped time up back to normal and the boys sped past them.

Turning, Gabrielle yelled at them, 'Jerks!' Turning back to Theo, she whispered, 'I swear we wouldn't have gotten out the way in time then.'

'Well, surprisingly, we did, and there's nothing like an adrenaline rush to make one hungry!' Theo joked in an attempt to change the subject.

Gabrielle laughed and they continued on their way to the bakery.

After getting their food, Theo scanned his surroundings until something caught his eye across the road from him. But it wasn't so much a 'something' as a 'someone'. The guy looked about his age and was walking toward the centre of the town.

'That kinda looks like Nicholas from Halls Gap,' he said under his breath, Gabrielle not hearing him at all as he continued to look at the guy.

'Nah, it can't be.'

He immediately dismissed it and turned back to Gabrielle.

***

Heading straight for his trampoline, Dylan walked out into the backyard to practice his wrestling moves. But before he got too far, his phone started to vibrate in his pocket.

'Hello?' he answered.

'Hey, you,' came the seductive reply of his girlfriend, Kelsey.

'Hey, babe,' he smiled unconsciously.

'You home yet?' she asked.

'Yeah, just got home in fact,' Dylan replied with a nod.

'You wanna come around to mine?' Kelsey asked.

'Sure, babe,' Dylan replied with a grin.

'I got a little surprise for you,' Kelsey said, her voice going husky.

'Awesome, I'll be around soon,' Dylan replied.

After hanging up, he quickly headed inside and changed into some cleaner clothes before heading straight to Kelsey's house. On his way there, he noticed the shadows skewing toward him as if they were being pulled his way. Smiling, he reached out and pulled at them more, noticing their eagerness to obey. Making sure no one was around, he pulled them from their resting places and swirled them around him, wreathing his fists in them as well. He laughed as he felt the power surge through his body, the euphoria of it before he finally let them go back to their original places. Shrugging off the power high, he continued to Kelsey's and a few minutes later, he walked through her front gate.

Noticing the absence of her parents' cars, he grinned as he knocked on the door. Seconds later, she opened it.

'Hey, sweet-cheeks!' she teased.

Kelsey was a relatively short girl, coming up to his lips in height, but she was fit and had short dark hair. Today, she was wearing a white button-up shirt and a short skirt.

'Hey, I told you not to call me that!' he growled playfully, taking her into his arms.

'Why not?' She giggled, looking up at him.

'Because I don't like it,' he grumbled out.

'Aww, Mister Grumpy,' she stirred before kissing him and leading him inside her bedroom.

She sat on her bed and beckoned Dylan to sit next to her, lust plain as day in her features. He complied with the request, eyeing her with equal amounts of lust evident in his own body.

He suddenly remembered what she had said to him on the phone. 'So, you had a surprise for me?'

'Oh, yeah!' Quickly standing, she headed off to her wardrobe and began rummaging around. Once she found what she'd been looking for, she came back toward the bed. A bottle of vodka was in her hand, which she handed to him.

'How did you get this?'

'I got a friend to buy it for me,' she said dismissively.

'Fine by me.' He twisted the cap off and took a swig from the bottle. He gave a slight grimace as the alcohol burned down his throat.

'Smooth,' he said semi-sarcastically.

'Yeah,' she agreed, taking the bottle from his hand and taking a swig herself.

'So, any more surprises?' he said with a cheeky smirk.

'Of course.' She winked.

*****

Nicholas walked into the local supermarket and picked up a basket before walking the aisles and scanning the shelves for essentials. He loaded up the basket with milk, eggs, bacon, bread, fruit and a bottle of soft drink. Before walking to the cash register, he examined his basket, making sure he had everything he needed. The guy behind the register was tall and had unruly black hair. Looking closer, it felt like he was looking in a mirror, except this guy had a bit more weight on him. The guy's badge even read 'Nicholas'.

Now that's just odd, he thought, unloading his groceries.

'Hello, how are you today?' the guy asked, scanning the items through.

'Good, thank you,' he replied politely, digging his wallet out.

'Is that the lot?' the guy inquired as he scanned the last item through.

'Yeah,' Nicholas replied.

'That's twenty-two dollars and fifty cents.'

'Just on the card,' Nicholas stated, holding up his credit card. He paid for his groceries, grabbed the bags and headed back to the hotel.

***

Lance sat on his bed and looked out the window, a bored expression on his face and his chin resting on his face. Both of his brothers had left him at home to hang out with their girlfriends.

'I need a girlfriend,' he said in exasperation, then sighed at his loneliness.

Standing up, he looked around the room for something to do. He spotted his wallet and picked it up, deciding to go to the supermarket for some snacks and drinks.

'Mum! I'm going down the street! Do you need anything?' he yelled as he started walking out the door.

'No, dear!'

'Okay,' he said as he shut the door and headed toward the supermarket.

Lance loved it here in Cobden. It was quiet and peaceful. He and his family had moved here two years ago after their father had left his family and gone to the United Kingdom to join a massive government project, the name of which Lance could not remember. Their father was a world-renowned scientist, specialising in human anatomy. So, he had been highly sought after and the project had paid top dollar to get him. A fight had broken out between his parents, his mother not wanting to move to the UK, and as a result, their relationship had broken apart in an instant and his father had left without a word. Lance frowned and tried to shake the thoughts of his father from his mind. They only brought more hurt.

Continuing his walk, he forced his thoughts back onto what he was going to buy. Walking into the supermarket, he bumped into someone.

'I'm sorry—' Lance started as he looked up, staring Nicholas straight in the face.

CHAPTER 13

Norman stepped out of the limousine, thanking Adam as he opened the door, and strode into the Palace Hotel of Tokyo. He quickly checked in, arranging for his luggage to be taken up for himself and Adam before making his way up to the suite.

The room was luxurious, to say the least. Two king-sized double beds sat closer to the doorway, a comfortable-looking three-seater comforter resting by the window that overlooked the city and as requested, a round table sat in the middle with elaborate-looking chairs surrounding it. The colour scheme of the room was neutral, with whites, light browns and soft reds mixed throughout.

'Nothing less than expected,' Norman said, slightly impressed.

After having his luggage delivered, Norman changed out of his suit and into clothes more suitable for exploration. Then he went back to his bag and retrieved the copied pages from the pages on the three swords.

'Is that going to help, sir?' Adam asked as he spied Norman walking toward the table, pages in hand.

'I hope so,' he answered, spreading out the copies on the table. 'Did you bring the laptop?'

'Yes, sir, would you like me to bring it out?' Adam asked.

Sitting down, Norman replied, 'Please, and start researching Japan.'

Adam pulled out the laptop, booting it up. 'And what, precisely, should I look up, sir?'

'Ancient ruins, caves, anything along those lines...' Norman murmured as he studied the copies.

Adam immediately got to work, sitting at the opposite end of the table. Norman searched for the part about the Sword of Time. The words were hard to read as they were a jumble of English and other languages.

Pulling out a notebook, he started translating the passage. First, there were mentions of the sword, then of something about a 'trial of three'.

Norman pondered this for a moment. 'Trial of three? I wonder what that means.'

Next, there was a mention of 'stone', followed by something he didn't recognise. Shortly after, the word 'Nue' was written.

Where have I heard that before? Norman thought.

He looked up to find Adam staring at the laptop screen intently.

'Have you found anything, Adam?' Norman asked, looking up from the pages.

'No, sir,' he replied 'Though I have only found three places that may suit the specifications we're looking for.'

'And what would they be, Adam?'

'The Haikyo Ruins, the Taya Caves and the Yonaguni Monument, sir.'

'Well, it can't be the Haikyo Ruins as they are too modern,' stated Norman matter-of-factually. 'We're looking for something more ancient.'

'I see.' Adam paused. 'Where did we find the other two swords?'

'The Sword of Darkness was located in ancient ruins; whereas, from what Nicholas has told me, the Sword of Light was found in a rock formation behind a waterfall.'

'Well, the Taya Caves are classified as ruins and the Yonaguni

Monument is a rock formation,' said Adam.

'Wait, how did you spell Yonaguni?' Norman asked.

Adam spelled it out as Norman looked over the image, immediately finding the word 'Yonaguni'.

'It's there!' Norman shouted as he hurriedly stood in his excitement, his finger still on the page as the chair fell over behind him.

'Yonaguni, sir?'

'Yes, Adam.'

'Well, in that case, there is one problem, sir,' Adam said, a grim look crossing his face.

'And what may that be?'

'The Yonaguni Monument, sir…'

'Yes?'

'It's a rock formation that is underwater, sir. On the sea floor.'

'Oh, that won't be a problem, Adam, You and I shall just dive down to it!'

'Me?'

'Yes, you. I'm going to need you to come with me.'

'Why me, sir?'

'Because I believe that the Sword of Time will be the hardest to retrieve. From what I have translated from these images of the book, there are going to be trials, and I know we made a deal; however, I think I may need you to use your power down there. That is how difficult I believe these trials to be.'

'But, sir, we agreed that I would never have to use it again!'

'I know, Adam, I know. You may not even need to, though I am warning you now so you are prepared if need be.'

'Very well, sir,' Adam replied, his low tone being one of disappointment.

'Alright, I now need you to call the pilot and organise a flight to the closest airport near Yonaguni Monument for tomorrow.'

'Yes, sir, and that would be the Yonaguni airport.'

'Could you also arrange for some diving gear?' Norman asked. 'Oh, and ring room service for a bottle of wine.'

'Yes, sir,' Adam replied with a nod, then left the room to begin making the phone calls as Norman leaned back in his chair, a grin spreading across his face.

***

The following day, both Adam and Norman packed waterproof bags with both clothes for exploration and fighting and left the hotel for the airport. Half an hour later, they arrived at the airport, boarded the plane and took off.

Once the plane had risen to height, Adam got up and made Norman his usual tea, delivered it to him and then sat back down. Thoughts plagued his mind. He was nervous, he hadn't been out in the field for a long time and he hadn't used his power since before then. Adam looked out the window, looking over the clouds as he reminisced.

He had been born in a suburb of London called Hounslow, to parents who didn't do anything for a living other than drink and smoke drugs for a living, living off welfare payments. When he had been born, his new brother and sister were already teenagers and ready to leave home, so by the time he had turned six, his siblings had left to live their own lives and with that, his parents had become abusive, giving him hell and starting to hit him. At the age of eight, he'd discovered Batman comics and used them as an escape from his brutal reality. But his favourite was neither the caped crusader nor his sidekick Robin; no, his favourite character was Batman's ever-faithful butler, Alfred Pennyworth. This character was his role model and ultimately, this led to him deciding that when he grew up, he wanted to become a butler to a wealthy family, like the Waynes in the comic, which could provide him with rare insight and opportunity to interact with professionals at the highest level and travel and work in the most amazing places around the world. That was what drew Adam to the profession.

Years went by and at the age of sixteen, Adam had made his dream a reality. He enrolled himself into the School of Butlers, completing the course at the top of his class and not long after that, a rich family had taken him in immediately. He moved into the rich family's mansion, away from his parents and their abusive ways. The rich family had even provided him with everything he needed to do his job. It was bliss.

Then a year later as he was carrying a cup of tea to the master of the mansion, the cup and saucer started to shake in his hand. He looked down at his hand to see that it wasn't him shaking, only the cup and saucer.

What the hell? he had thought at the time.

He swapped it to the other hand but the shaking did not stop. He hurried to the study, unsure of what was happening as the shaking got worse.

He knocked before opening the door to the study.

'Thank you, Adam, just…' was all the master could say before the cup and saucer exploded into a thousand pieces, splashing the tea all over himself and the master.

'I-I'm s-so sorry, s-sir,' stammered Adam, shocked at what had just happened.

The master stood, face red with fury as the tea and porcelain slid down his clothing.

'Get out! You're fired!' he screamed, pointing toward the door.

Adam left the room, head hung in shame and disbelief as he packed his belongings and left the mansion.

Over the next few months, he acquired other butler jobs but they all ended the same way with something around him shattering. But then one day, he got another interview with another family. He tentatively strode into the manor of the family and waited with the other applicants. The numbers slowly dwindled until he was finally called. He entered the room, nervous as he sat down in front of the master.

'So, you must be Adam,' the master began.

'Y-yes sir,' Adam stammered.

'Don't be nervous, son,' reassured the master. 'My name is Norman Quinzel and as you may have guessed, I am the master of this manor. I also see from your resumé that you are more than qualified to take the job, but I want to see you in action.'

'What would you like me to do, sir?' Adam asked.

'I'd like for you to bring me a cup of tea – the Earl Grey is sitting just over there on the table,' Norman said, motioning toward the table sitting in the corner of the study.

Adam's eyes widened in terror, knowing what would happen once he fetched the tea.

'Is there a problem, Adam?' Norman asked.

'No, sir,' Adam said, trying to calm himself as he made his way toward the tea.

Just relax, he thought to himself as he poured the tea. He picked the cup up and started walking towards Norman, the cup starting to shake. He looked down in horror as the cup shook more and more before exploding and spilling the tea all over his hand.

'I'm so sorry, sir!' Adam burst out, on the verge of tears.

'It's fine, Adam,' Norman said, grinning like the Cheshire Cat. 'Do it again!'

'What?' Adam asked, flabbergasted.

'Bring me another cup of tea, please,' Norman said with a grin.

Confused, Adam slowly walked back to the pot and poured a new cup. From the moment he picked it up, it began to vibrate violently before exploding on his hand once again. Adam grimaced and bowed his head in shame.

'I believe I know what is happening,' Norman said as he stroked his beard, still grinning.

'What would that be, sir?' Adam asked, now curious.

'Adam, would you place your hands on this table and try to vibrate it?' Norman asked, pointing toward his desk.

'Sir?' Adam questioned, confused.

'Oh, just amuse this old man, would you?' Norman chuckled.

'Okay…' Adam did as he was asked, but nothing happened.

'Concentrate, Adam. Visualise it, feel it, make the table vibrate!' Norman encouraged.

Concentrating more, Adam started feeling the table vibrate beneath his touch. He watched on in astonishment as the vibrations intensified to the point where the table splintered into shrapnel.

'Oh, my. I-I'm so sorry, sir!' Adam stood back from the mess he'd created.

Norman laughed. 'It's okay, Adam! I've figured it all out! You're a very special person young man. You just have an ability no one else does. Powers, as you may call it.'

'Really?' Adam asked in shock and alarm.

'Yes, I believe you control vibrations. You may just be limited to smaller vibrations such as this,' Norman said calmly as he gestured toward the table, 'or you may even have the potential for something on a massive scale, like an earthquake.'

'How do you know this? How do you know about powers?' Adam asked, disbelief still plastered on his face.

'I, too, have such abilities.' Norman raised his hand, the pieces of the shattered table rising with it, and as he closed his fist, the pieces rearranged themselves back into the desk. 'I control things with my mind. This is also known as telekinesis. Here, I can help you develop your abilities and control them. If you agree, you can have this job.'

'Sir, I will happily take the job and the training,' Adam cracked a small smile, his dread almost completely gone.

Norman reached out his hand and Adam took it, shaking it to seal the deal.

Adam started immediately and for the next year, Norman and Adam trained hard. Adam mastered his power but in the process, he learned that it was extremely dangerous and that he should only use it under extreme circumstances.

Suddenly, Adam broke out of his daze as he felt the plane begin to descend.

'Here we go,' he breathed, rubbing his hands together.

CHAPTER 14

Lance stood back in shock, mouth agape.

'Well, hello, Lance,' Nicholas grinned.

Lance couldn't reply, he was too stunned, his mouth just opening and closing.

'Are you alright?' Nicholas asked, confused.

Lance managed to shake his head.

'Ah! So, you're surprised to see me?' Nicholas laughed, confusion vanishing off his features.

Lance nodded.

'Alright, well, I suppose you want to know why I followed you and your brothers back here?'

'Err, yes, why?' Lance asked, finally having found his voice.

'That is because you are quite intriguing. I have never seen powers like yours and your brothers' before now.'

'Really? You find us interesting?'

'Yes, and yes.'

'Well, we only discovered our powers the other day,' Lance murmured, just loud enough for Nicholas to hear as he rubbed the back of his neck.

'Really?' Surprise was evident on Nicholas's face. 'But you guys were using your powers like you'd been training for years…'

'Huh? I've only been doing what feels right.'

'This level of control comes naturally to you?' Nicholas pondered as Lance nodded. 'Alright, well, you still need training. You all still need training.'

'Would you do that?'

'Do what?'

'Train us!'

'Oh! Umm… Look, go get your brothers and we can discuss it further with them present.'

'Alright, we can do it that way.'

'Here is my phone number,' He handed Lance a card with his mobile number on it. 'Let me know when you guys are ready to talk this over.'

'Cool, we will,' Lance said, taking the card.

Nicholas nodded before turning around and walking away.

Grinning, Lance walked out of the supermarket and immediately dialled Theo's number.

'Hello?' Theo answered after a couple of rings.

'Hey, bro, where you at?'

'Just got home, why?'

'Alright, I'll be home in five. I've got something huge to tell you!' Lance said excitedly.

'See you in five then.'

Lance hung up and hurried home. He made it to the front gate in just under five minutes, the pent-up excitement giving him extra speed.

'You were quick,' called out his mother as soon as the door closed behind him.

'Yeah, I know!' Lance replied, hurrying to Theo's room before knocking and letting himself in.

'So, what's up?' Theo asked, turning to face Lance.

'You'll never guess who I ran into at the supermarket!' Lance exclaimed, leaning back on the door as he caught his breath a little, his eagerness from earlier catching up to him.

'No, I won't. Who did you run into?'

'Nicholas.'

'But we always see Nicholas at the supermarket. He works there and you also play cricket with him.'

'No, not him! The one from Halls Gap!'

'What? You're joking, right?'

'I'm not joking, Theo. I ran into him in the supermarket. He followed us back here.'

'Wait, he followed us? Why? Is he here to silence us?'

'No, actually, he wants to meet with us. All three of us.'

'Why?'

'He offered to train us. Teach us how to control our powers better.'

'What?' Theo blanched, still not believing what Lance was saying.

'Yeah, you heard me right.'

'But, is that what we want? To be a part of this new world we've stumbled on?'

'Well, I think it's what I want. We aren't normal anymore and I feel like we belong in this new world!'

'Maybe, but I like my normal life. I don't feel like putting my life, or our loved ones, in constant danger.'

'I understand, Theo, but please, just come and meet him. Hear him out.'

'I don't know,' Theo said, crossing his arms.

'Come on, please? We're brothers, we do everything together!' Lance continued, adding with a grin, 'Well, almost everything.'

Theo groaned but cracked a small smile at the quip. 'Fine, but you owe me.'

'Yes!' Lance jumped out in excitement. 'Now, where is Dylan?'

'I have no idea, and you're on your own there.'

Walking over to the window, Lance looked out over the street and spotted Dylan stumbling toward their house.

'Well, there he is,' he said, pointing him out to Theo.

'Really?' Theo walked over to Lance and looked where Lance was pointing.

'Yeah, see? He's coming through the gate now.'

They watched on as Dylan stumbled through the gateway, falling over once he was through it and proceeding to crawl to the nearest garden bed where he vomited.

'Is he…' started Lance.

'Yup, he is drunk… again,' Theo confirmed. 'That damn girlfriend of his. Come on, let's go drag him inside.'

They quickly raced down the stairs and out the front door, crossing the front yard to where Dylan lay, still vomiting.

'Dylan, are you okay?' Theo asked as he placed a hand on Dylan's shoulder, pulling him to face them.

'Oh, hey, guys. Guess what?' Dylan slurred, clearly still drunk with no sign of sobering and grinning from ear to ear.

'What, mate?' Lance laughed at Dylan's current state.

Dylan chuckled before turning and vomiting in the garden bed again.

'Nice,' Lance said, his nose scrunching up at the smell.

'Yeah, it was,' mumbled Dylan, 'but I think I'm gonna lay down now…'

He went limp, face hitting the grass before the garden bed, and lost consciousness.

'And… There he goes!' Lance chuckled.

'Yeah,' Theo agreed. 'Now, come and help me with him.'

They picked Dylan up off the ground and slung him over their shoulders before carrying him inside. They just got past the kitchen when their mother stuck her head out and saw them.

'What the hell is going on here?' she asked, furious. 'Is he drunk again? And it's still early!'

'Yeah, we found him in the front yard,' answered Theo, glancing over his shoulder. 'We're just taking him upstairs to bed so he can sleep it off.'

'Right, well, I'm going to have a serious talk with him in the morning,' she muttered, going back into the kitchen.

Theo and Lance proceeded to haul their brother up the stairs, into his room and then dump him on his bed.

'Well, it looks like we won't be meeting Nicholas tonight,' said Lance, disappointed.

'Yeah.'

'I'll have to call him and let him know so he knows not to wait for us,' Lance murmured, fishing out the card and his phone from his pockets before he dialled the number and hit call.

'Hello?' answered Nicholas.

'Hi, Nicholas, it's Lance.'

'Ah, hello, Lance, what's up?'

'Just letting you know we won't be able to meet up with you tonight.'

'That's okay. How about we meet up tomorrow instead?'

'Yeah, sure. Meet you at the park near the supermarket then? Same time?'

'Perfect. I'll expect you and your brothers there tomorrow.'

'Righto, see you tomorrow. Bye.'

'Bye.'

Lance hung up and looked at Theo.

'So, we'll meet him tomorrow then?' Theo asked.

'Yeah, at the park.'

'Cool.'

'Boys! Tea is ready!' their mother called from downstairs.

'Alright, Mum!' Theo yelled back before getting up and heading down, Lance quick on his heels.

***

Waking to a splitting headache the next day, Dylan was not feeling good at all. He managed to set himself up on the edge of the bed, grunting in disgust when he smelt the mixture of vodka and vomit waft off himself.

'I regret yesterday now…' he muttered to himself as he rubbed the dreariness from his face, simultaneously shielding his eyes from the light pouring in from his window. As more of his senses came back to him, he heard someone coming up the stairs and stopping outside his door.

'Aww, crap,' he groaned quietly, thinking it was his mum coming to lecture him again.

'You awake yet, Dylan?' called Lance from the other side of the door.

Groaning loud enough for Lance to hear, Dylan flopped back down on the bed.

Taking that as a yes, Lance let himself in.

'Come on, dude,' Lance said. 'We have to go!'

'Go where?' Dylan asked, confused.

'We are going to the park.'

'What?' Dylan propped himself up. 'Why?'

Lance leaned against the door. 'We are meeting someone there.'

'Uhhh, who?'

'We're meeting with Nicholas.'

'Wait… what? That guy from the supermarket?'

'No, the guy from Halls Gap,' Seeing Dylan about to cut him off, he continued, 'And before you ask, yes, he followed us back here. I ran into him yesterday and went over all that with him. Now we're going to meet with him again to discuss his offer to train us.'

'Really? Train us? To do what?' Confusion was still set on Dylan's face.

'Yes. To use our powers better,' explained Lance. 'Now, get up, take a shower and get some clean clothes on. You reek! We'll leave in ten, so you better hurry.'

Lance nudged himself off the door and let himself out as Dylan, headache forgotten, jumped off the bed and gathered some fresh clothes before heading to the bathroom. He quickly had a shower, dressed in fresh clothes, sprayed on some deodorant and raced down to join his brothers at the front door.

'Morning,' Theo greeted, looking up from his phone.

'Morning,' returned Dylan.

'By the way, you owe us,' Theo said, motioning between Lance and himself.

'Err, why?' Dylan asked, an eyebrow raised.

'Because we hauled your sorry butt from the garden bed you passed out near up to your bed,' Theo said with a pointed look.

'Oh. Yeah. Thanks for that, and I'm sorry,' Dylan hung his head in shame at the thought.

'Oh, and Mum wants to talk to you when she gets home since you were still comatose this morning,' Lance chimed in.

'Ah, crap,' Dylan groaned.

'Alright, we all ready to go?' Lance asked.

'Yeah, let's go,' Theo said, Dylan nodding as well.

With that, the brothers left the house and made their way to the park near the dam. They found Nicholas sitting on a park bench, slightly hunched over with his back to them. Moving around the side of Nicholas, they found him twisting a hand between his knees. Below that twirled a mini-tornado, less than half a metre high.

'Hi, Nicholas,' called Lance.

Nicholas turned and smiled, the mini-tornado dissipating immediately. 'Hello, boys, how are we this fine morning?'

'Good, thanks,' Theo said, returning his smile before getting serious. 'Now, why are we here? And more importantly, why are you here?'

'I like you, straight to the point,' Nicholas laughed.

Theo and Dylan glared at him, unimpressed.

'Alright, alright. The reason I'm here is, essentially, you three. You are unique. I have never seen powers like yours and to top it off, for only having wielded them for a few days, somehow you can use your powers better than people who have trained for years!'

Theo crossed his arms, his face unchanged, as Dylan stepped forward.

'You mean that there are more people like us?' Dylan said excitedly.

'Yes, there are whole communities with people who have powers,' Nicholas stated.

'Cool!' Dylan's grin widened.

'And...?' Theo started, waiting for Nicholas to get to his point.

'Well, here is what I'm offering. I will train you three to control – and truly master – your powers, as well as train you in hand- to-hand combat and swordsmanship.'

'I don't know about you guys, but I'm in!' cheered Dylan.

'So am I.' Lance smiled.

'Excellent.' Nicholas grinned and turned to Theo. 'But what about you?'

'I guess I'll take you up on that offer, though I don't get why would you do this if you gain nothing from it?' replied Theo, arms still crossed.

'Curiosity's sake. And who's to say I gain nothing from it?'

'I still don't trust you.'

'I understand.' Nicholas bowed his head in acknowledgement. 'Alright, we start training tomorrow. Let's say here and at the same time?'

'Ye—' Lance started before Theo cut him off.

'Maybe not here. I know a place that'd be a bit more hidden. I'm guessing that this whole "powers" thing needs to be kept on the low-down, right?'

'Indeed, it does. There are rules about this and there is a governing body around the world that enforces these rules,' Nicholas said and turned to Lance. 'Just message me the place.'

'Right! See you tomorrow!' Lance said, excitement returning to his features.

Nodding, Nicholas stood and walked away.

Once he was out of sight, Dylan murmured, 'Well, that just happened.'

'Yep, our foot to this world is in the door.'

Theo nodded slowly, arms still crossed as he watched Nicholas round a corner and disappear.

CHAPTER 15

It was late afternoon by the time Norman and Adam disembarked from their plane. They quickly made their way to the car that had been organised for them before Adam drove Norman to the dive site of the Yonaguni Monument. On the way to the site, Norman continued to research the monument. The bulk of it read:

'The Yonaguni Monument is an underwater rock formation off the southernmost point of the island. It has staircase-like terraces, with flat sides and sharp corners.

Some people believe that it is a man-made structure, while others believe it to be a natural geological phenomenon.'

Norman looked up and asked, 'How long until we arrive?'

'I'm not sure, sir, but we are not quite halfway yet,' Adam answered.

'Very well then,' Norman dismissed, returning to his research. About twenty minutes later, they arrived on the edge of the coast, a small pier in front of them. Adam got out of the car and opened the door for Norman. He waited until Norman was out of the car before he closed the door behind him and went to retrieve the equipment.

'Do you have everything in order, Adam?' Norman asked.

'Yes, sir,' Adam replied with a nod.

'Let's go then,' Norman said.

They walked down to the pier and spotted the boat that they had rented for the day, a man waiting where it was moored. When they reached the boat, Norman greeted the man and made sure all other preparations had been made as he retrieved the keys for the vessel. Adam lifted their gear onto the boat before making his way below deck, changing from his usual attire into swim shorts and squeezing into a wetsuit, leaving the arms off until later. Not a moment later, Norman met him below and did the same.

Adam went above while Norman was changing and made sure everything was secure before calling down to Norman, 'Ready?'

'Yes, Adam, let's go!' Norman yelled back, excited.

Adam untied the mooring ropes and pushed the boat away from the pier. Quickly going back to the controls, he put the boat into gear and steered the boat toward its destination.

Once the boat reached the destination with its GPS navigation, Adam brought the boat to a stop, cutting off its engine and lowering the anchor so it would stay. Seconds later, Norman came up from below deck, two packs in his hands.

'Everything in order, sir?' Adam asked.

'Yes. These packs have food and water, a change of clothes for us, a first aid kit, flares and any research I might need down there. Are we above the monument?' Norman asked, placing one pack on the floor for Adam.

'Yes, sir,' Adam answered.

Norman nodded, strapping one pack to his weight belt and put that on around his waist. Adam did the same with the remaining pack when he returned after he'd put on the rest of the wetsuit and did it up. After that, they sat on the side of the boat and put on the remaining gear – the snorkel masks, flippers and torches – and helped each other with the oxygen tanks. Once the gear was on, they turned on and tested the oxygen before giving each other the 'thumbs up' and rolled backward off the side of the boat into the water. They quickly righted themselves and began swimming down toward the underwater, flat-topped pyramid-like structure known as the Yonaguni Monument. Adam hung back and admired the monument from afar, keeping a subtle eye out as Norman swam closer. He inspected it closely and began to notice the markings on it.

Maybe that is how we get inside. Perhaps one of those markings could be the entrance to the Sword of Time's chambers, he thought.

Continuing toward the monument, Norman indicated for Adam to start searching as well.

While Norman searched in one direction, Adam took the other. It wasn't long before Adam came across a wall of symbols that he recognised. Swimming closer to it, one symbol, in particular, caught his eye. Using the flashlight on his arm, he caught Norman's attention and motioned for him to come over. Once Norman got then, Adam pointed out the symbol. Norman immediately gave Adam the thumbs up.

Norman swam to the symbol and placed his hand on it. As it began to glow a bright blue, they swam away from it. There was a loud but slightly muffled crack before the wall started to move. It gave way to reveal an opening, the churned-up muck starting to settle. Then something moved from within the cavern beyond the opening.

What is… That was all Norman could think before a grey mass shot out, barely missing the pair of them. They immediately turned to face whatever it was.

It was a giant shark-like creature with huge, sharp teeth, metallic barbs on the edges of its fins and a tail hooked like a scythe.

The creature wheeled about and charged back at them, Norman and

Adam needing to swim in opposite directions just to dodge the massive beast.

An Isonade? Here? Norman thought, worried.

The beast turned around again, charging towards what appeared to be the weakest prey, Norman.

Norman concentrated, reaching out with his power. He pushed against the seafloor behind him to steady himself before pushing against the Isonade, trying to shove the creature back. But this only served to make it angrier and push back harder and harder until Norman couldn't hold it back anymore. Norman quickly swam away as the beast charged past, straight toward Adam. Norman watched as Adam began to vibrate the water around him, causing it to bubble and foam.

Smart, Norman thought as the Isonade slowed its charge, confused at the loss of its prey. Norman continued to watch as the Isonade swam into the foaming water, when Adam lashed out a punch. When his fist connected with the Isonade, the vibrations that Adam had surrounded his fist with erupted, blasting the beast back through the water. Norman then used his power to pick up a boulder from the seafloor and send it hurtling toward the Isonade, but it missed.

Damn, Norman thought, the beast beginning to recover before he concentrated on the boulder once again and used it to strike down the creature from behind. Dazed, it sunk to the seafloor.

Norman then swam toward the Isonade, using his power to push himself through the water like he did when bracing himself against the Isonade. Once he got there, he blasted the creature with a telekinetic shove, sending it tumbling across the seafloor.

Knocked out of its daze, it quickly recovered and charged the first thing it laid its eyes on. Which happened to be Adam, swimming toward the monument.

Bollocks, thought Norman before using his powers to try and bring the beast around to charge him instead. Noticing this, it went with it and headed for Norman.

Norman once again swam to the side to dodge it but the heavy use of his powers had drained him enough that he was slower, the barbs on the Isonade's fin catching his leg and tearing open a wound. Air and screams of pain tore out of his mouth as he clutched at the gash in his leg.

Turning around again, the creature charged ferociously at Norman, believing him to be easy prey now he was injured and bleeding out.

With his leg wounded bleeding and unable to be bound, Norman had no choice but to use his powers to keep himself distanced from the creature, whilst staying as close to the monument as possible. While he was being pushed about the water by the beast, Norman looked for Adam and spotted him by the monument, his hands braced up against it. There was a muffled crack before a piece of stone broke off. Understanding what Adam had done, Norman used his powers to push himself out of the path of the Isonade, while staying between it and the monument. Focusing on the rock that had broken off, he launched it at the beast once it came to charge back at him. Like a cannonball from a canon, it hurtled through the water and into the Isonade's mouth, keeping the creature's mouth stuck wide open.

Perfect shot, Norman thought.

The Isonade stopped and thrashed about, trying to dislodge it. While this had happened, Adam had swum up behind Norman, noticing his bleeding leg and weakened stature.

Adam then concentrated on the rock, increasing the vibrations is it to a violent level. This caused the piece of rock – along with the Isonade's head, jaw and neck – to blast apart, killing the beast instantly.

Norman motioned for Adam to swim from the cavern within the Yonaguni Monument. Obeying, he swam quickly. Norman used his power to tether himself to Adam telekinetically, following closely behind. Adam lit up his torch and brought them through the underwater cavern and into a higher, dry cavern. Once he got to the ledge, he broke the surface of the water and hauled himself up. He removed the oxygen tanks, flippers and mask before lighting a flare and helping Norman out of the water.

'My goodness, sir, your leg!' Adam exclaimed, clutching the leg in his grip to slow the bleeding.

'It's fine, Adam, just a scratch,' Norman replied, a pained look crossing his face as he took off the tanks and his mask.

'That's more than a scratch, sir,' Adam countered. 'Now, let me patch it up for you. Where's the kit?'

'Here,' Norman said, tugging the pack off his weight belt and pulling out the kit, dropping it next to Adam's leg and applying pressure to his leg, taking over for Adam while he patched it up.

'What on Earth was that thing?' Adam asked, cutting into Norman's wetsuit around the wound. Thankfully these suits were quick to drain.

'That was an Isonade,' Norman explained, pain leaking into his voice. 'Expect more monstrous creatures like that down here, Adam.'

Adam nodded, continuing by wrapping the wound. Norman grunted as the wrap tightened.

'Alright, all done,' Adam announced when he'd finished.

Looking down at the dressing, Norman smiled. 'Well done, young man.'

'Thank you, sir,' Adam nodded.

They sat there for a few minutes, having a much-needed snack while they recovered a little bit.

'Now, can you stand?' Adam asked as he stood, offering Norman a hand.

Norman took it and stood, grunting in pain but that was the only other sign that he was wounded other than the dressing on his leg.

'See? Naught more than a flesh wound.' Norman chuckled.

Adam chuckled with him before undoing the weight belt and stripping off his wetsuit, changing into the dry clothes they had brought with them. Norman followed suit, albeit a bit slower.

When he was done, Norman slung the now dry pack over his back, picked up the flare and said, 'Alright, let's find this sword.'

'You sure you're okay?' Adam asked.

'Yes, Adam, I'm fine,' Norman reassured him, walking, with a slight limp, toward the tunnel carved into the cavern wall.

'If you say so, sir.'

Before they even got to the tunnel, the flare died out. Adam went to light a new one when Norman stopped him. The symbols on the wall had begun to glow as the light died out, providing enough light without the need for a flare or torch.

'It's like they're there to show us the way,' Adam said, awestruck.

'Yes. Where the Sword of Darkness was located, these symbols were also present but they didn't glow,' Norman explained.

'Still cool, though.'

Norman chuckled at the words.

They continued through the tunnel until they came out into another, smaller cavern. This cavern was empty, except for a two-metre-tall stone statue of a samurai in the centre of the room, two katanas strapped to its back.

'The Sword of Time isn't here,' Adam said.

'Hmmm,' Norman pondered. 'It must be in another cavern, past this one. You can tell this place has not been disturbed for centuries, so it must be here.'

Norman tried to see past the statue and sure enough, there was another tunnel, which he pointed out to Adam.

'Let's go then,' Adam said.

Together they continued through the cavern. As they passed the samurai statue, Adam looked up at it, a shiver running down his spine making him stop in his tracks.

'Are you coming, Adam?' Norman asked, limping ahead.

'Yes, sir,' he replied, tearing his gaze from the statue and walking after Norman.

Norman made it into the cavern well before Adam got close. Once Norman crossed the threshold, there was a loud rumbling sound. A solid stone slab slammed down behind Norman, blocking off the tunnel entrance. Adam stopped, standing before the slab in shock. As the dust settled, he realised that he was trapped in this cavern while Norman was in the tunnel.

Then he heard a scraping noise. Adam turned but saw nothing else other than himself and the statue in the small cavern. Another scraping noise echoed through the cavern, the samurai statue's head turning to face him, a symbol on its forehead glowing red.

CHAPTER 16

A light-sucking, ink-black armour covered Dylan as he stood over an unconscious Pyro, Sword of Darkness raised to deliver the final blow.

'Wait! Dylan, stop!' Lance yelled, Sword of Light drawn as his golden armour shone into existence.

'Why?' he sneered.

'Because you're not that kind of person!' Lance pleaded as he inched toward Dylan.

'Yeah, well, this son-of-a-bitch started it all!' He spat, face contorted in anger as he continued. 'I don't care what you say, he deserves it.'

He started to bring the sword down over Pyro's neck but a blast of ice hit Dylan and quickly encased him in ice, the blade stopping barely a couple of inches above Pyro.

Glacia then quickly dove at Lance, tackling him to the ground. Lance, caught unprepared, dropped the sword, his armour dissipating the instant it left his hand. He threw Glacia off of him and fired twin beams of light at her, both striking her in the stomach. This lifted Glacia off her feet once again, sending her flying down a tunnel.

Lance scrambled to his feet and snatched up his Sword, golden armour appearing instantly. But before he could do anything, he was struck by a powerful torrent of water, making him crash into a wall and knocking him unconscious.

An orange-haired woman walked into the room, laughing arrogantly. She was slim but curvy, young and about average height. Her clothing, a tank top that stopped at her mid-riff and a skirt that seemed like an ultra-mini skirt at the front but drooped down to her knees at the back.

Suddenly, there was a loud crack. The ice encasing Dylan shattered and exploded outward, sending ice all over the cavern.

Dylan rose his head slowly, eyes locking with this new opponent, the other forgotten. The woman grinned as she brought the water back to surround her arms.

Dylan stepped forward, throwing a fist of darkness at her. She dove out of the way and retaliated with a whip of water. He blocked it with a shield of darkness and swiped at her with the sword as he dashed in close. She dodged her way behind him and rushed at him from behind, trying to knock him off his feet. But spikes erupted from his armour and impaled her. As he retracted the spikes, the woman's body slumped to the ground.

Then, with a scream, Glacia dove at Dylan, her ice daggers barely missing his neck as he sidestepped her; the sword flashing in the air before the sound of steel cutting through flesh and bone was heard. Glacia's arm had been cut off from the elbow down, blood dripping from the open wound and…

Theo jolted awake, sweat dripping from his forehead.

'It was just a dream,' he muttered to himself. But what a weird dream, felt so real…'

He sat up and moved to the edge of his bed, feet on the floor as he shook his head.

'It was just a dream,' he repeated, trying to reassure himself. He then stood and headed for the shower.

***

Dylan awoke to the sound of someone starting up the shower.

He rolled over and groaned.

'Oh god, I feel like crap,' he muttered.

He slowly sat himself up and groaned again when he heard a knock at the door.

'Yeah?' he mumbled, loud enough that Lance heard him and walked in.

'You ready?' he asked.

'Ready for what?'

'Our first day of training with Nicholas.'

'Oh, right. Give me five minutes then.'

'Righto, I'll meet you downstairs,' Lance said, walking out of Dylan's room and shutting the door.

Dylan dragged himself out of bed and stretched slowly. Then, finding some clean clothes, he quickly got changed and headed downstairs.

***

Theo pulled on his t-shirt and looking at himself in the mirror, he mumbled, 'Well, today is going to be interesting…'

He then left the bathroom and headed downstairs to find his brothers sitting at the dining table eating breakfast.

'Morning, guys,' Theo said as he entered.

'Morning,' they both replied.

Theo prepared himself a bowl of cereal and sat down at the head of the table beside Lance. Dylan sat on the other side of Lance.

'Ready for today?' Lance asked.

'Yeah, I guess,' Theo replied.

'It's gonna be awesome,' Dylan said, one side of his mouth turned up in a grin.

'I wonder what he'll have us doing,' Lance pondered.

'Hopefully using our powers.' Dylan's grin grew at the thought.

'Maybe,' Lance nodded.

Theo finished his cereal and looked up at them. 'Ready to go?'

'Yeah, let's do this!' Dylan said as he stood up.

The other two followed, all of them going to place their dishes in the dishwasher before leaving the house and heading for the park.

They found Nicholas sitting on the same park bench that he'd been sitting on where they'd all met the day before.

Having heard them approach, Nicholas stood and turned to face them, a smile on his face. 'Hey, guys!'

'Hey,' Dylan replied with a slight wave.

'You three ready for today?' Nicholas said as he picked up a bag and slung it over his shoulder.

'I think so,' Lance nodded.

'I'm ready,' Dylan smirked.

'Alright, let's go then,' Nicholas said.

'Where are we going?' Theo asked, arms crossed and an eyebrow raised.

Nicholas rolled his eyes. 'Out of town, somewhere people won't see us.'

Nicholas led the brothers out of the park and headed out of town until they came out into an open field where Nicholas abruptly stopped.

'Here we are,' he said, removing the bag that was over his shoulder and the jacket he'd been wearing.

'What's in the bag?' Dylan asked.

'You'll find out,' Nicholas grinned. Opening the bag, he pulled out a pair of MMA gloves and strapped them on his hands. Adjusting them, he continued, 'To start, I thought I would tell you guys a little bit about us meta-humans and our powers, then I'm going to test out what you three can do.'

'With our powers?' Dylan replied, a little too eagerly.

'No, with hand-to-hand combat. Hence the gloves,' Nicholas raised his hands slightly, doing a few air punches. 'No powers yet.'

'Oh, okay then,' Dylan said, deflating a little bit.

'So, with people like us, we are different from regular humans. We can control different aspects of different elements. Like, for example, I can control the weather and anything related to it. So, I can create tornadoes, fire lightning from my fingers and fly on currents of wind,' Nicholas explained.

'Is there anything else that is different about us besides the control over something?' Dylan asked.

'Yeah, there is, Dylan. Your metabolism is a lot higher now. Like, you've probably noticed that you're slightly faster and that your mind is more focused. Also, your body is a lot stronger now, like, you can take a lot more damage than a regular human and you will heal a lot quicker. A cut will heal in minutes, a deep cut in an hour and a broken bone would heal in about a day,' Nicholas answered.

'That makes sense,' Theo said. 'Like that other night where I watched you and that Pyro guy take blows that I thought would knock someone out but you just got back up. And that Bunyip cut you deep but you had healed by the time we saw you next.'

'Exactly,' Nicholas nodded. 'Another thing, with certain powers, their element can be absorbed into their body and make them even stronger. I think you, Dylan, and you, Lance, can be able to do this, but you, Theo, and myself can't do this as you can't absorb time and I can't absorb the weather. But there is a downside to doing this; it can cause people to become uncontrollable as it isn't their element that they create from their hands so it can corrupt if not done properly.'

Theo glanced at Dylan, remembering the night they discovered their powers; that is exactly what Dylan had done.

'Alright, that's probably all I can tell you for now. The rest I will tell you guys as the training progresses,' Nicholas said. 'Alright, let's get down to see what you can do in hand-to-hand combat. Who's going first?' Nicholas pulled out the second pair of gloves and held them out.

'I will,' Dylan replied before either of his brothers had the chance, snatching the gloves from Nicholas and strapping them on.

He tested the feel of them before imitating what Nicholas had done earlier.

'Alright, Dylan, you ready?' Nicholas said calmly, bringing his arms up into a ready position.

'Yeah, let's go!' Dylan replied, a look of determination set in his eyes as he punched his gloves together.

They cautiously approached each other, sizing their opponent up. Nicholas went on the offensive and threw the first jab. Dylan deflected it and came in with a punch of his own, catching Nicholas in the stomach.

Slightly winded, Nicholas stepped back, but Dylan didn't give him any time to recover. He ran at Nicholas, jumped up onto his shoulders and wrapped his legs around Nicholas's neck before back-flipping and throwing Nicholas to the ground.

Nicholas coughed as he rose. 'Nice head scissors.'

'Thank you,' Dylan smirked.

They began to circle each other. This time Dylan began the offensive with a roundhouse but Nicholas caught his leg and spun it outward, Dylan losing his balance and falling onto his back. Taking advantage, Nicholas jumped on top of him and started driving his elbows into Dylan. He blocked most of them before rotating his hips to throw Nicholas off. He then rushed to grab one of Nicholas's legs, drape it over his shoulder and pulled down on each side of the leg with his arms as he rose.

'Alright, that's enough,' Nicholas ordered.

Dylan let go and Nicholas stood up.

'That was good, Dylan. How'd you learn to fight like that?' Nicholas asked.

'Thanks. I'm a professional wrestler,' Dylan replied, a grin on his face.

'Ah, even though that isn't real fighting, the moves that you have learnt can be applied to inflict pain,' Nicholas nodded. 'Okay, Lance, you're up next.'

Dylan removed the gloves and tossed them to Lance with a smirk. 'Good luck.'

Lance strapped on the gloves and approached Nicholas.

'Are you ready?' Nicholas asked.

'I guess,' Lance replied nervously.

Nicholas brought his arms up to the ready, Lance imitating but sloppily. They approached each other and Lance was the first to throw a punch. Nicholas easily dodged it before dropping into a powerful sweep kick that took Lance off his feet, causing Lance to let out an 'oof'.

The air left his lungs as he landed on his back, a couple of half-suppressed sniggers sounding in the air. He took a minute to get back his breath before standing.

'Damn it!' Lance cursed.

'It's alright Lance,' Nicholas reassured him. 'Have you done this sort of training before?'

Lance shook his head.

'That's alright. I will teach you. I think we might move onto Theo then,' Nicholas said.

Lance pulled off the gloves and gave them to Theo. Theo strapped them on and approached Nicholas.

'Ready, Theo?' Nicholas asked.

He nodded, raising his fists into a half-guard, half-aggressive position before beginning to circle Nicholas. Nicholas circled with him, not willing to give Theo any advantages. Not finding any openings, Nicholas lashed out with a kick but Theo danced backwards, dodging the kick before rushing in and throwing two left jabs into Nicholas's ribs.

'What the hell?!' Lance cried out in shock.

'Yeah, since when could he fight?' Dylan asked, puzzled.

Nicholas stepped back, right guard dropping to his ribs, but Theo re-advanced and swung a left hook aimed for the head.

Nicholas quickly ducked under it and tried pulling Theo down onto his rising knee, but he blocked it with his left leg and shoved Nicholas back.

Not wasting any time, Theo twisted his body to the left to unleash a powerful right roundhouse kick at Nicholas, which caught him on the chin. Nicholas spun and fell to the ground, landing face-first.

'Holy crap! Theo knocked him out!' Dylan cheered, albeit prematurely as Nicholas groaned, rolling around slowly to sit up and lightly rub his chin.

'That was spectacularly done, Theo,' Nicholas praised him. 'Although, I do wonder who taught you.'

Theo just shrugged as he undid the gloves and tossed them back into Nicholas's bag.

'Alright, it's good to know at least two of you know how to handle hand-to-hand combat, or at least enough to defend yourselves.'

Dylan and Theo bumped fists as Lance groaned.

'And don't worry, Lance, I will teach you how to defend yourself,' Nicholas reassured him.

'Thanks,' Lance huffed in embarrassment.

'What else are we doing today?' Dylan asked, eager to continue training.

'That's all I planned for today,' Nicholas said, wincing slightly. 'Let's head back to town.'

'Okay,' chorused the brothers as Nicholas quickly packed the gloves and jacket into the bag before slinging it back over his shoulders. They all shook off the evidence of their bouts and headed back into town.

CHAPTER 17

Adam watched as the statue stepped off the podium, unsheathed the two katanas strapped to its back and advanced toward him. After assessing it, he smiled.

'This should be easy enough,' he mumbled to himself.

Concentrating and drawing on his ability, he punched the air toward the statue. A large crack sounded through the air as the shockwave passed through it and slammed into the statue, shattering it to pieces. The echoing clang of the katanas hitting the ground was the sound of victory.

'Done,' Adam laughed as he dusted himself off. He returned to the stone slab that was barring his way back to Norman.

'Hmmm, maybe I can run vibrations through it and break it apart,' he muttered.

He started mulling over the thought when suddenly, he heard the sound of stone scraping on stone.

'What on Earth…' he started, turning around to see the pieces of the statue tumble toward the point where the statue had been and begin to reform.

It looked eerie, as even the dust and the smallest of the debris swirled around the statue and found its place. Once reassembled, the samurai statue bent down, picked up its katanas and looked directly at Adam.

'Oh, bollocks!' Adam cursed.

The statue charged him, one sword raised in front of it, the other ready at its side.

Adam dove to the side, narrowly missing the downward slice of a katana as the statue passed him. He rolled, came up to face the statue and sent another punch shockwave at it but missed.

The statue came back, swinging its blades in quick succession. Adam ducked under the first and dodged to the side of the second as he gathered power in his arm.

Seeing an opening, he struck, punching the statue's upper arm. Once it connected, the vibrations exploded out, pushing the statue back and obliterating its arm and a chunk out of his side. The katana it was holding dropped to the ground.

Adam cartwheeled around it, picking up its sword.

'Now we're even,' Adam grinned, raising the katana to point at its chest.

It gave a nod in acknowledgment, stood forward into an attack position and raised its sword. Its arm and side started to regenerate once more.

Adam smiled and mimicked its stance, eager to test his sword skills once more.

Not a second later, they both made their move, the swords singing their metallic song as they clashed.

***

Norman cursed the stone slab and sighed.

'Looks like I'm on my own,' he mumbled to himself, turning back to the glowing symbols on the walls. Norman limped onward, examining the symbols on the way. But it wasn't too long before the tunnel opened up into a cavern. This cavern's walls were lined with more glowing symbols. They even made a pathway to, surrounded, and covered a podium located in the centre. Floating above the podium was the Sword of Time. It was a deep blue, the colour of sapphires, with three orange topazes embedded in each side of the hilt.

'There you are,' Norman said in awe, grinning ear to ear. 'You are the most beautiful sword I have ever laid eyes on. Looks like you were made entirely of sapphire.'

He took another step toward the Sword of Time before a loud growl rang through the cavern.

And of course, there must be a guardian, he thought before noticing a black smoke starting to work its way through the cave.

The creature stood in sight, making Norman's eyes widen in fear. It was about a metre and a half in length, and half a metre in height with the head of a monkey, the body of a dog, legs like a tiger's and a snake for a tail. Thick black smog billowed from its mouth and skin, the snake's head poised to strike.

'How wonderful,' muttered Norman semi-sarcastically. 'A Nue.'

The Nue growled, ready to strike. Norman breathed, readying himself when he inhaled some of the smog and began to cough violently. The more he inhaled, the more violently he coughed.

Bollocks, that smog is poisonous… Need to… isolate myself from it…

Norman quickly used his power to form a skin-tight barrier around himself, then pushed it out to form a clean air bubble around himself. His coughing eased as he got clean air.

Thwarted, the Nue growled again and began stalking toward Norman.

Noticing its advance, he prepared himself.

The Nue lunged.

Norman shoved at it with his telekinesis, the barrier blinking out momentarily as the Nue was flung into the stone wall behind it. A sickening crunch was heard as it crashed into the wall and then the thud of it hitting the ground once gravity took over. Smog continued to waft up from its body.

Thinking the Nue was down for the count, Norman allowed himself a small smile as he began limping for the sword once again.

Unnoticed, the Nue silently got up and lunged for Norman. It knocked him down, breaking his focus on the bubble, which then winked out of existence.

It clawed at Norman with its large tiger paws, more and more smog pouring from the beast.

Dazed, he sought to defend himself from its paws with his arms, deep gashes bringing him the pain needed to gather himself once more. With his mind regained, he blasted it off of him.

Now back to his senses, the smog began to smother him. Coughing, he struggled to get up and look around, looking for signs of the Nue, but the smog was now too thick, making his eyes itch and water.

He rubbed them as he contemplated his situation before opening his eyes again and trying to once again see signs of the Nue through the smog.

Mid-turn, the Nue dove at him from behind, taking him down once again before vanishing back into the smog, toying with him.

Turning over onto his side, a coughing fit wracked through his exhausted body, his eyes left watering by both the smog and his fit.

This is not going according to plan at all.

***

Adam darted back as the samurai statue slashed at him before dashing back in to stab at it. But the statue easily deflected it.

Adam continued in, getting into close quarters and letting his fist fly into the statue's chest, concentrating intense vibrations around his fist as it flew. As soon as his fist connected, the vibrations exploded, shattering the statue.

He stood back and caught his breath as the statue began to reform once again.

'How on Earth am I meant to defeat this thing?' he muttered to himself as he watched the statue rise and pick up its remaining katana.

Adam lunged at it, sword swinging to strike.

The statue stepped back, dodging Adam's katana and then advanced on him, sword flashing as it went for Adam's neck.

He deflected and kicked out with some added vibration to strengthen it. The statue was knocked backward but recovered enough to block Adam's slash.

Adam continued his assault while he had the upper hand but was quickly losing his advantage as the statue fully recovered its balance and started its offensive once again.

The shrill screams of the blade on blade settled into a rhythm as they continued their macabre dance – slashing, deflecting, parrying and blocking.

One slice of the samurai's blade nearly took Adam's nose after a miscalculated advance. Another from Adam nearly took its leg.

But the pair were evenly matched.

Until Adam went for a quick slash at its chest. The statue parried but Adam, with a flick of his wrist, took its less-dominant hand off at the forearm.

The hand sailed across the room and shattered upon impact with the ground but it did not reform.

'I think I've just found your weakness,' Adam grinned, twirling his borrowed katana.

The samurai looked down to where its hand once was, then to where its pieces remained before returning its gaze to Adam. It then lunged at him and swung with a newly found ferocity. Adam found himself falling into a defensive pattern as it continued its ferocious onslaught. He tried to slash out offensively but the statue wouldn't have a bit of it. Its blade was searching for a weakness and finding one every time Adam tried to lash out.

Blood was now leaking from Adam's right forearm, chest, left thigh and right calf. The pain and continuous onslaught from the statue now sent him off balance.

Before he knew it, its blade knocked the katana from Adam's hand. The follow-up slash had him diving to the side. He quickly rolled back to his feet and ran for the katana.

But something heavy struck him from behind, knocking him down and slightly winding him.

Rolling to his side with a groan, he saw the samurai's arm tumble back toward it.

'It threw its arm?' Adam exclaimed in disbelief as he watched the arm reattach.

The statue then launched itself at Adam, sword raised above its head. Adam quickly rolled away, the sword crashing down in the place he'd just been. He kept rolling till he got to his feet.

With a quick tug and the sound of stone grinding on stone, the samurai removed its katana from the ground it had dug itself into and began to advance on Adam once more.

Adam readied the vibrations in his palms and clapped, sending an explosive vertical shockwave rippling out in an arc in front of him, slicing the statue in half, as well as leaving a cut in the floor and ceiling of the room. The two halves of the statue remained there for a second before falling in toward each other and resealing, making the statue whole once more.

The samurai charged at him, katana raised.

Adam concentrated a haze of intense vibrations between his palms, then threw his arms wide, expanding the haze so it was like a wall. The statue hit it, disintegrating as the vibrations wreaked havoc on its stone body and the katana was sent flying back the way it had come.

He then turned and ran for the other katana as the statue fragments began to piece back together. Picking it up, he turned to face the samurai.

It had just picked up its other sword, the last few pieces flying back into place.

'This ends now,' Adam declared.

It nodded and charged at him once more, Adam following suit, both with their weapons raised. The blades hissed and sang as each gave it their all. Adam tried to keep the offensive, trying to find an opening to exploit but with no luck; the statue kept deflecting each slash.

He nearly missed the sudden shift of the statue's stance as it went onto the offensive. He instinctively found himself blocking and trying to lash out with an enhanced kick to its knee, but it danced out of reach. The next strike aimed to take his head, but he knocked the blade away as he skipped back and punched out, the shockwave blowing apart its unarmed side.

Adam quickly followed up, taking advantage of the distraction and its recovering side to slice off its other arm with his katana.

The arm fell, still holding the sword. The statue looked at its fallen arm and then back up to Adam. It fell to its knees and gave him the nod, acknowledging it had been defeated. Adam then took off its head and watched as the statue crumbled to dust, not to reform.

However, the katanas and their sheaths remained intact.

Adam placed down his sword, then picked up both sheaths and

strapped them to either side of his waist. He then picked up both katanas, slid them both into their sheaths and took a moment to breathe.

Sighing, he muttered to himself, 'Time to find Master Norman.'

Turning to the stone slab that blocked his path, he then approached it. Placing a hand on it, he began to send vibrations through it, increasing the intensity of the vibrations until it cracked. He then stood back and aimed a punch at the wall, the shockwave blasting a hole through the slab.

Adam stood through it and into a black smog.

***

Norman, bleary-eyed and coughing, tried to scan his surroundings. But the black smog surrounding him grew thicker with each passing minute as he waited for the Nue to strike.

The smog continued to build up in his lungs, forcing him to cough harder and harder as his body tried to eradicate it. It gave him an idea. Focusing on the soreness of his airways, he mentally followed the pain to the bottom of his lungs; then, using the same method as the bubble he'd made earlier, he pushed all the smog, and most of the air, from his lungs and maintained a small bubble as he gasped for the air he'd pushed out.

Catching his breath once more, he sighed in relief. 'Better, but unfortunately, it won't last long.'

Scanning his surroundings again, he spotted a soft blue glow through the dark smog. A small smile formed on his lips as he got up and began limping toward the glow.

Out of the corner of his eye, he saw something close in on him. He quickly flung out his hand and grabbed a hold of the thing with his telekinesis. He turned to face it, the Nue, and began to choke it as it struggled, trying to get out of his mental hold. He began coughing again, noticing that his barrier had slipped with his concentration on the Nue. He then threw the Nue up and then blasted it away with a telekinetic pulse. As it disappeared back into the smog, Norman turned back and began limping back toward the sword once again, the coughing steadily growing worse.

'Bloody smog,' Norman cursed as the smog got to his eyes. 'Need to get to the sword.'

The Nue, having recovered, pounced on Norman from behind and then back into the smog, leaving him on the ground and winded once more.

He slowly rose to his feet again and muttered some more curses under his breath when his vision dimmed as dizziness hit him, making him stumble. The Nue dove at him again but he just flicked his arm out, blasting it back as he continued limping. He then used his ability to levitate himself slightly off the ground and float to the Sword of Time. Grabbing the hilt, he pulled it out of its levitating state and immediately froze time, instantly feeling like gravity had increased. He dropped back to the ground and began limping toward the direction he flicked the Nue. Finding it, he stood in front of it, restarted time and grinned when he saw its eyes widen. Before it could leap away, he lopped the beast's head off.

It crumpled to the ground and Norman's vision dimmed once again.

'Bollocks,' was all he could let out before he fainted.

CHAPTER 18

Realising that the black smog he'd walked into was dangerous, Adam quickly tore off his shirt and tied it around his head so that his nose and mouth were covered. He then continued down the smog-filled passage, one hand against the wall, until it came to an open cavern.

Eyes beginning to water, he peered into the seeming dark oblivion, his eyes spotting a slow-moving dim blue light. The light then swung in a vertical arc, momentarily vanishing before reappearing and then dipping lower, where it appeared to stay.

'Norman!' Adam shouted, rushing toward the blue light, the smog beginning to dissipate.

He found Norman unconscious on the ground, next to the glowing Sword of Time. He felt for a pulse at Norman's neck, breathing a sigh of relief when he found one.

'He's still alive, thank goodness,' he breathed, picking up the sword and slipping it into his belt. 'But he will need to regain consciousness before we can leave here.'

Adam then pulled on Norman's arm and swung the unconscious man up onto his shoulder, then turned around and walked in the direction of the tunnel; the smog had dissipated enough for the opening to become just visible.

Passing through the cavern of his battle, he smiled, remembering his still-fresh victory over the samurai.

Continuing onward, he soon arrived back in the cavern they had arrived in; their wetsuits, diving gear and bags were still sitting beside the water's edge. Adam walked over to it and gently lowered Norman onto the ground beside the gear. Grabbing the longer of the two bags, he took the cloth from inside and wrapped the sword in it, then placed the wrapped sword into the bag. After putting the bag down, he began to remove his new swords when he heard a groan from behind him. Adam quickly placed his katanas in the bag with the wrapped sword and then rushed to Norman's side, Norman's eyes fluttering open.

'Good to see you conscious again, sir,' Adam greeted softly, unsure of Norman's state.

Norman tried to sit up but his body was immediately wracked with a coughing fit. Noticing his struggle, Adam quickly aided him and got him to sit as upright as possible against the softer of the two bags.

'Sir, I believe that smog has had a detrimental effect on your health. We should rest here for the time being until your health improves,' Adam cautioned.

Norman just gave a slight nod before closing his eyes and focusing on his abilities internally. Adam watched in shock as wisps of black smog were expelled from Norman's mouth, immediately dissipating. As soon as the last wisp evaporated, Norman sucked in a large breath as if he'd been winded, panting until his breathing returned to normal.

'Much better,' Norman sighed.

'I'm glad,' came the awed reply.

'Where is the Sword of Time, Adam?' Norman asked as he scanned the cavern.

'It's in the bag, and departure preparations are almost complete,'

Adam reassured him.

'Thank you, Adam,' Norman said, reaching for his nearby wetsuit.

'What are you doing?' Adam asked, reaching for Norman's arm.

'Well, we're done here, so I believe we should be leaving,' Norman stated, moving from Adam's reach as he began to put on his wetsuit.

'But, sir, you need to rest,' Adam stood, concerned. 'You are not well and we don't know the extent of the damage that poisonous vapour has done.'

'I am well enough to continue, Adam,' Norman asserted in a tone that left no room for further argument. He then zipped up his wetsuit and hauled on his oxygen tanks.

'Very well then, sir,' Adam said dejectedly and began to put on his wetsuit. Soon enough, they finished preparations and were ready to leave.

'Ready to depart?' Norman asked, attaching the smaller of the bags to his chest.

Adam nodded, the larger pack already strapped to his dominant side. They walked backward into the water, fitting their masks and breathers into the correct position before diving down further into the water and swimming out of the Yonaguni cavern. As they began their ascent toward the boat, Adam looked back at the sandstone formations of the Yonaguni Monument, sea turtles, a variety of fish and other wildlife swimming carefree around the stone. Adam spotted the Isonade's body lying on one of the stone platforms, starting to be picked at by other sea life. Adam shuddered and turned, swimming up to the surface. Once their heads broke the surface, they removed their masks and breathers and swam back to the boat. Adam boarded the boat first and helped Norman back aboard, then proceeded to strip off his gear.

'Home time, sir?' Adam asked as he fetched some dry clothes, a towel and a blanket for Norman.

'Indeed, let's head home,' agreed Norman, accepting the parcel from Adam and heading below deck to finish changing.

'Sir, are you sure you're alright?' Norman heard Adam call.

'Yes, Adam, I'm just going to take a nap,' he replied, finishing up and laying down on the couch, curling up beneath the blanket.

With an affirmative grunt, Adam started up the engine and turned the boat around, heading back toward Yonaguni Island.

***

Norman awoke with a jolt as the plane touched down on the tarmac.

'Sir, we have arrived back in London,' Adam stated, removing the empty cup Norman had in the holder.

'Ah, finally! Thank you, Adam,' Norman replied with a nod.

Once the plane had come to a full stop, Norman stood and followed Adam out of the plane. The pair quickly crossed the tarmac, Adam opening the rear door of the limousine for Norman to slide into. Once Norman was inside, Adam shut the door behind him and proceeded to the driver's seat.

'Home, sir?' Adam asked.

'Yes, Adam,' Norman nodded.

'Right, sir,' Adam confirmed before setting off.

Norman sat back and watched the familiar streets of London fly in and out of view. Luckily there were no delays, the mansion coming into view mere minutes after leaving the runway.

'We're home, sir,' Adam stated as he pulled up in front of the mansion. He then exited the car and let Norman out. Quickly closing the door behind him, Adam retrieved the packs from the limo before rushing up to the front door and letting Norman inside the mansion.

'Thank you, Adam,' Norman said as he strode through the door.

'May I have the sword?'

'You're welcome, and of course,' Adam replied as he retrieved the cloth bundle that contained the Sword of Time from within one of the packs. 'Would you like some tea, sir?'

'Yes, please,' Norman sighed with a grin, thankful for his butler's thoughtfulness. He retrieved the sword from Adam and began ascending the stairs, telling Adam, 'I will be up in the study.'

'Very well, sir,' Adam returned and quickly made his way to the kitchen. He immediately trayed up the tea set, filling the pot with boiling water, adding the leaves to the pot, plating up some biscuits and filling the milk pourer.

Retrieving the tray, Adam swiftly returned to Norman's study, opening the door as his master unwrapped the sword he had stowed in the bag.

'It's beautiful,' Adam commented, placing the tray down on the desk as his eyes appraised the shimmering sapphire sword.

Norman placed the sword down on the table. 'Thank you, Adam, it is beautiful indeed.'

Adam bowed slightly. 'Now that you have all three swords, what shall you do?'

'Firstly, Nicholas has to bring the other two swords. But once I have all three, I do not know yet. With one I would be near unbeatable; with the three at my disposal, I would be the most powerful man in the world,' Norman answered, the last half being not more than a mutter under his breath.

'Well, I suggest you best call Nicholas and see how he is progressing, sir.'

'Yes, thank you for reminding me, Adam.'

Adam bowed, then turned to leave the room; Norman looked away from the sword and reached for the phone.

***

Nicholas awoke to an annoying buzzing noise.

'What on Earth?' he mumbled as he reached for the offending noisemaker. Finding his phone, he mumbled, 'Who could be ringing me at this time of night?'

'Hello?' he answered groggily.

'Hello, Nicholas, how are you?' Norman asked.

'Still half asleep but doing well, Father,' Nicholas replied, sitting up.

'Good, good. I have some good news, my boy,' Norman announced, his excitement evident.

'And what would that be?'

'I have successfully retrieved the Sword of Time.'

'That's excellent news.'

'Indeed, but now I require those other two swords that you have retrieved. So, when shall you be returning?'

'Yeah, about that... I may not be returning for a little while.'

'What?'

'Well, to cut a long story short, as I was retrieving the Sword of Light, I came across three brothers with powers that I have never seen before.'

'So, you're training them then?'

'Yes, I think they could be a great asset.'

'Good plan.'

'I shall come home soon though, Father. I just wish to teach them basic control before they hurt themselves or others.'

'Very well, Nicholas, that is probably for the best. I do hope to see you very soon though.'

'No worries. Goodbye, Dad.'

'Goodbye, son.'

Nicholas hung up and put the phone back down, releasing a breath he didn't realise he'd been holding. He then rolled over and went back to sleep.

***

Putting the phone back down, Norman turned to Adam. 'It sounds like Nicholas won't be home for a while.'

'Oh?' Adam queried.

'He has found a set of brothers with abilities and has seen fit to train them.'

'Sounds like a good idea. We wouldn't want people running around with untamed and untrained powers willy-nilly; it'd be on the front page of the newspaper.'

'Yes, indeed.'

'Although, I am curious as to what powers these brothers possess.'

'As am I. Nicholas didn't say much about them other than they were unique, and that he'd never seen ones like them before.'

'Oh?'

'Yes.' Norman picked up his teacup and took a sip as he turned back to the Sword of Time.

Noticing that his master was staring at the sword, Adam asked, 'Have you used the sword yet, sir?'

'Yes, I have Adam,' he replied, picking up the sword once more.

'Any side effects?'

'Not that I could tell; although, I only used the sword's ability very briefly. The effect may be delayed in comparison to the Sword of Darkness's immediate reaction.'

Norman held the sword up in the light, rotating it so they could both marvel at the beauty of the sapphire sword and its topaz gemstones shimmering brightly.

He then placed the sword back on the stand and smiled slowly. 'I need to be alone now, Adam, thank you.'

'Very well, sir,' Adam said, bowing before turning on his heel and leaving the study.

CHAPTER 19

Theo fell backwards as a tall, strongly built man dove at him. Quickly rolling away, he stopped time briefly. Picking himself up off the ground, he examined the man closer.

Other than being tall and strong looking, the man looked rough, had long black dreadlocks and carried four cutlasses. Two were strapped to his hips with the others crossed over his back.

Theo walked toward him and unfroze time as he swung a well- aimed punch to the man's stomach. As the man bent over trying to suck in air, Theo lashed out with a roundhouse kick that smashed into the side of the man's head, knocking him down.

Theo turned to the sound of another person approaching him. It was another man, an older man. He was about as tall as the guy with dreads but had short, white hair with a matching beard and a jagged scar over his right eye. In his hand was a sword of deep blue, orange gems peeking out at the top and bottom of the hilt.

'The Sword of Time,' Theo mumbled to himself in wonder.

'Ah, you must be Theo!' the older man announced.

'And you are?' Theo asked.

'My name is Norman Quinzel,' he bowed.

'Nicholas's father?' Theo questioned sceptically.

'Indeed,' Norman nodded.

'What do you want?' Theo asked.

'The other two swords, of course,' Norman replied simply.

'Well, we have a problem then,' Theo stated as he placed himself in a defensive position, readying himself for battle.

Taking note of his stance, Norman smiled. 'You wish to fight me, boy?'

'You want the Swords of Light and Darkness, and you don't appear to be one to take no as an answer, so I'll do what I must,' Theo growled.

'As you wish,' Norman raised his sword and charged.

Theo froze time, but Norman kept coming.

'What?' Theo exclaimed, confused, as he was forced to dodge Norman's slash.

An unseen force then threw him to the ground. Landing on his side, Theo winced in pain and released time once more.

'What the hell?' Theo whispered as he stood, a puzzled expression appearing on his face.

'You can't best me, Theo. With this sword in my grasp, your abilities are rendered useless,' Norman laughed.

Changing tactics, Theo rushed Norman. Once again, an invisible force pushed him, but this time it pushed him toward Norman even faster. Faster than he could react as the point of the sword thrust toward his chest…

Violently thrown from his dream and his bed, Theo awoke with a groan. Picking himself up off the floor, he sat back on the edge of his bed and rubbed his eyes.

'Another weird dream,' he mumbled to himself, checking his body, 'It felt so real again.'

Standing up, he disabled the alarm that hadn't gone off yet and got changed.

'Were these dreams because of my powers? Could they be of the future?' Theo wondered out loud before he shrugged it off with a light laugh and said, 'Oh well, another day of training with Nicholas.'

He then left his room and went to the kitchen, finding his brothers already down there eating.

'Morning,' they greeted him as he walked in.

'Morning,' he replied. 'Where's Mum?'

'She's already gone to work,' Lance answered.

'Ah, right.' Theo nodded.

Theo placed two slices of bread in the toaster and flicked the lever down. 'What did Nick say we were doing today?'

'I think we're working on our powers today. Finally!' Dylan said, dramatising the last word in eagerness.

'Sounds good,' Theo replied as the toaster popped the toast out. He quickly grabbed the pieces, spread them and put them on a plate at the table before joining his brothers. He ate in silence, enjoying the crisp and perfectly buttered toast before washing it down with water as he went over the dream in his mind.

Noticing his unusual silence, Lance asked, 'What's up, man? You seem a little off.'

'Oh… nothing. Just some weird dreams lately,' Theo replied.

'Really?' Dylan questioned, eyebrow raised. 'What about?'

'Us,' Theo sighed. 'In battle.'

'Against who?' Dylan asked, intrigued.

'To be honest, I don't know,' having finished his toast, Theo sat back and crossed his arms. 'I don't think I've ever seen these people outside of my dreams.'

'Right…' Dylan snorted, his excitement diminishing.

'You know, you might be seeing the future, right? With your powers and all,' Lance said. 'Sounds even more possible since you said that you'd never seen these people before.'

'Yeah, I'd thought of that too,' Theo frowned. 'And if that's the case, then we're in trouble.'

'Pssh, it'll be fine,' Dylan said dismissively. 'We'll be trained enough by then!'

'I hope so,' Lance said at the same time Theo chimed in, 'Maybe.'

'Ah, well,' Lance said, looking at the clock. 'We better go train.'

'Yeah, sounds like a plan,' replied Dylan and Theo.

The three brothers placed their dishes in the dishwasher and left, heading out of town to the place they had been training. They arrived to find Nicholas waiting for them.

'Morning, lads,' Nicholas greeted them warmly.

'Morning,' replied the brothers harmoniously.

'Today's the day, boys!' Nicholas announced, spreading his arms out.

'For what?' questioned Theo.

'You will show me what your powers can do,' Nicholas replied.

'Finally,' Dylan smirked, cracking his knuckles.

'Alright! Theo, you're up first. Show me what you've got!' Nicholas readied himself as Theo put some distance between himself and his brothers, loosening his body of any tension before coming to a stop.

Nicholas smirked and thrust out the palm of his hand out, sending a concentrated blast of wind. Theo just shrugged as he stopped time. He casually side-stepped just out of range of the blast and lifted the freeze, the wind blasting past him.

'Interesting move,' pondered Nicholas. 'Try this one!'

Nicholas thrust out both his palms out; two more concentrated blasts of wind sped off in Theo's direction. Once again, Theo froze time. This time, however, he walked to a now-frozen Nicholas and moved him into the path of his attack. Theo stood off to the side and admired his work before resuming time. Nicholas's eyes widened in shock as the two blasts of wind struck him in his shoulder and stomach, sending him tumbling back with the wind knocked from his lungs. Coughing and trying to regain his breath, he stood before brushing himself off.

'Well played, Theo,' said Nicholas, bowing his head toward Theo.

'Thank you,' replied Theo with a small smirk.

'I think we are done. You have me beat.'

Theo nodded and re-joined his brothers, high-fiving their awaiting hands.

'Alright, Lance, you're up!' Nicholas called out, preparing himself once again.

'Alright,' replied Lance, clearly uneasy as he walked out to where Theo had been minutes before.

'You ready?' Nicholas asked.

'Not really,' Lance replied.

'You will be fine, Lance, just do what feels natural.'

Lance nodded and readied himself. Nicholas thrust out his palm and the blast of wind shot straight at Lance. Lance's eyes widened and he dove to the side as the blast flew past him, the wind rustling his clothing with the proximity.

'Come on, Lance, you can use your light to block my attacks and fight back!' encouraged Nicholas, sending another blast of wind at Lance. Lance gritted his teeth and used his light to form a shield on his arm. He raised the shield and blocked the wind the power of the wind still knocked him flat on his back. Lance coughed as he stood back up to see lightning strike Nicholas, but instead of it instantly incinerating him, the lightning crackled between Nicholas's hands before he levelled his hand out and sent it in Lance's direction. Lance dove to the side, rolled, brought his hands up and fired two beams of light at Nicholas. He dodged them, using the wind to propel his body away and sent another powerful gust of wind at Lance but Lance thrust out both of his hands and a wall of light formed, blocking the wind. Nicholas smiled and used the wind to propel himself into the air and hover above the wall and Lance.

'You doing great, Lance!' cheered Nicholas before closing his eyes and concentrating.

The air suddenly became heavy, water droplets beginning to form around the two of them, the other brothers staying dry.

'Is he making rain?' asked Dylan, looking at Theo.

'Somewhat,' replied Theo, as more and more water droplets formed.

Nicholas opened his eyes, the droplets freezing rapidly into hailstones. Lance cursed as Nicholas pointed at him. The hail propelled itself straight at Lance. Lance wrapped the wall into a small dome around him, blocking the hail, then brought the dome into a large orb in front of him, firing it straight at Nicholas.

Nicholas dodged it using the wind to propel himself from the orb, then straight at Lance, coming in for a running landing and lashing out with a kick. Lance stumbled back a bit but ducked underneath the kick, retaliating with an orb of light straight into Nicholas's chest. The orb exploded on impact, sending him tumbling backwards, to which Nicholas used the momentum to recover, rolling back onto his feet and clapping.

'Well done, Lance! See, you're getting better already,' Nicholas said with a smile.

Lance dipped his head toward Nicholas as a small smile appeared on his lips.

'Alright, that will do. Dylan, you're up!' Nicholas announced.

Lance walked back to Theo as Dylan strode out, darkness already swirling around him.

'Ready?' asked Nicholas, preparing himself.

'Yep, let's go! This oughta be fun,' Dylan replied eagerly but mumbled the last part to himself.

Dylan sent a fist of darkness at Nicholas, who dove to the side, rolled to his feet and flew up into the air. Tracking his movement, Dylan threw two spears of darkness at Nicholas but he dodged both of them before thrusting out his hand, lightning arcing off his fingers and straight at Dylan. Dylan brought up a wall of darkness, blocking the lightning before he pushed the wall up into the air and straight at Nicholas. Nicholas flew over the wall and sent a powerful blast of wind at Dylan, but Dylan just blocked it with another wall, then morphed the wall into two massive orbs of darkness and fired them at Nicholas. Nicholas nose-dived straight into the attack but slipped between the orbs and spun around to drop-kick Dylan. Dylan instead caught his leg, pulled him from the air and threw him across the field, sending him tumbling across the ground with the momentum. Dylan sent two tentacles of darkness after Nicholas, wrapping them around his arms and pulling him back to Dylan. Nicholas struggled against the tentacle's grip, two more of them gripping his legs before they stretched him out in front of Dylan. He watched as darkness seeped beneath Dylan's skin and bled into his eyes. Dylan flashed an evil grin and looked up at Nicholas.

'Dylan?' Nicholas asked, a smidgeon of fear leaking into his voice.

Dylan didn't respond other than maintaining the grin.

Beginning to sense something was off, Nicholas concentrated a powerful downdraft on Dylan, knocking him down and startling him enough to release Nicholas. Landing on his feet, he followed up with a concentrated gale toward Dylan, sending him tumbling away before he could recover.

'Something isn't right,' Nicholas mumbled as Dylan stood up, his face contorted with rage.

'Oh, no,' said Theo, dread creeping in.

'What is it?' replied Lance.

'Dylan has lost control,' Theo informed his brother.

'Like on the night we discovered our powers?' Lance asked, worried.

'Yeah, except I think this is much worse,' Theo replied.

Dylan raised his arms to stretch out either side of him, darkness rose up and around him and started to swirl off his back. Four tentacles burst out of the swirling darkness behind him. Nicholas turned to take off into the air again but a tentacle shot out and swatted him in the back, sending him sprawling. The other tentacles shot forward and wrapped around his arms and legs once more, pulling him back in front of Dylan.

'Alright, Dylan, that will do for the day,' Nicholas said, but Dylan replied with a brutal, darkness-coated punch to Nicholas's exposed solar plexus.

The wind was driven from his lungs, a choked gasp of pain following it out as he sagged in the hold.

'We have to stop Dylan. He isn't going to stop!' Theo yelled to Lance.

'I'm on it!' replied Lance as he summoned an orb of light, hurling it at Dylan.

The orb zipped through the air and crashed into him exploding on impact and sending him flying. Nicholas crashed back down to the ground as the darkness evaporated but Dylan quickly recovered. Tentacles rose out of his back and raced toward his new target, Lance. Lance dodged the first, but the second and third struck him in the chest and knocked him on his ass. The fourth snaked towards Theo, but Theo just shook his head and froze time. He walked over to Lance and touched his shoulder, unfreezing him.

'You okay?' asked Theo.

'Yeah, just a tad winded,' Lance replied, puffing heavily.

'Come on,' Theo said, pulling Lance over to a frozen Dylan. 'Alright,

I'm gonna unfreeze time and I want you to blast him.'

'Sounds good,' Lance smirked.

'Ready?' asked Theo.

'Go!' Lance nodded. Orbs of light appeared in each of his hands.

Theo unfroze time and Lance brought his hands together, making a twisting motion in front of him, as if to put a spin on a ball. The orbs melded together to form a powerful orb of swirling light before Lance thrust it out at Dylan. The light struck Dylan, exploding with such force that it blew everyone off their feet. Theo quickly recovered his footing and ran over to Dylan. The darkness faded from his eyes and skin before he opened his eyes groggily.

'What happened?' groaned Dylan, sitting up.

'You don't remember?' asked Theo.

'Not really,' replied Dylan. 'The last thing I remember is catching Nicholas's leg.'

Theo looked at Dylan as Nicholas walked over.

'You fought very well, Dylan, but unfortunately, I managed to catch you off guard and got you with a blast of wind,' he praised him.

'Damn,' mumbled Dylan.

'That will do for the day, lads,' Nicholas informed them.

Dylan stood up and began to walk towards town, Lance joining him.

'We aren't telling him what just happened?' Theo asked, concerned.

'Not yet,' replied Nicholas, slinging his bag over his shoulder. 'I'm starting to get a good understanding of the powers you and your brothers have.'

'Well, that's just dandy for you but what if Dylan loses control again?' Theo asked, his anger building.

'Let's just hope it's against someone that we don't like!' Nicholas laughed and jogged to catch up with Dylan and Lance. Theo shook his head and followed behind him.

CHAPTER 20

Nicholas slid the room key into the keyhole and turned it, opening the door to his hotel room.

'What a day,' he mumbled to himself, placing his bag on the couch. He walked over to the bed, knelt and reached under to pull out the Swords of Darkness and Light. He placed them on the table and stared at the two swords, pondering what he was going to do. He picked up the Sword of Darkness, closing his eyes for a second, resisting the power that the darkness offered.

Maybe that's how Dylan lost control, he thought, opening his eyes.

Darkness curled and dripped off the obsidian blade as Nicholas rotated the sword in his hand.

Maybe he let the darkness take over? Nicholas put the sword back on the table, his eyes lingering on it a moment before turning away. *I need to know more about the brother's powers. These swords have the same powers as Lance and Dylan. Maybe I should go home and get the book my father used to find the swords; it might have more information on the powers within them.*

He walked over to his bag, pulled on a blue hoodie and smiled.

Looks like I'm going home!

He picked up the two swords and placed them back under the bed, and then left his room, locking the door behind him.

Nicholas walked outside and looked up at the starry night sky.

'London, here I come,' He sighed happily, rising off the ground and taking off into the night sky.

***

Nicholas hovered above the entrance gate to the mansion that he called home but didn't land.

Hmmm, Dad still thinks I'm still in Australia. Maybe I should get the book when he is asleep. I don't want him to know I was here; if he does know then he will want to know about the brothers and their powers and then I will have to tell him that they are the exact same powers as the swords. He can't know, not yet, not until I figure all this out and that book should help.

He had become fond of the brothers and if he told his father about them, he would use them, along with the swords, to further his ambitions, not that Nicholas knew exactly what those ambitions were.

Nicholas nodded to himself, turning and flying a bit further away, out of sight of the mansion before landing somewhere inconspicuous and calling a taxi.

Five minutes later, the taxi arrived and picked him up.

It wasn't long before the taxi arrived at Nicholas's destination. He paid the taxi driver and stepped out. He looked at the house he had arrived at and grinned before he walked up the path to the door. He knocked and was answered by a tall, skinny man with dark hair.

'Ah, hello, Nicholas,' the man greeted him warmly.

'Hello, Mr Ryan,' replied Nicholas, smiling. 'Is Kate home?'

'Yes, she is. Come on in,' Mr Ryan stood back and motioned

Nicholas in. He entered after he removed his shoes by the door.

Mr Ryan closed the door behind him and motioned up the stairs. 'Kate is in her room.'

'Thank you,' replied Nicholas.

Nicholas climbed the stairs and made his way to Kate's bedroom. He opened the door quietly. Kate was sitting at her desk, headphones in her ears, back to Nicholas. He smirked and snuck up behind her, tapping her on the shoulder once. Kate screamed in fright, throwing her pen and phone up in the air. Nicholas caught the phone as she turned, ripping the headphones out.

'What the hell?' she yelled. 'You scared the crap out of me!'

'Hello to you too,' He chuckled, smirking. Kate crossed her arms and stared at Nicholas. 'Alright, I'm sorry.'

Kate stood and wrapped her arms around Nicholas, hugging him tightly and burying her head into his chest.

'I'm glad you're home,' she said, lifting her head and kissed him.

He lifted a hand to cradle her jaw softly and when they finally broke the kiss, he replied almost breathlessly, 'As am I.'

Smiling, she pulled away and returned to her desk, sitting down on her chair. He opted to sit on her bed.

'How was Australia?' she asked.

'It's a beautiful country and I'll be going back shortly,' Nicholas replied.

'How soon?'

'Not sure yet. My father is still over there.'

'Why'd you come home then?'

Nicholas hesitated for a second, thinking about what he was going to say. 'I came to grab a couple of things and see you.'

She smiled at the last part. 'Where'd you go in Australia?'

'Well, I'm currently staying within the Grampians.'

'What're the Grampians? Where are they?'

'How much Australian geography do you know?'

'I know the states and capital cities of each state.'

'Well then, the Grampians are located in the mid-western region of Victoria. They are a localised mountain range filled with gaps, waterfalls, trees, trails and springs.'

'Sounds beautiful.'

'It is. But enough about me, what about you? What have you been up to?'

'Not a whole lot, just this uni work,' she replied dully, gesturing to the paperwork he'd distracted her from earlier.

Nicholas smiled sympathetically. 'How's uni going?'

'Yeah, not too bad, but it's keeping me busy,' she said, turning back to her work.

'Ah, good,' he said, getting up off her bed to encircle her in his arms from behind and whispered in her ear. 'I've missed you.'

'I missed you too,' she said as she lifted her arms to hold onto his while she turned her head slightly. She looked into his eyes before leaning in slowly for a kiss.

***

After having dinner with Kate and her father that night, Nicholas said his goodbyes and took a taxi back to the mansion.

'All the lights are off, good,' Nicholas muttered to himself. 'They must be asleep.'

Concentrating, he used the wind to lift himself up and over the boundary wall surrounding the mansion he called home. Landing softly, he began to sneak up to the building. Looking up, he spotted the chimney that led straight into the library and grinned. He took to the air once more, flying up to the top of the wide chimney stack and looked down within.

'This could get messy,' he sighed, releasing his hold on the wind, and he dropped into the chimney, using his hands and feet, wrapped in dense wind, to slow his descent and protect his hands. This, unfortunately, created a lot of dust and soot to come loose and shower him in his descent, making him gag and cough. He soon reached the bottom, ducking and rolling out of there as quickly as he could to avoid the rest of the debris that followed him. Rising out of the roll, he quickly shook off what he could, pulled his hood over his head and made his way into the darkened library.

'Now, where could that book be…' He trailed off as he began searching the shelves. But after what felt like ages of searching time, he still couldn't find the book he was looking for.

'Damn it, where else could it be?' He cursed and pondered. 'Maybe it's in Father's study?'

Careful not to make any noise, he made his way out of the library and through the halls of the mansion until he found the door he was looking for. Opening the door a crack, he peered in to ensure the coast was clear. Seeing no one, he slipped into the room. He walked over to the desk and gasped in amazement. Laying on a soft cloth was a sword of shimmering sapphire, three topaz gems embedded down the hilt.

'The Sword of Time!' Nicholas quietly said in awe before shaking his head. 'Can't get distracted, that's not what I'm here for.'

Sitting not too far from the sword was the book he'd been looking for. Smiling, he quickly grabbed it and stashed it under his clothes.

'Time to go,' he said as he began to sneak back to the library, leaving the doors as he found them. But just as he reached the fireplace, the lights flicked on behind the door, a couple of low voices slowly getting louder. Using a quick gust of wind, he blew back the evidence of the chimney being used and darted behind a row of shelves.

Not a moment too soon, it seemed, as the door opened, Adam's voice instantly becoming clear. 'I swear I heard footsteps, sir.'

'Adam, I'm sure it was nothing,' Nicholas heard his father trying to reassure his butler.

Something odd caught Nicholas's eye.

What happened in here? he thought as he saw parts of the shelves surrounding him charred and blackened.

'What if Pyro is back again?' Adam asked his master, unknowingly answering Nicholas's question.

And that's how he knew the location of the Sword of Light; he'd broken in here, Nicholas realised.

'If it were Pyro, he'd make himself known, Adam; however, if there is an intruder, remember our agreement,' Norman said, looking to his butler.

'Yes, sir, I shall not attack them. I am an ordinary butler with no powers and little self-defence skills.'

'Good. Now, shall we continue our little check?' Norman said, gesturing into the library.

'Sir,' Adam nodded as he led Norman into the library, flicking the lights on in the room.

Damn it, Nicholas cursed and crouched low. *Can't let them find me.*

He quickly crept his way toward the fireplace and his escape.

'Norman!' Adam called out, having appeared behind Nicholas, and began chasing him.

Nicholas broke out into a sprint, his goal within reach. Suddenly, an invisible force pulled him backward, sending him hurtling into a charred section of shelves, which gave way, swallowing him in burnt tomes and shelving.

Two shadows slid over him as his father and the butler loomed over the mess. Norman's power then began to lift him out of the debris pile and make him float in front of the pair.

'Who are you?' Norman growled.

Nicholas didn't answer; this prompted Norman to reach out for Nicholas's hood. Nicholas lowered his head as the hood came off.

The pair gasped and Nicholas felt himself being lowered to the floor.

'Nicholas?' Norman queried, not quite believing his eyes.

'Hello, Father,' Nicholas mumbled, head still lowered.

'What are you doing here?' Norman asked as he crossed his arms.

Nicholas didn't answer.

'Why did you break in? Why didn't you just come in the front door?' he asked again, but still no reply.

Norman's eyes widened with a realisation, then anger swept over his face. Nicholas was suddenly blasted off his feet.

'You son of a bitch! You're here for the Sword of Time!' Norman screamed at him as he tried to regain his footing, but couldn't before another telekinetic blast sent him flying into a more solid shelf.

Nicholas crumpled to the floor and cried out in pain.

'You want the swords for yourself!' Norman yelled, two tables nearby rising into the air. 'You've betrayed me!'

Nicholas stumbled to his feet and looked up at Norman, just as he sent the tables through the air at him. He dove to the side and rolled to stand, the tables having barely missed him. He then closed his eyes in concentration.

'You are not my son anymore! What son betrays his father?' Norman shrieked.

Nicholas's eyes snapped open – a miniature but powerful tornado tearing into existence in the middle of the library.

Nicholas watched as Norman and Adam dropped to the floor, narrowly avoiding the now-flying furniture and debris; then, using the chaos as a cover to get away, he darted for the fireplace, ducked under the ridge and created a powerful updraft to launch his body out into the night sky. Feeling around his torso, he found the book still within his clothes to his relief. This allowed him a brief smile before his tears began to form and fall away into the breeze.

***

Pyro rapidly spun the wheel of his hot red 2012 Chevrolet Camaro, sending the car into a drift around the corner before continuing down the streets of Melbourne.

'Why do you insist on driving like this?' Glacia groaned, not happy being in the passenger seat with this maniac at the wheel.

Pyro just laughed.

'Where are we going anyway?' Glacia huffed, crossing her arms.

'To the warehouse. We're meeting the others there.'

'So, we're finally bringing the others into this mess?' Glacia smiled at the thought of the whole gang back together again.

They drove for another ten minutes, arriving at an old graffiti-covered warehouse in an outer suburb known as Northcote. They both got out of the car and walked up to the warehouse.

Glacia, noting the graffiti, snorted in disgust. 'Damn kids.'

Pyro fished a key from his pocket and unlocked the door before entering, holding the door for Glacia to enter. She too slipped inside, Pyro closing and locking the door behind them.

Glacia looked around the empty warehouse.

'Couldn't we at least put some stuff in here?' she started. 'You know, make it seem less suspicious?'

'Why?' Pyro replied, walking to the far wall. 'The building is only here to hide this.'

Pyro then placed his hand on a secret panel on the wall, his handprint triggering one of the small concrete slabs on the floor in the centre of the building to drop and slide beneath another. This exposed a stairwell leading underground.

'Ladies first,' Pyro smirked, gesturing toward the staircase.

Glacia began her descent, Pyro following behind. It wasn't long before the stairwell stopped its descent and exited into a large room. The room was almost full of computers, monitors covering the walls, a single swivel chair at each monitor, and in the centre sat a large, round metal table with five chairs. Three of those chairs were occupied.

'Took your time!' taunted the man with long, black dreadlocks, his feet sat up on the table.

'Nice to see you too, Gale,' Pyro chuckled, grinning at his mate.

'Hey, bro,' called out the orange-haired woman sitting beside him, barely a striking resemblance to Pyro.

'Sis!' Pyro walked over to her and gave Assana a tight hug.

'Hey, Terra,' Glacia greeted the large, brown-haired muscular woman with a wave, earning a grunt in reply.

'Alright, greetings are done,' Glacia began. 'Let's get down to business.'

At that, the whole team settled into their seats. Glacia indicated for Pyro to start.

'So, this is what we know. Nicholas Quinzel – a weather manipulator and the son of Norman Quinzel, a telekinetic from England – has both the Sword of Light and Sword of Darkness. We don't know if they've managed to locate or acquire the Sword of Time yet.'

'We have reason to believe that Norman has just retrieved the Sword of Time,' Gale interjected, rolling his chair over to the nearest computer. He quickly flicked an image of Norman up onto the screen at the tail end of the table.

'This was taken in Japan, at the Palace Hotel,' Gale said, brushing a few stray dreadlocks from his face. 'He only stayed in Japan for a couple of days. He didn't appear to have any business there. Only personal reasons could explain his trip, meaning he has most likely discovered and retrieved the sword.'

'Damn it,' Pyro muttered.

'This means he will soon have all three Swords. He will be unstoppable,' stated Glacia.

'Alright, Assana, what about Nicholas? Where have we tracked him to?' Pyro asked, gesturing for his sister to share.

'Well, he is currently…' She trailed off, pointing a remote at the screen at the end of the table.

The image changed to that of a map. It started as a map of Australia before shrinking down to just a map of Victoria, one of its southwestern states.

'Here.' A small area in the southwestern region of the state became highlighted. 'In a small town named Cobden.'

'Alright, good work,' Pyro dipped his head to his sister. 'Do we know if he still has the two swords?'

'No, we haven't made contact yet,' Assana replied.

'Okay, looks like we're going for a drive,' Pyro grinned maniacally at Glacia, whose eyes only narrowed in return.

CHAPTER 21

Lance awoke to the sound of the shower starting up in the bathroom on the other side of the wall. He cursed and rolled out of bed.

'Why did I pick this room again?' he mumbled to himself, running his hand through his hair. 'Well, silver lining, a day off from training today.'

He quickly changed into a plain blue shirt and jeans before making his way downstairs for his breakfast. He placed two slices of bread in the toaster and pushed the slider down. As he waited, he pondered what he was going to do for the day. He turned as he could hear footsteps approaching and Dylan appeared from around the corner, his newly won championship belt slung over his shoulder. He had won the title on the previous night at a wrestling event he had competed in.

'Morning,' Dylan greeted him with a grin.

'Morning,' Lance replied. 'You ever going to put that down?'

'Hell no!' Dylan laughed, grinning from ear to ear and holding the title closer. Lance just rolled his eyes and turned back to the toaster as it clicked, his toast shooting up, ready to eat. He grabbed his toast, wandered over to the couch and turned the TV on. Dylan laid the belt on the counter and poured himself a bowl of cereal and joined his brother on the couch.

'You lied,' Lance chuckled.

'What?' Dylan replied, spoon halfway to his mouth.

'You lied,' Lance repeated, smirking.

'And what did I lie about?' Dylan asked, confused.

'You said that you wouldn't put that belt down,' Lance replied.

'Oh, piss off! I'm not going to get food on it,' Dylan replied irritably.

'Oh, look at you with the excuses,' Lance mocked.

'Shut up!' Dylan shot back.

'Why?' Lance asked with a grin.

'Because you are annoying,' Dylan seethed.

'But it's my job. I am your twin after all!' Lance replied with another laugh.

Dylan rolled his eyes and stood up, walking away from Lance, making him chuckle.

'Hey, you two! Stop fighting,' Theo said. 'We have to go.'

'Where?' Dylan replied, turning to look at Theo.

'Nick just messaged me saying he needs us over at his hotel room,' Theo explained, heading towards the door.

'I thought it was our day off,' Lance groaned, standing up.

'He said it isn't any kind of training, but he said it was extremely important,' Theo insisted, opening the door. 'So let's go!'

Lance and Dylan both looked at each other, shrugged and followed Theo out the door.

'Did he say what he wanted us for?' Dylan asked, walking up next to Theo.

'No, he didn't,' Theo replied. 'He just said it was important.'

Dylan shrugged and the three brothers walked in silence to the hotel. They arrived at the hotel and knocked on the door of Nicholas's room.

'It's open,' they heard Nicholas yell from inside. They entered the room and they found Nicholas sitting on the couch, watching TV, the Swords of Light and Darkness laying on the coffee table in front of him.

'Hi, guys,' Nicholas mumbled, rubbing his eyes and yawning.

'Hi, Nick. You okay? Dylan replied.

'Yeah, just didn't sleep,' Nicholas replied, switching off the TV. Dylan nodded.

'So, what did you want to talk about?' Lance asked, sitting down in one of the chairs.

'Well, if I am honest, there is a lot of stuff I want to talk to you guys about,' Nicholas replied. 'But first, there is something I have to show you.'

Nicholas stood up and walked over to the bed and picked up a black, metal-bound book, brought it back over and placed it down on the coffee table, between the two swords.

'What is that?' Dylan asked, sitting down and leaning closer to the book.

'Well, this book is how these two swords were found,' Nicholas replied, running a hand across the cover.

'Where did you find that?' Lance whispered, clearly in shock.

'Before I answer that question, I need to tell you guys something else,' Nicholas replied. 'So obviously, I haven't told you guys much about myself and where I come from.'

The brothers nodded and Nicholas took in a breath and began his story.

'So, I was born on the tenth of March in Manchester, but my parents were involved in a car accident when I was six months old. So, I was placed in an orphanage and that's where I stayed until I was adopted by a man called Norman Quinzel.'

'Wait, as in the world-famous surgeon Norman Quinzel?' Theo asked, shock once again on his face.

'Yeah, that's my father,' Nicholas replied, nodding.

'My girlfriend left yesterday to go over there to his house for some sort of program for future surgeons,' Theo replied.

'Yeah, he does that program every year for particularly gifted students,' Nicholas replied with a dismissive wave. 'Anyway, I will continue my story. So, Norman adopted me and for the next seven years of my life, I was happy as could be and had everything I could ever ask for; then, when I turned eight, the training began.'

'Training?' Lance asked.

'Yeah, to become a weapon, my father trained me in every combat style imaginable. He paid for experts from all over the world to train me in martial arts, the use of particular weapons and other things, and then four years into my training, my powers over weather surfaced.'

'But how did Norman know how to train your powers?' Lance asked.

'Well, he also has a power, like us,' Nicholas replied.

'He does?' Theo asked.

'Yeah, telekinesis,' Nicholas replied.

'You mean he can control things with his mind?' Dylan asked.

'That's right,' Nicholas replied.

'Well, that probably explains why he is one of the best surgeons in the world,' Theo replied.

'Anyway, over this time, Norman was also researching these swords, finding this book in the process of his research and searching. Then last year, he comes back from one of his adventures with this.'

Nicholas picked up the Sword of Darkness.

'He presented me with this, telling me I was ready and that's when I started going out on missions for him, killing rogue monsters and retrieving more information for Norman's research, and that brings us to right now and, of course, you guys know the rest,' Nicholas finished, taking a deep breath.

The brothers breathed out and all nodded.

'Now, onto how I got the book,' Nicholas exclaimed, putting the sword down and picking up the book. 'So, last night, I was sitting in this exact spot, thinking about you guys' powers, when I realised that your powers and the swords could be linked. I thought I would go home and retrieve this book. I snuck in at night and grabbed it from my father's study, but also found something else.'

'What was it?' Theo asked.

'The Sword of Time,' Nicholas replied.

Theo instantly looked up, a sensation running down his spine.

'What?' Dylan questioned. 'There is a third sword?'

'Yeah, it is true,' Nicholas exclaimed, sighing. 'He retrieved it while I was retrieving the Sword of Light. He did say he was away, anyway, so I grabbed this book and as I was leaving, I was caught by my father and he thought I had betrayed him and I was there to steal the Sword of Time, so he disowned me on the spot and attacked – we fought and I barely escaped.'

'Wow, man, that's rough. Are you okay?' Dylan asked.

'Yeah, I will be okay,' Nicholas replied. 'But now I can guarantee one thing and that is my father is coming for us now.'

The brothers all looked at each other.

'Well, I guess we are going to have to keep training then,' Dylan exclaimed, standing up.

'I agree with that but not today. You guys do deserve a break and we do have a few days since he is holding the program,' Nicholas replied.

'Maybe the book can help us,' Lance exclaimed, pointing at the book.

'Well about that…' Nicholas exclaimed, opening the book. 'I can't read it at all.'

The brothers looked at the opened book and gasped at the swirling unreadable words on the page.

'What language is that?' Dylan exclaimed.

'I have no idea,' Nicholas replied. 'I was kinda hoping that something might happen when it was close to the swords.'

Lance reached over and touched the book and the instant his fingers touched the page, the words on the page morphed into English.

'Whoa!' Lance exclaimed, quickly pulling his hand back.

'What the…' Nicholas exclaimed. 'Do that again.'

'It must react to us,' Theo said. He reached out and touched the corner of the book and once again, the words morphed into English.

'What does it say?' Dylan asked, leaning over Theo's shoulder.

'Looks like this page is on the Sword of Darkness, explaining it and what it can do,' Nicholas exclaimed, spinning the book to face him but making sure Theo's touch stayed.

'According to this, the sword has a spirit in it and that's where its power comes from,' Nicholas said, excitement filling his voice. 'It also says that it is destined for a certain person and that person will be able to defeat the spirit inside and take full control of the blade and any who isn't worthy of it can wield it but will suffer certain consequences.'

'What kind of consequences?' Lance asked.

'Well, I can tell you that sword attacks me when I use it more and more,' Nicholas replied, looking over at the black blade and rolling up his sleeve, showing the scars up and down his arm.

'Who do you think the destined user is, Nick?' Theo asked.

Nicholas looked up at Dylan.

'Me?' Dylan questioned, taking a step back.

'Yes, Dylan, I think it is destined for you,' Nicholas nodded.

'But last time I touched the sword, it also attacked me,' Dylan countered.

'I don't think that's the case. When you touched it, someone else took over. I now believe that that was the spirit in the sword and you instantly succumbed to it,' Nicholas explained.

'Well, who's to say that that won't happen again?' Dylan asked with concern.

'Well, you are stronger now and we also know to make this next time different,' Nicholas replied.

'Right… well, I guess we can give it a shot,' Dylan nodded.

'Excellent, but first, I'm hungry. Are you guys?' Nicholas asked.

The brothers all nodded, so Nicholas quickly hid the swords and the book behind a loose board in the wall and they all set off in search of something to eat.

***

Pyro parked his car and he and Glacia stepped out of the car and looked around.

'So, this is Cobden,' Glacia muttered, looking around the small main street.

'Kinda boring, isn't it?' Pyro replied, folding his arms and leaning onto the car. 'Do we know where Nicholas is?'

Glacia reached into her jeans pocket and pulled out her phone and brought up a picture of a map that Assana had sent her.

'He is staying at a motel on the outskirts of town, next to a service station,' Glacia explained, showing Pyro her phone.

'Alright, we go there,' he responded.

They both got back into the car and drove to the motel.

'It's a tad small,' Pyro exclaimed, stepping out of the car and looking at the small hotel.

'Well, there are only eight rooms, so it shouldn't be hard to find Nicholas's room,' Glacia replied and began walking towards the motel to begin their search.

***

Nicholas and the brothers walked back towards the motel, finishing off the last of the sandwiches.

'So, when we get inside, Dylan will try to conquer the spirit in the sword,' Nicholas explained, opening the door into the corridor.

'That's going to be interesting,' Dylan mumbled, fear creeping into his voice.

'What the hell?' Nicholas exclaimed as he approached his room. The door was gone; pieces of frozen wood were scattered around the entrance. He raced to the entrance and growled as he spotted Pyro and Glacia searching under his bed.

'What the hell are you two doing here?' Nicholas growled, lightning suddenly arcing between his fingers.

Pyro shot up and turned to Nicholas.

'Whoops, busted,' Pyro exclaimed with a laugh and he hurled a fireball.

CHAPTER 22

Seeing the fireball hurtling toward him, Nicholas let the lightning fade and summoned a mini whirlwind in the doorway, extinguishing the fireball before it could get close. Seeing an opening, Dylan quickly dashed into the room, clouds of roiling darkness surrounding his arms.

Not missing a beat, Pyro threw two fireballs in Dylan's direction.

The dark masses sloughed off Dylan's arms and formed a shield, it absorbed the fireballs before bearing down on Pyro and Glacia in the shape of a wave, knocking them both back against the wall.

'Why are you here?' Dylan growled.

Glacia threw sharp shards of ice at him in reply. Dylan cursed, not expecting the attack, as the shards dug into his arms.

Nicholas barrelled in to assist Dylan, blasting a gale at the opposing pair. This blew Pyro through the wall where the window was meant to be, debris raining all over him, and sent Glacia crashing through the table.

'Pyro!' Glacia screamed, clutching her side as she regained her footing and ran over to assist the coughing and groaning man. 'Are you alright?'

'Yeah, I'm fine,' Pyro replied, sitting up with another slight groan. 'Damn him!'

Then he spun on his heel and dove through the open window to the outside, Glacia following him out.

'You're just not going to give up, are you?' Nicholas barked out as he and Dylan followed them through the window.

'Of course not. If I want something that is going to make me rich, then I will stop at nothing to get it,' Pyro laughed, rolling his shoulders and neck, the joints cracking as flames flared into existence around his closing fists.

Glacia followed his lead and sunk into a fighting stance, drawing out two blades of ice in her hands.

'And you'll fight four of us for it?' Nicholas asked with an eyebrow raised just as Lance and Theo rounded the corner of the building.

'We want those swords, so if we have to, then yes,' Glacia replied, raising one hand further in front of her, dagger ready.

'So just do yourselves, and us, a favour and hand them over!' Pyro smirked.

'You know we aren't going to do that,' Nicholas replied, falling back into a defensive stance.

Pyro shrugged and brought his arms together and fired an x-shaped blast of flames at Nicholas. He blocked the flames with the wind, then he sent a burst of wind at Pyro, but he dodged the wind. Glacia dove at Nicholas, knives outstretched, but Dylan intercepted her with a mass of darkness, knocking her back. She tumbled back to her feet and threw the knives at Dylan. He blocked the blades with a shield of darkness, but Glacia rushed Dylan, ducking under the shield and tackled him to the ground, then she straddled him and started to throw punches, but he brought his arms up around his head to block, then he rotated his hips, sending Glacia tumbling off him and they both scrambled to their feet and Dylan blasted her off her feet with another mass of darkness.

Pyro ran at Nicholas and swung a flame-covered fist at his head. Nicholas ducked under and Lance was behind him, orbs of light in each hand. Lance brought his hands together, one in front of the other, and thrust them out, sending a beam of light at Pyro, striking him in the chest, blasting him off his feet and sending him tumbling backwards.

'Nice shot,' Nicholas grinned, giving Lance a thumbs up.

Lance nodded, grinning.

Glacia stood up and turned to face Dylan again and he sent another stream of darkness at her, but she rolled under the darkness and sent a stream of ice at him; it struck him in the legs and ice quickly spread down his legs, freezing him in place. She ran up and drop-kicked him in the chest, sending him flying backwards.

Pyro stood up, his chest still smoking.

'They are much stronger than before,' he mumbled to himself. Glacia cartwheeled backwards and stood next to Pyro.

'What are we going to do? Keep fighting?' Glacia asked as Theo helped Dylan back to his feet.

'Yeah, we keep fighting,' Pyro replied. 'These brothers are still inexperienced; they might be stronger, but we can take them.'

'And what about Nicholas?' Glacia asked.

'We take out the brothers first, then we both get Nicholas,' Pyro instructed.

'Let's do it then,' Glacia said, nodding.

Pyro summoned an orb of fire in each hand and threw them at Dylan and Theo and Glacia sent spears of ice towards Lance and Nicholas. Theo quickly stopped time and moved himself and Dylan out of the path of the fireball, then restarted time, the fireball sailing past them. Lance created a barrier of light in front of himself, protecting himself and Nicholas from the spears. Nicholas dashed forward and sent pillars of wind on each side of him, slamming into Pyro and Glacia, sending them tumbling away. Theo instantly dashed forward as Pyro hit the ground and jumped on top of him and began to rain punches down. Pyro quickly brought his arms up, blocking the punches, and his eyes began to glow. Theo saw it and stopped time, moving off Pyro, and stepping back, restarting time again and beams of fire burst out of Pyro's eyes but only struck empty air.

'What the…' Pyro exclaimed, jumping to his feet and turning to face Theo. 'How are you doing that?'

But Theo didn't answer the question; he just prepared himself to fight again. Nicholas suddenly appeared and spear-tackled Pyro to the ground. Glacia rolled backwards onto her feet and turned to face Lance and Dylan. She placed her hand on her hip and smiled seductively in their direction.

'You boys wanna go?' she asked, licking her lips.

Dylan and Lance both blushed and looked down at the ground. Glacia's smile turned evil and ice began to crystalise around her hands, forming claws. Lance and Dylan snapped out of their dazes as Glacia raced towards them and slashed at them with the claws. They both dodged back and Lance fired a beam of light. Dylan threw a stream of darkness at her, but she dove between the light and darkness, landing next to Lance and she lashed out at him again. Lance panicked and stumbled backwards, the sharp claws barely missing slashing his stomach to shreds. Glacia then danced back as Dylan tried to get her again with another mass of darkness. Lance fired another beam of light at Glacia but this time she changed her claws into a shield of ice. The beam struck the shield and it reflected off, nearly striking Dylan on the reflection. Glacia looked down at the shield in surprise and then she smirked, realising her advantage. Lance and Dylan nodded at each other and Dylan charged, darkness surrounding his fists, and he punched at Glacia. She brought the shield up, blocking his punch, then ice surrounded her fist and she drove it towards Dylan's ribs, but darkness rose, blocking the punch. Dylan then dashed to the side, revealing Lance firing another beam of light at Glacia. She brought up the shield at the last second and the light reflected off, angling the shield at the last second towards Dylan. The light burst through Dylan's darkness and struck him front on, sending him flying backwards. Then Glacia dashed towards Lance again and she managed to run her hand along his stomach and down his thigh; ice instantly formed, freezing down his legs.

'Damn,' Lance exclaimed, struggling to move.

Glacia cartwheeled backwards and smirked.

'You're looking a bit stuck,' Glacia said, trying not to laugh.

Lance glared at her and continued to struggle. Glacia summoned a spear of ice and lined Lance up.

'Well, boys, this is your end,' she announced.

Lance threw an orb of light at her in desperation but she easily dodged it, shaking her head.

'Pathetic.' She sighed and she threw the spear.

Lance summoned a barrier of light, the spear breaking on impact. Lance then dropped the barrier and thrust both his hands out and two beams of light fired at Glacia, but again she brought up a shield on each arm and reflected the light in front of her, the beams striking each other and forming an orb of light. Lance cut off the beams but before the orb disappeared, Glacia stepped forward and encased the orb of light in ice.

'Now I am going to use your power against you,' she announced, laughing maniacally, but Lance reached out, splaying his hands and the light inside the orb exploded outwards, shattering and melting the ice in an instant and knocking Glacia off her feet and throwing up a cloud of dust.

Glacia coughed as she got to her feet and as the dust began to settle, her eyes widened in alarm. She was surrounded by hundreds of shards of light floating in the air. She looked over at Lance; both his hands were raised and open and a grin was on his face.

Glacia sighed, realising her mistake, and Lance threw his arms down and all the shards shot down and all struck Glacia, making her scream in agony. Every part of her body was ravaged by the torrent. She stumbled for a second then fell to the ground, passing out from the pain. Lance breathed a sigh of relief and he collapsed to the ground, the ice melting around his body. Suddenly a fireball was flying at him but it was stopped by a mass of darkness. Dylan stepped in front of Lance and Pyro stalked towards them. Lance could see both Nicholas and Theo struggling back to their feet behind Pyro, a ring of fire around them, preventing them from going anywhere.

'No one is going to stop me from getting those swords!' Pyro roared, pointing at Lance and Dylan. 'Not you,' Pyro pointed behind him. 'Not them, not anyone!'

'I got this, Lance,' Dylan growled, stepping in Pyro's direction.

'Fine! I will take you out and they will be mine finally,' Pyro yelled and he threw two fireballs at Dylan.

Dylan quickly extinguished them with darkness then charged at Pyro, a mass of darkness growing behind him. Pyro also charged and they met head-on and began to throw fists, blocking and countering until Pyro pushed Dylan back, but Dylan sent the mass that had formed behind him at Pyro, striking true and lifting him off the ground. Dylan quickly followed him, darkness lifting him off the ground. Pyro tumbled through the air until the bottom of his feet ignited, straightening him and he floated for a second before flying straight at Dylan like a bullet, tackling him, then spinning and driving his leg into Dylan's stomach, sending him tumbling to the ground and landing with a crash. Pyro descended to the ground once again as Lance got to his feet and prepared to fight.

'Just give up,' Pyro sighed. 'Those swords are now mine.'

Lance didn't say anything and just sent a beam at Pyro, but he dodged it easily.

'Damn it. I used too much in that last fight,' Lance mumbled to himself as he stumbled back a bit.

Pyro ran at Lance, his fists igniting with flame, and he swung a punch at Lance but Lance's training kicked in and he swayed to the side, avoiding the punch. He threw a punch of his own, but Pyro caught it with his flame-covered hand. Lance howled in agony as the fire burnt his hand. Pyro punched Lance in the side of the cheek, sending Lance stumbling backwards. Lance reached up and rubbed his cheek, feeling the burn that was now there too.

'Just give up, kid, you're in no condition to fight me,' Pyro laughed.

Lance ignored him and held his fist out and an orb of light formed around it, growing in size until it was the size of a basketball, then Lance thrust it towards Pyro and the orb flew off his fist and sped towards Pyro. Pyro began to laugh but Lance unclenched his fist and splayed his fingers and the orb split into six smaller orbs, causing Pyro's eyes to widen in surprise and alarm as the orbs rocketed with much greater speed towards him and struck him in different parts of his body, exploding on impact and sending him flying backwards with a howl of agony.

'Light shotgun,' Lance mumbled, remembering that the popular anime characters name their attacks.

Pyro coughed and groaned in pain as he got back to his feet.

'Damn, kid. Didn't expect that,' he mumbled. 'Enough of going easy.'

Pyro's hands ignited again and threw them out and dozens of tiny little balls of fire floated off his hands and floated in Lance's direction.

Lance looked around in panic and wonder as more and more of the fireballs floated around and past him. Pyro smirked to himself and suddenly the balls stopped floating and sped at Lance, each one striking different parts of his body, exploding on impact. Lance screamed in agony and fell to the ground as more and more of the fireballs exploded against and around him.

'Looks like you're done now,' Pyro said, crouching down next to Lance.

Lance groaned and looked at Pyro through half-lidded eyes, trying to not pass out from the pain.

'I will be taking those swords now,' Pyro exclaimed as he rose back up, but he was suddenly blasted off his feet by a mass of darkness.

'Forgetting something?' Dylan asked as he stepped in front of Lance again.

'I thought I had dealt with you,' Pyro growled, getting to his feet.

'Not quite, mate,' Dylan grinned.

Pyro threw his hands out in anger and streams of fire burst from his hands, but Dylan blocked them with a wall of darkness, then he turned the wall into a dozen of spears and sent them at Pyro, but he tumbled out of the way and struggled back to his feet.

'Damn. They have taken too much out of me,' Pyro mumbled to himself. 'I can't keep this up.'

Dylan had tentacles of darkness formed around him but Pyro held up his hand.

'Stop. I give up,' he exclaimed. 'I'm too weak to continue fighting you.'

Dylan ignored Pyro's declaration of surrender and sent the tentacles speeding in Pyro's direction. In desperation, Pyro flung up his arms and a wall of flames blocked the tentacles.

Dylan tried to blast the wall apart but to no avail. Cursing, he tried again and again until the wall suddenly dropped, revealing empty space behind it.

'They're gone,' he mumbled as his darkness faded away. He walked over to Lance to check on him.

'Are you okay?' Dylan asked.

Lance sat up and groaned in pain.

'I've been better, but I'll be fine,' Lance replied.

Nicholas and Theo walked over, joining them.

'Everyone okay?' Nicholas asked, holding his ribs.

'Yeah,' the brothers all replied.

'Good. Let's get inside and let our bodies rest and heal.'

And with that, they helped each other walk back to Nicholas's room.

CHAPTER 23

The plane made its descent and landed on the runway of Heathrow Airport in London, making Gabrielle breathe a sigh of relief and she finished off the glass of straight vodka, the only thing that kept her somewhat calm during the flight.

'Thankfully that's over,' she mumbled. 'This flying thing sucks.'

She quickly disembarked the plane, making her way into the airport. She got through security easily; she quickly retrieved her bags and made her way through all the different shopping and fast-food outlets, towards the area where most people meant their particular rides. She pulled a printout of the information she needed to find her ride to Mr Quinzel's. The information said that she needed to go towards the Qantas check-in area. She folded the paper and followed the overhead signs to that area until she spotted a man in a three-piece suit holding a sign with her name on it.

'Hi, I'm Gabrielle,' she said, approaching the man.

'Hello, Gabrielle, I am Adam. Mr Quinzel has sent me to take you to his mansion,' Adam replied.

'Sounds good, but where are the other people?' Gabrielle asked.

'They are already at the mansion. You are the last person to be picked up,' Adam said.

'Ah, right,' Gabrielle replied, a tad embarrassed.

'Are you ready to go? Or is there anything else you need to get?' Adam asked.

'No, no, I am ready to go,' Gabrielle replied with a grin.

Adam nodded and picked up her luggage. 'Shall we?' he asked.

Gabrielle nodded and followed Adam out of the terminal and to the parking out the front, Adam walking up to the parked limousine.

'Is this the ride?' she asked, clearly trying to not show her excitement.

'Yeah, it is. First time in a limousine?' Adam asked as he opened the car boot and placed her bags in it.

Gabrielle nodded and Adam smiled.

'Well, I hope you enjoy it,' he said, opening the door for her and she gasped as she stepped inside.

She couldn't believe the size of the area, with seats on the edges, a mini-fridge and a television. She sat down and looked around in wonder as Adam sat down in the driver's seat.

'What do you think?' he asked from the front.

'This is so cool,' Gabrielle replied, still in awe.

Adam laughed and started the engine.

'If you are thirsty, there are refreshments in the fridge. You are more than welcome to have as many as you like,' he said as he pulled the limousine out into traffic. 'It will take us about half an hour to get to Mr Quinzel's home, so sit back and relax.'

Gabrielle nodded and reached for the fridge. She grabbed a bottle of water from it.

'So, what part of Australia are you from, Gabrielle?' Adam asked.

'Oh, I'm from a small town called Cobden in the state of Victoria,' Gabrielle replied.

Gabrielle saw in the rear-view mirror Adam's eyes widened in surprise, mumbling something that Gabrielle couldn't hear.

'What was that?' Gabrielle asked.

'Oh, nothing,' replied Adam. 'Is that anywhere near the Grampians?'

'It's about two hours to the southeast of the Grampians,' replied Gabrielle. 'My boyfriend was there recently.'

'Your boyfriend?' Adam queried.

'Yeah, his name is Theo,' Gabrielle confirmed.

Adam took in a sharp breath.

'Is something wrong?' Gabrielle asked.

'Nothing, sorry,' Adam replied quickly.

Gabrielle opened the water and took a drink, watching the streets of London fly by.

'It is so beautiful out there,' Gabrielle exclaimed in awe.

'Yes, it is,' Adam replied.

'Have you lived here your whole life here, Adam?' Gabrielle asked.

'Yeah, I was born in Hounslow,' Adam replied.

'I will be honest with you, Adam, I don't know where that is,' Gabrielle replied.

'You're lucky that you don't,' Adam replied, images of his horrible childhood flashing through his mind. 'It isn't a nice part of London, Gabrielle.'

'Oh, right,' Gabrielle said.

'Ah, we have arrived,' Adam announced.

Gabrielle gasped in amazement as the large ornate gates opened and Adam drove the limousine through and up the driveway towards the mansion. Adam parked up at the front door and Gabrielle waited as Adam turned off the engine, stepped out of the driver's seat and made his way around to open the door for Gabrielle.

'Thank you,' she said as she stepped out of the limousine.

'You're welcome,' Adam replied. 'Don't worry about your bags; they will be brought up to your room later.'

'Sounds good,' she replied.

'Allow me to show you inside,' Adam exclaimed, motioning to the front door.

Gabrielle nodded and followed Adam up the steps. She gasped again in amazement, looking around the main foyer as she walked inside.

'This house is amazing,' Gabrielle exclaimed.

'That it is,' Adam replied. 'Allow me to show you to your room. You will be getting a tour later on.'

'Okay,' she replied. She followed Adam up the stairs to the second floor and into the west side of the mansion.

'Alright, here is your room,' Adam announced, opening the door to the bedroom.

'Wow,' Gabrielle muttered, looking inside. There was a king-sized bed, a large flat-screen television, a fridge, a table with a variety of books and a beautiful view out the large window of the grounds.

'Is it to your liking?' Adam asked, stepping back.

'Oh, yes,' Gabrielle replied.

'Good. I will leave you to get comfortable and I will be back later,' Adam said as she stepped into the room and closed the door behind him.

'This is amazing,' Gabrielle said to herself, spinning around and then flopping down on the bed.

***

Adam pulled the last piece of paper out of the printer and carried the papers to the study. He walked into the study and placed the stack of papers on the desk next to Norman.

'Here, sir. Here are all the medical records of the people who have come here,' Adam said.

'Thank you, Adam,' replied Norman, moving the papers in front of himself. 'Can I get some tea?'

'Right away, sir,' replied Adam.

He quickly left the study and Norman grabbed the first page off the pile and read through the page but he shook his head.

'Not the right blood type,' he mumbled to himself. He grabbed the next page. 'Same again. Why do I have to be looking for a rare blood type?' he mumbled to himself. He looked through the next few pages with no luck. 'Is this gonna be like every other year?'

Then he picked up the page about Gabrielle.

'Hmmm, Gabrielle Morrison. Lives in Cobden, Victoria, Australia. Well, things just got very interesting,' Norman mumbled.

'Yes, she is an interesting girl,' replied Adam, walking into the study.

'Did she tell you anything? Does she know the brother Nicholas is meant to be training?'

'She is the girlfriend of one of the brothers – Theo.'

'What? It is a small world. Guess I better check her blood type.'

Norman returned to the page and scanned the page and gasped.

'Finally,' he mumbled.

'She is a match?' asked Adam.

'Yes, Adam. Blood type AB negative. This is perfect.'

'Now what, sir?'

'Well, I'm going to put a bag of blood I have into her and see what happens,' replied Norman, an evil look crossing his face.

Adam took a step back, a little scared.

Norman opened the drawer and pulled out a container with pills in it.

'Alright, Adam, at dinner tonight, I want you to place one of these in her drink,' Norman commanded, throwing the pills to Adam.

'What? Why?' replied Adam, looking down at the white container of pills, a simple label that read 'Zolpidem'.

'Those pills will put her to sleep for a while and it will look like she fainted. While she's out, I will perform a blood transfusion,' Norman informed his butler.

'Okay,' Adam replied slowly.

'Good, now leave me,' replied Norman.

Adam walked out of the study, eyeing the bottle in his hand.

He is getting worse. His research of people with powers is making him push the boundary more and more. I know he has done this to someone before but that was a full-grown adult, but I have to do what the master wishes, Adam thought, pocketing the pills and heading for the kitchen.

***

Gabrielle stood in front of the mirror and admired herself. She had a long, silky, strapless blue dress on. She was waiting for Adam to collect her for dinner. Then there was a knock.

'Gabrielle, it's Adam. Are you ready for dinner?' Adam asked through the door.

'Yes, I'll be out in a minute,' replied Gabrielle, quickly heading out and joining the group of other people following Adam.

'Alright, everyone, let's go to dinner,' Adam said.

Everyone walked down the stairs and walked into the large, dining room. A long table ran down the middle of the room with ten wooden chairs on either side with a single, high-back chair at the head of the table. Four suits of armour, two on each side, stood against the walls and the walls were adorned with artwork from a variety of different artists. Gabrielle sat down and looked around the room in amazement.

'This room is amazing, isn't it?' exclaimed the guy next to Gabrielle.

'Yes, it is,' Gabrielle replied, smiling at him. He was a tall man with short brown hair.

'I'm Mike,' Mike introduced himself with an American accent.

'I'm Gabrielle,' Gabrielle replied.

'Where are you from?' Mike asked.

'Australia,' Gabrielle replied.

'I'm from America,' Mike said with a smile.

Gabrielle and Mike continued their conversation, as Adam stood up and walked to the door. Norman approached the other side.

'Are you ready, sir?' Adam asked through the door.

'Yes, Adam,' replied Norman.

Adam loudly cleared his throat and a hush fell over the room.

'Ladies and gentlemen,' announced Adam. 'It is my honour to introduce to you, Mr Norman Quinzel.'

Adam opened the door and Norman walked into the dining room.

'Hello, everyone,' exclaimed Norman. 'I am very pleased to welcome everyone to my home. I hope to get to have a conversation with each of you and hope you all enjoy your stay.'

There was a round of applause and Norman took a seat at the head of the table and everyone continued their conversation.

'Those two up there are lucky,' muttered the other guy next to Gabrielle, pointing to the two people seated next to Norman.

'I guess so,' replied Gabrielle, looking up at Norman. The other guy looked back at her and smirked.

'You are from Australia,' he said.

'Yeah, I'm Gabrielle,' replied Gabrielle. 'You are from here in London?'

'Yes, I am. I'm Dexter,' replied Dexter.

Dexter was a thin man with light brown hair; he was wearing a blue suit and a pair of curved sunglasses with blue lenses on his head. He was playing with a small ball of string, rolling it between his fingers.

'Nice to meet you,' replied Gabrielle.

'I bet it is,' Dexter replied smugly.

'Wow, what a jerk,' Gabrielle muttered as the entrée was placed in front of her.

'Awesome food,' Gabrielle mused.

The next hour went by quickly for Gabrielle; she ate her meals and had different conversations with different people from around the table. Adam walked around with a trolley, collecting all the plates and utensils.

'Adam, can I get another drink?' exclaimed Gabrielle.

'Sure,' replied Adam. He walked around, grabbed her glass and went into the kitchen and minutes later, he returned with her drink.

'Thank you,' Gabrielle said.

'No worries,' replied Adam, looking a little pale.

Gabrielle looked up and noticed that the two people who were sitting around Norman had left for bed.

'Here's my chance.' She stood up and walked to the head of the table and sat down next to Norman.

'Hello, sir. My name is Gabrielle,' exclaimed Gabrielle, extending her hand. Norman took her hand and shook it.

'Ah, yes. Gabrielle,' replied Norman. 'I believe you are from Australia.'

'Yes, I am,' replied Gabrielle, taking a sip of her drink.

'Excellent. I have always loved Australia,' replied Norman.

'Yeah. It is a beautiful country,' replied Gabrielle.

'Yes, it is. I was actually thinking of moving there when I was younger but I love London too much,' Norman said with a laugh.

'That's fair enough. It is quite nice here,' replied Gabrielle.

'Do you like London?' Norman asked.

'Well, from what I've seen, it's a lovely city,' replied Gabrielle.

'Yes, it is,' replied Norman. 'So why have you come here to do my program?'

'Well, I've always wanted to be a doctor – in particular, a surgeon – then I received an email about this trip and I thought, why not learn from the greatest surgeon in the world? You,' replied Gabrielle. The edges of her vision started going a bit fuzzy.

What is going on? she thought but she shook it off.

'Good answer,' replied Norman, smiling.

Gabrielle shook her head again as the fuzziness and dizziness got worse.

'Are you alright?' Norman asked. 'You look a bit pale.'

'I'm fine,' replied Gabrielle, but she wasn't as black spots danced in front of her eyes.

'Are you sure you're alright?' exclaimed Norman as Gabrielle swayed in her chair.

'I don't think so…' was all she could say before darkness took ever and she passed out.

***

Norman looked up; no one else was in the room – all had left for bed – and he smirked.

'Adam,' Norman called, standing up.

'Yes, sir?' replied Adam, stepping out of the kitchen.

'Good job,' replied Norman. 'I'll be back.'

Norman walked out of the dining room and Adam frowned.

'Why is he doing this?' Adam muttered to himself.

Minutes later, Norman returned with a wheelchair. Norman concentrated and Gabrielle lifted off her chair and into the wheelchair.

'Come along, Adam,' Norman commanded.

Adam grabbed the handles of the wheelchair and pushed it, following Norman to the elevator. Norman pressed the button for the underground lab and the elevator went down. Adam wanted to ask what was going on, but he remained silent. The elevator stopped and the doors opened. They walked out of the elevator and up the narrow passage, towards the double doors. Norman pushed open the doors and allowed Adam to wheel Gabrielle in.

'Adam, welcome to my lab,' exclaimed Norman.

Adam remained silent.

'Alright, let's get to work,' exclaimed Norman.

Norman looked around; it looked like a surgery room from a hospital. There was a hospital bed in the middle of the room and drawers and cupboards surrounding the walls with a single light above lighting the room. Norman walked over to the drawers and pulled out a syringe, and then he walked over to the fridge and pulled out the blood bag. Suddenly, Gabrielle was lifted out of the wheelchair and onto the bed.

'Whose blood is that, sir?' exclaimed Adam.

Norman held up the bag and it read 'Nicholas Quinzel, Blood type AB negative'.

'Nicholas's blood?' Adam questioned, and then he realised what Norman was doing. 'You're going to try and give her powers.'

'Well, theoretically, yes,' replied Norman. 'That is the plan; it is a theory I am testing.'

Norman placed the blood bag on a hook and placed an IV line on it, then he attached the line to the needle in his hand.

'Here it goes,' exclaimed Norman and he pushed the needle into the back of Gabrielle's hand and the new blood began to flow.

***

Adam watched from behind the window, looking at Gabrielle still laying in the bed. It had been three hours since she had passed out and Norman had said she would wake up any minute.

'Do you think she will have powers now?' Adam asked.

'I hope so,' Norman replied. 'I have waited too long for this to fail.'

Then Gabrielle started to stir.

'Finally,' Norman mumbled.

Gabrielle opened her eyes and looked around the room.

'Where am I?' she mumbled, still a bit groggy, and Norman walked into the room.

'How are you feeling?' asked Norman.

'Alright, I think,' replied Gabrielle. 'Where am I?'

'You are in my lab underground. When you passed out, I brought you down here to make sure you were alright,' replied Norman.

'I passed out?' asked Gabrielle, the light above her flickering.

'Yes,' replied Norman.

'How the hell did that happen?' she exclaimed angrily, her eyes starting to glow blue, then she threw her arms up and electricity arced out of her fingers, flying around the room. Norman used his telekinesis to protect himself. Her eyes widened in alarm and she quickly thrust her arms down and hid her hands under them.

'What has happened to me?' she asked, tears in her eyes.

'It is as I thought,' replied Norman. 'The reason you passed out is that your powers have manifested themselves.'

'My powers?' she whispered, more to herself, looking down at her hands.

'Yes,' replied Norman.

'How do you know this stuff?' Gabrielle asked.

'Because I am like you,' replied Norman and he used his power to lift the bed she was on.

'Whoa, okay, put me down,' she exclaimed and the bed lowered to the ground again.

Norman stepped forward. 'Gabrielle, I believe you and I were destined to meet. I can train you to use your power and control it.'

Gabrielle looked down at her hands again.

'What do you say? Would you like to stay here for a bit and I can help you?' Norman asked.

Gabrielle looked over and he nodded.

'Alright. Please train me, Norman,' she exclaimed.

Norman extended his hand and she grabbed it, giving him a small shock.

'Whoops, sorry,' Gabrielle said, blushing slightly from embarrassment.

'We will work on that,' Norman smiled.

CHAPTER 24

Pyro placed his hand on the panel and the entrance opened up in the centre of the room. Glacia and himself descended the stairs into the meeting room.

'You're back?' Assana asked with surprise, taking her attention away from the computer and spinning around in her swivel chair to face Pyro and Glacia.

'Yeah,' replied Pyro, sitting down at the metal table in the centre of the room and reaching for one of the bottles of water that were in the centre of the table.

'How did you go?' replied Assana. 'And why are you limping, Glacia?'

'If it had gone well, I would have been carrying two swords,' Pyro replied, frustrated, running his hand through his hair.

'It didn't go well,' Glacia sighed, sitting down. 'And I'm limping because we got our asses kicked.'

'Nicholas beat you both? By himself?' Assana asked, some shock in her voice.

'Not just Nicholas,' Pyro replied, opening the bottle of water and taking a mouthful.

'What?' Assana questioned.

'The three brothers I told you about from the falls were with him and it looks like he is training them,' Pyro replied, after he had swallowed.

'Well, that's just great,' replied Assana, sarcastically.

'We are still gonna get those swords,' Pyro snarled, slamming his fist down on the table, making the bottles of water in the centre topple and roll off the table.

'Alright, Pyro. I've got to ask; how did you find out about these swords?' Assana asked.

'I was given a tip by an associate of mine,' replied Pyro.

'Which associate?' replied Assana. 'It better not be Strings.'

'Ummm, well,' muttered Pyro, looking away.

'Oh god, it is Strings,' exclaimed Assana, standing up. 'I am out of all this.'

'Wait, Assana, you can't just leave,' Pyro said, also standing up and reaching for his sister.

'If Strings is involved, I don't want anything to do with this. Remember what happened the last time we did a job for him? We were almost killed,' Assana replied, pointing a finger at Pyro.

'We almost died, but we didn't,' replied Pyro. 'And Strings isn't involved in this; he only told me about Norman receiving the Sword of Darkness and the other swords, okay?'

'Are you sure?' replied Assana.

'Yes, I am sure. He isn't involved, he just told me about this stuff,' replied Pyro.

'Alright, if this Strings isn't involved, then I guess it's okay,' Assana sighed, sitting back down.

'Good. Now, we need a new plan to get those swords,' exclaimed Pyro.

'Well, maybe someone else should go and take them on,' replied

Assana. 'Maybe Terra should go, you know, give them a power they haven't faced yet.'

'That's not a bad idea,' replied Pyro. 'Where is she?'

'I'm right here,' replied Terra, walking into the room.

'Well, good,' replied Pyro. 'Are you ready for a fight?'

'Always,' she replied, cracking her knuckles.

'Alright, I need you to go to the town where Nicholas is and retrieve the swords,' replied Pyro.

'Fine,' she replied and the floor underneath her opened up. She descended through the floor, into the earth underneath.

***

Nicholas awoke and moaned.

'Ah, I feel like I have been hit by a truck,' he muttered.

'Well, not a truck, but a few fireballs,' Dylan replied.

Nicholas sat up and rubbed his forehead.

'Smart arse,' Nicholas replied.

'Ah, you're awake,' exclaimed Theo as he and Lance stepped back into the room.

'Yeah, I'm awake,' replied Nicholas. 'Sorry, I am a heavy sleeper.'

They had a good laugh at that.

'So, what is the plan now?' Theo asked.

'Well, things aren't looking good, if I am honest,' Nicholas replied. 'People are going to attack us now that they know that we have these swords.'

'Well, we've been reading this book,' exclaimed Lance, holding up the book Nicholas had retrieved from Norman.

'And what did you find out from it?' Nicholas's eyes widened in enthusiasm.

'Well, the book starts with a legend of three brothers with the same power as us that sealed themselves in the swords after they were defeated by a great evil,' Theo explained. 'Then it went on to explain the swords, their powers, their locations and that they can only be used by certain brothers and for anyone else who uses them, there are side effects.'

'Yeah, I know about that,' replied Nicholas, lifting his sleeve and showing the scars on his arms. 'This is what the Sword of Darkness does to people who are not meant to use it.'

'What does the Sword of Light do then?' Lance exclaimed.

'I don't know yet,' replied Nicholas. 'I haven't used the Sword of Light yet.'

'Oh,' replied Lance. 'Will there be side effects if I use it?'

'I don't think so,' Nicholas replied, deep in thought.

'And why is that?' replied Theo.

'Well, I think that clearly, you guys are the certain brothers that the swords are meant to go to,' replied Nicholas.

'We don't know that for sure,' replied Theo.

'Well, have you read any more of the book? Is there anything about these certain brothers taking full control of the swords?' Nicholas asked.

'Yeah, there is,' replied Theo. Nicholas stood up, walked into the bedroom and knelt, reaching under the bed. He pulled out the bag that contained the Sword of Light and Darkness from under the bed, strapped it over his shoulder and walked back into the room.

'Alright, let's go,' Nicholas said.

'Where are we going?' replied Theo.

'To the field, where we train,' replied Nicholas. 'It is time for Dylan and Lance to take full control of the Sword of Darkness and the Sword of Light.'

'Finally,' Dylan grinned, standing up. Lance and Theo also stood up.

'Don't forget the book, we might need it,' Nicholas said.

Theo picked up the book and they all left the hotel. They walked for five minutes out of town to the field where they had been training. Nicholas dropped the bag and turned to the brothers.

'All right, here we are,' he exclaimed, smiling. He knelt and unzipped the bag and pulled out the Sword of Darkness.

A shiver ran down Dylan's spine and he stared at it.

'Alright, Dylan, do you know what to do?' Nicholas asked.

'Ummm… not really,' Dylan replied, shrugging.

'Oh, right, what does the book say?' Nicholas asked, turning to Theo.

Theo opened the book and flicked through the pages till he came to the page he wanted.

'Alright, here is the page. It says to take control of the swords, you have to hold your thumb on the centre gem of the sword and then, in Dylan's case, pour your darkness into the gem and then something should happen. That's all the book says; it doesn't say what will happen, all it says is that you'll duel the spirit in the sword once whatever happens,' Theo explained.

'Alright,' replied Nicholas, shrugging. 'Are you ready, Dylan?'

'I guess so,' replied Dylan.

'Good,' replied Nicholas. 'Let's do it then.'

Nicholas walked up to Dylan and held out the Sword of Darkness.

'Here you go,' exclaimed Nicholas.

'Ummm, I'm not sure,' exclaimed Dylan.

'You'll be fine,' replied Nicholas. 'You have the training necessary to fight.'

Dylan nodded and reached out, wrapping his hand around the hilt of the sword. He placed his thumb on the centre ruby and started to pour darkness through his thumb into the ruby. The ruby started to darken. The sword buzzed in Dylan's hand and his body was pulled towards the ruby. In that instant, Dylan knew that this was his destiny. Darkness burst out of the sword, but instead of the darkness surrounding Dylan's body, it surrounded the area around Dylan, forming a cocoon of darkness.

Nicholas, Lance and Theo stepped away as the cocoon of darkness quickly enclosed Dylan. Inside the cocoon, Dylan looked around and then looked down at the sword. It was vibrating violently. Dylan gasped and with that, his spirit was absorbed into the blade.

***

Nicholas, Lance and Theo looked on at the cocoon.

'Do you think he is okay?' asked Lance.

'Yeah, he should be fine,' Nicholas replied. 'I would say this is all a part of taking control of the Sword of Darkness.'

'I hope so,' replied Lance. 'What do you think is going on in there?'

'Have no idea,' replied Nicholas.

'Pity. I'm just curious for when it is my turn,' replied Lance.

'Well, we will find out when Dylan is finished in there,' replied Nicholas.

'Yeah, I guess so.'

Then the ground beneath them started to shake and rumble.

'What the?' exclaimed Lance. 'We don't get earthquakes here.'

A woman tore out of the ground and stood in front of them. She was a tall, muscular woman with short brown hair.

'Damn, another one. Who are you?' Nicholas asked with a sigh.

But she didn't reply to Nicholas and she looked around.

'You are Nicholas Quinzel, correct?' she asked.

'Yes, I am,' replied Nicholas, slightly confused.

'Where are the swords?' she asked flatly.

'What?' Nicholas asked, confused by her abruptness.

'Where are the swords?' she asked again.

'But I don't even know your name,' Nicholas exclaimed. 'If you want that information, then I would at least like your name.'

'Fine, it's Terra,' she replied.

'Nice to meet you,' Nicholas said.

'Now, where are the swords?' Terra asked once more.

'And why would I tell you that? Pyro sent you, didn't he?' Nicholas challenged.

'Because if you don't, there will be a world of hurt waiting for you three,' Terra growled.

'Is that supposed to scare us?' Nicholas asked.

Terra didn't respond and a mass of earth rose out of the ground.

'For the last time, where are those swords?'

'You're gonna have to beat it out of me,' replied Nicholas, readying himself.

Terra sighed and fired the mass of earth at Nicholas, but Nicholas destroyed the mass of earth with a blast of wind.

***

Dylan opened his eyes and he was standing in a domed room, the colour of the ruby. Dylan turned and standing in the centre was a tall man with long dark hair like Dylan, wearing an expensive-looking pure black suit.

'Hello, Dylan,' Heolster said with a grin.

CHAPTER 25

Dylan approached Heolster and asked, 'Who are you?'

Heolster laughed and stepped forward, extending his hand to Dylan.

'Heolster,' he introduced himself, grinning.

'Wait… as in the Heolster in the book?' Dylan asked, shaking Heolster's hand.

'The very same,' replied Heolster, his grin stretching.

'As in, according to the book, the Heolster that lived and died a thousand years ago?' Dylan asked, trying to comprehend what was happening.

'Yeah, that's me.'

'But how are you even here?'

'Well, Dylan, I am merely a spirit. I did die over a thousand years ago, but just before I died, I sealed myself in this sword, which was later named the Sword of Darkness, due to the power my spirit gave it.'

'But if you're from a thousand years ago, then why are you wearing a suit?' Dylan asked, confusion crossing his face.

Heolster laughed again.

'I like you, Dylan. You're a thinker,' replied Heolster. 'Well, since I'm a spirit, I can change my appearance at a whim and I saw this suit one day while this sword was in the possession of Nicholas.'

'So, you can see everything that happens out of the sword?' Dylan asked.

'When someone is holding the blade, yes,' Heolster nodded.

'Well, there you go. So, how do you know me?'

'Well, Dylan, I have known about you for a thousand years; just like you, Dylan, I had two brothers too and they also controlled light and time, and my brother that controls time foresaw you and your brothers in this time.'

'So, if your brothers controlled light and time, does that mean you…' Dylan mused, making Heolster smile and raised his arms and darkness began to swirl around him.

'Yes, Dylan, I control darkness,' replied Heolster.

Dylan grinned and raised his arms and darkness started to swirl around him.

'Impressive, but do you have what it takes to defeat me and claim this sword for yourself?' Heolster asked.

'Well, Heolster, I don't mean to be rude but I am going to kick your ass to get this sword,' replied Dylan.

'Good to hear, Dylan, because I am not going to make it easy. Are you ready, Dylan?'

Dylan smirked and nodded.

'Alright, this battle will not be to the death; it is a battle for me to merely test you and decide whether or not you are worthy of this sword and its powers,' Heolster explained.

Dylan nodded again and darkness rose and wrapped around his arms.

'Alright, Dylan, we begin now!' Heolster shouted and he threw his hands out and multiple streams of darkness flew at Dylan. Dylan smirked and prepared for the darkness to absorb into his body, but the streams struck him and sent him flying backwards. Heolster laughed and Dylan scrambled to his feet.

'What the hell?' Dylan mumbled to himself.

'Hahaha, I knew you would try that,' Heolster said. 'You see, Dylan, your darkness and my darkness are different, which means you can't absorb or control my darkness and I can't absorb or control your darkness.'

'That would have been nice to know before,' Dylan replied, smirking.

'Shall we continue then?' Heolster asked, nodding.

Dylan nodded back and sent a mass of darkness at Heolster.

'That's more like it,' Heolster laughed as he blocked the mass with a wall of darkness, then Heolster pushed the wall of darkness at Dylan.

Dylan ran along the wall and dove, the wall barely missing him. Dylan rolled to his feet and sent two streams of darkness in Heolster's direction. Heolster used darkness to propel himself through the two streams and sent multiple orbs of darkness at Dylan. Dylan weaved between the first two orbs, but the other orbs struck him, sending him stumbling, then a mass of darkness slammed into Dylan front on, sending him sliding across the floor, then the mass slammed down on top of him, pinning him to the floor. Heolster laughed as he walked up to Dylan.

'And here I thought you would provide more of a challenge,' he exclaimed, crouching down.

***

Nicholas and Lance dodged backwards as a mass of earth flew between them.

'She's good,' exclaimed Lance.

'But we're better,' Nicholas growled, thrusting his hands down, blasting himself into the air, and he began to fly down at Terra.

Terra summoned balls of earth and threw them up at Nicholas, but he weaved in and out, dodging the balls of earth and continuing in her direction. As that happened, Lance summoned orbs of light and threw them at Terra, but she raised her arms and earth shot out of the ground, surrounding her and blocking Lance's orbs. Nicholas stopped and looked down at Terra, through the top of the pillar.

'Looks like I can still hit you from here,' mumbled Nicholas to himself and he felt lightning charge through his fingers. He threw his hands down and lightning arced out of his fingers straight down but the top of the pillar sealed, blocking the lightning.

'Of course,' mumbled Nicholas, lowering himself to the ground.

'Now, what are we going to do?' exclaimed Lance.

'To be honest, I'm not sure,' replied Nicholas. 'I haven't faced someone who could control the element of earth before.'

Then the ground began to rumble beneath them and Terra burst out of the ground between them, thrusting her hands out at Nicholas and Lance. Two pillars of earth shot out of her palms, striking Lance and Nicholas each in the chest, sending them flying backwards.

'That was too easy,' Terra mumbled to herself, shaking her head and turning to the bag on the ground, then Terra froze.

Theo walked to where Lance and Nicholas lay, hand raised at Terra, freezing time around her.

'Are you guys alright?' exclaimed Theo.

'Yeah, I'm fine,' replied Nicholas, getting back to his feet. 'I've been hit harder than that before.'

'Yeah, I'm good too,' replied Lance, standing up.

'Alright, good,' Theo said. 'I can't hold her for much longer; you two better do something.'

'Alright,' replied Nicholas. 'Lance, you ready?'

'Yeah, let's do this,' Lance nodded.

Nicholas quickly ran over and grabbed the bag that contained the Sword of Light and slung it over his shoulder, strapping it in place.

'Alright, release her now,' Nicholas commanded.

Theo nodded and lowered his hand and Terra started to move again.

'What the hell?' she exclaimed, looking at where the bag was.

'Looking for something?' Nicholas mocked.

Terra turned and scowled.

'Is this what you're after?' Nicholas laughed, waving the bag in his hands.

Terra shook her head and threw her arm out in Nicholas's direction and a mass of dirt shot out of the ground and flew straight at Nicholas. He smirked and prepared to blast the mass apart with a pulse of wind, but the mass of dirt split in two flying on either side of Nicholas, stopped, then flew inwards, but Nicholas sent two blasts of wind on either side of him, blowing the earth apart, but that didn't stop the particles of earth slamming into Nicholas on both his sides and the earth spread across Nicholas's body completely encasing him from the neck down, trapping him.

Nicholas cursed, trying to break free.

Terra then turned to face Lance and Theo.

'Looks like it's up to us,' Lance said.

'Yep, you ready?' Theo asked.

'I hope so,' Lance nodded.

Theo placed his hand on Lance's shoulder and froze time. The brothers quickly ran behind Terra and Lance summoned an orb of light. Theo unfroze time and Lance threw the orb at Terra, but Terra instantly turned, blocked the orb of light with a shield of earth and then raised her arms and two pillars of earth shot out of the ground behind Lance and Theo, striking them in the back. They both cried out in pain, being propelled forward.

'Ah, crap,' Theo exclaimed, falling to the ground, clutching his ribs.

'You alright?' Lance asked.

'I think my ribs are broken,' Theo hissed through clenched teeth.

'Well, shit,' Lance cursed, standing up and facing Terra. 'Looks like it's on me.'

Lance summoned two orbs of light. Terra threw her arms down and rocks rose out of the ground and attached to her fists, forming gauntlets, then Terra rushed at him. He threw the two orbs, but she easily dodged them and threw a right hook at Lance's cheek. Lance panicked and fell under the right hook, but Terra instantly punched him in the stomach with a crunch, making Lance gasp as all the wind was knocked out of him and he fell to the ground, clenching his stomach. Terra smirked and punched down. Lance's eyes widened and he rolled out of the way at the last second as Terra punched the ground where he was, forming an impression in the ground. Lance struggled to his hands and knees, trying to recover but Terra approached and kicked him in the side of the head. Lance's eyes rolled into the back of his head and he dropped to the ground unconscious. Terra smirked and turned to Nicholas, the earth around him moving slightly, revealing the bag containing the sword.

***

'Come on, Dylan, I thought you would be better than this,' Heolster taunted.

Dylan struggled underneath the pillar of darkness and Heolster walked around him, laughing.

'You'll never beat me at this rate,' Heolster laughed.

Dylan thrust his hands down at his sides, darkness bursting out of his hands, propelling him out from underneath the pillar and then he flew like a missile in Heolster's direction and tackled him to the ground. They both rolled and Dylan was first up, throwing a ball of darkness into Heolster's chest as he rose, making him stumble back. Then he sent out a tentacle of darkness that wrapped around Heolster's ankle and Dylan pulled the hard with the tentacle, pulling Heolster off his feet. He ran at Heolster, darkness surrounding his fists, but darkness rose, surrounding Heolster, and then was dispersed and Heolster was gone. Dylan stopped and concentrated, trying to sense where Heolster was, then the back of his neck started to tingle and he turned and sent a mass of darkness straight at Heolster as he stepped out of a mass of darkness, striking him front on and throwing him backwards. Heolster rolled, then stopped and didn't get up.

'I think I put a bit too much into that one,' mumbled Dylan, tentatively walking towards Heolster, then Heolster burst out laughing.

'That was fantastic, Dylan,' Heolster laughed, jumping back to his feet. 'I haven't had a fight like that in a thousand years.'

Heolster nodded and walked to Dylan.

'I think we are done,' he exclaimed, placing a hand on Dylan's shoulder and looking him in the eye. 'Congratulations, Dylan, you have beaten me. I deem you worthy to wield this blade.'

'What happens now?' Dylan asked, but Heolster didn't respond. Darkness burst out of the ground under Dylan and he felt himself leaving the blade and going back to his body.

***

Terra walked up to Nicholas, who was still struggling against the earth that encased him.

'You can't take it,' Nicholas snarled, but Terra ignored him and reached out for the bag, but suddenly she felt the ground pulse behind her.

'What the hell is that?' she muttered to herself as she turned to face the cocoon of darkness.

It pulsed and started to collapse in on itself and this continued until the darkness surrounded Dylan's body, forming the armour from the neck down. Dylan opened his eyes and looked down at himself.

'Wow, this is amazing,' Dylan mumbled, admiring the armour and the sword in his hand.

'Hey, Dylan, can you hear me?' Heolster's voice said in Dylan's mind.

'Yeah, Heolster,' Dylan replied in his mind.

'Good. Alright, this is what will happen when you hold the sword. This armour will form; I will be able to talk to you and you have full control, not like last time you held the sword,' replied Heolster.

'Alright, sounds good,' Dylan replied as he turned and looked over at Terra.

'Who are you?' he exclaimed.

'You have the other sword,' she replied. 'Hand it over.'

'Yeah, I'm not going to do that, not now,' Dylan said, shaking his head.

'Then I will have to take it from your corpse,' Terra snarled.

Dylan looked around and saw his brothers down and Nicholas trapped in a cocoon of earth.

'Did you do this?' Dylan growled, his anger beginning to boil.

Terra didn't reply and she thrust her hands out. A mass of earth burst off the ground and flew at Dylan. He raised the sword and swung it down; a wave of darkness flew off the blade and cleaved the mass of earth in two, each piece flying past him.

'I'll take that as a yes,' he shrugged.

CHAPTER 26

Dylan flexed his fingers and rotated his wrists, noting the weightlessness and flexibility of the armour.

'Wow, this armour is amazing,' Dylan murmured, looking down at the armour.

'The armour is made of pure darkness, so it has no weight and moves with you,' Heolster replied.

Terra scowled, getting annoyed at Dylan ignoring her, and raised her hands, masses of earth rising out of the ground. Dylan snapped out of his thoughts and focused on Terra.

'Dylan, I can help you with combat and such,' Heolster explained.

Dylan nodded as Terra flicked her hands at Dylan, the masses of earth flew at him. Tentacles of darkness instantly rose out of the armour and lashed out, destroying all the masses of earth, and then the tentacles coiled and shot out in Terra's direction. She dodged the first tentacle, but the second tentacle struck her in the chest, sending her flying back. Dylan smirked, raised his head, closed his eyes and felt the power surge through him.

'This feels good,' he mumbled to himself.

He lowered his head and walked towards Terra as she rose to her feet and he sent a wave of darkness at her. She brought up a wall of earth in response, protecting her from the wave, and then she pushed the wall at Dylan, but he propelled himself over the wall, using his darkness to push him over and then used darkness to levitate in the air. Terra looked up at him, anger clear on her face. She summoned more masses of earth and threw them in at Dylan, but Dylan easily weaved in and out of the masses, and then he sent a mass of darkness at Terra. Terra dove to the side, the darkness barely missing her. She came up and raised her arms and a wave of earth rose out of the ground underneath her and carried her up and level with Dylan.

'Welcome to my level,' Dylan mocked, laughing.

Terra didn't reply; instead, she reached down into the wave and pulled out a sword of solid rock. Dylan smirked and raised the Sword of Darkness. Dylan then swooped at Terra, swinging his sword and the two swords met, chips of rock flying off Terra's blade. Terra pushed with her sword out, shoving Dylan back, but he quickly sent two streams of darkness at her. Shields of earth rose out of the wall to intercept the streams of darkness. Dylan used the moment of distraction to fly straight at Terra, swinging the Sword of Darkness again. Terra blocked the slash with her sword, but the momentum from Dylan caused Terra to stumble. Dylan then flew around in an arc and flew at her again, sword poised to strike. Dylan swung and Terra brought up her blade at the last second, managing to block the strike and stumbling again, bringing her to the edge of her platform. Dylan saw this and sent a stream of darkness that struck her front on, knocking her off the platform and sending her plummeting to the ground below. A pillar of earth quickly rose from beneath her, catching her. She hit the pillar hard with an 'oof', driving the air from her lungs. She lay on top of the pillar, groaning as it slowly descended to the ground and laid Terra in the grass. Dylan descended to the ground and landed in front of Terra as she got to her feet, coughing up blood.

'Looks like I'm not getting these swords today,' Terra sighed, wobbling slightly on her feet.

'No, you're not, and you never will,' Dylan replied, preparing himself again.

'I will take my leave, but I will be back,' Terra replied and with that, she descended to the ground. Dylan looked around, waiting for Terra to appear again. Once he realised that she wasn't coming back, he breathed a sigh of relief and walked over to Nicholas, who was still trapped in rocks.

'Nice work, Dylan,' Nicholas said. 'Reckon you can help me out of this?'

'I suppose I can do that,' replied Dylan. He let darkness seep into the rocks around Nicholas, and then he pushed the darkness out, causing the rocks to crack and break, releasing Nicholas.

'Thank you,' Nicholas nodded to Dylan. He walked over to his bag and reached inside and pulled out the Sword of Light.

'Good, she didn't get the Sword of Light,' he sighed in relief. He then reached into the bag again and pulled out the scabbard that belonged to the Sword of Darkness.

'I guess this is yours now,' Nicholas said, holding out the scabbard to Dylan.

Dylan took it, strapping it to his hip and as he sheathed the Sword of Darkness, the armour dissipated into the blade as it slid into the scabbard.

'Better check on your brothers now,' Nicholas said, turning and walking in Theo and Lance's direction.

'Are you alright?' Nicholas asked, kneeling next to Theo.

'Give me a sec,' mumbled Theo. Theo concentrated on the pain in his ribs and began to reverse time around his ribs. He felt his ribs click back into place and repair themselves. Theo breathed a sigh of relief and stood up.

'Alright, I'm good now,' Theo said.

'Good,' replied Nicholas. They turned to Lance, who began to stir.

'Are you alright, Lance?' Theo asked.

Lance sat up and rubbed his cheek.

'I guess so,' Lance groaned, standing up.

'Alright. Well, we managed to survive her onslaught,' Nicholas sighed.

'Yeah, thanks to me,' Dylan bragged, slightly puffing out his chest and tapping the sword.

'Only because you have that,' Lance replied, a bit of snark in his voice.

Dylan turned, ready to challenge his brother before Nicholas interjected.

'Alright, boys. I think we are a bit tired and in need of some rest. Let's go back.'

Dylan glared at Lance before they all nodded and began their trek back home.

***

Pyro sat at the computer monitor, doing research for Assana, trying not to fall asleep. Then the ground underneath him began to shake; he spun around in his chair as Terra rose out of the small section of bare earth they had exposed for her to come and go and collapsed against the wall.

'Whoa, Terra!' he exclaimed in surprise. 'Are you okay?'

'I will be,' she breathed. 'Just a tad beat up.'

'I take it they beat you too,' Pyro frowned, crossing his arms. Terra nodded and collapsed into a chair.

'Tell me what happened,' Pyro said, standing up and joining her at the table.

'Alright, so I arrived there and I found them looking at a weird dark orb thing and there were only three of them – Nicholas and two of the brothers. Well, I fought them, trapped Nicholas in a rock and took out the other two and just as I'm about to take possession of the Sword of Light, the dark orb burst open and the missing brother appeared out of it and he had the Sword of Darkness in his hand and a dark armour surrounding his body,' Terra recounted to Pyro.

'So, he lost control again,' replied Pyro, remembering what had happened at MacKenzie Falls.

'No, this was different to what you told us. He had full control over the sword and he was too strong for me, so before I could be defeated, I left and that was that,' Terra explained further.

'Well, isn't that a shame?' Gale laughed, walking into the room, clapping his hands slowly and sarcastically.

'What's that supposed to mean?' Terra barked, spinning to face Gale.

'Nothing. Nothing at all,' Gale replied, smirking. 'So, you didn't get the swords?'

'No, I didn't,' Terra muttered, turning away.

'I knew you wouldn't be able to,' Gale laughed.

Terra slammed her fists down on the table with a bang and stood, facing Gale.

'Alright, that's enough from both of you,' Pyro exclaimed, raising his hand in placation.

Terra eyed Gale; he just smirked back at her. She shook her head and sat back down.

'Alright, we need a new plan and fast,' Pyro stated.

'I got one,' Gale announced.

'And what would it be, Gale?' replied Pyro.

'I will go this time,' Gale boasted, looking straight at Terra.

Terra snorted and shook her head.

'What?' Gale asked.

'If I can't get the swords, what makes you think you can get them?' Terra replied, crossing her arms.

'First, remember who beat you last time we sparred,' Gale retorted.

'Hey, you cheated last time,' Terra fumed.

'Me? I would never do such a thing,' Gale responded, mock shock lacing his words.

'Whatever,' Terra fumed.

'Anyway, I plan to go now and take the swords at night when they are asleep,' Gale stated.

'Actually, that's not a bad plan,' Pyro replied, pondering the idea. 'Alright, Gale, you take a crack at getting them.'

'Awesome, I'll go get my cutlasses,' Gale beamed, running out of the room.

Pyro turned to Terra. 'It's a pretty good plan,' he confirmed.

Terra just grunted and stood up, exiting the room.

Gale walked back into the room a few minutes later, four cutlasses strapped to him, two on his hips and two across his back, the hilts poking out over his shoulders, and he also had two weird-looking steel poles strapped to his lower back.

'Finally, I get to test that out?' Pyro asked, pointing to the poles.

'Yeah, it's as good a chance as any,' Gale replied, patting the poles.

'Well, good luck,' Pyro said.

'I don't need luck,' Gale said as he walked past Pyro and up the stairs, pushing the button to open the cement trapdoor across above him and he walked out into the warehouse and outside. He breathed in the night air and smiled as air flew up underneath him and lifted him in the air and he flew off in a west direction.

***

Nicholas awoke suddenly, sweating and breathing heavily.

'Damn nightmares,' he mumbled to himself, trying to shake the mental image of a Manticore tail pointing in his direction. He reached down beside his bed, feeling for the Sword of Light sitting next to him. He wrapped his hand around the hilt and lifted it to sit on his lap.

'Guess I'll have to give this one to Lance soon too,' he mumbled. 'And I haven't got to use it yet.'

He chuckled to himself until he heard a click come from his door.

'What was that?' he mumbled. Then he heard more clicking and scratching.

'Someone is picking the lock,' he muttered. He rolled over and pretended he was still asleep, hiding the sword under the blanket, pressing it against his body. He heard the door click open, then footsteps that walked into the room. Nicholas rolled over, raising the sword. It cast a bright light over the room and standing there was a tall, muscular man with dark dreadlocks, two cutlasses strapped to his hips and two to his back.

'Gale?' Nicholas asked, shocked and sitting up.

'Hey, Weatherman,' replied Gale, lifting his hand to block the light.

CHAPTER 27

Nicholas lowered the sword, sitting up and swinging his legs out of the bed. 'What are you doing here?' Nicholas asked. 'I haven't seen you since the day you and Norman had that fight and you left the mansion.'

'Ha, ha. Good times,' Gale replied, chuckling. 'The old man used to piss me off two ways to Sunday.'

'Yeah, I will never forget those fights,' Nicholas replied, nodding. 'But why are you here, Gale?'

'Ummm… well…' Gale hesitated, looking away.

'Oh, you are here for this?' Nicholas replied, holding up the Sword of Light.

'Yeah, kinda,' Gale muttered.

'You are working for Pyro, aren't you?' Nicholas stated, already knowing the answer.

'Yeah, I am. I am sorry, man.'

Nicholas sighed and stood up off the bed.

'I can't let you take this sword, Gale,' Nicholas said, determination now in his voice.

'I thought you would say that,' Gale sighed. He then thrust out his palms and a pulse of air lifted Nicholas off his feet, tumbling over the bed and hitting the wall, the Sword of Light cluttering to the floor.

'So, it's going to be like that then,' Nicholas sighed, getting back to his feet.

'I guess so.' Gale shrugged.

'Just like old times,' Nicholas replied, nodding to himself, briefly remembering their training together, then he dove over the bed and tackled Gale to the ground and they rolled around the floor, trying to wrestle control over the other.

Gale kicked Nicholas off him, stood up and drew one of his cutlasses. Nicholas stood up and used his power to pick up the Sword of Light. It flew into his hand and he held it out, readying himself. Gale smirked and he attacked first, slashing at Nicholas, but he blocked the slash and the battle began. Nicholas swung with viciousness, making Gale stumble back, more in shock, out of the room and out into the corridor. Nicholas followed him and Gale threw a nearby folding chair. Nicholas slid under the projectile, instantly coming back to his feet, slashing at Gale again with his sword. Gale blocked this slash and then he drew his second cutlass with his other hand and used it to slash at Nicholas with that, but he quickly jumped back, narrowly avoiding the blade.

'Now, that just isn't fair,' Nicholas objected.

'Yeah, well, bad guys cheat,' Gale laughed. 'Now, come at me, Weatherman, because I know you are better than this.'

Nicholas balled his fist in anger and slashed another vicious slash at Gale's throat.

'Ah, there we go,' Gale laughed, blocking the slash. 'Let the anger flow.'

Nicholas lashed out with a kick, catching Gale in the knee and he fell to the floor, howling in pain. Nicholas stomped down, but Gale rolled out of the way and threw one of one his cutlasses at Nicholas. Nicholas pushed the cutlass to the side with a gust of wind, then he ran at Gale and drop-kicked him further down the corridor, his other cutlass flying from his hand. Gale scrambled back to his feet, turning and running. Nicholas gave chase, out of the building and outside into the warm night air. Nicholas looked around, the oncoming sunrise illuminating the ground, but Gale was nowhere to be seen.

'Where did he go?' he mumbled to himself. Nicholas turned and a cutlass flew straight at him; Nicholas dodged it at the last second, but he was then blasted off his feet by a jet of air, the sword flying from his grasp.

Gale landed next to Nicholas and began to laugh.

'Predictable,' Gale sneered down at Nicholas. 'You will never change and here I thought Norman would have taught you better.'

Nicholas moaned and crawled towards the Sword of Light, but Gale just laughed and placed his foot on the sword.

'That's mine now,' Gale proclaimed. 'And you know what? I never liked you anyway.'

Nicholas rolled onto his back and blasted Gale off his feet with his own jet of wind.

'Ah, you sneaky bastard. Looks like you have learnt a little bit more than I thought,' Gale chuckled as he got back to his feet.

Nicholas placed his hand on the Sword of Light and stood up, turning to face Gale. Gale grinned maniacally and raised his hands, and his four cutlasses flew from where they lay and began to float around Gale, being held up by air.

Nicholas scowled and prepared himself for the battle to come.

'You don't like these, do you?' Gale asked, motioning to the blades around him. 'Well, they are going to be your end.'

Gale flicked his hand in Nicholas's direction and all four cutlasses flew at him. Nicholas dove to the side, avoiding the first volley of the cutlasses, rolling as the cutlasses circled back, making him roll again to avoid the second volley.

'Ah, excellent work,' Gale laughed and he threw his arm again and the cutlasses flew at Nicholas again. Nicholas sent a blast of wind that split the cutlasses, sending them flying off in different directions, then Nicholas sent another blast of wind at Gale, but he swiped his hands across, redirecting Nicholas's attack around him.

'You forget I control air,' exclaimed Gale, raising his arms. 'Your wind is useless against me.'

'Doesn't matter,' Nicholas replied through clenched teeth.

'And why is that?'

'I have plenty more tricks up my sleeve.'

Nicholas raised his hands and clouds began to form above them and it began to rain.

'Oh, nice trick. You made it rain,' Gale teased.

'Is it?' replied Nicholas, thrusting his hand out and lightning arced out of his fingers. Gale's eyes widened as the lightning struck him in the chest, blasting him off his feet. Gale rolled and stood up, smoke coming off his chest.

'Ha, ha, that was good,' Gale said, patting his chest. 'If it wasn't for the layer of air over my skin, that could have done so much more damage.'

He raised his hand and the four cutlasses rose off the ground once again and flew straight at Nicholas, but Nicholas propelled himself into the air, dodging the cutlasses and then Nicholas thrust out his hand again and more lightning flew at Gale. Gale dodged the lightning and smirked. The air that Nicholas was using to float suddenly disappeared and he fell to the ground with a crunch.

'Hahaha, you forgot again,' Gale cackled. 'You can't do anything related to air – you can't fly me or use wind against me but those are your go-to moves, aren't they? You're nothing else but lightning.'

Nicholas groaned and Gale approached him, kneeling down to Nicholas.

'You wanna know why I despise you so much?' Gale sneered, standing up and kicking Nicholas in the stomach. 'You have everything.'

And he kicked again, lifting Nicholas off the ground and sending him rolling away.

'You had the father.'

Another kick.

'You, kid, wanted everything and got everything.'

Another kick.

'And worst of all, you got the girl,' Gale growled, kneeling again. 'I liked her and you made it your mission to take her from me.'

Nicholas coughed up blood and turned his head to face Gale.

'I did nothing like that,' Nicholas breathed through the pain. 'Kate made her choice and she told you that. You were just too caught up in yourself to see that she didn't want to be with you.'

'LIAR!' Gale screamed and he kicked again. 'You…'

Kick.

'Son…'

Kick.

'Of a…'

Kick.

'Bitch!'

Kick.

'You know what?' Gale breathed. 'I'm gonna end you now.'

Gale reached behind him, pulling out the two steel poles that were strapped to his back. He locked them together and pressed a button and the poles extended into a staff with four locking mechanisms on the end. Gale raised his free hand and the four cutlasses flew through the air. Gale raised the staff and the four cutlasses slotted into the locking mechanisms, the bladed edges facing outwards, creating a weapon that looked like the combination of a mace and a bladed staff.

'Remember this?' Gale asked, laughing menacingly.

Nicholas looked up, groaning in pain, and cursed when his eyes locked onto the weapon.

'Ah, you do remember,' Gale exclaimed. 'Well, you would remember my sketches anyway and now I'm going to use it to end you.'

Gale casually strolled up to where Nicholas lay and placed the bladed end over his chest.

'Well, it's been nice knowing you, but I'm afraid this is your end.' Gale laughed, muscles tensing, preparing to push the weapon down.

'Not yet,' Nicholas muttered and he placed his finger on the blade and electricity flew up the metal.

Gale screamed in agony as the electricity coursed through his body, dropping him to the ground, muscles twitching and convulsing, dropping the staff as he fell, it falling next to Nicholas. Nicholas coughed and slowly stood up, clutching his ribs.

'Ah… god damn it,' he breathed, trying to block out the pain.

Gale rolled over and cursed.

'You bastard,' he seethed as he also slowly got to his feet. 'You always find a way to get out of those spots.'

Nicholas shrugged and held out his hand, wind picking up the Sword of Light and placing it in his outstretched hand. Gale did the same and his staff flew into his hand.

'You seriously think you can fight me in your current state?' Gale asked, shaking his head.

'Well, I'm gonna try,' Nicholas replied, pointing the Sword of Light at Gale.

A beam of light out of the tip of the blade struck Gale in the chest, knocking him off his feet. Nicholas screamed in pain as the blade burned his hand and wrist.

'Damn side effects,' he breathed, examining his wrist.

'That damn sword!' Gale raged, leaping to his feet and charging at Nicholas, blade staff poised to strike. Nicholas blocked the blades, pushing back with all his strength, the blades separating and he swung his blade at Gale, but Gale used a burst of air to flip backwards and out of harm's way. Then he sent a burst of air at Nicholas, knocking him back. Nicholas howled in pain and Gale laughed.

'I told you; you have no chance in your state,' Gale stated, but Nicholas just ignored him and concentrated.

Suddenly the rain around them changed into hail. Then Nicholas directed the hail straight at Gale and Gale howled in pain as the golf ball-sized hailstones struck his body. Nicholas leapt to his feet and ran at Gale, tackling him to the ground. Nicholas sat on Gale's chest and began to punch Gale in the face. Gale tried to block the punches, but Nicholas was relentless and Gale's attempts at protecting himself failed, so Nicholas continued to rain down punches until Gale's face looked like mincemeat. Suddenly, Gale placed a hand on Nicholas's chest and a pulse of air sent Nicholas flying off him and tumbling away.

'God damn it,' Gale moaned, breathing through broken teeth. Nicholas stood up and placed the Sword of Light on Gale's throat.

'I win,' Nicholas said through clenched teeth.

'What? You gonna kill me now?' Gale asked, with a slight lisp.

'No, Gale. I'm not like you,' Nicholas replied. 'But I want you to leave right now and don't even think about coming back.'

'Fine,' Gale growled, getting back to his feet. Nicholas nodded and stepped away as Gale's staff flew into his hand and he quickly disassembled it.

'I will admit, you've gotten better,' Gale mumbled. 'Till next time, Weatherman.'

'There isn't going to be a next time, Gale,' Nicholas growled, causing Gale to laugh and then cough in pain.

'Oh yes, there will be, you just don't know it yet,' Gale answered.

'Well, you tell your boss that he needs to stop these attacks because it clearly isn't working for him,' Nicholas said.

Gale shrugged, lifting off the ground and flew up and away. Nicholas looked up as the sun began to crest the horizon and sighed.

'This isn't over… it's only the beginning.'

CHAPTER 28

Gabrielle ducked as Adam swung a right hook at her head, making her dance back to get away from his attacks.

'Good, Gabrielle,' Norman called, standing in the corner of the room, observing the combatants' every move.

Gabrielle nodded to him, then dashed in and kicked out at Adam, but Adam caught her leg, spun, lifted her off the ground, and threw her. She hit the mats with a thud, then tumbled across the floor and hit the wall with another thud. Gabrielle slowly stood, legs wobbling but she gritted her teeth and stand up to her full height, ready to fight again.

'She bounces back well,' Adam said, turning briefly to face Norman, clearly impressed. Norman nodded to Adam, agreeing with him.

'You are doing well,' exclaimed Adam, turning back to face his opponent, but Gabrielle was already running at him. She ducked under a swing, then lashed out with a kick that caught Adam in the side, making him gasp, the wind being driven out of him. Then Gabrielle tackled him to the ground and transitioned that into her wrapping her legs around Adam's neck and trapping one of his arms. She then pulled on that arm, applying a triangle choke.

'Alright, that's enough for today,' Norman announced, clapping his hands. Gabrielle instantly released the hold and Adam rolled over, gasping for air.

'Sorry, Adam. Are you alright?' Gabrielle asked, concern in her voice, offering him her hand.

'Yeah, I'm fine. I've had a lot worse things done to me,' Adam replied, briefly looking over at Norman, then he grabbed Gabrielle's offered hand and she helped him up.

'From what you have been telling me, I believe that,' Gabrielle replied.

They walked over to Norman, each grabbing a towel that Norman offered them.

'You did really well, Gabrielle. You are taking to this combat training very easily,' Norman congratulated.

'Thanks, Norman,' Gabrielle replied, blushing slightly, using the towel to wipe some sweat from her face.

'Alright, you go have a shower and I'll see you at dinner,' Norman said, nodding.

'I will,' replied Gabrielle, leaving the gym and making her way through the mansion and back to her room, flopping down on the bed and groaning.

'Those training sessions are getting tougher,' she mumbled to herself. She held up her hand and watched the electricity arc between her fingers, grinning, then looked up at the clock.

'Looks like I have time for a nap,' she laughed to herself. She set an alarm on her phone and within minutes, she was asleep.

A few hours later, Gabrielle awoke to the sound of her alarm. She rolled over, groaning in discomfort, feeling the aches and pains in her body.

'Damn, I've gotta go to dinner,' she mumbled. She rolled off the bed and changed out of her training clothes and into a pair of jeans and a blue blouse.

'At least this is the last dinner before everyone goes home,' she smirked.

Gabrielle walked out of her room, headed downstairs and entered the dining room. Everyone was already seated, including Norman. Gabrielle sat down next to Norman and looked around the table.

'How you feeling, Gabrielle?' exclaimed Norman.

'A tad sore, but I'm alright – had a nap,' Gabrielle laughed. Norman laughed with her. Then she noticed that Dexter was staring at her, smirking. Gabrielle glowered at him and turned away.

'You are doing very well with your training,' Norman told her, grinning. 'But I do have something to tell you, but it can wait till after this dinner.'

'Okay, Norman,' Gabrielle responded, looking over Dexter again. 'What is his problem?'

'Whose?' Norman asked.

'That guy on the end, Dexter,' Gabrielle replied, inclining her head in Dexter's direction.

'The one staring at you with the sunglasses on his head?' Norman asked.

'Yeah, that's him,' Gabrielle confirmed, frowning.

'Actually, there wasn't much on him in his file, just a name and date of birth,' replied Norman, puzzled.

'Wait, you have files on us?' Gabrielle exclaimed, shocked.

'Of course, I have to do my background checks,' Norman replied, smirking.

'Okay, that does make sense,' Gabrielle replied. 'Then how did he get into this program? You have no information.'

'I have no idea,' Norman replied, scratching his chin in thought. 'Might have to look into that after dinner.'

'Maybe a good idea,' Gabrielle replied, nodding as Adam placed their dinner in front of them.

'Ah, good. Food,' exclaimed Norman, standing up. 'Attention. I would like to make a speech. First, I would like to thank everyone here for coming here for the past couple of days, enjoying my hospitality and learning about the life of a surgeon. I do hope these past couple of days have convinced you to become surgeons or something like that in the future. Once again, thank you and please enjoy Adam's fantastic cooking.'

Everyone clapped as Norman sat down.

'Now, everyone, dig in!' exclaimed Norman, raising his glass and everyone began to eat.

After an hour of eating, talking and laughing, everyone started to file off to bed for their last night in the mansion. The only people left were Norman, Gabrielle, Adam, Mike and Dexter.

'What is Australia like?' Mike exclaimed.

'It's a beautiful country, to be honest. I love living there,' Gabrielle replied, smiling.

'Maybe I should come to visit you there sometime,' Mike smirked.

'I think that would be nice,' Gabrielle replied. 'Excuse me.'

Gabrielle stood up and walked back to the head of the table and sat back down next to Norman.

'He's still staring at me,' Gabrielle growled, motioning in Dexter's direction.

'I've noticed. I've been keeping my eye on him all night,' Norman replied. 'And so has Adam.'

'Yes, I have,' Adam confirmed, stepping up to the other side of Norman, nodding his agreement. With that, Dexter stood up and left the room, not saying a word.

'Anyway, what was it you wanted to speak to me about?' Gabrielle exclaimed.

'Oh, that will have to wait. We will discuss that in my study,' Norman replied. 'Meet me there in twenty minutes.'

'I will, Norman,' Gabrielle said, nodding. Norman stood up.

'I will see everyone in the morning. Goodnight, everyone,' Norman announced, standing up and leaving the dining room.

'Think I'm going to head to bed too,' Mike exclaimed.

'Yeah, I think I will too,' Gabrielle agreed. They both stood up and left the dining room together, leaving Adam to do the clean-up.

'Alright. Goodnight, Mike,' Gabrielle exclaimed and walked into her room. She sighed and looked up at the ceiling.

'I wonder what Norman wants?' Gabrielle mumbled to herself. 'Guess I better find out.'

Gabrielle stood and left her room once again, walking down the hall towards Norman's study. Just as she walked past the library, she heard noises from inside.

'Huh? That's odd. No one should be in there and Adam should be still in the kitchen, and Norman's in his study,' she mumbled. She crept towards the library and she heard another noise. She quietly opened the door and crept inside and began to search around. She heard the noise again, so she moved in that direction and there she found Dexter, rummaging through the shelves, looking for something.

'Dexter?' she asked, stepping into his view. 'What are you doing?'

Dexter looked up and just smirked.

'Are you looking for something?' Gabrielle asked.

Dexter didn't reply and walked towards her, sweeping his hand across. Gabrielle felt something wrap around her ankle and she was taken off her feet, screaming in shock.

'What the hell?' she exclaimed, hanging upside down. 'You have powers?'

Dexter just smirked and went back to looking through the bookshelves. Gabrielle reached up and felt around her ankles, finding what was holding her up off the ground.

'String?' she mumbled. 'He controls string?'

She pointed her finger at the string and electricity arced out of her finger, burning through the string and she fell to the ground. Dexter turned and frowned as she stood up, raising her hand and electricity arced off her fingers, making Dexter dive to the side. He rolled and ran out of view behind the dozens of roof-high shelves.

'Damn,' Gabrielle growled, making chase. She ran around the library, looking down all the shelves, but couldn't find Dexter anywhere.

'Where did he go?' she mumbled to herself. She turned and a mass of white flew out of nowhere, striking her and knocking her back. She landed hard on her side, groaning, then string quickly wrapped around her entire body, cocooning her.

'Damn,' Gabrielle mumbled as Dexter walked towards her. He looked down at her and smirked.

'Pathetic,' he exclaimed, walking away from her. Gabrielle struggled against the string, but she couldn't move. She cursed, then she felt a hand on her shoulder. She looked up and Adam was kneeling next to her.

'Are you alright?' he asked.

'Yeah, Adam,' she replied. 'Can you help me with this?'

'Give me a sec,' he replied and she felt the strings loosen.

'Thanks, Adam,' she said, standing up. Adam nodded.

'Now, who did this?'

'Dexter.'

'Okay. Norman's looking for him right now.'

Then there was a loud bang.

'What was that?' Gabrielle asked.

'Let's find out,' replied Adam. They ran to the area of the library where the noise came from and found Norman standing near the door.

'What happened, sir?' Adam questioned.

'I found him, he attacked. I fought back, he ran,' Norman explained.

'Are you alright?' Gabrielle asked.

'Yeah, I'm fine, Gabrielle,' Norman said, waving off her concern. 'Are you alright?'

'I'm fine,' Gabrielle replied.

'Good,' Norman nodded 'Let's take this conversion to my study.'

They all left the library and walked down the hall into the study. Gabrielle's mouth opened in shock, looking at the sapphire sword on Norman's desk.

'That is beautiful,' Gabrielle exclaimed.

'What? This?' Norman replied, picking the sword up.

'Yeah,' Gabrielle nodded.

'Well, this is the Sword of Time,' Norman explained, holding the blade up to the light.

'The Sword of Time?' Gabrielle asked, slightly puzzled.

'Yes,' Norman replied. 'Actually, this is part of the reason that I wanted to talk to you.'

'Right,' Gabrielle nodded, confused.

'Yes, alright, here is the story: I've been hunting for three legendary swords, the Swords of Darkness, Light and Time,' Norman began.

'Wow, that is kinda cool,' Gabrielle said in awe.

'Yeah, well, I found the Sword of Darkness and gave it to my son,' Norman continued.

'Wait, you have a son? Where is he?' Gabrielle asked in shock.

'Yes, he is Nicholas. Anyway, recently he found the Sword of Light and I found the Sword of Time, but he also found something else,' Norman continued.

'What did he find?' Gabrielle asked.

'Three brothers with powers,' Norman stated.

'Three brothers?' Gabrielle asked.

'Yes, brothers, from where you are from actually,' Norman said.

'No…' Gabrielle breathed, realisation dawning on her face.

'Yes, you know them as Dylan, Lance and Theo,' Norman explained.

Gabrielle took a step back, holding her head in shock.

'Are you alright?' asked Norman.

'No, I'm not… ummm… my boyfriend is Theo,' Gabrielle muttered.

'I know,' Norman replied. 'I'm sorry to say your boyfriend is a bad person now.'

'No, he isn't. He is kind,' Gabrielle exclaimed, her fists balling.

'My son and these brothers have taken the Swords of Darkness and Light from me,' Norman explained.

'No…' she breathed.

'Yes, Gabrielle. I know this is hard to hear, but it's true,' Norman stated.

Gabrielle turned to Adam.

'Is this true?' she asked, anger beginning to fill her voice.

'I'm afraid so,' replied Adam.

'Alright,' Gabrielle breathed. 'Then, what are we going to do?'

'Well, I want to go to Australia after Nicholas and I want to get my swords back, and I want your help.'

'Alright, I'll help. I'll come with you,' Gabrielle exclaimed, conviction now in her voice.

'Excellent. Now, you know you might have to fight against Theo.'

'Good. I need to find out the truth about him and kick his ass.'

'Good. Alright, we will leave for Australia tomorrow.'

'Sounds like a plan,' Gabrielle growled.

CHAPTER 29

Theo ran down the passage, lights illuminating the basalt walls of the labyrinth in front of him, the Sword of Time slapping against his leg in its scabbard. Theo turned a corner and ran into someone; they both fell to the ground from the impact. Theo scrambled his feet, preparing to fight, but found Nicholas getting back his feet.

'Nick?' Theo asked, surprised.

'Run!' Nicholas wheezed, terror on his face.

'What? Why?' Theo asked, now confused. Nicholas then took off past him, screaming for him to run.

'What's up with him?' Theo mumbled, then he heard the rumbling coming from the tunnel. Theo turned and his eyes widened in fear as a giant snake, roughly the height of him, slithered down the hall towards him.

'Holy crap!' Theo yelled out, turning and running the way Nicholas ran. Theo drew the Sword of Time on the run and a deep blue and orange armour materialised around his body. Theo looked behind him and the giant snake was right behind him, hissing in hunger, ready for its meal.

'I'm not going to be your meal,' he shouted and thrust the sword forward, freezing the snake in time. Theo nodded in satisfaction, turning and

running forward again and away from the snake. Once he felt he had put enough distance between himself and the snake, he sheathed the sword again, unfreezing time.

'Alright, now to find the others and get out of this place,' he mumbled. Theo walked run down the hall, but suddenly he stepped on something foreign. He stopped and looked down, seeing that he had stepped on a vine and the vine instantly sprang to life and wrapped around Theo's ankle, ripping him off his feet, draping him across the floor and up and over the wall into complete darkness and…

Theo fell out of his bed, instantly waking up. He leapt to his feet, preparing to fight whatever was there.

'Whoa, whoa, Theo, calm down,' Nicholas exclaimed, standing in the doorway. 'You were having a nightmare?'

'Yeah,' Theo replied, steadying his breathing, trying to calm down. He breathed out and sat down on the edge of his bed. 'It's been happening a lot lately.'

'How long have these nightmares been happening?' Nicholas asked, stepping into the room.

'A week or two.'

'Since you discovered your powers?'

'Actually, yeah.'

'Theo, these nightmares could be your power. You could be seeing the future or possible future. Now, tell me about these dreams,' Nicholas said, grabbing the chair from the desk and sitting down.

'Are you alright?' Theo asked, noticing the bruises on Nicholas's face.

'Yeah, I'm fine,' Nicholas replied, waving off Theo's concern. 'I'll tell you about it later when your brothers are awake. Now, tell me about these nightmares.'

'Well, they are always in the same place, in a maze or a labyrinth underground and we are all there – you, me, Dylan, Lance – but each dream is a different scenario.'

'Hmm, interesting. Please, continue.'

'Well, the first dream I had was myself, Lance and Dylan, and Dylan was standing over an unconscious Pyro, ready to strike him down and Lance was trying to talk him down, but they were both attacked by Glacia and a woman I didn't recognise. They took out Lance, but then Dylan killed the women with spikes of darkness and then sliced Glacia's arm off.'

'Hmmm, very interesting. How did the next dream go?'

'Well, it started with me and a guy with dreadlocks in battle…'

'Gale…'

'You know who he is?'

'Yeah, I do. But that can wait. Please, do continue.'

'Well, I managed to beat him, turned around and your father was walking towards me.'

'My father?'

'Well, I assume it was your father as he held a sword of deep blue crystal that I am assuming is the Sword of Time. Anyway, he said he was after the other two swords and then I said that that wasn't going to happen and we began to battle. I tried to freeze time, but it wouldn't work due to him having the sword and he used his telekinesis to pick me up and draw me towards him and that's when that dream ended.'

'Was that last night's dream?'

'No. Last night's dream started with me running through the labyrinth, with the Sword of Time strapped to my hip, when I turned a corner and ran into you and you told me to run, terror on your face. You ran past me and as I turned, a giant snake was slithering towards me,' Theo began, eyes going distant again.

Nicholas's eyes widened in fear.

'A Basilisk?' Nicholas stammered out, fear starting to take his voice.

'Is that what that snake was?'

'I think so. Personally, I've never seen one before and I hope I never do.'

'You're afraid of snakes?'

'Yes, I am. Now, continue with the dream,' Nicholas replied quickly, clearly not wanting to discuss the topic.

'Alright, well I ran and the Basilisk chased me until I drew the Sword of Time, an armour forming like what happened with Dylan, and then I used the sword to freeze the Basilisk in time and used that to get away. I unfroze time when I was a safe distance away, sheathed the sword and stepped on a vine and the vine instantly wrapped around my ankle and dragged me away somewhere, but that is where the dream ends,' Theo recounted.

'That's it?' Nicholas asked.

Theo nodded.

'Hmmm… well, the vine sounds like an Assassin Vine – a very dangerous carnivorous plant,' Nicholas explained. 'Can kill easily.'

'Well, that's just great to know,' Theo replied, sarcasm evident. 'Shouldn't I have frozen to stone because I looked at the Basilisk, though?'

'Ah, that is just a legend. They don't actually turn people to stone, but they do breathe fire.'

'Great. Am I seeing the future?'

'Well, Theo, you do control time, so it would make sense that you are seeing the future, but it could be one of many futures you are seeing also.'

'The future doesn't look good for us then.'

'Going off these dreams, no, it doesn't, but as I said, it could be one of many futures. Anyway, I'll leave you to get dressed. Meet me downstairs. I need to talk to you and your brothers about something.'

'This about what happened to you?'

'Mostly,' Nicholas nodded, leaving Theo's room. Theo got up off the bed and quickly got changed into some better clothes.

Theo walked out of his room and down the stairs into the kitchen, where Lance, Dylan and Nicholas were waiting.

'Took your time,' Dylan exclaimed.

'Only 'cause you are up early for once,' Theo teased, waggling a finger in Dylan's direction.

Dylan huffed and crossed his arms, causing Lance to laugh in amusement.

'Alright, I guess I'll tell you guys what's going on,' Nicholas said.

'That would be good,' Dylan replied, turning to face Nicholas.

'Alright, so last night, someone else tried to steal the Sword of Light,' Nicholas began.

'Someone else working for Pyro?' Dylan asked.

'As it turned out, yes, they did work for Pyro and this person did put up a good fight but I was lucky enough to defeat them and send another one packing, keeping a hold on the sword,' Nicholas recounted.

'So, who was it?' Theo asked.

'That doesn't matter right now,' Nicholas replied. 'What matters are that these attacks are not going stop until Pyro gets what he wants, which is the swords.'

'Yeah, it seems like it,' Lance replied, looking down. 'Why do they want the swords anyway?'

'In all honesty, Lance, I don't know. There could be multiple reasons for them wanting the swords: dominate the world with the sword's powers or sell them for a heavy price. As I said, there are multiple different reasons,' Nicholas replied.

'So, you think that someone else will come and try and get the swords?' Dylan asked.

'Well, we've had four different people attack us for the swords in the last couple of days, so yes, I do think someone else will try to get the swords for Pyro,' Nicholas replied.

'Well, that's just great,' Dylan replied, throwing his arms up in frustration.

'Where is the Sword of Light now?' Theo asked.

'Over there, on the couch,' Nicholas replied, pointing to the bag on the couch.

'So, they're gonna come here now?' Dylan asked, his anger rising.

'They shouldn't. They probably think that I'm still at the hotel,' Nicholas replied.

'But they were able to find you there, so they will find you here,' Dylan replied, standing and coming face to face with Nicholas. 'So, you are leading the danger straight here to our home.'

Theo stepped between them and pushed Dylan back.

'That is enough,' Theo remarked. 'If that is the case, then we need to prepare ourselves.'

'You're right,' Nicholas replied, nodding. 'So let us get our training in for today because they could strike at any time.'

***

Pyro heard the roof above them slide across and Gale descended the stairs.

'How did you go?' Assana asked, turning in her chair to face Gale. Gale didn't reply; he walked past Pyro and Assana and to his room.

'Not good,' Pyro growled, shaking his head.

'Obviously,' Assana replied. 'Well, it looks like it's my turn to have a go, I guess.'

'Yeah, I guess so,' Pyro mumbled, now lost in thought.

'What is it, Pyro?' replied Assana.

'Do you think you can do it?' Pyro asked.

'Oh, yeah,' Assana grinned. 'Remember, I am the strongest one out of the five of us.'

'Well, that's debatable,' Pyro replied. 'Do you have a plan?'

'As a matter of a fact, I do,' Assana exclaimed. 'And I'm going to need your help with it.'

'Oh?' questioned Pyro.

'Yes, my dear brother,' Assana replied, standing up. 'Now, I'll get changed and we can go.'

Assana walked out of the room and after five minutes she walked back in. She had changed out of her business suit and into a short shirt that exposed her stomach and a blue skirt that was long at the back and short at the front.

'Ah, that's better,' She grinned. 'Ready to go?'

'Yeah, let's go,' Pyro replied, nodding.

CHAPTER 30

Theo danced backwards as Nicholas advanced towards him, fist ready to strike. Theo threw a kick and Nicholas blocked the kick with his arms and then he lashed out with a kick of his own, but Theo jumped back and froze time and breathed a sigh of relief and then smirked. He approached a frozen Nicholas, crouched down like a line-backer, unfroze time and tackled Nicholas to the ground, with a thud. Theo laughed as he rolled off and stood up.

'Excellent move,' Nicholas said as he stood. 'All right, time for a break.'

Nicholas and Theo bowed to each other and then walked back into the house and into the kitchen.

'When do you think the next attack will come?' Theo asked.

'Who knows? To be honest, it could be in five minutes, it could be in five days – we just have to wait and find out,' replied Nicholas. 'All we know is that they are coming.'

'Most likely,' Theo replied glumly.

'How did you guys go?' Dylan asked as they stepped into the lounge room.

'Just fine,' Nicholas replied. 'Couldn't do much in that backyard though, but it will do.'

'What are we going to do when the next person comes after the swords?' Lance asked.

'Do what we have done the last few times,' replied Dylan. 'We fight!'

'Actually, I agree with Dylan on that,' Nicholas replied, nodding. 'We can't run; they clearly will just find us, so we fight until they give up and realise we can't be defeated.'

The brothers all nodded, grinning at each other.

'The one thing we need to do is for Lance to master the Sword of Light,' Nicholas exclaimed.

'I agree,' Theo replied, nodding and smiling at Lance.

'It would make it easier for us to protect ourselves and the swords,' Nicholas exclaimed.

'I guess you are right,' Lance mumbled, not convinced. 'Let's give it a try.'

***

'He's not here,' Pyro said as he walked out of the hotel.

'Oh, I know he's not here,' Assana replied, examining her nails in boredom.

'What do you mean? Why didn't you tell me?' Pyro asked in frustration.

'You didn't ask,' she replied, shrugging.

Pyro grunted, opening the car door and getting in, making Assana laugh as she got into the passenger seat.

'So, where is Nicholas then?' Pyro asked.

'Hang on a minute, let me at least track his phone. Damn, you're impatient,' Assana replied, pulling out her phone. 'Alright, by the looks of it, he is still in town.'

'Good. He must have the Sword of Light with him because it wasn't in his room.'

'Then let's go.'

Pyro turned his car on and quickly sped away from the hotel and back into the town.

'Alright, which way?' asked Pyro.

Assana pointed down a street to the right and Pyro spun the wheel and turned down the street.

'Alright, he's up here in one of these houses,' Assana announced, pointing to a two-storey home with a nice front yard. 'Stop here.'

Pyro pulled the car over and Assana stepped out.

'Wait here,' Assana commanded. 'I will send you a sign when I need you.'

'The usual sign?' Pyro asked.

'Of course,' Assana grinned. She closed the car door and walked towards the two-storey house across the road.

'He must be in there,' she mumbled to herself. She walked through the front gate and noticed the pond in the garden. She smirked and the water swirled out of the pond and formed a ball in the palm of her hand and threw the water at the front door.

***

Nicholas walked to the couch and reached into the duffel bag and pulled out the Sword of Light, the gold gleaming in the light.

'You ready, Lance?' Nicholas exclaimed.

'I guess so,' Lance replied nervously.

Nicholas nodded and walked towards Lance, Sword of Light in his hand, when all of a sudden, the front door was blasted off its hinges and careened into Nicholas, knocking him off his feet. The Sword of Light was flung from his hand and impaled itself, hilt deep, in the wall.

'What the hell?' Dylan exclaimed. The brothers looked forwards to the doorway and standing there was a striking, beautiful woman with long, orange hair and a ball of water floating in her hand.

'Hello, boys,' she said, a smirk on her face and cocking her hip. Lance just stared at her.

'Who are you?' Dylan growled.

'Oh, straight to the point,' she laughed. 'Assana.'

And she held out her hand for someone to shake it.

'You are here for the swords,' Theo growled.

'Aw. Ruin the surprise,' Assana replied, laughing, taking her hand back since no one moved to reciprocate the gesture.

'You are working for Pyro too,' Dylan exclaimed, slowly moving towards the stairs.

'I wouldn't say working,' Assana replied. 'He is my brother after all.'

'Well, you aren't getting the swords,' Theo said, trying to sound intimidating.

'Sorry to disappoint you, boy, but I am,' Assana laughed.

Dylan bolted for the stairs but Assana threw the ball of water across the room, striking Dylan square in the back and knocking him to the floor.

'Not going to happen, big shot,' Assana chastised. 'I know you need that Sword of Darkness to be stronger.'

Nicholas pushed the door off himself and stood up, throwing a blast of wind at Assana but she dove forward, rolling under the blast and stood up.

'Ah, Nicholas Quinzel, how are you feeling today?' she asked knowingly. 'I bet not good, after what happened last night.'

'That's what you think,' Nicholas said.

Lance didn't move; he just continued to stare at Assana.

'Hey, hotshot, like what you see?' she asked, turning to face Lance.

This caused Lance to snap out of his daze and blush.

'Come on, Lance, focus.' Nicholas scowled. This made Assana laugh and Lance blushed again.

'Quickly, get the Sword of Light,' Nicholas commanded and Lance nodded, turning and running for the wall where the sword was embedded.

'Ha-ha, not gonna happen,' Assana laughed and the tap in the kitchen began to groan. It burst off, water spraying out and forming a stream as it flew to swirl around Assana.

'Try this,' she exclaimed and threw her arms in Lance's direction and two streams of water flew straight at him, but Nicholas stepped in front of the streams and blocked them with a barrier of densely compressed wind.

'Get the sword, Lance!' Nicholas yelled, struggling to fold off the streams.

Lance wrapped his hand around the hilt of the sword and was about to pull it out of the wall when a third stream of water snuck past Nicholas, wrapping around Lance's ankle and pulling him off his feet. Then the stream wrapped around the hilt of the sword and pulled the Sword of Light out of the wall and back towards Assana.

'Ha-ha, you can't stop me,' she announced with a laugh.

Theo instantly stopped time, walked up to pull the Sword of Light out of the water stream's grip and stepped towards Lance and unfroze time. Assana gasped in shock, noticing the sword wasn't in her water's grip anymore.

'What?' she exclaimed as Nicholas took advantage of her distraction and blasted her off her feet with a blast of wind. Theo leant down next to Lance.

'Here you go,' Theo said, handing Lance the sword.

'Thanks, Theo,' replied Lance. Lance reached out and wrapped his hand around the hilt. He placed his thumb on the centre sapphire, sending light from his thumb into the gemstone. Theo stepped back as light began to leak out of the sword. Lance looked down at the sword, pulses of a weird feeling spreading from the sword into his body. He felt himself being drawn towards the blade and with one last pulse, Lance felt himself being sucked into the sword. Theo watched as the light from the sword seeped into Lance's body and his eyes began to glow brightly.

'Lance?' Theo asked, reaching out to touch him, but Theo found an invisible barrier surrounding Lance.

'Well, at least she won't be able to get to him,' Theo mumbled to himself, turning back to the battle as Assana got to her feet.

'What the hell?' she asked, looking at Lance. Nicholas turned and smiled.

'Looks like you won't be getting that sword anytime soon,' he announced.

'No? Well, I'll just go after the other sword then,' she replied. Then a stream of darkness struck her, lifting her off the floor and into a wall.

'That's not gonna happen either,' Dylan said as he turned and ran up the stairs and into his room. He walked up to his desk, where the Sword of Darkness was laying. He picked it up and darkness swirled around, an armour instantly forming.

'Hello, Dylan,' Heolster said in Dylan's mind.

'Hello, Heolster, we've got some work to do,' Dylan replied with a grin.

***

Lance opened his eyes and sat up, looking around a blue sapphire room and standing in the centre of the room was a tall man with white-blonde hair and wearing a white suit. Lance stood up and the man turned towards him.

'Hello, Lance,' the man said.

'How do you know my name?' Lance replied, confused.

'Oh, Lance, the moment you touched this sword, I knew everything about you,' he replied.

'Really? That's a tad creepy,' Lance hesitated.

'Yes, and trust me, Lance, I can't hurt you anyway. Now, to business – my name is Apollo,' Apollo announced, spreading his arms wide in greeting.

'It is nice to meet you, Apollo. Where are we anyway?' Lance replied, looking around the room.

'We are inside the sapphire of the sword – the centre one to be precise. The one you placed your thumb on,' Apollo explained, also looking around.

'That is amazing.'

'Yes, so have any of your brothers spoken to any of my brothers in the swords?'

'Yes, one of my brothers has spoken to Heolster.'

'Ah, right. In that case, you are probably expecting a battle between you and me.'

'Yes, actually, that is what Dylan had to do with Heolster.'

'Of course. That is my brother. A fight-first, talk-later kind of guy. Well, that's not what is going to happen. I'm not like my brothers.'

'Well, that's a relief. To be honest, Apollo, my fighting skills are still a work in progress.'

'Oh, I know. Anyway, for me to hand over the mastery of this sword, I just want you to answer one question for me.'

'Okay, what is the question?'

'What is evil to you?'

'What is evil to me?'

'Yes.'

'Well, evil is to me is anyone or anything threatening the wellbeing of the world and, more importantly, threatening my family and friends,' Lance said with conviction, looking Apollo square in the eye. Apollo stared at Lance, not giving away anything.

'Well, Lance, that is a great answer.'

'Really?'

'Yes, it was all I needed to hear. It shows me that you have a kind heart and are a good person. I knew that before you came here but I wanted to hear your answer to that question.'

'Does this mean I pass?'

'Yes, Lance, the control of the Sword of Light is officially yours,' replied Apollo, extending his hand to Lance.

'Thank you, Apollo,' Lance said, shaking his hand.

The room began to glow around them and Lance closed his eyes and when he opened them, he was standing in his house again, a white-gold armour surrounding his body, the Sword of Light in his hand. Lance looked up and Assana stared at him in shock. Lance looked around and noticed Nicholas and Theo were laying on the ground, barely moving.

'You did this?' Lance asked, anger crossing his face.

'Of course,' Assana replied, now laughing. Lance roared in anger, raised the Sword of Light and charged straight at Assana.

CHAPTER 31

Pyro groaned and leant back in his seat as he looked over at the house where Assana had just destroyed the front door and entered.

'I'm so bored,' he mumbled, now twiddling his thumbs in his lap.

Then there was a bright flash of light from within the house.

'That's probably not good,' Pyro said, excitement now in his voice as he opened the door and ran to the house.

***

Lance raised his hand and a beam of light fired at Assana, but she dove to the side, dodging the beam, rolled and came up on her knees and then she sent a stream of water at Lance, knocking him back. Nicholas then dove at Assana but she grabbed him in mid-air with a hand of water and threw him over the couch.

'Alright, Shiny, hand over the sword,' Assana said, pointing at Lance.

'Not gonna happen,' Lance growled, preparing himself.

'Hahaha, you think you can beat me?' Assana asked.

'Actually, yes I do,' Lance replied. 'I'm stronger now.'

'Is that right?' Assana asked, placing her hand on her hip and smiled seductively. Lance blushed and looked away and with that distraction, Assana threw a large stream of water at Lance, knocking him off his feet and into the wall. Assana laughed and walked towards Lance as he slowly got back to his knees.

'Look at you now,' Assana said, kneeling down next to Lance. 'And you thought you could beat me.'

'I will,' Lance snarled, lashing out with the sword.

Assana laughed again, just out of range of the slash and sent another stream at Lance, knocking him into the wall again.

'Come on,' Assana taunted. 'Where is that spirit?'

Then a mass of darkness flew down the stairs and struck Assana, knocking her across the room and Dylan descended the stairs, darkness swirling around his armour.

'Are you alright, Lance?' Dylan asked, kneeling next to his brother.

'Yeah, I'm fine,' replied Lance, standing up, armour pulsing with light.

'Let's do this together,' Dylan grinned, standing back up. Assana stood up and looked at her two adversaries.

'Well, this is now unfair,' she said, motioning to the pair. Then a fireball flew out of nowhere, striking Lance in the chest plate, exploding on impact, making him stumble back.

'Well, you took your time,' Assana said as Pyro stepped through the doorway and into the house.

'I thought you had things under control,' Pyro replied, smirking.

'Apparently not.'

'I told you you would need me.'

'Shut up,' Assana grumbled, crossing her arms across her chest. Pyro laughed again and he turned to face Dylan and Lance.

'Hello, lads, long time no see,' Pyro greeted, smirking.

'Pyro,' Dylan sneered.

'Oh, chilly, even I felt that and I control fire.' Pyro laughed, rubbing his arms in a mocking gesture. Dylan snorted and threw a mass of darkness at Pyro, but Assana summoned a wall of water, blocking the darkness.

'Yeah, that's not gonna happen,' Assana shook her head.

'Thanks,' Pyro said, nodding at his sister. 'Looks like this will be interesting.'

'I think so, yes,' Assana replied.

'Are you ready, Lance?' Dylan asked, looking down at his brother.

'Yeah, sure,' Lance replied, standing.

'You boys have no chance,' Pyro laughed menacingly, summoning a fireball in each hand.

'I agree with my brother,' Assana agreed, water streams now swirling around her body.

'Bring it,' Dylan growled and he sent a stream of darkness at Assana and Lance fired a beam of light at Pyro.

Assana blocked the darkness with a wall of water and Pyro dove to the side, dodging the light. Assana then changed the wall into spears and sent them at Dylan. He used the same tactics as her and blocked the spears of water with a wall of darkness, then he changed the wall into multiple blades of darkness and threw them at Assana, but she ducked under the blades. Pyro leapt at Lance, fireballs in each hand, but Lance fired a beam of light, striking Pyro and sending him flying back, but he used the momentum to slide across the floor and threw fireballs in Lance's direction, but he used a shield of light to snuff the fireballs out.

Assana rolled to the side as a mass of darkness slammed down where she once lay. She rolled back to her feet and threw a stream of water that struck Dylan, making him stumble back. Dylan looked up and smirked.

'I thought you would have been stronger,' he laughed.

Assana raised an eyebrow as darkness swirled around Dylan until she couldn't see him anymore.

'What is he doing?' she mumbled. She threw another stream of water but it just bounced off the swirling darkness. Then the darkness dissipated and Dylan was gone.

'What the hell?' Assana exclaimed, whirling around. 'Where has he gone?'

Then darkness swirled up behind Assana and Dylan stepped out of the darkness and sent the swirling darkness at her, striking her in the back, knocking her down.

'Son of a bitch,' Assana exclaimed in anger, getting up.

Lance fired another beam at Pyro but he rolled away to the side and sent a stream of fire in Lance's direction, but Lance continued to block the flames with a shield of light.

'Aw, come on, kid,' Pyro teased. 'Just let me kick your ass.'

Lance didn't reply and he disappeared in a flash of light.

'What?' Pyro exclaimed and Lance appeared behind him, lashing out with a kick, foot surrounded by light, striking Pyro in the back, the light exploding on impact, sending Pyro flying across the room, over the couch and crashing into Assana, sending them both tumbling across the floor.

'Let's finish them,' Dylan said to his brother.

Lance nodded and they both charged at them as they stood. They both looked up and saw the brothers coming at them so they dodged to either side of the brothers.

'Now!' Assana yelled and she threw water in the direction of Pyro and Pyro thrust out his hand sending a stream of fire in Assana's direction, the water and fire striking each other and changing to steam, instantly billowing out and blanketing the room.

'Crap,' Dylan cursed as the room was completely filled with steam. He looked around, but he could not see anything through the steam, then something moved next to him. Dylan spun but there was nothing there. He spun again and a fist of water burst out of the steam, striking him in the face, knocking him down, cursing.

'Damn,' Dylan mumbled, rubbing the side of his face and standing up again. Dylan sheathed the Sword of Darkness, the armour dissipating.

'Think I'm going to need both my hands for this,' Dylan mumbled, summoning darkness around his fists.

Lance spun in circles, trying to see through the steam that surrounded him.

'I can't see a thing,' he said.

'That's right,' came Pyro's voice from inside the steam.

'Where are you?' Lance asked, whirling around again.

'Oh, you won't find us,' replied Pyro's voice. 'This steam is too thick for you to see anything.'

Lance heard Pyro laugh and he gritted his teeth.

'Yeah, well, take this,' Lance yelled, pointing the Sword of Light out into the steam and firing a beam of light out of the sword and then he swept the beam across the room. From within the steam, Pyro and Assana saw the beam of light coming and ducked under it, but Dylan wasn't so lucky. He turned and the beam struck him in the chest, blasting him off his feet.

'Damn it, Lance,' Dylan groaned, struggling to get back up.

Lance cut off the beam and grinned to himself.

'That should have done the job,' he mumbled to himself.

'Really?' came Pyro's voice again. 'You missed me.'

'And me,' came Assana's voice.

'But I'm pretty sure I got someone,' Lance mumbled, looking around, straining to see through the steam.

'You did. Your brother.' Pyro laughed.

Lance cursed, then Pyro and Assana dove out of the steam, in front of Lance, and they sent streams of fire and water, striking Lance in the chest, sending him flying backwards through the steam. Lance felt the Sword of Light fly from his grasp, the armour instantly dissipating. Lance hit the wall hard and fell into a heap onto the floor with a groan.

'Where did that sword go?' Pyro exclaimed, suddenly growing frantic, knowing the Sword of Light was within his grasp.

'Calm down, Pyro,' Assana replied. 'The sword should be over there.'

Then there was a gust of wind that filled the room, blowing away the steam and standing in the middle of the room was Nicholas, breathing heavily.

'Oh, hello again,' Assana greeted, grinning.

Pyro looked down and halfway between himself and Nicholas was the Sword of Light. Pyro instantly charged for it but was knocked off his feet by a blast of wind. Assana sent a stream of water at Nicholas, but he blocked the water with a wall of wind.

'You can't keep this up much longer, can you?' Assana laughed.

'You would be surprised what I can still do,' Nicholas replied, smirking.

Assana smirked back and sent another stream of water at Nicholas, but he blocked it again, but with that distraction, she used another stream of water to snake forward and grab the Sword of Light.

'Got it!' she exclaimed, using the stream to throw the sword to Pyro. He caught it and stared down at his prize.

'Finally,' Pyro breathed in awe. 'Let's get out of here.'

Pyro quickly ran out of the house and straight for the car outside. Assana turned and followed her brother out of the house. Nicholas cursed and dashed after them out of the house, lightning now crackling in his fist. Pyro threw the Sword of Light into the back of his car and jumped into the driver's seat and started the car.

'Drive!' Assana yelled, jumping into the passenger side as lightning arced across the hood of the car.

'Damn it, my car!' Pyro yelled, slamming his foot down on the accelerator. The car roared to life and sped off.

Nicholas ran out onto the road as the car turned the corner at the end of the street.

I've gotta go after them, Nicholas thought as he began to run down the road, a powerful updraft propelling him into the air and he flew after Pyro's car.

CHAPTER 32

'Wait, Nick!' Dylan yelled, jumping to his feet as Nicholas ran out the door, chasing after Pyro and Assana. Dylan ran after Nicholas out the door and watched as Nicholas took off into the air and flew off in an eastern direction.

'Damn it,' Dylan cursed. 'I won't be able to chase him now.'

Dylan turned around and walked back inside.

'What a mess,' Dylan sighed, looking around the room. The room was a disaster zone, the chairs and couches were flipped over, the television screen smashed, scorch marks covered the walls and floor and the sink was completely destroyed from Assana's water manipulation.

'How are we going to explain this to Mum?' Theo moaned, standing up from behind the overturned couch.

'I have no idea. Thankfully, she is away on business right now,' Dylan said. 'Are you alright?'

'Yeah, I am fine. Just a tad sore,' Theo replied, walking over to Lance.

'Damn it,' Lance mumbled in pain, sitting up.

'Lance, are you okay?' Theo asked.

'No. No, I'm not. They took the Sword of Light,' Lance fumed.

'What?' Dylan exclaimed, instantly placing his hand on the hilt of the Sword of Darkness and breathing a sigh of relief.

'How?' Theo asked, placing his hand on Lance's shoulder.

'They both attacked me when I had my guard down when the steam was blanketing this room and after I thought I had taken them out, but it turned out I had missed them and had only got Dylan,' Lance replied.

'Oh, yeah, thanks for that by the way,' Dylan grumbled.

'Ignore him,' Theo said, staring daggers at Dylan. 'How did you lose the sword?'

'As I said, they both attacked me together, hit me with their powers together, knocking me back and causing me to let go of the sword,' Lance replied, looking down guiltily.

Dylan cursed and Theo held his hand to Lance, Lance taking it and Theo helping Lance up.

'I am so sorry, guys,' Lance grumbled.

'Don't worry about it, Lance,' Theo replied. 'What matters is what we do next.'

'Wait, where's Nicholas?' Lance asked, looking around for him.

'Ummm… well… he flew off,' Dylan replied.

'Wait, what?' Theo asked, turning to face Dylan. 'Where did he go?'

'He flew off chasing after Pyro and Assana,' Dylan replied, pointing out the front door.

'Well, what do we do now?' Lance asked.

'We wait,' Theo replied.

'We what?' Dylan replied, turning to Theo, looking at him as if he had gone insane. 'We should go after them.'

'How, Dylan?' Theo replied, turning to face his brother. 'We have no idea where they have gone. Do you know where they have gone?'

'No,' Dylan mumbled, turning away.

'See. So we wait. Clearly, Nicholas flew off to find out where they are going and once he finds where they are, where their base of operations is and where the sword is, he probably will call us, tell us where they are and we will go back to him up,' Theo replied, nodding.

'Well, you do have a point there,' Dylan nodded.

'Exactly,' Theo replied. 'So that gives us time to rest and regain our strength, 'cause I think we have a big fight coming and it also gives us time to clean this mess up as best we can.'

***

Pyro turned the corner and the warehouse came into view.

'Finally,' he mumbled.

'I don't think they followed us with all the detours you did,' Assana replied, looking a tad queasy.

'Yeah, I think we are good,' Pyro replied, parking this car out the front of the warehouse.

'Let's get out of sight,' Assana said as they both stepped out of the car and dashed to the entrance, Pyro holding the Sword of Light close to his chest.

They quickly entered the warehouse and made their way underground into their base.

'Ah, good to be back,' Assana sighed, instantly heading to her room for a change of clothes. Gale poked his head out of his room.

'How'd you go?' he asked. 'Fail like the rest of us?'

Pyro smirked and held up the Sword of Light.

'What?' Gale exclaimed, in shock. 'You guys managed to get the swords?'

'Only one,' replied Pyro. 'This one is enough though.'

'What are you going to do with it then?' Gale asked.

'For now, I'm taking it down into Terra's labyrinth,' Pyro replied.

'Hide it down there for now.'

'Is that a good idea?' Gale asked.

'I think it is. I've had Terra create a special room to seal the sword away in,' Pyro replied.

'Well, that explains where she has been this whole time,' Gale said.

'Yeah, I've asked her to make some changes,' Pyro replied, walking towards the entrance of the labyrinth.

'As long as she doesn't release that beast down there,' Gale replied.

'Don't worry, Gale. You know it is only for emergencies,' Pyro explained, grinning. 'And besides, she isn't working in that area of the labyrinth anyway.'

Pyro left Gale to his thoughts and walked down the stairs that led further underground, the Sword of Light in his hand. He lit a fireball as he reached the bottom of the stairs and the entrance of the labyrinth, Terra standing there, waiting for him.

'Knew I was coming?' Pyro asked.

Terra grunted a 'yes' and turned, walking into her labyrinth. Pyro ran to catch up with her and fell in step beside her.

'I see you finally managed to get a sword,' Terra mumbled, not looking at him.

'Of course. You have to have some faith in me, Terra,' Pyro replied, jovially, but Terra just grunted at him.

'Is the room ready for it?' Pyro asked.

Terra grunted another 'yes' as they rounded a corner.

'Is the beast still sealed away?' Pyro asked, hesitantly.

Terra instantly stopped walking, spinning to face Pyro. 'Of course!' she snapped. 'What do you take me for?'

'Sorry, Terra,' Pyro apologised, holding his hand up in placation and stepping back. 'I was just checking. We don't need that thing running around here unless it's a last resort.'

Terra grunted, turned, and continued walking further into the labyrinth. Pyro breathed a sigh of relief and followed after her. After walking for another fifteen minutes, they finally reached the centre of the labyrinth.

'Here you go,' Terra grumbled, crossing her arms. A slab of earth slid across, revealing the room Terra had created for him. Pyro stepped into the room and the only thing in there was a small pedestal made of shimmering rocks. Pyro grinned and placed the Sword of Light on the stand.

***

Nicholas landed next to Pyro's car and looked around.

'Well, this is an interesting area,' he mumbled. He peered through the windows of the car but it was completely empty inside.

They must have taken the sword inside, he thought.

Nicholas walked up to the door of the warehouse and tried to open it.

Locked, but I should be able to blast it off.

Nicholas hunched down and pointed his finger at the lock, a small stream of lightning burst from his finger, destroying the lock. He pushed the door and it swung open, revealing an empty warehouse.

Empty. Hmmm, Nicholas pondered. *Where could they have gone?*

Nicholas walked to the far wall and felt along it but couldn't find anything out of the ordinary. He scratched his chin, thinking, then looked down at the floor.

What if they are underground? Nicholas thought. *Surely that means there is a way to open the hatch then.*

He looked around again until he spotted the hidden panel on the wall.

Bingo.

He walked over to it. He felt around it and found the finger sensors.

Well, that doesn't help me. I wonder where the entrance is?

Nicholas closed his eyes and concentrated on the air around him to try to find anything odd, then he sensed a breeze coming up through the concrete floor.

There, but I can't open that myself. Think I might need Dylan for this.

Nicholas pulled out his phone and dialled Theo's number.

***

Theo flipped the couch over and sighed.

'Mum is gonna kill us,' he mumbled.

'You're not wrong,' Lance replied, trying to sweep away the water.

'Well that massive scorch mark around the room is definitely your fault,' Dylan said, picking up the TV.

'I had to do something,' Lance argued. Then Theo's phone began to ring in his pocket. He pulled it out and answered it.

'Hello?' he answered.

'Theo!' he heard Nicholas exclaim on the other end of the line.

'Nick! Did you find them?' Theo asked, now listening intently.

'Yeah, I did. They have a warehouse in the suburbs of Melbourne and their base is underground, underneath the warehouse,' Nicholas replied.

'And what about the Sword of Light?' Theo asked.

'They still have it and I can't get into their base underground. I need you three here! ASAP!' Nicholas exclaimed, excitement in his voice.

'We can be there, just send me the address,' Theo replied, then he looked up at his brothers. 'You two okay to do battle again?'

Dylan and Lance both nodded.

'Yeah, we're ready,' Theo said into the phone.

'Good, I'll send you the address,' Nicholas replied.

'Alright, we'll be there as soon as we can,' Theo replied.

'I'll be waiting.' And with that, Nicholas hung up.

'Alright, let's go,' Theo exclaimed. The boys left the house and got into Theo's car, speeding off, starting their drive to Melbourne.

***

'Tea, sir?' Adam asked, carrying a tray with a steam pot of tea on it.

'Please, Adam,' Norman replied, nodding.

Adam nodded back and poured a cup of tea for Norman, then he turned to Gabrielle.

'Tea?' he asked.

'Thank you, Adam,' Gabrielle said, nodding and Adam also poured her a cup.

'How long till we get to Melbourne?' she asked, now looking out the plane window. She could see land beneath them, meaning they must have been close.

'About two hours,' Adam replied.

'Well, I was wrong then,' she muttered.

'What was that?' Adam asked.

'Oh, nothing, Adam. Sorry,' Gabrielle replied. He nodded and sat back down, opposite Norman.

'Sir, we just got another ping from Nicholas's phone,' Adam whispered, leaning over to Norman so Gabrielle wouldn't hear.

'Ah, good. I take it he has moved from the town of Cobden,' Norman whispered back.

'Yes, sir. He is now in Melbourne,' Adam whispered.

'Excellent, that just made this much easier,' Norman replied, rubbing his hands together.

CHAPTER 33

'Are we nearly there?' Dylan asked, boredom evident in his voice.

'If I hear you say that one more time, I swear I'm going to stop this car and put my foot in your ass,' Theo threatened, spinning the steering wheel as Lance directed him to turn down a narrow road.

'By the GPS, we are close,' Lance replied, holding his phone up to show Dylan the maps app. 'It's just around this corner.'

Theo turned the car around the next corner and in front of them was Pyro's car and the warehouse that Nicholas had told them to come to. Theo parked his car behind Pyro's car and the brothers all stepped out, stretching after the long drive.

'You finally made it,' Nicholas called as he stepped out from the shadows nearby.

'Of course,' Dylan replied, lifting the Sword of Darkness out and strapping it to his back so the hilt poked out over his shoulder. Lance also reached back into the car and retrieved the empty scabbard, strapping it to his hip.

'So, where are Pyro and his lackeys hiding?' Dylan asked.

'In this warehouse,' Nicholas replied, motioning to the warehouse.

'Alright, let's do this,' Dylan said, clearly excited for the fight ahead.

They walked inside the warehouse, revealing the emptiness within.

'It's empty. Now what?' Dylan groaned, looking around.

'Patience, Dylan, they are underground,' Nicholas replied. 'I can sense the air coming up through gaps in the door that is a part of the floor.'

'Well, how do we get down there?' Lance asked, looking down at the floor.

'Well, I can't find anything to open it up,' Nicholas replied. 'So, I thought that Dylan could use his darkness to open this up.'

'I was hoping you would say that,' Dylan grinned, darkness beginning to swirl up and around his body. 'Now, where did you say this door is?'

Nicholas moved into the centre of the room.

'It's about here,' Nicholas said, pointing down.

'Alright, stand back,' exclaimed Dylan, walking to where Nicholas once stood.

Nicholas, Theo and Lance all moved away from Dylan to the walls of the warehouse. Dylan spread darkness across the floor until he felt the gaps in the floor, indicating where the door was. The darkness seeped into the gaps and underneath the slab that was the entrance.

'Alright, here we go,' Dylan announced and he began to lift the darkness up from underneath, but the slab on concrete wouldn't budge.

'Damn it,' Dylan growled. 'Time for Plan B.'

Dylan brought the darkness back up above ground, forming a mass above the concrete slab, then he slammed the mass down, sending a resounding 'boom' and the slab began to crack.

'That's more like it,' he smirked, admiring his work, as he brought the mass up for another strike.

***

Gale looked up as there was a loud 'boom' above his head.

'What the hell was that?' Assana demanded, stepping out of the room, now dressed in a different shirt and skirt.

'I think we have company,' Gale replied, rushing over to the computer monitors. He turned them on and quickly switched to the security cameras in the warehouse.

'Well, would you look at that,' Gale said, humour in his voice.

Assana walked over to the monitors. 'Well, if it isn't Nicholas and these brothers,' Assana laughed. 'They must be here for the Sword of Light.'

'They must have followed you back here,' Gale replied.

'What's going on?' Pyro asked, walking up the stairs.

'We have visitors,' Gale smirked, looking up at Pyro.

'Of course, we do,' Pyro sighed, looking at the security feed from above. 'You know what to do. Into the labyrinth – we protect the sword at all costs.'

They all nodded, stood and made their way downstairs.

'What's going on?' Glacia asked as she stepped out of her room.

'Into the labyrinth. You know what to do,' Pyro replied, nodding.

***

Dylan lifted the mass again and slammed it down, the crack in the slab widening.

One more should do it, he thought as he lifted the darkness up one last time, slammed it down and the concrete slab split clean in two, caving inwards, revealing stairs that led underground.

'Bingo,' Dylan grinned as Nicholas stepped up beside him, looking down the stairs.

'Nice work,' Nicholas congratulated, patting Dylan on the back. He looked at Lance and Theo, motioning down the stairs. 'Down we go.'

They all climbed over the broken pieces of cement and made their way down the stairs into a room.

'What the hell?' Dylan asked, looking around. The room had TVs and computer monitors across the walls and a table in the centre of the room, two corridors leading off the room, one to the left and the other further underground.

'Look, they have been watching us the whole time,' Lance said, pointing to the monitor that displayed the security feed from in the warehouse.

'Damn it,' Nicholas cursed. 'They know we are here.'

'That doesn't matter,' Dylan said. 'We are still stronger than them. They just aren't here 'cause they already know that they are defeated.'

Theo shook his head at Dylan's arrogance.

Then all the monitors around the room flickered on, revealing a video feed of Pyro.

'Hello, boys,' Pyro said, a grin on his face.

'Pyro,' Dylan growled.

'Welcome to my humble abode,' Pyro welcomed. 'I would ask why you are here, but I already know the answer to that,' he lifted the Sword of Light in view.

'My sword!' Lance exclaimed.

'Your sword? Nah, not anymore, kid,' Pyro replied, laughing.

'We will get that sword back!' Dylan retaliated.

'Not likely, but if you would like to try and get this sword back, then walk to the stairs that lead further underground and into my labyrinth.'

'A labyrinth?' Theo questioned, looking over at Nicholas, but he was intent on the monitors.

'Is that fear I hear?' Pyro mocked. 'Well, if you want this back, then come down here and find me.'

And with that, all the monitors turned off.

'Well, let's go,' Dylan said, taking a step towards the corridor that led down.

'Wait, what?' Theo retorted. 'We can't go down there.'

'We have to,' Nicholas replied, beginning to follow Dylan. 'If we want the sword back, it can't stay in his hands.'

'I agree,' Lance piped up. Theo turned to Lance and sighed.

'Fine,' Theo said, holding his hands up in surrender. 'But you guys do know this is a trap, right?'

'Oh, of course,' Nicholas replied, smirking.

'It's kinda obvious,' Dylan shrugged.

'Alright, let's do this, I guess,' Theo sighed.

They nodded to each other and walked down the stairs that led further underground. They got to the bottom of the stairs and stepped into the underground room made of solid basaltic rock, lights above illuminating the area. In front of them were four different tunnels leading off in different directions.

'Aw, great. Which one do we choose?' Dylan groaned.

'No idea,' Lance replied, looking at each in turn.

'We are going to have to split up,' Nicholas said.

'What?' Theo replied, dumbfounded. 'How is that a good idea?'

'Well, we cover more ground that way and you three are ready to do this so I have faith,' Nicholas replied, smiling.

'Sounds like a plan,' Dylan replied, cracking his knuckles.

'Fine,' Theo scowled.

'Alright, lads, choose a lane and let the race begin,' Nicholas announced.

Nicholas took the far left tunnel, Theo took the close left. Lance took the far right and Dylan took the close right.

'Alright, meet back here with the Sword of Light,' Nicholas said.

And with that, they all enter their tunnels and into the unknown beyond.

***

Pyro placed the Sword of Light back on its stand smirked to himself.

'This is going to be interesting,' he mumbled to himself. Suddenly, Terra rose out of the ground next to him, but Pyro didn't even flinch; he was used to Terra's way of transport.

'They have entered the labyrinth,' she informed Pyro.

'Excellent,' he replied, rubbing his hands together. 'Is everything ready?'

'I guess so.'

'Is everyone in their places?'

'Yes. They are and that's where I'm going now.'

'Good.'

Terra shrugged and descended back down into the earth.

'So it begins,' he mumbled to himself.

***

Theo made a right turn and continued down the tunnel ahead.

'This labyrinth must be huge,' he mumbled, looking around at the earth around him. He made another right turn, then a left turn, then he continued straight ahead, then another left turn.

Looks like there is a room up ahead, Theo thought and he continued until the tunnel opened into a room.

'Where am I?' Theo asked, looking around the room and finding a man with long, dark dreadlocks, two cutlasses strapped to his back and two that strapped to his hips and two steel poles strapped to his lower back.

'Hello, lad,' he said, waving to Theo. Theo's eyes widened, recognising him from one of his dreams.

'Who are you?' Theo asked.

'The name's Gale,' Gale laughed, bowing slightly. 'And you one of those pesky brothers.'

'You are the one who attacked Nicholas during the night.'

'That is me. And you know I can't let you find that sword, right?'

'I guessed that.'

Gale drew one of his cutlasses and grinned.

'Fine,' Theo said, preparing himself to fight.

***

Adam parked the limousine behind a white car, turning the engine off. Norman and Gabrielle stepped out and she gasped.

'What is it?' Norman asked.

'That's Theo's car,' Gabrielle replied, pointing at the white car.

'Well, I did tell you there would be a chance they would be here,' Norman said, reaching back inside the car and pulling the Sword of Time out.

'Yeah, I know,' Gabrielle mumbled, still looking at the car.

Norman walked over to Adam as he grabbed his katanas out of the car also. 'Is this where Nicholas's phone last sent out a signal?' Norman asked.

'Yes, sir, inside that warehouse,' Adam replied.

'Alright, let's look inside,' Norman said. 'Come on, Gabrielle.'

Gabrielle snapped out of her daze and the three of them walked inside the warehouse.

'Well, something has definitely happened here,' Adam said, pointing to the broken cement slab in the centre of the room. Gabrielle nodded and Norman stepped up to the broken pieces of concrete.

'Let's go,' Norman commanded, moving down the stairs, past the broken cement, and they descended into the ground.

CHAPTER 34

Dylan made a left turn and continued following the tunnel, the lights above illuminating the way ahead.

'Where the hell am I?' Dylan mumbled to himself. He turned right and came to a T-intersection.

'Great, now which way do I go?' he mumbled. He decided to go to the right, he walked on, turned left and then right.

'Looks like there is something up ahead,' he mumbled. He turned left and the tunnel opened into a room. Standing in the middle of the room was Pyro and behind him was the Sword of Light.

'Well, if it isn't Dylan?' Pyro laughed. 'Didn't think you would be the first one to find me here.'

'Pyro,' Dylan growled.

'At your service,' Pyro replied, bowing with a flourish.

'Just hand over that sword,' Dylan commanded, taking a threatening step towards Pyro.

'What? This sword?' asked Pyro, motioning to the Sword of Light behind him. 'Nah, not gonna happen. Why don't you hand over your sword to me?'

'In your dreams,' Dylan growled, placing his hand on the hilt of the Sword of Darkness.

'Well then, I'll just have to pry it from your dead hands,' Pyro threatened, his expression instantly changing.

'Come on, give it your best shot,' Dylan replied, darkness leaping from the corners of the room and surrounding Dylan.

Pyro laughed and sent a stream of fire at Dylan, but Dylan brought up a shield of darkness to block the flames, then Dylan charged at Pyro, darkness surrounding his fists and he swung a punch at Pyro's face, but he dodged backwards and sent a fireball at Dylan, the fireball exploding on impact, sending Dylan flying backwards. Dylan rolled back to his feet, patting out the flames on his chest. Dylan scowled, his shirt now just smouldering. Dylan then drew the Sword of Darkness, shadows bursting from the blade and wrapped around Dylan's body, forming the armour, making Dylan grin in anticipation, feeling the power course through his body, renewing his strength and stamina.

'Now, things are gonna get interesting,' Pyro grinned, flames surrounding his fists.

Dylan sent two streams of darkness in Pyro's direction, Pyro dodged the first stream, but the second came flying in, striking him front on, sending him spinning back. Dylan took advantage of the situation and sent spears of darkness at the fallen Pyro. Pyro looked up, cursing and then using his power to propel himself across the floor, avoiding the spears. Pyro stood and began to clap.

'Excellent, Dylan, just excellent,' Pyro congratulated. 'You are stronger than the first time I met you.'

Dylan slightly blushed at the compliment, and then Pyro's expression changed on a dime and he thrust both his hands out, streams of fire bursting out of his palms and the flames completely engulfed Dylan.

'Turn to cinders!' Pyro screamed in triumph, increasing the intensity of the flames, then cutting his flames, them instantly dissipating and Dylan was gone, small amounts of darkness swirling in the place where Dylan was.

'As I said, cinders,' Pyro said, nodding.

Then darkness rose up behind Pyro and Dylan stepped out of the darkness, sword raised. Pyro's neck suddenly tingled, as if something was behind him and he turned as Dylan slashed down. Pyro tried to dodge back, but the sword still cut through his shirt and opened up a cut across his chest. Pyro cried out in pain as blood began to leak from the wound. Pyro used a burst of flames to drive Dylan back, then he concentrated, flames forming across his wound, cauterising the wound and stopping the bleeding. Pyro tore off his ruined shirt, flames burning in his eyes, turning around and picking up the Sword of Light.

'That was one of my favourite shirts,' Pyro growled, pointing at the ruined clothes. 'You are going to burn now.'

***

Nicholas turned right and looked ahead to the long tunnel in front of him, green vines hanging from the walls.

'I hope that's not what I think it is,' Nicholas mumbled, eyeing the vines. He picked up a rock and threw it at the appendages, the rock striking the fleshy surface and the plant burst to life, slithering around the walls and floor, searching for whatever had hit it.

'Damn, Assassin Vines,' Nicholas cursed. It slowly settled down and stopped moving again. Nicholas moved slowly moved through the tunnel, slowly stepping with caution, trying not to touch the greenery.

'Nearly there,' he muttered, but as he stepped over the last vine, his heel lightly brushed against it. Nicholas cursed as the plant sprang to life again and quickly wrapped around Nicholas's ankle. Nicholas was torn off his feet and dragged across the floor. Nicholas closed his eyes and concentrated, then he thrust his hands down, creating a burst of wind that made him shoot forward, tearing the vines apart. He quickly leapt to his feet and ran down the tunnel, getting away from the sinister thing. He turned left and continued to run down the tunnel until he was satisfied he was far enough away, so he stopped to catch his breath.

'Those damn vines,' Nicholas rasped. 'I hate those things.'

Nicholas turned right and then turned left, revealing a room.

'Hello, Nicholas,' Assana greeted as Nicholas walked into the room.

'Nice to see you again, Assana,' Nicholas replied.

'What brings you here?'

'I think you know what.'

Assana laughed in response and water began to swirl around her.

'I do, but you won't be doing anything else from here. I won't allow you to go any further.'

'I look forward to seeing you trying to stop me.'

Assana smirked and sent a stream of water at Nicholas, but he blocked the water with a wall of dense wind, then Nicholas sent a pulse of wind, but she dove to the side, flinging her arm in Nicholas's direction, sending another stream of water at Nicholas, but he used a burst of wind to dodged to the side and clapped his hands together, creating a clap of thunder. Assana covered her ears and Nicholas used the distraction and ran at her, lashing out with a kick when he came within range, which she blocked, grabbing hold of Nicholas's leg and began to swing him around, but Nicholas sent a burst of wind into Assana, knocking her back, making her release him. They both tumbled away from each other.

'Well, it looks like you were holding back in the house,' Assana called out, standing up.

'I can neither confirm nor deny that fact,' Nicholas replied, also standing.

'You're still not going to beat me,' Assana replied and four tentacles of water rose around Assana and she sent each of them at Nicholas.

He dodged the first and second tentacles, but the third struck him in the stomach, lifting him off his feet and knocking him back. He landed in a heap. He looked up and rolled to the side as the fourth tentacle came down in the spot where he had just been.

He quickly stood and ran around Assana, dodging her tentacles then he raised his hand and a bolt of lightning arced out of the palm of his hand and flew straight for Assana. She used the tentacles to vault herself to the side, the lightning bolt flying past her and striking the wall behind, exploding with a loud crack and rock debris flying across the room. She turned to face Nicholas again and sent all four tentacles speeding towards him again, but he used a large gust of wind to blast the tentacles of water apart, sending water droplets flying everywhere. Assana laughed as she raised her hands, all the water droplets stopping their fall and hanging suspended in the air. Assana rotated her hands and the droplets changed into knives, spinning to face Nicholas.

Nicholas cursed and he closed his eyes, concentrating. Assana shrugged, seeing this as her perfect chance to be rid of him once and for all. She threw her hands down and the hundreds of blades all sped straight for Nicholas, but at the last moment, he raised his hands and his eyes shot open and the temperature in the room instantly dropped to freezing, the blades all instantly froze, falling to the floor and shattering into pieces of ice.

'No!' Assana cried out, wrapping her arms around herself to keep warm. She tried to summon more water but it just froze in an instant.

Nicholas looked up at Assana and smirked. She growled in response and charged at him and swung a punch at his head. He blocked it with his arm, but this broke his concentration on the temperature and it began to increase back to normal again. Nicholas then swung a punch of his own, but Assana also blocked it, spinning and driving a knee into Nicholas's stomach. He gasped as the breath was driven out of him, then she spun again and struck him in the side of the face with a backhand, making him spin to the ground. She then stomped down at Nicholas's neck but he rolled away at the last second and he blasted her off her feet with a pulse of wind. Nicholas slowly got to his feet, clutching his stomach and wheezing.

'Just go down,' Assana complained, also standing up.

'No,' Nicholas replied.

'Persistent bastard,' Assana growled, shaking her head.

'That I am,' Nicholas laughed.

Assana sighed and water began to swirl around her once again. Nicholas also sighed and began to float off the ground, lightning crackling around his hands.

***

Theo dove to the side as Gale slashed at him with his cutlass, then Theo froze time and caught his breath. Theo cursed, eyeing Gale. He walked up to where Gale was frozen and unfroze time, lashing out with a kick that caught Gale in the chest, sending him stumbling back.

'Crap,' Gale cursed. 'How did you do that?'

Theo shrugged, not replying. Gale sheathed the two cutlasses and held his hand out in front of him and air began to swirl in the palm of his hand, forming a ball of spiralling air.

'Take this!' Gale yelled, running at Theo, but Theo just froze time again. He walked up to Gale, unfroze time again and kicked him in the chest again, but Gale used the air to keep himself upright, then he thrust the spiralling orb into Theo's stomach. Theo howled in pain as the spiralling air ground against his stomach, then the orb detonated, sending Theo flying backwards, bouncing across the ground and hitting the wall with a loud crack.

'That's what I thought,' Gale proclaimed, walking towards where Theo now lay. Gale raised his foot, ready to stomp Theo, but Theo rolled out of the way, leaping to his feet with a grunt of pain and tackling Gale to the ground. They rolled across the floor and Gale kicked Theo off him. Theo fell backwards and Gale dove at him, but Theo rolled to the side and froze time around Gale and Theo stood and walked up, unfroze him and Theo punched him in the stomach then the jaw, sending him spinning to the ground. Theo breathed a sigh of relief, turning away from Gale, only to come face to face with a strongly built man with white hair and beard, a scar over his right eye as he walked into the room, a sapphire-coloured sword with orange gems embedded in the hilt in his hand. A shiver ran down Theo's spine.

'The Sword of Time,' Theo breathed, then his eyes widened in realisation. 'Wait, this is similar to one of my dreams.'

'Hello, boy,' Norman Quinzel greeted, motioning to Theo.

'You must be Norman Quinzel.'

'Ah, you have heard of me?'

'Yeah, your son told us about you.'

'Of course he did.'

'Why are you here?'

'I'm here for the other two swords.'

'I can't let you do that,' Theo replied, taking a boxer's stance.

'You're going to fight me, boy?' Norman laughed. 'Alright, let's see what you can do then.'

Theo froze time and walked towards Norman, but time unfroze

and Theo gasped in shock. Norman blasted Theo off his feet with a telekinetic blast.

'What the hell?' Theo muttered, slowly standing up.

'Your powers over time won't work against me as long as I have this sword,' Norman replied with a chuckle.

Norman concentrated and Theo began to rise off the floor as Norman lifted him with his telekinesis and then he pulled Theo towards him and Norman ran Theo through with the sword through the chest. Theo tried to scream, but nothing came out of his mouth as Norman tilted the blade down, dropping him to the floor. Norman then turned and began to walk away. Theo felt the life leaving his body, numbness taking its place and with his last dying thought, he reversed time around himself.

CHAPTER 35

Lance came to an intersection and groaned.

'Aw man, not another intersection,' he groaned. 'This maze is huge.'

Lance decided to go right and he continued along the tunnel until he came to another intersection. Lance cursed and decided to turn left, grumbling to himself. He turned left, then right, and left again, revealing a room ahead. He walked into a room and standing in the middle of the room was Terra.

'Terra?' Lance asked, recognising the woman. Terra turned, facing Lance and grunted.

'Where is the Sword of Light?' Lance asked. Terra smirked.

'Not here,' Terra replied.

Lance cursed, looking away from Terra.

'Fine, I will go through you then to get to it,' Lance declared, turning back to Terra.

Terra laughed, shaking her head. 'Not going to happen.'

Lance sighed, clenching his fists, orbs of light forming around them.

'I'm not going to lose, not anymore,' Lance proclaimed. He thrust both fists at Terra, the orbs flying off his fists and sped towards Terra.

'That's not going to work,' Terra sighed.

Lance smirked and splayed his fingers. Each of the orbs split into six smaller orbs. Terra's eyes widened as the twelve orbs flew towards her and all twelve orbs struck Terra, exploding on impact and sending her flying backwards.

'Well, that was easier than I thought,' Lance said, then Terra's body crumbled into dirt.

'What the hell?' Lance gasped, walking up to the pile of dirt. Then a hand burst out of the ground and grabbed hold of Lance's ankle.

'Ah, shit,' Lance cursed, as the hand tried to pull him down into the ground.

Lance pulled his leg out of its grasp and backed away from the hand. Terra rose up out of the ground, sending a mass of earth at Lance. He dove to the side, but another mass of earth shot up from underneath Lance, knocking him across the room. Lance tumbled across the floor and Terra laughed, raising her hand. The floor underneath Lance quickly changed into quicksand and Lance began to sink into the sand. Lance cursed as he struggled but continued to sink.

'You will never get out of that quicksand,' Terra declared. 'You are going to die here.'

'You're wrong,' Lance replied, descending chest-deep into the quicksand.

'You want to know what's funny?' Terra asked. 'You boys, you are so naïve. You think that 'cause you have these powers that you can be heroes, that you can save people, but the world isn't a comic book. You aren't a hero. You're just a child in a world that you have no idea about.'

Lance closed his eyes as the sand came up to his neck then his chin until his head descended into the sand.

'And that's the end of a so-called hero,' Terra declared, walking away from the quicksand. Then there was a flash of light and Lance appeared in front of her and he sent a beam of light that struck Terra in the chest, making her stumble back, then there was another flash of light and Lance teleported behind Terra and fired another beam that struck Terra in the back. Then there was another flash of light and three Lances appeared around Terra.

'What the hell?' Terra faltered, looking around at the three Lance's surrounding her.

'What were you saying about me being a boy?' all three of the Lances said as they cupped their hands in front of them, an orb of light forming in their cupped hands.

Terra cursed and all the Lance's fired a beam of light straight at Terra. All the beams struck Terra and she howled in pain dropping to her knees. The Lance copies disappeared and Lance walked up to Terra.

'Where is the Sword of Light?' Lance asked.

Terra looked up at him and smirked. 'Find it yourself,' she replied.

'Fine,' exclaimed Lance, light surrounding his hand. Terra smirked and raised her hand and the wall behind Lance slid across, revealing another room beyond.

'Good luck with that,' Terra said and she descended into the ground.

'Damn, she's gone,' Lance turned and looked in the other room; something began to move in there.

'Wait, there is something in there,' Lance gasped.

There was a loud hiss and a giant snake's head appeared out from the gloom. Lance stood there, frozen in shock as the snake began to slither out of the room and reared up in front of Lance. Its head alone was the same size as Lance's height and the rest of it would have been at least twenty metres long. Lance snapped out of his fear, turning, and he began to run back into the labyrinth. The snake hissed in anger and began its chase.

***

Dylan raised the Sword of Darkness and more darkness surrounded him. Pyro laughed and ran straight for Dylan again, slashing at Dylan with the Sword of Light and Dylan blocked with the Sword of Darkness. When the blades met, there was a pulse of power but it didn't affect Dylan or Pyro. Dylan sent a mass of darkness, sending him flying away from him. Pyro flipped in mid-air, using a blast of fire from his feet to align himself and landed on his feet and instantly sent a fireball straight for Dylan, but he batted it aside with the sword, then Dylan thrust the sword at Pyro and streams of darkness burst off the blade and spun through the air, straight for Pyro. Pyro dove to the side, the streams barely missing him, rolled back to his feet and pointed the Sword of Light straight at Dylan.

'Take this,' Pyro snarled and fired a beam of light, roaring in pain as the sword burned his hand and wrist. Dylan laughed and raised a wall of darkness to block the beam, but instead of the beam being blocked, the beam blasted through the darkness and struck Dylan in the chest, sending him flying back, roaring in pain as the beam had also gone through the armour.

'What the hell?' Dylan said from where he now lay, perplexed, the hole in his armour reforming.

'And there is your weakness,' Pyro smirked, rubbing his now-burnt wrist. 'But looks like the blade doesn't like me, so you can deal with this instead.'

Pyro concentrated, holding his hand out in front of him and a ball of fire formed in front of him. He concentrated harder and the ball of fire began to morph until it resembled the shape of a person.

'What the?' Dylan exclaimed.

'Say hello to my fire golem,' Pyro chuckled, taking a step back as the golem began to grow taller and bigger until it was double the height of Pyro and double the width.

'Now die!' Pyro snarled and the golem charged for Dylan and swung a punch of fire at him. Dylan danced back, raising a hand and a wall of darkness rose. He then pushed the wall at the golem, forcing it backwards, but the golem morphed into streams of flames, moving around the wall and reforming on the other side. Dylan cursed as the golem dashed at him, swinging a massive fist, striking Dylan front on and sending him flying backwards. Dylan hit the wall of the cavern with a loud crack and crumpled to the ground.

'Finish him off,' Pyro ordered and the golem ran at Dylan again, but spikes of darkness erupted out of the shadows throughout the room, striking the golem, impaling it and stopping it in place.

Dylan stood up and the golem morphed out of the spikes and formed in front of Dylan again. The golem swung its fist at Dylan again, but this time, Dylan blocked the attack with a shield of darkness, then he changed the shield into a block of darkness and sent it straight at the chest of the golem but the darkness went straight through the golem this time and the golem raised its hand and a stream of flames burst forth at Dylan. Darkness rose behind Dylan and he stepped back into his shadow realm. The golem and Pyro looked around as the spikes lowered and formed puddles of darkness on the floor. Dylan stepped out of the shadows on the far side of the room and placed his hand on the floor and the pools of darkness spread and combined, covering the floor underneath the golem with shadow.

'Black hole!' Dylan yelled and the darkness under the golem began to swirl. The golem began to be sucked down into the darkness. The swirling intensified and the golem was sucked down into the darkness, disappearing for good.

Pyro looked at Dylan in shock as Dylan turned to face him.

'Your turn,' Dylan growled.

'You will die here!' Pyro roared in anger, raising the Sword of Light and his other hand. A beam of light fired from the sword and a stream of fire burst from his other hand. The light and the flames spiralled around each other, forming together, creating a stream of golden flames that sped towards Dylan. Dylan tried to block the stream with a shield of darkness, but the stream burned straight through, striking Dylan in the chest and the golden flames burned away the front of his armour and began to burn his clothes and skin underneath. Dylan howled in pain as the armour began to form again, cutting off the flames and putting them out.

'This is it for you!' Pyro snarled, raising the sword at Dylan.

'I couldn't have said it better myself,' Dylan replied and multiple streams of darkness with rounded ends formed in front of Dylan and they all flew straight at Pyro, striking him all over his body, sending him flying back, out of the room and into the tunnels. Dylan quickly stood up and ran out of the room, following the direction Pyro had flown.

'Damn, he has run,' Dylan cursed, looking around for Pyro. Dylan snarled and charged down the tunnel, giving chase after Pyro.

***

'Well, that takes care of one of them,' Norman muttered to himself, taking a silk handkerchief from out of his pocket and wiping the blood off the sword.

Suddenly Norman was tackled to the ground, losing grip of the Sword of Time, it sliding across the floor. Norman scrambled to his feet and looked across at Theo as he stood.

'What?' Norman exclaimed. 'How are you alive?'

'I think you know that answer,' replied Theo and he froze time around him, freezing Norman in place.

Theo looked around and spotted what he wanted. He walked over to where the Sword of Time was, picked it up and placed his thumb on the centre gem of the hilt. Instantly, Theo felt weird sensations course through his body and he was drawn towards the bright orange gemstone and his consciousness was sucked into the sword. He opened his eyes and he was in a completely orange room and standing in the centre of the room was a tall man with light brown hair and was wearing a sapphire-coloured suit.

'Hello, Theo,' he said, a broad smile on his face. 'I have been waiting for this day for a long time.'

'How do you know who I am?' Theo asked, now confused.

'Theo, I have known about you and your brothers for a very long time,' the man replied.

'So, you are one of the legendary brothers from the book?' Theo asked.

'Yes, my name is Horace,' Horace replied, grinning.

'Horace,' Theo breathed, committing the name to memory. 'Do you control time as I do?'

'Yes, I do.'

'Is that how you already know about myself and my brothers? Have you seen the future and seen us?'

'That is correct. I declared a prophecy a thousand years ago about you and your brothers from a vision I had of you and your brothers. I saw that you three were destined for great things and would be able to defeat any evil that was put in front of you and that is why I am giving you mastery of this sword – no test or anything – because I know who you are and what you will become. Now, take my hand and make a difference in this world.'

Theo nodded to Horace and took Horace's hand and the room began to glow around them and Theo closed his eyes and when he opened them, he stood back in the room in the labyrinth. He looked down and gasped at the sapphire-blue shimmering armour now covering his body, the Sword of Time faintly glowing in his hand. He turned back to face Norman and Norman stared at him in shock and with a little awe.

'How did you…' Norman began, but Theo froze time, walking up to him, unfreezing time again and punched Norman across the cheek. Norman stumbled back, clutching his jaw and Theo froze him in time, walking over to him and removing the scabbard for the sword from his person.

'Time you had a taste of your own medicine,' Theo growled, looking over at a frozen Norman.

Suddenly, Theo heard the crackle of electricity and it struck his body, sending him flying back, freeing Norman from Theo's frozen time. Theo's body convulsed, but he quickly used his power to reverse the effects and the convulsions disappeared. He stood and turned to face his attacker and he nearly fell to his knees in shock and horror. Gabrielle stood next to Norman, an orb of crackling electricity in her hand.

'Leave him alone,' she growled.

'Gabrielle? What are you doing here? And you have powers?' Theo gasped in shock.

'Yes, I do,' Gabrielle growled. 'And so do you. Why didn't you tell me?'

'To keep you safe,' he replied.

'Safe? Well, it looks like that backfired, now, didn't it?' Gabrielle snarled. 'You lied to me!'

'That may be true, but it was to keep you safe!' Theo cried out. 'Why are you here?'

'I'm here to help Norman, help him get those swords, to keep them out of the wrong hands, like yours,' she snarled back.

'He is the evil one, Gabrielle. He wants the swords for world domination,' Theo pleaded with her.

'Liar!' Gabrielle roared. 'Stop it, Theo, stop your lies. You and your brothers are the evil ones. You were about to attack an unarmed and defenceless man.'

'He had it coming,' Theo growled, tears forming in his eyes. 'Come on, Gabrielle. I thought we were a team.'

'Not any more,' she replied, anger and sorrow lacing her voice. 'I am not going to be with someone who lies to me. I told you that, but you didn't listen!'

And she threw the orb of electricity at him. Theo shook his head.

'He's brainwashed you,' he mumbled, a tear rolling down his cheek. He froze the orb, moved out of the way and then let it fly past him, exploding against the wall behind him.

'Fine, if that's the way you're going to be about this then fine,' Theo growled. 'I'll just have to beat both of you.'

Gabrielle's face fell at Theo's response, tears forming in her eyes, so she turned and ran out of the cavern, back into the labyrinth.

'Wait, come back!' Theo called out, running after her. Norman watched as Theo ran out of the room and scowled, knowing he couldn't do anything now that Theo had the Sword of Time. He cursed when suddenly he was blasted off his feet by a column of air. Norman landed with a cry of pain and groaned.

'What now?' he muttered, looking across the room as he spotted Gale walking towards him, four cutlasses floating around him.

'Finally,' Gale breathed. 'I have been waiting for this moment for a long time, old man.'

CHAPTER 36

Adam looked around and saw what looked like a room up ahead.

Hopefully, something is in this room, Adam thought. He stepped into the room and looked around, shivering as the cold in the room hit him.

Something's not right here, he thought, drawing one of his katanas.

Suddenly, he spotted movement in the shadow and he dove to the side as knives of ice flew just past his head.

'Who's there?' Adam called out. 'Show yourself.'

Adam turned as he felt the vibrations of someone moving behind him and Glacia stepped out of the shadows.

'Why are you here?' she asked, crossing her arms across her chest.

'That is none of your concern,' Adam responded.

'So, you are here for the swords?' she asked.

Adam shrugged, not answering Glacia's question.

'Well, I can't let you pass if you are.'

'Well then, it seems we are at an impasse.'

'It would seem that way.'

'Looks like we are going to have to do this the hard way.'

'It looks that way,' Glacia replied, ice forming and surrounding her fists.

Adam readied himself, dropping into a stance, katana pointed at Glacia. She growled and ran at Adam, swinging her fists at him, but Adam dodged back and swung his katana at her, but she dodged to the side, then drove her fist into Adam's stomach, driving the wind out of him, then she hit him with an uppercut to the chin, lifting him off his feet, sending him falling onto his back.

'Ha, you are good,' Adam chuckled, rubbing his jaw as he sat up.

'I hope that hurts,' Glacia growled.

'Oh, it did!' Adam laughed.

Glacia threw her arm out in Adam's direction and the blades of ice flew off her arms and sped straight at him, but Adam raised his hand, forming a wall of vibrations and the blades disintegrated into ice powder as they struck the wall.

'What? How?' Glacia exclaimed in shock.

Adam smirked and punched at the air, feeling it crack, and sent a shockwave through the air, straight at Glacia. She tried to dodge, but the shockwave caught her on the side, sending her spinning across the room, but she planted her hands on the ground and flipped herself back to her feet.

'What the hell was that?' she mumbled, eyeing Adam.

Adam concentrated, forming an orb of vibrations in his hand and ran at Glacia. She sent a stream of ice at him, hitting him in the arm that held the orb, freezing his arm, causing the orb to dissipate. Adam looked down at the ice on his arm and vibrations caused the ice to shatter. He swung his katana at her as she charged in close to him. She ducked under the blade and placed her hand on his stomach.

'Now freeze!' Glacia yelled and ice spread over Adam's body, completely encasing him.

'That is now your grave,' she muttered, but then the ice began to vibrate.

Glacia cursed as the ice around Adam exploded outwards, freeing him once again. Any ice that flew at Glacia stopped in front of her and fell to the floor.

'That's not going to work on me,' Adam said, shaking his head.

'So, your power is something like vibrations?' Glacia asked, curiosity getting the better of her.

Adam nodded and Glacia sighed, knowing now that her ice would be useless, but a sword of ice still formed in her hand and she ran at him, swinging the ice sword and Adam his katana in defence and the two swords met, but Adam's katana sliced straight through Glacia ice, making Glacia have to stumble back in shock to avoid the blade.

'And that won't work either,' Adam said. 'This sword negates powers that we have.'

Glacia stood, scowling.

'Fine, try this then,' she yelled and she thrust her hands down and ice began to spread across the floor of the room. Adam sheathed his katana and jumped up into the air, avoiding the ice and orbs of vibrations formed around his fists and he fell to the ground, slamming his fists down on the ground of ice, the vibrations exploding outwards, destroying the ice, the room shaking and large cracks formed in the floor that spread across and up the walls. The room rocked again and pieces of rock began to fall from the roof.

'Whoops, overdid it,' Adam mumbled, watching Glacia run out of the room. Adam turned and ran out of the room as it collapsed behind him.

'Well, that's one way to destroy a room,' He chuckled to himself.

***

Nicholas weaved through the air as Assana sent spears of water at him, dodging each spear in turn, then he raised his hand as he flew and lightning arced from his palm, straight for Assana. She dove to the side, dodging the lightning and rolled back to her feet, scowling up at Nicholas.

'Are you going to stay up there or come down here and fight me on even ground?' Assana challenged.

'I think I'll stay up here,' Nicholas replied. 'It is nice up here, plus I have the high ground.'

'Really? You're making references now?' Assana scowled.

Nicholas laughed and raised his hands and clouds began to form around him. Assana prepared herself as the clouds darkened and spread around Nicholas, obscuring him from Assana's view and it began to rain from the clouds.

'Idiot,' Assana mumbled, raising her hands, the droplets of rain stopping in mid-air.

'Take this,' Assana mumbled to herself and all the droplets sped toward all the clouds that Nicholas was in.

Nicholas smirked to himself in the clouds, snapping his fingers. All the droplets froze, turning to hail. The hail rotated in the air, rotating to face Assana. She cursed, turning to run, but the hail flew down, striking her in the back, making her cry out in pain. She turned and raised a shield of water to protect herself from the hail. Nicholas lowered himself from the clouds and landed on the floor as the clouds continued pelting Assana.

'Time to take her out,' Nicholas mumbled, bringing his hands together, crossing all his fingers across each other except his index and middle finger, which stayed pointed.

Nicholas concentrated and lightning began to spark and arc around his hands. Nicholas raised his pointed fingers, aiming at Assana, who was still defending herself from the hail. Lightning arced around his hand with more intensity and then a concentrated beam of lightning blasted from the tips of his pointed fingers and flew straight for Assana with accuracy. Assana continued to try and block the hail, but out of the corner of her eye, she saw the lightning speeding towards her and she dove out of the way, the lightning barely missing her. Nicholas cursed and ran at Assana, the clouds now dissipating. Assana leapt back to her feet and dodged back as Nicholas swung a punch and she sent a stream of water into Nicholas, sending him flying backwards. Then she raised her hands and water began to form an orb in front of her, the orb growing bigger and bigger until it was the same height as her.

'I hope this hurts,' Assana smirked and she sent the large ball of water at Nicholas.

Nicholas frowned, realising that he couldn't dodge this attack. He concentrated, raising his arm up above him and then sliced it down, a wave of wind flying off his arm that sped across the room and it sliced through the ball of water into two, making the two balls of water start to go around him, but Assana raised her hands and the two balls of water stopped on either side of Nicholas. She then brought her hands together, making the balls fly towards Nicholas again, but he thrust both his hands at the balls of water, blasts of wind bursting from his hands, blasting the balls apart. Assana raised her hands again and all the droplets from the balls were suspended in the air. She threw her hands down again, making the droplets speed towards Nicholas, striking him all over his body all over. Nicholas cried out in pain and fell to his knees. Assana walked to him, hands on her hips.

'Is that it?' she asked, grinning. Nicholas groaned.

'I'll take that as a yes,' she laughed and suddenly the air rippled between and Assana was shot off her feet and flew across the room, landing in a heap.

'Got ya,' Nicholas muttered, slowly getting back to his feet. He brought his hand together again, his index and middle fingers pointed and another beam of lightning began to form at the tip of his fingers.

'I'm going to finish this now,' Nicholas yelled at Assana, but suddenly the room began to shake and rumble.

'Ah, what now?' Nicholas groaned and a giant snake's head appeared from one of the tunnels. Nicholas's eyes widened in fear, lightning dissipating.

'Oh, no. It can't be,' Nicholas stammered. 'The Basilisk.'

The Basilisk slithered into the room and rose up in front of him. Nicholas stood there, frozen with fear and it hissed at him. Assana stood and looked up at Nicholas and the giant snake.

'Oh, god, she unleashed it,' she breathed. She turned and ran out of the room.

The Basilisk opened its mouth and a glow began to form, deep in its throat. This glow made Nicholas snap out of his fear, turning and running towards one of the tunnels leading out of the room. He looked over his shoulder and a stream of fire burst out of the Basilisk's mouth. Nicholas dove to the side, the flames barely missing him. He scrambled to his feet and ran out of the room and down one of the tunnels. The Basilisk hissed in anger and began to slither after him.

***

Lance turned a corner and continued to run, adrenaline and fear coursing through his body.

'I can't run anymore,' he breathed, slowing down and leaning against a wall. Lance turned and listened for any sound of the snake following him.

'I think lost it,' He signed in relief. 'I thought I was a goner for a second there. I guess I better keep moving; I have to find my sword.'

Lance stood up again and continued through the tunnel, around a corner and then he heard footsteps running towards him.

'Someone is coming,' he mumbled, hiding back behind the corner, watching the tunnel ahead.

Suddenly, Pyro came running around the corner and ran in the direction of where Lance was hidden.

'The sword,' Lance gasped, spotting the Sword of Light in Pyro's hand.

Pyro stopped and leant over, catching his breath.

'Looks like it's now or never,' Lance mumbled. He stepped out from his hiding place and walked down the tunnel, towards Pyro.

'Pyro!' Lance yelled.

Pyro sighed, coming back to his full height and turning to face Lance. 'Of course, I run into another one of you,' Pyro sighed, not believing his luck.

'Give me that sword back.'

'No.'

'I am going to have to take it from you then,' Lance challenged, orbs of light surrounding his fists. Pyro began to laugh.

'You are going to take this from me?'

'Yeah, I will.'

'Oh, this will be good,' Pyro laughed. Lance raised his fists and orbs flew off his fists and they sped towards Pyro, but Pyro raised the Sword of Light and the orbs were absorbed into the blade.

'Looks like that isn't going to work,' Pyro chuckled.

'How am I going to get that sword back?' Lance mumbled to himself. 'Guess I am going to have to use my fists.'

Pyro threw a fireball at Lance and Lance used a shield of light to block the flames, then he ran at Pyro, throwing a punch, but Pyro ducked under the punch and he kicked out, catching Lance in the thigh, causing Lance to drop to one knee and Pyro kicked again, but this time Lance caught his leg and drove an elbow into Pyro's thigh, making him cry out in pain. Lance rolled backwards, stood up and dove at Pyro. They tumbled across the floor and The Sword of Light flew from Pyro's grip and slid across the floor, away from the two of them. Lance felt his foot on Pyro's belly and he kicked out, sending Pyro flying off him, but Pyro flipped back, landing on his feet and he turned, running for the sword. Lance raised his hand and fired a beam of light that struck Pyro in the back, making him stumble. Lance charged forward, throwing another punch, catching Pyro in the cheek. He stumbled back, seeing stars and Lance kicked Pyro's knee out, making him howl in pain as it buckled, dropping him to the floor. Lance stomped down, but Pyro rolled away, rose and threw a punch at Lance. He caught Pyro's wrist and wrenched it to the side, making Pyro flip over Lance and he hit the floor with a loud thud. Pyro groaned and Lance walked up to the Sword of Light.

'Finally,' he breathed, a grin forming across his face. He reached down and picked up the sword. The blade glowed and the golden armour formed around Lance's body.

'Welcome back, Lance. I knew you would get the sword back,' Apollo said in his mind.

'Hello, Apollo,' Lance replied in his mind. He sheathed the sword and continued down the tunnel, looking to find his way out, leaving Pyro behind.

CHAPTER 37

'Gabrielle!' Theo yelled, running through the tunnels, but there was no answer back. 'Damn, I think I lost her.'

'Don't worry, Theo,' Horace said in Theo's mind. 'You will find her.'

Theo nodded, stopping.

'I think you need to find your brothers and get away from here,' Horace said.

'Yeah, I think so too. Hopefully, I'll find her along the way,' Theo replied.

Theo slid the Sword of Time into the scabbard on his hip, the armour disappearing around him, and ran back down the way he had come. He turned a corner and ran into someone; they both fell to the ground. Theo scrambled to his feet, preparing for battle one once again, but Nicholas stood up in front of him.

'Run!' Nicholas cried, terror on his face.

'Wait, why?' Theo asked.

'Just run!' Nicholas screamed, running past Theo and disappearing around the corner.

'What's up with him?' Theo pondered, then his eyes widened in realisation. 'Wait, I dreamed this.'

Theo turned, knowing what we would be behind him, and the

Basilisk slithered down the hall towards him.

'Oh, my dreams are coming true. They are the future,' he sighed, turned and ran, following the direction Nicholas had gone. He turned the corner and drew the Sword of Time and looked back and the Basilisk was still behind him. He cursed, turning and froze time.

I should be able to get away. With this sword power boost, I can freeze time much longer now, Theo thought, then turned and ran through the labyrinth, getting away from the Basilisk. He continued to run until he felt he was far enough away from the snake. He unfroze time and sheathed the sword again.

'Alright, now I have to find the others and get out of here,' he mumbled. 'But I feel like there was something more in dreams.'

He ran down the hall, not noticing the vine that ran across the floor until he stood on it. He cursed again, remembering what it was in his dream as the vine sprang to life and wrapped around his ankle, tearing him off his feet and dragging him up the wall and into the darkness of a small gap above. Theo clawed at the ground, trying to find something to grab, to stop the vines from pulling him further into the abyss. Suddenly, the vine began to slow and curl further up his leg and around his body, pinning his arms to his side until the tunnel opened up into a small room.

Where am I? he thought. He looked around and spotted a large plant in the centre of the room and noticed all the vines came from its centre mass.

That must be the plant that controls these vines, I need to get free of these vines.

Theo struggled against the vines and tried to move his arm and grab the Sword of Time.

'Come on,' Theo growled in frustration. Suddenly, he felt the hilt of the sword.

He wrapped his hand around the hilt of the sword and his armour formed around his body, stretching the vines, causing them to snap, freeing Theo. He stood up and the floor beneath him began to crack.

This floor isn't stable, Theo thought, balancing himself.

Vines rose around the room and shot towards Theo. He dodged the first two and sliced through the next three that came at him. Then he ran at the plant in the centre, the floor cracking beneath each step, then he jumped and sliced down with the sword, cleaving the plant clean in two. The floor cracked again and gave way with the force of Theo's slash. Theo and the plant fell through. Theo landed in another room, hitting the floor hard, but his armour protected him from any injury. Theo groaned, standing up. He looked down at the two slices of the plant, the vines not moving. He shrugged, turning and running down the closest tunnel.

***

Norman slowly stood up and Gale walked towards him, his four cutlasses floating around him.

'Hello, Gale,' Norman greeted. 'When did you get here?'

A look of anger crossed Gale's face.

'I have been here the whole time!' Gale growled.

'Have you?' Norman replied. 'I didn't even notice.'

Gale clenched his fists.

'See, this is why I left your training. This is why I hate you!'

'No, Gale, you left because you were weak.'

Gale screamed in anger and threw his hand at Norman and the four cutlasses sped straight for Norman, but Norman raised his hand and the cutlasses stopped in the air.

'Ah, Gale, you know that's not going to work,' Norman chastised.

The cutlasses rotated in the air and pointed back towards Gale. Norman flicked his wrist and the cutlasses flew towards Gale, but he threw his hands to the side and a burst of air blew the cutlasses to the side. Norman raised his hands in Gale's direction and Gale felt an invisible force begin to wrap around his body. He cursed and as Norman pulled his hand back, the invisible force pulled Gale off his feet and threw him across the room and Gale hit the far wall with a thud, crumpling to the ground. Then Norman picked Gale again and pulled him towards him. Gale concentrated as he flew and a ball of concentrated air formed in front of him and when the ball touched Norman, it exploded outwards, sending Norman and Gale flying backwards. Norman was first to his feet and he reached out with his telekinesis and picked Gale up off the floor again and pulled Gale towards him again and Norman extended his arm out, swinging it as Gale flew past, clotheslining Gale, making him flip and land with a loud thud. Gale groaned and Norman picked Gale up again with his telekinesis and threw him across the room, where he impacted the wall again with a loud thud and crumpled to the ground again. Norman laughed in amusement, walking towards Gale, picking up one of the cutlasses as he passed.

'I hate to do this, Gale,' Norman said, a tinge of regret in his voice. 'You had potential, but you were always so arrogant and didn't care about what's important.'

Norman raised the cutlass above Gale, ready to strike him down, but suddenly Gale leapt back to his feet, a spinning orb of air in his hand and he thrust the orb into Norman's stomach.

'Take this, old man!' Gale screeched and Norman howled in pain as the ball expanded, grinding into Norman's body, then the orb exploded in a maelstrom of swirling air that sent Norman flying back, cutlass flying from his hand and bouncing across the floor. Norman groaned, getting back to his hand and knees.

'You were saying, old man?' Gale laughed, raising his hand and his four cutlasses rose off the ground and surrounded him.

'It's time to show you the one thing you wouldn't let me create,' Gale announced, drawing the two poles from the small of his back. He locked the two poles together, pressing the button and the two ends extended out, the locking mechanism for the cutlasses at one end. The four cutlasses slide into each mechanism, locking into place, creating his unique blade staff. Norman slowly made his way to his feet and his eyes widened.

'You actually made that thing?' Norman said, shocked.

'Yes, I did,' Gale replied. 'And it is going to be the end of you.'

Suddenly a stream of darkness came flying from one of the tunnels, striking Gale in the stomach, making him fly backwards.

'What was that?' Norman exclaimed and Dylan ran into the room, the armour of darkness and the Sword of Darkness in his hand.

'The Sword of Darkness!' Norman gasped.

Gale scrambled back to his feet, picking up his blade staff.

'What the hell?' Gale bellowed. 'What gives you the right to come barging in here and knocking me down? You must be Dylan, considering your power.'

'Yeah, that's me,' Dylan replied, nodding. 'And you helped take something from us so I thought it would be a good idea to knock you down. I am assuming that you are Gale.'

'Another one being told about me,' Gale laughed.

'What's so funny?'

'You and your brothers.'

Dylan's face darkened and darkness began to swirl around Dylan. 'Say that again,' Dylan growled.

'You and your brothers are a joke!' Gale yelled to Dylan.

This made Dylan roar in anger and sent a mass of darkness at Gale. Gale laughed and blocked the darkness with a wall of air. Gale continued to laugh as he and Dylan began to circle each other.

'You haven't got any chance against me,' Gale challenged.

'Watch me,' Dylan snapped back. 'I've already beaten one of your friends.'

'Oh really? I believe you will find that I am much different than the others.' Gale laughed. He suddenly shot forward, using the air to propel him forward, swinging his blade staff and Dylan brought up his sword and the two blades clashed.

'Nice reaction,' Gale congratulated and the air between them rippled. Dylan was blasted off his feet from a pulse of air.

'But not good enough,' Gale laughed.

Dylan stood, face contorted in rage, darkness now swirled around him and began to absorb into his body.

'Be careful, Dylan. With the amount of darkness that you absorb, you can't lose control,' Heolster said in Dylan's mind.

Dylan ignored Heolster and he ran at Gale, masses of darkness surrounding his fists. Gale chuckled, shaking his head and sent a blast of air that knocked Dylan back again. Then Gale and Dylan were knocked off their feet by an invisible force.

'You boys didn't forget about me, now, did you?' Norman called, walking forward. Dylan looked up and his eyes widened.

'You are Norman,' he exclaimed in shock.

'Indeed, I am, my boy. Now, hand over that sword to me,' Norman commanded.

'Not going to happen,' Dylan replied, preparing himself.

Gale stood up and pointed his staff at Norman. 'Stay out of this old man,' he commanded.

'Oh, but I can't do that. That is what I'm after,' Norman replied, pointing at the Sword of Darkness.

'Well, neither one of you are going to get it,' Dylan declared.

'Well, it looks like we have reached an impasse,' Norman said.

'It would seem that way,' Gale replied.

'Well, I guess it will come down to who's the strongest then,' Norman said.

They looked at each other, waiting for the first one to strike. Dylan decided he wasn't waiting and attacked first, sending a mass of darkness at each of the other men. Gale laughed and blocked the darkness with a shield of air and Noman redirected the mass with his telekinesis, the mass flying past him. Then Norman blasted Dylan off his feet, then he ran at Dylan as the Sword of Darkness left his hand, but Norman was blasted aside by a blast of air.

'That sword is mine,' Gale announced and ran for the sword, but Dylan sent out a tentacle of darkness that quickly slithered across the floor, wrapping around the hilt of the blade and pulling it back into his grasp, the armour forming again.

'These guys are too strong,' Dylan mumbled to himself. 'How am I going to beat them?'

Dylan looked down at the Sword of Darkness.

'I thought when I took control of this sword, I would be stronger than anyone else.'

Then his eyes widened as an idea formed in his mind.

'Heolster?' Dylan asked in his mind.

'Yes, Dylan?' Heolster replied.

'What is this sword made of?' Dylan asked.

'Pure Darkness, why?' Heolster answered. Dylan smirked to himself.

'No, Dylan, you can't do that. If you do, darkness will corrupt you for good,' Heolster said.

'But it's the only way,' Dylan replied, raising the Sword of Darkness in front of him.

'Dylan, you can't do this,' Heolster exclaimed.

'Well, I'm going to do it anyway. It is the only way to beat these two,' Dylan replied, the armour disappearing.

'Dylan, no!' Heolster exclaimed, but Dylan didn't listen and pressed the Sword of Darkness against his chest and stomach.

Dylan howled in pain as the Sword of Darkness sank into his body and was absorbed. Darkness erupted out of Dylan's body, like a wave, knocking Norman and Gale off their feet. The darkness then retracted and surrounded Dylan, as he hunched over, still howling in pain, forming a cocoon around him.

'What has he done?' Norman questioned, looking over at Dylan.

'What the hell is going on?' Gale exclaimed, looking over at Norman.

The cocoon pulsed and the colour of the darkness began to change from black to a blood-red. The cocoon pulsed again and exploded out, sending dust and debris everywhere. The dust settled and was standing in the middle of the settling dust was Dylan, black lines covering his skin. He looked up and his eyes were completely black, blood-red darkness beginning to swirl around him.

'So much power,' Dylan mumbled, looking down at his hands, the black lines on his skin where his veins were.

'Hey, where did the sword go?' Gale yelled at Dylan, but Dylan ignored him, still looking down at his hand.

'Hey, I'm talking to you!' Gale yelled angrily, taking a step toward Dylan. Then suddenly a blood-red mass struck Gale in the chest, sending him flying back and he hit the wall hard and crumpled to the ground.

'So much power,' Dylan mumbled again and he began to laugh.

'He has become a lot stronger now,' Norman mumbled. 'What is this new form though?'

Dylan turned towards Norman, blood-red darkness swirling around him.

'Your turn,' Dylan laughed. Blood-red darkness flew from Dylan at Norman, but Norman smirked and raised his hand, using his power to redirect the darkness, but the darkness wouldn't redirect and continued towards Norman.

'What the…?' was all Norman said before the blood-red darkness struck him, sending him back, head over heels. Norman tumbled across the floor and hit the rock wall behind him. Dylan laughed.

'This power – this form – is amazing,' Dylan muttered, flexing his fingers.

Norman groaned and stood up. *Why didn't my telekinesis work?* Norman thought. *Has he become so powerful that other powers don't work on him now?*

Suddenly there was a loud rumble.

'What now?' Norman signed, turning to the tunnel from which the rumbling was coming from and Adam ran into the room.

'Adam!' Norman exclaimed, waving Adam over to him.

'Sir!' Adam replied, running towards Norman.

'What's going on?' Norman asked as Adam joined him.

'That!' Adam replied, pointing behind him and a giant shake head appeared from the tunnel.

'A Basilisk!' Norman exclaimed in shock and horror.

'Yes, sir. Our powers don't work on it either,' Adam said. 'I tried.'

Dylan turned as the Basilisk reared up in front of him, hissing at him.

'A giant snake?' he questioned, then he smirked. 'Time to test what I can now do.'

CHAPTER 38

Pyro groaned and rolled onto his back, breathing heavily.

'Man, I've got to stop underestimating those brothers,' he mumbled. 'They are stronger than they look.'

He sat up, rubbing his head.

'Especially the one who controls light.'

Pyro stood and looked around.

'Better find my swords,' he grinned and ran the way Lance had gone.

***

Terra sat in the underground, dirt, rocks and other detritus surrounding her, her eyes closed, concentrating on the vibrations in the earth around her.

'Hmmm, there is a lot of activity coming from over there. That must be where the Basilisk is, but there are others there too – about four people by the feel of it. Looks like that is happening in Gale's room,' she muttered to herself. 'And it seems that everyone else is heading in that direction, except for one…'

Terra opened her eyes, the earth opening up above her and she rose up into the tunnel above, finding Assana walking ahead of her.

'Assana!' Terra called.

Assana turned to face Terra. 'Terra, where did you come from?' Assana asked, walking up to Terra.

Terra sighed and pointed down at the ground.

'Ah, of course,' Assana shrugged. 'I can't believe you unleashed the Basilisk. I thought Pyro said only in extreme circumstances.'

'This is an extreme circumstance,' Terra replied, annoyance crossing her face.

'How so?'

'Well, there's more than just us and those brothers down here now.'

'What? Who?'

'I think it is Norman Quinzel and whomever he has brought with him.'

'Well, Pyro's whole plan has turned to shit.'

Terra nodded, looking away and down one of the tunnels.

'Where is Pyro?' Assana asked.

'I'm not sure, but everyone else seems to be heading for Gale's room,' Terra replied, turning back to Assana.

'Well, that is where we go too,' Assana replied, determination crossing her face. She turned to run down one of the tunnels but then she stopped and turned back to Terra. 'And which way do I go exactly?'

'This way,' Terra grumbled with a sigh and a shake of her head, walking in the right direction. Assana let out a laugh and followed Terra.

***

Gabrielle turned a corner and stopped, bending over to catch her breath, tears rolling down her cheek.

'I can't believe him,' she sobbed, standing up straight and wiping the tear away. 'I have to get out of this nightmare.'

Gabrielle turned and began to run back the way she came, trying to remember the turns she had taken to get there. She turned a corner and looked down the tunnel.

This looks familiar, she thought. She continued down the tunnel until she spotted someone up ahead of her.

'Hey!' she called out. 'What are you doing down here?'

She walked towards them and they turned, Glacia looking Gabrielle up and down.

'Who are you?' Glacia growled, her piercing blue eyes looking at Gabrielle.

Gabrielle opened her mouth to reply but she stopped, remembering something that Norman had told her.

'Never tell anyone who you are until you know they are trustworthy,' he had said.

'Who am I?' Gabrielle asked in response. 'That's none of your business.'

'Why are you here?' Glacia asked, her temper starting to bubble over. Gabrielle eyed her but didn't answer. Glacia's eyes narrowed and blades of ice formed in her clenched fists.

'Ice?' Gabrielle questioned.

'I can't let you pass,' Glacia warned, raising the blades threateningly. Electricity began to arc around Gabrielle's fingers. Glacia grunted and then charged forward at Gabrielle.

***

Lance down ran the tunnel, the welcome feeling of the Sword of Light bouncing against his back.

'Dylan? Nicholas? Theo?' he yelled. 'Where could they be?'

Then he heard a voice ahead of him.

'Hello? Is anyone there?' he yelled.

'Lance? Is that you?' came Theo's voice from around the corner. Lance ran around it and Theo was standing there, waiting for him.

'Theo!' Lance exclaimed.

'Good to see you again, Lance,' Theo replied, nodding to his brother. 'I see you got the Sword of Light back.'

Lance nodded with a grin, then he looked down and saw the hilt of the sword strapped to Theo's hip.

'Is that the Sword of Time?' Lance asked in awe.

'Yeah, it is,' Theo replied with his own grin. 'Norman Quinzel is here.'

'Really?'

'Yeah, so we have to get out of here.'

'I agree, we need to find the others and go.'

'Right, then let's go and find the others and go,' Theo replied, nodding to Lance and they set off.

***

The Basilisk hissed and Dylan laughed, the blood-red darkness swirling and coiling around him.

'You don't scare me,' Dylan laughed and he sent streams of red darkness at the Basilisk.

'That won't work,' Adam said to Norman as they watched. 'Powers don't affect that monster.'

'I wouldn't be so sure about that,' Norman replied, pointing as the darkness struck the beast, driving it back with a hiss of anger.

'How did he do that?' Adam whispered in shock.

'He is a lot stronger with that red darkness. I can't use my telekinesis against him with it,' Norman replied.

The Basilisk rose again and opened its mouth, a glow forming deep in its throat and a stream of fire burst out of its mouth, straight at Dylan. Dylan smirked, blocking the fire with a wall of red darkness, then the wall changed into a sickle-like wave and he threw it at the side of the Basilisk's face, slicing through its skin, spilling hot blood across the floor, causing it to hiss in pain and thrash about, hitting the walls.

'That thing has to be taken out before it crushes us all from all that thrashing,' Adam said.

'I agree, Adam, and I have a plan,' Norman replied.

'What are you thinking?' Adam asked.

'I want you to bring the roof down on it,' Norman commanded.

'You got it, sir.' Adam nodded and ran in the direction of the Basilisk.

'What are you doing?' Dylan growled as Adam ran past him.

'Helping you,' Adam called over his shoulder as he ran.

'I don't need your help,' Dylan called back.

'Everyone needs help now and again,' Adam whispered to himself as he stopped, raising his hands towards the roof above the still thrashing Basilisk. Adam concentrated and the roof above began to vibrate, so he pushed harder and suddenly a section of the roof collapsed, large pieces of rock falling onto the Basilisk, squashing parts of its body, pinning it to the ground. It still hissed, having not been killed by the fallen rocks.

'All yours,' Adam said, walking past Dylan and back towards Norman.

Dylan grunted, slowly walking up to the Basilisk. Dylan raised his hands and the blood-red darkness swirled around him, lifting him off the ground and above the beast's head as masses of blood-red darkness surrounded his fists. Dylan suddenly released the darkness that was holding him up and he fell straight down, the masses around his fists changing into large blades. He landed on the Basilisk's head, driving the blades through the top of its head and into its brain, killing it instantly.

'And that's that,' Norman muttered as Adam joined him once again. Dylan leapt off, the blades dissipating.

'Now it's time to take out the rest,' Dylan muttered to himself, then a sharp pain ran through his body.

'What?' he gasped, falling to his knees. Another sharp pain ran through his body and he howled in pain as the red darkness began to change back to black. The Sword of Darkness materialised from Dylan's body and fell to the ground and Dylan fell, face-first, to the ground, breathing heavily.

'What just happened?' Adam asked Norman.

'Clearly, that new power of his only has a time limit,' Norman explained. 'And he has reached his limit.'

'Then he is done, sir?' Adam asked.

'Yes,' Norman smirked. 'We will take that sword now.'

Norman and Adam began to walk towards where Dylan now lay.

'Leave him alone, Father!' Nicholas bellowed as he ran into the room. 'That sword doesn't belong to you!'

'Is that so, my wayward son?' Norman asked with a laugh. 'And who's going to stop me?'

'I will do what I must to protect these brothers, Father, even from you,' Nicholas replied.

'You? I would like to see you try,' Norman laughed.

'I think you are in over your head, Weatherman,' Gale called out as he stood up once again.

'That may be so, but I won't give up,' Nicholas replied. This made Norman laugh.

'I wouldn't expect anything less from you, Nicholas,' Norman said. 'But that won't help you now. I will take that sword and the other two.'

'No, you won't. Not on our watch,' Theo called out as he and Lance ran into the room and stood beside Nicholas.

'Ahahaha, excellent. Now all the swords are here,' Norman laughed. 'It's my lucky day.'

Lance and Theo both drew their swords and their armour shone into existence, ready for battle once again.

'Sir, they now outmatch us,' Adam whispered to Norman.

'I know, Adam,' Norman whispered back. 'Don't worry; this scene will change.' And with that, Pyro ran into the room and Terra rose out of the ground with Assana and they all stood next to Gale.

'Don't worry, we are here,' Pyro exclaimed. 'Now hand over those swords.'

'See, I told you Adam,' Norman whispered.

'So, what's the plan, sir?' Adam whispered back.

'We will let this fight play out and once they are done, we will swoop in and take the swords.'

Adam nodded.

'That isn't going to happen, Pyro,' Nicholas responded.

'Nick, we are outnumbered,' Theo whispered to Nicholas. 'It's four against three and that isn't including Norman and his butler over there.'

'I know, Theo. We need Dylan right now, but I don't think he is fit to fight,' Nicholas whispered back.

'I can fight,' Dylan wheezed, slowly standing up, picking up the Sword of Darkness, the dark armour forming again.

'You sure?' Theo asked, looking at his brother.

'Yeah, the sword is helping,' Dylan breathed.

'Alright, Pyro, if you want these swords, come and get them,' Nicholas challenged.

'Ah, one final battle to decide who gets these swords, is it?' Pyro asked with a laugh.

'It looks to be that way,' Nicholas replied, watching out of the corner of his eyes as Norman and Adam stepped back to the edge is the cavern.

'Are you guys ready?' Nicholas asked the brothers and they all nodded. 'Then let's do this.' And with that, they charged forward at Pyro, Assana, Terra and Gale.

'Time to put an end to this!' Pyro roared. 'Terra! Take them out.'

She nodded, kneeling down and placing her hands on the ground.

'Quickly, everyone, dodge!' Nicholas yelled and they all dodged to the side as pillars of earth shot out of the ground where they all were.

'Damn, Assana?' Pyro cursed and turned to his sister. Assana nodded and streams of water burst forth and flew straight at the brothers. Theo froze time and moved out of the way, restarting time again once he was out of the way and the others blocked the water with each of their own powers.

Pyro cursed again.

'Fine, you all know what to do,' Pyro growled.

Gale raised his hand and his blade staff flew into his hand and they all charged forward and the two teams clashed. Gale and Dylan's blades clashed, Assana sending water at Lance, Theo charging at Terra, and Nicholas and Pyro charging at each other – fire in Pyro's hand and an orb of lightning in Nicholas's hand.

CHAPTER 39

Norman watched as Pyro's and Nicholas's teams clashed, then he turned and walked towards the exit of the room.

'What's going on?' Adam asked, following after Norman.

'We are leaving,' Norman replied.

'Why?' Adam questioned.

'We need to find Gabrielle,' Norman responded. 'By then, they should be finished fighting and we will grab the swords.'

'Sounds like a plan,' Adam nodded. Norman nodded back and they both exited the room.

'Alright, Adam, can you please use your power over vibrations to find Gabrielle?' Norman asked.

Adam nodded, kneeling and placing his hand against the floor. 'Alright. Obviously there are a lot of vibrations coming from the room we just left, but there are some minor vibrations coming from over there.' He stood up and pointed down the left tunnel. 'She must be down there.'

'Ah, good.'

'But she is not alone.'

'She must be battling someone!' Norman exclaimed. They both

turned and ran down the tunnel that Adam had indicated.

'I hope she's okay,' Adam huffed as they ran.

'So do I,' Norman agreed. They turned a corner and the tunnel in front of them split into two.

'Which one, Adam?'

'Left one.' They both took off down that tunnel.

'She's just up ahead,' Adam called out as they turned another corner and that is where they found Gabrielle, electricity crackling around her body, facing off with Glacia.

'Glacia! Gabrielle! Stop it now!' Norman yelled. Glacia's eyes widened in shock.

'Master Norman?' Glacia questioned in confusion. 'Is that you?'

'Master?' Gabrielle and Adam both exclaimed at the same time.

'Hello, Glacia,' Norman replied. 'Would you kindly stop attacking my new apprentice?'

'Oh, of course. I am so sorry,' Glacia replied, stepping away from Gabrielle. 'I had no idea.'

'Hang on. You two know each other?' Gabrielle asked.

'Yes. Glacia here is one of my spies,' Norman replied. 'I assigned her to keep an eye on a group of thieves who had begun to steal ancient artifacts and such. It turned out that it was Pyro and his associates.'

'Wait, you've known about Pyro?' Adam asked.

'Sort of. I didn't know he was going to attack us and neither did Glacia,' Norman replied.

'Nope. He just left out of nowhere, didn't say anything to anyone about where he was going,' Glacia agreed. 'Suddenly, he got intel from someone he calls "Strings" and he was off.'

'Anyway, Glacia, keep doing what I've told you,' Norman said. 'Keep helping Pyro with his ambitions until I tell you otherwise. Sounds good?'

Glacia nodded in response.

'You better go now, they need you,' Norman said.

Glacia nodded again, turning and running down the tunnel Norman and Adam had come from.

'You have spies?' Gabrielle asked.

'A few, yes,' Norman replied.

'Alright, what now?' Adam asked.

'We go back to the entrance,' Norman replied.

'Why?' Adam asked, confused.

'Because whoever has the swords at the end of that battle will try to exit the labyrinth and we will be waiting,' Norman replied.

Adam and Gabrielle nodded and they all set off.

***

Nicholas dodged to the side as Pyro swung his flame-covered fist in his direction and Nicholas thrust his orb of lightning at Pyro, detonated the orb near Pyro, a maelstrom of lightning exploding outwards, but Pyro managed to block most of the lightning with a shield of fire, but the force of the explosion sent Pyro flying across the room. Nicholas turned and sent a blast of powerful wind at Terra, causing her to stumble and distracting her for a second, allowing Theo to tackle her to the ground. They tumbled across the ground until Terra kicked Theo in the chest, sending him off her. They both stood and charged at each other again. Theo swung his sword at her as they got close to one another, but she blocked the slash with a shield of rock then rocks surrounded her fist and she took a swing at him, but Theo froze time. He stepped back and surveyed the area.

'What to do?' he mumbled to himself, then he spotted Assana was sending a stream of water at Lance.

'Perfect,' he mumbled, a grin on his face. He quickly moved Terra in front of the water stream and moved Lance out of the way. Theo smirked, then restarted time and the stream of water struck Terra, sending her flying backwards.

'What the hell?' Assana exclaimed. Theo smirked and Lance threw orbs of light at Assana, but she blocked them with a wall of water. Gale slashed down with his staff and Dylan jumped back, the blades barely missing him, but Gale thrust out his hand and Dylan was blasted off his feet by a pulse of air. He tumbled across the floor until he came to a stop, lying face down and groaning.

'I don't think I can do this much longer,' he muttered as he slowly got back to his hands and knees. Gale smirked as he walked towards him, spinning his staff but Theo froze time, walked up to Gale, unfroze time and punched Gale in the stomach. Gale let out a gasp, the wind being driven out of him and Dylan sent a mass of darkness in Gale, sending him flying back.

'Thanks,' Dylan said as Theo helped him back to his feet.

'Thank me later,' Theo replied. 'We have a fight to win.'

Dylan nodded and turned, spears of darkness forming around him and he flung them at Assana, but she saw them coming, using a wall of water to block the spears.

'You are going to have to do better than that,' Assana teased.

'Oh, we will,' Nicholas said as he sent lightning at her and she dove to the side, avoiding the lightning, but Dylan sent a mass of darkness and Lance sent a beam of light at her. Assana brought up walls of water, blocking the brothers' attacks. Then Nicholas dashed behind Assana and sent a blast of wind into her back, causing her to stumble forward, then Dylan sent a mass of darkness that struck Assana, sending her flying backwards.

'We have to get out of here,' Nicholas exclaimed.

'You're not going anywhere,' Pyro yelled, standing up, flames forming around him.

'Take this!' Pyro yelled and he thrust his hands out, a dome of flames forming around him. It grew and grew until it reached its limit and it exploded, sending flames across the room. Theo stepped forward and froze time, moving out of range of the flames, when Theo restarted time. Lance teleported out of range. Dylan summoned darkness behind him, stepping back into it and disappearing. Nicholas tried to block Pyro's attack with a wall of wind, but the force of the explosion pushed the wall back into Nicholas, sending him tumbling across the room.

Pyro began to laugh, but that quickly stopped when he noticed Lance and Theo still standing. Then darkness rose up behind him and Dylan stepped out. A tentacle of darkness swept Pyro's legs out from under him. Then darkness surrounded Dylan's fist and he brought his fist down into Pyro's stomach in mid-air, slamming Pyro into the ground with such velocity that it knocked him out. Then Dylan raised the Sword of Darkness, ready to deliver the final blow.

'Wait! Dylan, stop!' Lance yelled.

'Why?' Dylan sneered, looking over at his brother, malice in his eyes.

'Because you're not that kind of person!' Lance yelled back at him.

'But this son-of-a-bitch started all this!' Dylan spat, face contorted in rage. 'I don't care what you say, he deserves it!'

Dylan started to bring the sword down over Pyro's neck, but a blast of ice hit Dylan and quickly encased him in ice, the blade stopping inches above Pyro. Glacia then dove at Lance, tackling him to the ground.

'I've seen all this before,' Theo mumbled, frozen in sudden realisation, watching one of his dreams unfold. Lance, caught unprepared, dropped the Sword of Light, his armour dissipating the instant it left his hand. He threw Glacia off him and fired two beams of light at her, both striking her. This lifted Glacia off her feet once again, sending her down the tunnel she had just come from. Lance scrambled back to his feet and snatched up the sword, his golden armour appearing instantly, but before he could do anything, he was struck by a powerful torrent of water, blasting him off his feet and sending him crashing into a wall. Assana walked towards Lance, laughing arrogantly. Suddenly there was a loud crack and the ice encasing Dylan shattered and exploded outwards, sending ice all over the cavern.

'Nothing can stop me,' he whispered, raising his head slowly, eyes darkening as the inky black was absorbed into his body. Assana grinned as she brought it back to her and surrounded her arms. Dylan stepped forward, throwing his arms forward and tendrils of darkness burst forth, spiralling through the air towards Assana.

She dove out of the way, rolled back to her feet and retaliated with a whip of water. He blocked it with a shield of darkness, then dashed forward, swiping at her with his sword. She dodged to the side, then danced in behind him, then rushed at him from behind, ready to tackle him to the ground.

'No!' Theo yelled out, knowing what was going to happen next, but it was too late as spikes erupted from Dylan's armour, impaling Assana. As the spikes retracted, Assana transformed into water and sloshed to the ground.

'A clone?' Dylan questioned before Glacia dove at Dylan, her ice daggers barely missing his neck as he sidestepped her, the sword flashing in the air as the sound of a blade cutting through flesh was heard.

Glacia screamed in pain and anguish as she stared down at the bloody stump at her elbow, the rest of her arm now laying on the ground next to her, blood now dripping from the open wound and she fell to her knees. Dylan kicked her down and was about to finish her off, but a stream of water hit him, sending him stumbling back and the real Assana ran at Dylan, getting him away from Glacia. Glacia gritted her teeth, concentrating through the pain and ice formed over the wound, stopping the bleeding and numbing the pain. Assana leapt at Dylan, water forming in her hands, but Dylan blasted her away with more darkness, sending her tumbling through the air. Glacia stood, turned and walked towards Dylan.

'You're gonna pay for this,' she seethed, holding up the stump.

'Is that right, Stumpy?' Dylan sneered in response.

Glacia screamed in rage and ran at Dylan. He slashed at her with his sword, but she slid under the slash and, as she slid past, she ran her hand along his leg, ice instantly forming. She stood and a new arm and hand of ice formed from her stump. She flexed the fingers and then turned to face Dylan, a war hammer of ice forming in her hands. She swung it into Dylan's chest, sending him across the room, howling in pain. Then she changed the hammer into two blocks of ice and she threw them at him as he stood. Dylan sliced the first block with the sword, but the second struck, sending him staggering back.

'Damn, I'm not strong enough,' he mumbled as Glacia dashed towards him, two curved blades of ice forming in her hands.

'I can't do this,' he mumbled and darkness rose behind him. He stepped back into it and disappeared. Glacia stopped and looked around for him.

'Where did he go?' she growled. 'Coward!'

She turned as darkness rose up near one of the exits and Dylan stepped out and ran out of the room, sheathing the sword.

'Wait, Dylan!' Theo yelled to his brother, but it was too late. He had disappeared into the darkness of the tunnel.

CHAPTER 40

Dylan ran down the tunnel and turned a corner, stopped, leaned against the wall and slowly slid down it, tears forming in his eyes.

I'm not strong enough, he thought, his head in his hands. *How do I get stronger?*

He looked up and around the tunnel.

Maybe they are holding me back. He looked back down the tunnel he had just come from. *I should just leave and find a way to get stronger.*

Dylan stood up, nodding to himself, then he began to look for the exit. He ran down the tunnel, taking a right turn, then a left and then another right and the entrance of the labyrinth appeared up ahead.

'The exit,' he breathed. He ran out into the cavern where the entrance was, but he stopped in his tracks.

'Ah, no,' he mumbled as Norman, Gabrielle and Adam turned to face him.

'Dylan?' Gabrielle questioned, her surprise evident.

'Gabrielle? What are you doing here?' Dylan asked.

'I'm here with Norman,' Gabrielle replied, motioning over to Norman.

'Really?' Dylan questioned with his own surprise.

'Anyway, hello, Dylan,' Norman said, stepping forward.

'What do you want now?' Dylan asked, anger now in his voice.

'Well, in all honesty, I want that sword you have,' Norman replied, pointing at the sword at Dylan's hip.

'Well, that's not happening,' Dylan replied, placing his hand on the sword.

'Calm down,' Norman assured Dylan. 'I don't want to fight you. Where are your brothers?'

'I left them behind,' Dylan replied, looking away in shame.

'Why is that?'

'I panicked and ran.'

'And why did you run?'

'Because I'm not strong enough!'

'Really? You seemed like a strong person to me; I just watched you take down a powerful monster. Also, you're the first person to hit me as full-on as you did in a long time.'

'Really?'

'Yes, Dylan. I see a lot of potential in you.'

'You do?'

'Yes, Dylan, but you still need a lot of work – work I can help you with. I can help you, I can train you, train you to become stronger. Isn't that what you want?'

'Yeah, that's what I want. I want to become stronger.'

'Well, join me then. You've seen who I've trained – like Nicholas and Gale – and you've seen how strong they are,' Norman appealed to Dylan. 'Join me and I will make you as strong as them, if not even stronger.'

Dylan turned away from Norman, unsure what to do.

'This is what you want, Dylan,' Norman appealed. 'I will make you the strongest, even stronger than me. Join me.'

Norman extended his hand. Dylan turned back, looked down at the hand, then up at Gabrielle, who nodded to Dylan, then he looked back at Norman and nodded.

'Alright, I will. I'll join you. Please help make me stronger,' Dylan exclaimed, taking Norman's hand and shaking it.

'Excellent choice,' Norman grinned. 'And don't worry, I'll make you stronger.'

'Thank you,' Dylan replied. 'Are we leaving now?'

'Not quite,' Norman said. 'I need you to do something before we leave.'

'What is it?'

'I need you to go back in there and get the other two swords.'

'But they're my brothers. And I'm not strong enough.'

'Yes, you are. Use that red darkness you have.'

'Fine, I will do it, but can we please leave after I get them?'

'Of course.'

Dylan nodded, turned and ran back into the labyrinth.

***

Glacia turned to face Theo.

'Looks like your brother is a coward,' she mocked.

'Where did he go?' Theo asked in a whisper to himself.

'Hand over that sword,' Glacia commanded.

'No,' Theo replied bluntly.

'And you're going to stop me?' Glacia mocked with a laugh.

'Not just me,' Theo replied, motioning over to Nicholas as he stood and walked over to Theo.

'I will help him,' Nicholas said.

'And I will too,' Lance said, stepping up to the other side of Theo.

'I highly recommend that you give up now,' Nicholas commanded.

'She isn't going to do that,' Assana said as she stepped up next to Glacia.

'Two against three? I still like those odds,' Nicholas laughed.

'Ha, we thrive against odds like that,' Assana laughed. 'Right?'

'Right,' Glacia nodded and they bumped fists.

'Well, let's see how you go with these odds,' Nicholas replied.

Assana nodded and sent two streams of water at the brothers and Nicholas. Lance stepped forward raising his hands and a barrier of light formed around all of them, protecting them from the streams. Theo placed his hand on Nicholas's shoulder and froze time, then they both moved behind Glacia and Assana. Nicholas nodded to Theo and he restarted time. Nicholas flung his arms wide and a pulse of wind blasted Assana and Glacia off their feet. Assana cursed as she rolled across the ground.

'How did they get behind us?' Glacia asked as she rolled back to her feet.

'I think it is that brother in the blue armour. I think he controls time,' Assana said.

'That explains a lot,' Glacia replied.

'As I said before, you two should give up. You are outclassed.' Nicholas laughed.

'Glacia! Assana! Stop!'

Everyone turned and Terra walked towards them.

'He is right. We can't win this one,' she exclaimed. 'We are too exhausted to battle anymore.'

Assana and Glacia both looked at Terra in shock but quickly realised that she was right and they both slumped in exhaustion and they stepped back, joining Terra.

'Fine, I will admit I'm beaten,' Assana sighed.

Nicholas and Theo walked over and joined Lance.

'Alright, we give up. You win,' Terra said. 'We are going to leave now.'

'We are?' Glacia asked.

'Yes, we are,' Terra replied with a growl. 'Grab those other two.'

Glacia and Assana walked over to Pyro and Gale, picking them up with their powers and bringing them over to where Terra stood.

'Alright, we are going to leave now,' Terra exclaimed. 'But I promise that we will be back to get those swords.'

'And we will stop you then,' Nicholas replied.

Terra snorted and the ground beneath them opened up and Terra, Assana, Glacia and the unconscious Pyro and Gale began to descend into the ground.

'We will be back,' Terra said again and they all disappeared into the ground.

'Well, that's the end of that,' Lance said in relief.

'Yeah, but where is Dylan?' Nicholas asked.

'He ran off,' Theo replied, anger in his voice.

'What?' Nicholas asked in shock.

'He was getting beaten, so he ran,' Theo replied, sheathing his sword and crossing his arms.

'Well, we have to find him and get out of here,' Nicholas replied.

'Alright,' Lance nodded and the brothers turned and started to walk away when there was a strange sound and Nicholas gurgling. Lance and Theo turned around and gasped. Nicholas was standing there, looking down at the three blades of darkness that protruded from his stomach and he fell to his knees and then face-first to the ground, revealing Dylan behind him, blades protruding from his hand.

'Dylan?' Theo questioned in shock.

'Hello, boys,' Dylan replied with an evil grin on his face.

'What the hell have you done?' Theo exclaimed.

'I have done something we should have done at the Grampians.' Dylan snarled.

'What? You're joking right?' Theo replied, his anger beginning to bubble to the surface.

'Why would I joke?' Dylan asked with a shrug.

'Why are you doing this?' Lance yelled at his brother.

'Because I want the swords,' Dylan replied, pointing to the blades.

'Not going to happen after this sick display!' Theo snarled. 'You've become power hungry just like Pyro and Norman, our enemies!'

'There's nothing wrong with Norman,' Dylan replied with a shrug.

'You bastard! You've joined Norman!' Theo roared in outrage, realising what his brother had done in his brief time away from them.

'So, what if I did?' Dylan replied with another shrug. 'What are you going to do about it?'

Lance fired a beam of light that struck Dylan, sending him flying back. Dylan rolled back to his feet, drawing the Sword of Darkness with a snarl and he placed it on his chest. He howled in pain as the sword absorbed into his body and a cocoon of darkness formed.

'Theo, heal Nicholas with your powers,' Lance commanded as the cocoon pulsed and changed into a blood-red colour and it split open, revealing Dylan with black eyes and black lines covering his body and blood-red darkness swirled around him.

'What have you become, Dylan?' Lance asked in shock.

'Stronger than you can possibly imagine,' Dylan grinned. Theo knelt next to Nicholas and he began to reverse time around Nicholas's wound. It began to close up, the blood going back into his body and the skin returning to normal and Nicholas groaned.

'Stay down, Nick,' Theo said to him. 'You've been hurt.'

Theo stood up and joined Lance.

'You two can't beat me, not now,' Dylan said with a laugh.

'We will,' Theo growled and he froze time, but Dylan just laughed.

'What?' Theo exclaimed in shock.

'Your powers don't affect me now,' Dylan explained with an evil laugh and he threw a mass of red darkness into Theo, sending him flying back, breaking the time stop. Lance fired a beam of light at Dylan, but he just blocked it with his arm.

Lance stood there in shock and Dylan smirked. Spears of red darkness materialised above him and he threw them at Lance. Lance formed a barrier of light to block the spears, but the spears smashed through the barrier and continued straight at Lance. He quickly dove to the side but one spear caught Lance in the shoulder, smashing through the armour and sending him spinning back, howling in pain. The spear disappeared, causing Lance to cry out again, blood dripping down his arms and chest.

'Lance! Use your light to heal yourself!' Apollo exclaimed in Lance's mind.

'I can do that?' Lance replied.

'Yes, you can,' Apollo replied. 'Here's how to do it.'

Suddenly, images flashed in Lance's mind and he summoned an orb of light in his hand and applied it to his shoulder and the wound began to heal.

'Cool,' Lance breathed, standing up and rolling his shoulders.

'I told you that you can't beat me, Lance,' Dylan laughed.

Lance didn't reply and clenched his fists, orbs of light forming around them.

'Why are you doing this, Dylan?' Lance asked again. 'And don't give me the bullshit about the swords; it's not about them. It's something else.'

'You really want to know?' Dylan asked. 'I want power and the only way I am going to get that is to join Norman and have him train me because you are all holding me back.'

Lance sighed, shaking his head.

'Pathetic,' Lance sighed and he thrust his fists in Dylan's direction. The orbs flew off his fists and sped straight at Dylan. Lance then splayed his fingers and the two orbs burst into six smaller orbs each. Dylan just stood there, a grin on his face, and all the orbs struck him, exploding on impact, but they didn't affect Dylan whatsoever.

'No, you know what's pathetic?' Dylan yelled. 'YOU!'

And a pillar of blood-red darkness shot out from under Lance, knocking him into the air, then Dylan propelled himself into the air and sent a mass of red darkness into Lance, slamming him to the ground, the armour protecting him from any damage. Dylan landed next to Lance, a blade of red darkness forming in his hand.

'This is your end,' he announced in triumph, raising the blade above Lance, but suddenly a pain ran through his body.

'No, not now,' Dylan breathed as he stumbled back from Lance, clutching his chest. Then he fell to his knees with a scream of pain and the Sword of Darkness formed and fell from his body and Dylan fell to the ground, unconscious.

'What the hell?' Lance mumbled as he stood, watching Dylan closely, then there was a hand on his shoulder.

'You alright, Lance?' Theo asked.

'I think so,' Lance replied. 'Well, except for our brother betraying us.'

'Guess it is time to leave then,' Theo said.

'Yeah, but what about Dylan?' Lance asked.

'He betrayed us; he can stay here for all I care. I don't want anything to do with him. He tried to kill our friend so he can rot down here or his new friends can come and get him!' Theo growled as he walked over to Nicholas and placed his hand on him. 'Can you walk?' Theo asked.

'Yeah,' Nicholas replied with a nod and Theo helped him to his feet.

Nicholas walked over to Dylan and picked up the Sword of Darkness.

'I don't think he deserves this,' Nicholas said, touching the spot where Dylan had stabbed him. 'And it can't fall into Norman's hands.'

'I agree with that,' Lance agreed.

'Alright, let's get out of here,' Nicholas said, taking the scabbard off Dylan's body and they all walked out of the room. Fifteen minutes, they were outside.

Theo had frozen time around them so when they had walked outside, Norman was standing next to his limousine, staring back at the warehouse, clearly waiting for Dylan. Adam was already in the driver seat of the car and Gabrielle was nowhere to be seen. They all hopped into Theo's car and he started the engine and as he drove off, he restarted time.

***

Norman turned as Theo's car shed off down the street and out of sight. Norman cursed as Gabrielle got out of the limousine.

'That was them, wasn't it?' she asked.

'Yes. They must have used the time manipulation to get past us,' Norman replied.

'What about Dylan?' Gabrielle asked.

'He must be still down there,' Norman replied, beginning to walk towards the warehouse. 'Wait here. I will go get him.'

Ten minutes later, he walked into the room where the battle between the brothers and Pyro's group had taken place and that is where Norman found Dylan lying face down, unconscious.

'Dylan!' Norman exclaimed as he ran over to Dylan and performed a quick medical examination.

'He is alright, just exhausted,' Norman muttered to himself. 'And he has lost the sword.'

Norman cursed as he stood, lifting Dylan up with his telekinesis and they began to leave, Dylan floating behind him.

CHAPTER 41

Kate pulled into her driveway and turned off her car.

'What a day,' she muttered to herself. She had been at the university all day and been through three lectures and spent the rest of her time doing research. She opened the door and stepped out of her car and went inside the house.

'Hey, Dad,' she called out as she walked inside.

'Hello, sweetheart,' her dad replied. 'How was your day?'

'Long,' Kate replied, starting up the stairs. 'I'll be back, Dad, just going to get changed.'

Kate walked up the stairs and went straight into her room, dropping her bag and kicking off her shoes, and quickly changed into a pair of faded jeans and a Star Wars t-shirt.

'That's better,' she sighed, content. Then she felt something on her hand. She looked down and there was a green blob in the palm of her hand.

'What's that?' she mumbled. 'Eh, just something off my car.'

She wiped the blob on her desk and went back downstairs.

'What's for dinner, Dad?' she asked as she walked into the kitchen.

'I'm just making some spaghetti bolognese,' her dad replied.

'Cool,' she replied. 'I'll set the table.'

'Thank you,' he replied.

After a nice dinner, Kate went back to her room to study for the test that she had the next day. She opened her door and instantly smelt something funny.

'What's that smell?' she mumbled and looked around her room, trying to locate the source of the smell, then she turned to face her desk and there were small wisps of smoke rising from where she had wiped the green goo earlier. She walked over to the desk and examined a hole burned through the wood.

'Oh, shit,' she mumbled, grabbed a couple of tissues and wiped at whatever was left of the blob but it started to burn the tissue.

It's acid, I think, she thought, throwing it down into the bin and looking down at her hand.

If it is acid, then how didn't it burn my hand? she questioned, then she gasped as more of the green goo began to bead up in the palm of her hand.

What the hell is going on?

She walked out of her room, downstairs and out into their backyard.

'Where is this acid coming from?' she mumbled and she thrust her hand out. A stream of acid flew from her hand and landed on one of the garden gnomes and it instantly began to melt, the acid eating it down to nothing.

'Oh my god, it's coming from me!' she exclaimed in excitement. She looked down at her hands and smiled. 'I have superpowers,' she whispered. 'I must be able to produce acid.'

For the next hour, Kate stayed out in the backyard, using her power, learning to use it and control it until she was exhausted.

'Powers take it out of you,' she mumbled, walking back inside and back up to her room.

'I think it is time for some sleep,' she muttered sleepily.

***

The next morning, she woke up and quickly got dressed, sent a quick text to Nicholas, grabbed her bag and walked downstairs.

'Morning, Dad,' she exclaimed.

'Morning. How'd you sleep?' he replied as he put his shoes on, about to head off to work.

'Fine,' Kate replied.

'That's good. Don't forget, you've got to stop and check Norman's house.'

'Yeah, I know, Dad.'

'Good. I'll see you tonight.'

'Alright, Dad.'

He kissed her on the cheek and left for work. Kate quickly made herself some breakfast and left the house, locking the door behind her. She drove around to Norman's house. She pulled into the street and instantly knew something was wrong. As she got closer, she noticed the steel entrance gates were wide open.

Why are they open? she thought. *Norman shouldn't be home yet.*

She drove through the gates and up the driveway, pulled up at the entrance door and got out of her car. She fished the keys out of her pocket and walked up to the doors, but they were slightly open.

I think someone might be here, she thought. Kate edged the door opened and peeked inside.

No one there. She stepped inside and walked into the lobby. Then she felt something brush against her leg. She looked down and a strand of string was there.

String? she questioned, when suddenly the string snapped tight, coming to life and wrapping around her ankles and up her leg until it pulled her off her feet and more string wrapped around her body, pinning her arms to her side. Then she heard footsteps and someone shouting.

'Finally! Finally! Someone to play with!'

Kate watched upside down as a woman with blue and red hair slid down the banister of the stairs and skipped up to where Kate hung.

'Hi, I am Magna,' she introduced herself, extending her hand. 'Oh, wait, you're a little tied up for that.'

Kate struggled against the string, but it was strong.

'You won't get out of them,' Magna laughed. 'My babe's strings are too strong to break.'

'Your babe?' Kate questioned.

'Yeah, he's up in the library looking for particular books.'

'You're here for a book?'

'Yep.'

Kate cleared her mind like she had been taught by her martial arts teacher. She focused and she felt the acid form in the palm of her hand. She moved her hand up to some of the strings and the acid began to eat through the string until she felt the strings loosen. She stumbled to her feet, the strings falling off her.

'How did you get out of that?' Magna asked in shock.

'With this,' Kate exclaimed, thrusting her hands at Magna and acid burst from her hand, going straight for Magna.

'Oh, you have powers,' Magna laughed as she raised her hands.

Metal in the room flew from their places and surrounded Magna, protecting her from the acid.

'You are going to be more fun than I thought,' Magna laughed, a silver dinner tray melting from the acid. 'Oh, acid.'

'Magna, stop now!' came a voice, making Kate and Magna turn as a tall, rather thin man with light brown hair, wearing curved sunglasses with blue lenses descended down the stairs, a book and two scrolls under his arms.

'Would you put Mister Quinzel's belongings back where they were?' he commanded.

'Okay, babe,' Magna grumbled and all the objects returned to their place, except for the now-melted dinner tray.

'Sorry for all this. I'm Dexter,' he exclaimed. 'And you must be Kate.'

'How do you know my name?' Kate asked in confusion.

'Oh, that's easy. We work for a secret government project,' Dexter replied with a slight shrug. 'We research people with powers and the reason I know who you is that you are linked to Mister Quinzel.'

'Why are you here then?' Kate asked. 'Why are you taking these things?'

'Well, they are for our research and we have tried to get them from Mister Quinzel before, but he wouldn't cooperate so I got this warrant'— Dexter held up a warrant—'to search this place and retrieve these.'

'Oh, okay. Guess I can't stop you then,' Kate sighed.

'I see you have powers. How long have you known about your powers?' Dexter asked.

'Actually, I only discovered them last night,' Kate replied.

'So you wouldn't have much control then?' Dexter asked.

'Not really,' Kate replied.

'See, at our facility, we train people like us and offer them jobs,' Dexter replied. 'If you want, you can come around to our facility and we could not only help you with controlling your power but also offer you a job helping us.'

'I can't right now, Dexter,' Kate replied. 'I have to go to uni today, but I can come around after I finish this afternoon.'

'Alright, Kate, here is my card. Call me when you are coming,' Dexter replied, handing her a business card. 'Come on, Magna, we're leaving.'

'Yay,' Magna exclaimed and they walked out of Norman's house. Kate looked down at the card and grinned.

***

After Kate had finished at university, she rang Dexter and he told her the address of the facility. She drove to the address and pulled up to a shabby, run-down looking warehouse.

'This doesn't seem right, but this is the address,' she mumbled. She got out of her car and walked up to the door of the warehouse and pressed a button next to the door. Suddenly, the door swung open and Dexter was standing there, waiting for her.

'Welcome, Kate,' he said with a grin.

'Thank you,' she replied.

'Follow me,' he said.

Dexter walked into an elevator behind him and she joined him. Dexter pressed a button and the elevator began its descent down until it came to a stop and they walked out into a large lobby with multiple doors on either side. They walked past all the doors to the end of the lobby and into a corridor, turning right and following the corridor until Dexter stopped at a door.

'Alright, in you go. This is one of my bosses. He'll tell you more,' Dexter explained.

'Thank you,' Kate replied, opening the door and stepping inside. She looked around at the lab behind.

'His office is at the back,' Dexter said as he turned and left Kate to it. The lab was a large room with benches around the edges and a long table up the middle and the tables held a whole range of different medical equipment and science equipment. She walked to the door and knocked.

'Come in,' came a male voice.

Kate opened the door and stepped into an office and found a man with short dark hair and glasses sitting behind a desk, looking at a computer screen. He looked up at her and smiled.

'Ah, Kate, welcome,' he said. 'Please take a seat.'

Kate sat down.

'Alright. My name is Cameron Blackburn. Before we make this official, are you sure this is what you want to do?' Cameron asked.

'Yeah, I think so,' Kate replied with a nod. 'I want to control this power I have.'

'Okay. Your name is Kate Ryan, correct?'

'Yes,'

'And your father is Sebastian Ryan?' Cameron asked, beginning to type on his computer.

Kate nodded.

'And your boyfriend is Nicholas Quinzel?'

Kate nodded again.

'Are you aware that Nicholas has powers also?'

'Wait, what?'

'Yes, he goes around the world doing certain missions with his powers for Norman Quinzel.'

'I had no idea. He never told me.'

'And so he shouldn't. This can be a dangerous world we are in – he was just protecting you. I hope you understand.'

'I do understand and it makes sense.'

'That is good, Kate. I don't want to be the cause of any friction.'

Kate nodded.

'Anyway, back to it. Now, what are your powers?'

'Acid, I think,' Kate replied, holding up her hand and showing Cameron the green blob in her palm.

'Interesting,' he said. 'Well, that is everything I need. You are now an employee here.'

'So, what do I do exactly?'

'Not much to start with – you will mostly be training with your powers with either Dexter or myself and doing small jobs around here, but once you are ready, you will start going out on missions with others.'

'Right, sounds good.'

'And you will get paid well and we will cover your university fees from now on,' Cameron said, standing and extending his hand to Kate. 'Welcome to the Meta-Human Project.'

'Thank you,' Kate replied, also standing and shaking Cameron's hand.

CHAPTER 42

Theo turned off the tap and looked up at himself in the mirror, touching the remnants of the jagged cut on his cheek.

'Why?' he mumbled to himself, remembering Gabrielle's attack that had created the cut.

It had been two days since the labyrinth and they all were still recovering from the ordeal. After they had got home, they had completely cleaned the house, repairing any damage that was done and Nicholas had purchased a new TV to replace the broken one. After that, Nicholas had moved into Dylan's room for the time being. Then they had rung their mother, informing her that Dylan had to leave abruptly to go to Japan to wrestle, telling her that he was required earlier than expected and he had to go straight away. She had been upset but also understood that she would contact him as soon as she could as she was busy with her work and they told his girlfriend, Kelsey, the same thing when she called around, looking for him.

Theo walked out of the bathroom and into Dylan's old room, finding Nicholas lying on the bed.

'Ah, Theo,' he said, sitting up.

'Can we talk?' Theo asked.

'Of course,' Nicholas replied, motioning to the office chair. Theo nodded and sat down in the chair. 'What's up?' Nicholas asked.

'I am done,' Theo replied.

'You're done? Done with what?' Nicholas asked, confusion crossing his face.

'I'm done with all this, this world of powers and monsters. I want to go back to my normal life before all this started,' Theo stated. 'I didn't want this and after everything that happened in that labyrinth, I am done with it all.'

'I understand you are hurt, Theo, but that isn't a reason to quit,' Nicholas replied, spinning his legs off the bed and onto the floor so he was facing Theo directly.

'Actually, it is. After seeing my now ex-girlfriend and brother betray me and join your father, my heart was broken twice in mere hours. If that's what I get for using my powers and being a part of this world, then I want no part of it at all,' Theo replied solemnly.

'But Theo, you were born to belong in this world,' Nicholas pleaded.

'I will be honest, Nick. I don't care anymore. I just need to do this, alright? I need to be normal again,' Theo replied, standing and exiting the room, leaving Nicholas in stunned silence.

***

Dylan nodded to Adam and sat down in the limousine, sitting next to Gabrielle.

'You are going to love Norman's mansion, it is amazing,' Gabrielle said.

'I have no doubt,' he replied as Norman sat down opposite them.

'Home, sir?' Adam asked through the partition.

'Yes, Adam,' Norman replied with a nod and with that, the limousine took off from the airport.

Dylan smiled and pulled out his phone, turning it on for the first time since he had landed in London. Instantly, two text messages came through. The first text message was from his mother.

Hey, baby. Good luck wrestling in Japan. Call me when you can.

'So that's the excuse my brothers used,' he muttered silently to himself.

And the second text was from Kelsey.

I can't believe you did that, just left for Japan without so much as a goodbye. I am done with your bullshit and I am done with you. We are over.

That message made Dylan growl, making Gabrielle look over at him.

'What?' Gabrielle asked.

'Oh, girlfriend broke up with me. Whatever excuse my brothers used to explain my absence clearly pissed her off,' Dylan replied with a shrug.

'Oh, I'm sorry,' Gabrielle replied.

'Don't be,' he replied with a smile and he turned to look out at London, marvelling at the amazing city.

After fifteen minutes of driving, the limousine pulled up at the door of Norman's mansion.

'Dylan, welcome to your new home,' Norman exclaimed with a flourish as Adam pushed the door open.

They all stepped inside and Dylan looked around in amazement.

'This place is huge,' he exclaimed.

'I told you that this place is amazing,' Gabrielle whispered to him.

'Alright, Dylan, Adam will take you on a tour and show you to your bedroom. I have some business to attend to, so I will see you two later,' Norman said and he left them, walking upstairs to his study.

'Come on, Dylan, let us begin our tour,' Adam said with a smile.

Dylan nodded and they began their tour. After half an hour of touring, Adam stopped in front of a door.

'And this is your bedroom. I hope it is to your liking,' Adam said, opening the door. Dylan gasped in awe of the sight that greet him beyond the threshold.

'This is amazing!' he exclaimed.

'Good. I have to leave you for a bit and see to Master Norman,' Adam said with a bow.

'Thanks, Adam,' Dylan replied, walking into his room.

Adam left Dylan and made his way downstairs to the kitchen, made Norman his favourite tea, then walked back up the stairs and to Norman's office.

'Those bastards!' he heard Norman yell from the library. Adam opened the door and found Norman.

'What's wrong, sir?' he said.

'They took them!' Norman yelled, turning to face Adam.

'Who?' Adam asked.

'That damn government group, the Meta-Human Project. They took that book and scrolls that they've been badgering me for,' Norman replied, holding up the warrant that Dexter had left. 'Even had a warrant.'

'Well, there's not much else we can do,' Adam replied, handing Norman the cup of tea.

'I know, Adam, it is just frustrating,' Norman sighed, taking the cup of tea and taking a sip. 'Follow me to my study.'

They walked out of the library and into the study.

'So, what's next, sir?' Adam asked.

'I'm glad you asked that, Adam,' Norman grinned, putting the cup down and picking up a scroll off his desk.

'What is it?' Adam asked.

Norman rolled the scroll open slightly, revealing its title, but Adam couldn't read the language.

'What does that say, sir?' Adam asked, looking up at Norman.

'Well, Adam, I had it translated and it translated to three words,' Norman replied.

'And that translation says?' Adam asked.

'The Great Evil,' Norman replied with a grin.